THE

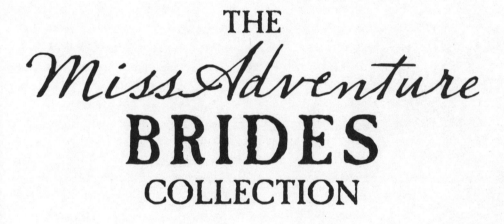

MissAdventure

BRIDES

COLLECTION

7 Daring Damsels Don't Let the Norms of Their Eras Hold Them Back

THE
MissAdventure
BRIDES
COLLECTION

Kimberley Woodhouse
Mary Davis, Cynthia Hickey, Kathleen E. Kovach,
Debby Lee, Donna Schlachter, Marjorie Vawter

BARBOUR BOOKS
An Imprint of Barbour Publishing, Inc.

Along the Yellowstone River ©2018 by Debby Lee
MissTaken Identity ©2018 by Kimberley Woodhouse
Lesson of Love ©2018 by Cynthia Hickey
Maddy's Llamas ©2018 by Marjorie Vawter
Zola's Cross-Country Adventure ©2018 by Mary Davis
Detours of the Heart ©2018 by Donna Schlachter
Riders of the Painted Star ©2018 by Kathleen E. Kovach

Print ISBN 978-1-68322-775-5

eBook Editions:
Adobe Digital Edition (.epub) 978-1-68322-777-9
Kindle and MobiPocket Edition (.prc) 978-1-68322-776-2

All scripture quotations, unless otherwise noted, are taken from the King James Version of the Bible.

Scripture quotations marked ESV are from The Holy Bible, English Standard Version®, copyright © 2001 by Crossway Bibles, a publishing ministry of Good News Publishers. Used by permission. All rights reserved.

This book is a work of fiction. Names, characters, places, and incidents are either products of the author's imagination or used fictitiously. Any similarity to actual people, organizations, and/or events is purely coincidental.

Published by Barbour Books, an imprint of Barbour Publishing, Inc., 1810 Barbour Drive, Uhrichsville, Ohio 44683, www.barbourbooks.com

Our mission is to inspire the world with the life-changing message of the Bible.

ecpa Member of the
Evangelical Christian
Publishers Association

Printed in Canada.

Contents

Along the Yellowstone River

by Debby Lee

Chapter 1

Heather Duncan had ground roughly three ounces of dried sage when she noticed the fire in the hearth dying. In spite of it being early spring, a chill settled in the air. She donned her shawl and exited the cabin to bring in another load of wood.

Fresh green blades of wild grass had recently sprung from the cold earth. Heather admired the beauty of the rugged landscape as she walked. With her eyes on the trees and her thoughts on budding leaves, she missed her footing and slipped on the rain-soaked ground. She took a tumble and rolled end over end down the small hill.

"Oh," she groaned. Unhurt, she stood up and repinned her long hair, sure that it contained as many twigs as hairpins. Mud coated her skirt, and her elbow had torn clear through her sleeve. Thankful for the absence of company while looking so unpresentable, she loaded her arms with firewood and went back to the house.

After rekindling the fire, she took the time to warm her cold hands and dry her wet skirt. Heat soon filled the room, and she went back to grinding her herbs. Moments later her dog, Rufus, let out a hearty growl, alerting her to someone's presence. She paused, mortar in one hand, pestle in the other, to listen. It couldn't be Papa; he wasn't due back from checking traps for another two days. The scruffy but loyal canine let out a series of barks that sent shivers down her spine. Heather dropped her tools and rushed out the log cabin's crude door.

"Rufus, what is it?" Heather lurched to a stop. The town doctor, wearing an expression of sorrow, rode into the front yard of the small homestead. Behind him, a black-haired man rode a pack mule. Both men dismounted their animals and tied them to the hitching post.

It was then Heather recognized the last horse in the train. Papa's. Her eyes took in the familiar deerskin coat on the body draped over the saddle, but it took a few seconds for her to realize that body was her dear Papa.

"No!" Heather screamed and stumbled to where her father lay over the horse. Running her fingers through his hair, she found dried blood caking the dark locks. A ragged gash ran from his temple to his ear. Her father's lifeless eyes stared back at her. Tears of bewilderment and shock rolled down her cheeks.

"What happened?" she finally managed to ask.

"Ma'am." The black-haired man pulled his coonskin cap from his head. "My name's Louie Renault. According to the Rocky Mountain Fur Company's supervisor, Theodore McGill, your father took a nasty tumble from his horse and smacked his head on a rock. Died on impact, or so I'm told."

Fell from his horse? Heather didn't believe that for one second. Theodore McGill was as crooked as Rufus's hind leg. As hard as Papa worked, his debt to the company should have been paid off three times over rather than have climbed like a zealous mountain goat.

"We'll help you bury him." The doctor strode toward a shovel resting against the wall of the cabin.

Heather caught sight of the bundle of beaver pelts tied with a leather strap sitting next to where the shovel was. Four additional skins were tied to hoops in the yard, and two deer hides were drying in the late afternoon sun. All were to be taken to the next Rendezvous even though it was a good two months away. Papa had always enjoyed singing and playing games at the events where the ale flowed as freely as a spring waterfall. Never again would he laugh and drink with his trapper friends. She bit her lip and turned away.

Mr. Renault pulled a shovel from his pack. Bleary-eyed, Heather traipsed to the backyard and pointed to a spot on the ground, next to where her mother rested. Mr. Renault drove his shovel into the ground with a strength Heather wished she possessed. The sound of her father's grave being dug tore through her.

Mama had passed only a few months ago, during the cold brutal winter, and now Papa was gone. She no longer had parents and faced the brutal wilderness alone. Pain seemed to swallow her, allowing a sob to escape. She slapped a hand over her mouth and ran into the cabin.

Dropping onto a chunk of oak log that served as a chair, she leaned forward, covered her face with her hands, and let the tears come. How many times had she asked to go along when Papa set his traps, or when he went into town to see McGill?

Papa had forbid it and said it was for her protection, but from what? Certainly not from the Shoshone Indians. They were kind people. Just last week Heather had exchanged information about local roots with their friend Red Feathers. Mama hadn't minded staying home and making the rustic dwelling a home, but Heather itched to get out and see the wilderness. Mr. McGill said the wilderness was no place for a lady.

Uneasiness swept over her as she thought of Mr. McGill. She, among others, believed the man balanced the company's books in his favor by underpaying the trappers and pocketing the extra money, thus contributing to the trappers' debt. She suspected he had something to do with Papa's death, but what? And could she prove it?

For several minutes she questioned God, wondered how He could allow harm to come to such devoted followers of scripture as her parents. Seeds of anger and fear swept through her, looking for a place to take root. Her heart told her to pray, but the message was lost somewhere in the feelings of abandonment and pain filling her. God wasn't someone she wanted to talk to, not after He called her folks to heaven, thereby shredding her trust in Him.

Heather stared out the open door at the mountains in the distance. The sun passed through several clouds as it slipped into the horizon, much like Heather's hopes and dreams for the future.

Mr. Renault called from outside, telling her they were finished and ready for a small service to begin. Heather dried her eyes and stood tall. She reached for the family Bible and strode out to lay her father to rest. She alone was now in charge of holding down the homestead. A plan took shape in her mind. She would trek into the wilderness herself and set Papa's traps. She would pay off her father's debt, no matter the dangers, and bring his killer to justice.

◆•——•◆

Louie Renault pulled off his coonskin cap as he stood before Old Man Duncan's final resting place. He ached for the man's daughter, a fiery red-haired miss no bigger than a halfpenny, but he also admired her spunk.

Two small twigs protruding from her hair pointed due north. The mud speckles on her dress added to the fabric's pattern, and yet she held her chin high. Freshly an orphan, yet she stood over her father's plot with strength he didn't see in many females. But then again, females needed to be strong in this rugged wilderness.

The melodious voice of Miss Duncan echoed through the cool evening air as she read the scriptures.

"Yea, though I walk through the valley of the shadow of death, I will fear no evil."

She read softly, with sorrow firmly in check. He admired that she knew how to read so well. Perhaps he could work around her homestead in exchange for some lessons. He should give her some time to grieve first, before asking, but the company's Rendezvous approached, and that didn't leave much time to dawdle. Once he knew how to read and do arithmetic, he could assess his own accounts with the Rocky Mountain Fur Company. It seemed as though every trapper in the region was in debt to the company, and that bothered Louie a great deal.

When Miss Duncan shut the Bible and bowed her head in prayer, Louie did the same. He believed in God, as his friend Jedediah Smith had. While Jedediah was alive, Louie's faith had never wavered. But now that Jedediah was gone, Louie struggled with doubt. For two weeks he had been plagued with fevers while setting his traps along the Yellowstone River. He'd asked the doctor for help and had prayed for healing. So far it hadn't happened. Did God really hear his prayers?

Rumor had it the Scottish Miss Duncan knew a thing or two about treating sickness and injuries. When Louie had visited the town doctor, the man had told him about her, how she'd stayed up all night with a sick Shoshone baby until the infant's fever broke.

Louie smiled and warmed at the thought of asking her about any remedies that would help. He suppressed a chuckle. If he wasn't careful, he'd be as in debt to her as he was to the fur company.

The lady cleared her throat and squared her shoulders. "I'd like to be alone for a while if you gentlemen don't mind."

Louie found his voice. "Miss Duncan, allow me to chop some wood for you and stock your woodbox for tonight."

"Thank you." She clutched the Bible to her chest. "You may call me Heather."

"I can help for a bit, and then I need to get back to town." The doctor donned his hat and strode toward the woodpile.

Louie ran his fingers through the soft fur of his cap while working up the courage to speak. "I can come back tomorrow evening to make sure you have enough wood and to see if you need any chores done."

Heather nodded. "Thank you."

When she smiled, he noticed a hint of pink in her cheeks. He watched her square her shoulders and walk around the corner of the cabin. So brave and yet so vulnerable. Louie's heart squeezed.

What was to become of a lone woman in such a wild place, with men like Theodore McGill and their dark intentions?

Chapter 2

Brash tactics likely wouldn't get her far, but Heather Duncan needed to pay a visit to Theodore McGill. First, she would try reasoning with him. She was well educated, in her opinion, and not some dimwit. If that failed, she wasn't beyond using her feminine wiles to gain access to the ledgers. If smarts and sass failed, well, she didn't know what she'd do.

Dressed in her Sunday best, she strolled toward McGill's. Tamping down her trepidation, she stepped into his office in the front room of his quarters and up to his desk. Her boots thumped on the plank floor with every step. The sound, she hoped, let him know she meant business.

A sweat broke out on her brow, and she paused. A smile creased McGill's face and competed with the scar snaking its way across his left cheek.

"Afternoon, Miss Duncan." McGill folded his hands, set them on his shiny desktop, and leaned forward. "I'm so sorry to hear of your father's passing." There was no sadness in his voice; if anything, glee seemed to lace his tone. The wicked grin stayed in place. She wondered how any member of the human race could be so cold. She could now see that Papa had good reason to keep her away from the man.

She squared her shoulders and lifted her chin. "I'm here to see the ledgers regarding my father's account. I can read well, and I'm quite good with numbers. I'm sure we can get the books settled in no time."

McGill stood, his fists clenched. The corners of his mouth finally turned down. His nostrils flared. Even in the dim light she could see his face take on a deep red hue. Then, as fast as a jackrabbit, his smile was back.

"Don't bother yourself about your father's accounts. I know how we can take care of everything. A woman alone in the wilderness needs some protection, and I, of course, being a gentleman, am more than happy to provide you with whatever you might need." He stepped from behind his desk and moved toward her.

Her breath caught in her throat as he reached for her. This man was slick as a weasel coated with bear's grease, and likely just as dangerous. She thanked God for her gloves as he took her by the hand. The touch of his skin on hers would have made her sick.

Heather recoiled from him. His eyes narrowed and he glowered at her. Then, quick as a wink, the wicked grin made its way back to his face.

McGill guided her to a chair much too plush for the rugged area, and set her down. Indignant at being coddled like a whimpering puppy, Heather gritted her teeth lest she tell him what she really thought of him. But she couldn't do that and expect to see the account books. No, she needed some finesse when dealing with him.

"This land is much too rough for a damsel of your beauty, Miss Duncan."

"Mr. McGill, I studied with a renowned physician in Glasgow, Scotland—"

"Oh piddle." McGill rolled his eyes and waved a hand at her.

So much for using her brains. Perhaps another approach would work.

She pulled a fan from her reticule, batted her eyelashes, and in her sweetest voice said, "Why, Mr. McGill, I simply can't rest until I've seen those ledgers. Won't you please, please let me have just a tiny peek at them?"

McGill harrumphed and then patted the top of her bonneted head so vigorously her hair pins poked into her scalp. It took every ounce of restraint she possessed to keep from pulling the pins from her hair and sticking him with them.

So much for using her feminine wiles. What else could she try?

He turned to face her and said, "Now don't you worry your pretty little head over those ledgers. I'm taking care of everything. Allow me to add some culture to your afternoon. I'll make you a cup of tea, and then we can talk about marriage."

Heather gasped. The contents of her stomach roiled. Papa wouldn't want her married to such a man. If Mr. McGill had broached the subject with her father, well, Heather didn't want to imagine how that conversation would have gone.

A plan formed in her mind. Why hadn't she thought of this earlier? With her sweetest simper, she replied, "Why, thank you, Mr. McGill. That's so kind of you."

"Wonderful." McGill clapped his hands together. The sound of his chuckle grated against her skin and raised the hair on her arms. He stepped to the fireplace and pulled two tin mugs from a shelf above. He set them on a nearby table.

A lump formed in Heather's throat and refused to go down no matter how hard she swallowed. She must keep her wits about her.

"Mr. McGill," she said. "I'm feeling a bit chilled. Why don't you gather some more wood for the fire, and I'll make the tea."

McGill puffed out his chest. "Of course, where are my manners?" He stepped outside.

Heather jumped to her feet. She rushed to the table. The teapot rested on a grill over the flames. She poured the water into the mugs. Quick as she dared, she fished in her purse for her vials of dried herbs she always carried with her. She grasped one and pulled it out.

Belladonna? Heavens no! Murder was a sin, and she didn't wish to kill the misguided fool, no matter how rotten his behavior. She pulled out another vial.

Pennyroyal? Meant for women's complaints, wouldn't that wreak havoc on the man's insides, as well as his emotional state? She shook her head and set it aside. There had to be something she could use.

Dried ground bark of cascara buckthorn. Now that would do the trick. Not enough to hurt him, just enough to keep him in the outhouse long enough for her to get to the account books. Of course, it wouldn't take effect until the next afternoon, but with the town doctor away for a week, she imagined when he got sick he'd send for her. She had patience; she could wait. She stirred a fair amount into his mug and tried, unsuccessfully, to suppress her smile.

◆—◆

The bright sun did little to heat the early morning air, even though April would soon be upon them. Louie stepped toward the company office on a mission. All night long he'd mulled over in his mind just what he planned to say to McGill. Not that his words could do much good. Until he learned to read, he'd have to take McGill at his word when he said the books were in order. Just what he hoped to glean from the meeting he didn't know, but he had to at least try.

Louie rubbed his arms to help ward off the chill. "Good morning, Red Feathers," he said to his Shoshone Indian friend who was mounting his horse in front of the boardinghouse. "Bring in a mess of pelts, I hope?"

The tall, black-haired man nodded. "But there's something you should know. My people promised Duncan that if anything happened to him, we'd take care of his daughter. When I turned in my furs, McGill bragged that he was keeping company with her, alone."

Louie's fists clenched. He struggled against saying something unholy. "Do you know if it's true or not?"

Red Feathers shook his head, his silver and beaded jewelry jingling. "I can't be sure. I can't imagine Duncan's daughter behaving that way, but I did see her come out of his office late yesterday afternoon and ride toward her homestead."

"Now I'm really going to have words with that man!" Louie tipped his coonskin hat to his friend and hurried along. If Duncan looked down from heaven, he surely was aghast at his daughter being alone with the likes of McGill. Louie growled. He had let his friend down. First he'd confront McGill, threaten him if he had to, to get him to leave Heather alone.

As soon as he was done with McGill, he'd check on Heather to make sure she was all right. Strong as she was, he still worried about her.

About ten paces from his destination, Louie stopped in his tracks. McGill burst through the front door, grasping his trousers about his waist. He stumbled into the street.

"Get out of my way, you fool!" he screamed.

Louie watched the man clamber toward the outhouse. He hadn't heard about McGill being sick. Louie laughed. It served McGill right. Conviction then swept over Louie. The Bible said to pray for your enemies. Louie sighed, ducked his head, and said a quick prayer for McGill.

Ill or not, it didn't matter. Louie would wait for the man in his office. Again he thought about his choice of words. If good graces didn't work, was he above using threats? He didn't want to cause trouble within the company and risk losing his contracts, but he knew enough trappers were complaining, and unhappy with McGill.

Walking through the front door, he shook his head. The stench in the room was enough to drop a pack mule. Louie yanked a bandanna from his pocket and held it over his nose, but what really made him suck in a breath was the sight of Heather Duncan.

She stood over McGill's desk, a pile of ledgers, maps, and papers before her. She stood, slack-jawed and mute, with parchment in one hand, quill in the other.

What was she up to?

Chapter 3

Heather couldn't think fast enough for words that would placate Louie Renault. His furrowed brows and arms folded over his ample chest demanded an explanation. The man had been kind enough to help her bury her father and had stopped by the homestead to chop firewood for her. He'd even mended her corral so Papa's horse and cow wouldn't wander off.

"Mr. Renault, I, um. . ." She didn't feel right keeping him in the dark regarding her plans to expose Theodore McGill, but what could she say? Perhaps the truth was the best option. "As you very well know, your accounts, my father's accounts, and several other trappers' accounts didn't add up, so to speak. So I thought I'd go over the ledgers myself and see if I could figure them out."

Mr. Renault raised his eyebrows as he spoke. "And Mr. McGill gave you carte blanche approval to do so?" He leaned back against the doorframe and tapped his foot.

"Mr. McGill is, uh, um, indisposed at the moment, but when he returns, I have every intention of sharing my findings with him as soon as I find what I think I'm going to find." She was rambling now and, guessing by the way Mr. Renault continued to tap his foot, he had to know she was up to something and doubted her story.

She really did intend to have words with McGill if she found any inaccuracies in the accounts, but not as cordially as Mr. Renault might think.

After a long, slow moment, he said, "I don't abide by the way McGill does business, but that doesn't give us an excuse to behave dishonestly."

Heather snorted. "How else are we going to prove his guilt?"

"The Good Book says we're not to lie or cheat, but to love one another."

"And what has God done for my family, besides let them die?" Heather could read the scriptures full well, but believing God answered her prayers was another matter altogether. Just how the man remained so devoted to his faith, in spite of hardship, was beyond her. Most mountain men drank and used coarse language, but not this one. And yet in spite of herself, she admired him for it.

"Miss Duncan?"

The sound of his voice sent shivers through her. "Oh, um, yes, Mr. Renault?" she stammered.

"If you don't have McGill's permission to view his ledgers, then you need to stop what you're doing this instant."

"But there are some missing pages, in at least four spots of the book where you can see that pages have been ripped out, and the dates don't add up. If I can find them in this mess, I might—"

"Heather,"

To her chagrin, she knew he was right. She threw the quill onto the desk and slammed the ledgers shut. Crossing her arms, she glared at him "Okay, Mr. Renault, now what do you propose we do?"

He cleared his throat and began again. "First of all, please call me Louie. Secondly, I can use some lessons in reading and figuring numbers. If you'd be so kind to help me learn, in exchange for work around your homestead, we could meet with Mr. McGill together, ask him to go over the ledgers with us, and get this mess sorted out."

"An illiterate accusing me of faulty record keeping?" The voice in the doorway boomed. McGill towered in the entryway, red-faced, his fists clenched at his sides.

Shivers of another kind coursed through Heather. She gulped and stepped away from the desk. A stack of parchment papers slipped to the floor.

"Sifting through my ledgers were you?" McGill glared at Louie. "Renault, I should have you arrested for this."

"Mr. McGill—" Heather's words were cut off as Louie stomped across the floor and grasped her by the elbow.

"We were just leaving," he snarled.

Heather tried to protest. After all, it was only a matter of time before McGill had to make another trip to the outhouse. If she could just convince Louie to let her gather more information, all she needed was another fifteen minutes or so. Her plans were dashed however. Once outside, Louie turned to face her. His dark eyes snapped with fire.

"Miss Duncan, you must promise me you won't compromise your reputation by being alone with a man of such ill repute as Theodore McGill."

Heather wrung her hands. Not only was Louie a handsome man, but he was concerned with her well-being. A warm blush crept into her cheeks, and it had nothing to do with the warmer temperatures. How this man could upend her senses was a mystery to her.

He scrunched down to meet her at eye level and gently held her by the shoulders. "Give me a few lessons, and together we'll go see McGill. If he doesn't listen to us, we'll go directly to his supervisor."

She relished the notion of giving him lessons in reading and arithmetic. His company at the homestead would soothe her fears of being alone. It would save her backbreaking work around the homestead. Besides, how could she say no to a man who had been her Papa's friend? She tried to convince herself those were the only reasons she wanted him around.

But she'd heard that Louie Renault lived and breathed his faith in God. She didn't dare tell him she slipped McGill some herbs that sent him racing for the outhouse. After all, if Louie was willing to help her, she didn't want to risk upsetting him.

◆━━━━━◆

Louie swallowed the lump in his throat. He hated the idea of Heather meeting with McGill alone. Not that the man would attack her, but Louie wouldn't put it past him to spread gossip and lies, or compromise her in some other way. He must be more diligent in watching over her. After all, he'd promised Old Man Duncan he would if anything ever happened to him.

Taking a deep breath of fresh mountain air, he calmed himself. "Miss Duncan, I'll be over tomorrow afternoon to tie up your father's pelts. And then, with your permission of course, you can give me some lessons. When we're finished I'll bring the pelts in for you and see to it McGill credits your father's account."

"That would be fine, Louie. And please, call me Heather." The smile on her face caused his heart to jump. Yes, he wanted to learn to read so he could study the Bible more, but she might prove more of a distraction than a teacher.

◆━━━━━◆

The following afternoon, Louie once again found himself at the Duncan homestead. After bringing in a load of kindling, he stood by the fire and watched Heather perusing her book of herbs and roots.

"Heather," he said, "I'd like permission to use your father's traps."

She looked up from her book, chewed on her lower lip as if she studied something other than medicinal herbs, and went back to her reading.

She hadn't given him a direct answer, but he decided to check them anyway. The spring mechanisms worked well. Still, he oiled them and set them aside.

From there he moved on to a stack of beaver skins. He scraped the backs and then bound the stack with a thick leather strap. Then he bound two bundles of tanned muskrat pelts, a few fox, and two large buckskins.

When the tasks were completed, he strolled into the Duncans' cabin, hoping he'd earned at least an invitation to dinner and perhaps a lesson on the alphabet. The smell of venison stew made his stomach rumble.

Heather bustled about the hearth, stirring the contents of a pot over the fire and pulling biscuits from a small stove.

"Louie, would you like to stay for dinner?" she asked.

"Sure," he replied. He leaned against the wall and watched her, thankful that, for once, he didn't have to cook. When she finally sat at the table for the meal, he noted her pink cheeks and smiled.

"Allow me to say the blessing." He folded his hands in prayer, hoping a moment with the Almighty would help him get his mind on dinner and the lessons to follow. Heather merely fixed her gaze on him and didn't so much as blink. He understood her anger at God for taking her parents, but he wasn't about to partake of a meal without first thanking the Lord and asking His blessing on the food.

"Louie," she finally said, "I'll have more pelts for you to tie up soon."

"But how, from where?" he asked.

"I'm taking over Papa's job as a fur trapper. I'm going into the woods and setting those traps myself."

Chapter 4

A week after Louie had been a guest at her dinner table, Heather found herself traipsing through the Yellowstone wilderness with him. He had tried to talk her out of fur trapping, but she was determined.

That evening the pouring rain drenched Louie and Heather's campsite but not her resolve. The half-moon in the sky illuminated the area outside the camp, but under the trees it was a bit darker. The sheltering trees kept most of the rain off the fire.

Heather huddled at the opening of her tent, added another stick of wood to the fire, and pulled the blanket tighter around her. She shivered. At least she didn't have to worry about animals attacking. No creature in its right mind would be out in this deluge.

Heather scoffed. What would her Papa say at her wanting to give up because of a little rain? He'd want her to be strong no matter the circumstances. She smiled at the memory of his twinkling eyes and robust laughter at the company's Rendezvous last year.

Determined to make the best of it, Heather decided to make a hot drink to help her stay warm. "Louie, I'm brewing some tea. Would you like a cup? It's the kind Red Feathers tried when he was here today. He seemed to like it all right."

Snoring from the tent next to hers served as her only response. The poor man was tired from the games he and his Indian friend had played all that afternoon.

No matter. She reached for a dry stick of kindling, wrapped a greased rag around one end of it, and held the other end in the flames. When the rag caught fire, she traipsed away from camp toward the creek's edge to get water for the teakettle.

Shadows danced along the dimly lit embankment only a hundred feet away. The makeshift torch didn't give much light. If she could just keep from tripping on rocks. Undaunted, she moved forward. To make a go of this fur-trapping business, she had to get used to harsh conditions.

Of course the presence of the handsome Frenchman made the cold and primitive conditions more bearable. He had taken well to his lessons, memorizing the entire alphabet in the first three days they had been out. Tomorrow they would go over sounds and rules of the English language. It wouldn't be much longer before he was able to read short words. All he needed was practice.

She hummed a few bars of an old Scottish hymn, "The Isle of Skye," to keep her mind from the pelting rain. The storm had made the ground slick. She slipped and fell on her bottom. Would she ever manage to keep her footing in this rugged wilderness?

Fumbling with the torch and teakettle in one hand, she hoisted herself from the ground and managed to steady herself. The sound of Louie's snoring reached her ears. He sounded just like her Papa. The rugged woodsman had many admirable qualities: brute strength balanced with a gentle kindness, adherence to his code of values, and even patience with her slow steps along the trail. Endearing warmth washed over her, a welcome feeling in the bitter wind.

She carefully stepped to the creek's edge and knelt beside it. She dipped the kettle into the rushing water. A shock of cold surged through her hand and up her arm. She sucked in a breath of icy air. The warmth she felt a moment ago fled. The sooner warmer temperatures arrived the better.

She yanked the brimming kettle from the water and rose, then proceeded back to camp. She hadn't made it more than three steps up the embankment when a series of growls met her ears.

"Louie, is that you?" Her skin tingled. Fear welled in her stomach. It wasn't Louie. It wasn't his friend Red Feathers either. Turning her head from left to right, she counted four sets of yellow, gleaming eyes.

Wolves.

After a long, hard winter without much food, they were likely hungry and capable of tearing her to bits. Why hadn't she thought to bring Papa's pistol?

◆•———•◆

Louie bolted upright at the sound of yelling.

"Heather," he bellowed. Tossing his wool blankets aside, he grabbed his gun and flew out of his tent. "Heather," he called again.

More cries sailed through the night air. They were Heather's cries, and they came from the direction of the creek. If anything happened to her, he'd blame himself forever. Why hadn't he done more to talk her out of this crazy idea?

The trees overhead obscured what scant bit of moonlight broke through the clouds. Louie couldn't see very well, but that didn't stop him from hurrying toward her as fast as possible. The first time he fell, he bit back a cry; the second time his knees hit the mud, his gun accidentally went off.

A yelp accompanied the screams. If he'd shot Heather in the melee, he'd never forgive himself. "Heather," he yelled a third time. Sure that she was being attacked by a grizzly bear, he sprinted from the wooded area and ran full force.

Darkness made it difficult to see what exactly the moving shadows were, but he heard the commotion. Growling, barking, hollering. She had to be in trouble, so why didn't she answer him? Would he have to bury her too alongside her mother and father? He feared the worst and panic drove him onward. The river was only a few feet away. Where was she?

"Oof!" He ran smack into someone, or something, before tumbling to the cold, hard ground.

Splash!

He groped along the embankment, searching for her, but was unable to find her. Had he knocked her into the creek?

More splashing, followed by, "Help, Louie! I can't swim!"

Wading into the icy water and flailing about, he called Heather's name again and again. The deluge of spring rains had swollen the waterways, and the currents ran fast. He had to find her before she was carried too far downstream.

Up to his waist in frigid water, he felt around for any sign of her. The rocky creek bottom made for uneven steps, and if he wasn't careful, he'd go downstream with her. Continuously he hollered for her. Where was she?

To his relief, he finally heard her voice.

"Louie!"

"Heather, I'm here." He grasped hold of what had to be her skirts flowing around him. Thank the Lord the water wasn't deep, but it was cold enough to give them their death of a chill. Motivated by fear-crazed strength, he hefted himself from the flowing waters, dragging her behind him.

The sound of her coughing calmed him. His heart quit racing. He lay on the riverbank, sucking in precious air. "What, what, h–h–happened?" he finally sputtered.

She let out a quiet sob. In the dim moonlight he could just make out her silhouette. The poor dear. He reached out to her. "You fell in the creek, but you're all right now." He suspected he'd knocked her into the creek, but that was a topic for later discussion.

Louie refused to focus on how cold he was. Heather was all that mattered. He pulled her into his arms, pushed her tangled hair from her face, and rocked her back and forth, a motion he hoped soothed her.

When her sobs ebbed, he asked, "What are you doing down here?"

"I came down to fill the kettle so I could make tea. I hadn't thought to bring Papa's gun, and a pack of wolves surrounded me. Then my torch went out. I was sure they were going to attack me. I threw the kettle at one of them, yelled at them, hoping to frighten them off. If your gun hadn't gone off when it did. . ."

In spite of his cold, wet clothing, anger bubbled up in Louie and he struggled to tamp it down. "You came down here unarmed in the middle of the night to get water for tea? What were you thinking?"

Chapter 5

The next afternoon Heather trudged alongside the pack mule. Louie led the way down the narrow path along the Yellowstone River. She remained silent. Since they were still in the wilderness together among hungry wild animals and disreputable characters, another misunderstanding wouldn't bode well for them.

Yes, it had been irresponsible of her to traipse around at night by herself, but in her mind the only thing she'd done wrong was neglect to take Papa's gun with her. Why, if she'd had Papa's pistol, she'd have shot those wolves and not had to worry about a thing. And she'd have a wolf skin, perhaps two, to show for her troubles.

There was so much to learn about trapping animals. It was a wonder any of the men survived the dangers. Appreciation and respect for Papa, and for Louie, swelled in her heart.

They came to a fallen tree on the trail, and Heather stifled a groan. Louie pulled a hatchet from his pack and hacked away at the log. The tool zinged and the wood cracked with every swing he made.

He still seemed upset, but she had reason to be upset as well. He's the one who had panicked, barreled down to the creek, and then knocked her into it. Thankfully, they were able to get changed into dry clothes and drink some hot tea to get warm.

"How many times must I say I'm sorry?" she asked.

"No need to keep saying it unless you think there's more to discuss."

"Is something else upsetting you?"

"No, that's not it." Louie finally cut through the tree trunk and moved it off the trail.

She met his gaze. His eyes shone with concern and compassion. "Why are you so silent today?"

His chuckling rang in the crisp air. "My apologies, Heather. I was spending some time with the Lord in my mind. I didn't mean to neglect you." Louie smiled at her as brightly as the rising sun and warmed her just as much.

He was so handsome, and she was relieved. There was no need to be upset. But there he went again with that religious rambling. Like Papa and Mama, his faith was woven through him so thoroughly she doubted it could be extricated without leaving a hole in his being. It was what made him strong, and even though she was angry with God, she liked that trait in him.

Louie could hardly read a word, yet he could quote scriptures to the letter with such ease. She, on the other hand, could read the Bible forward and back again, but believing the words was something else altogether. The irony confounded her at times.

"Are you all right, Heather?"

The sound of Louie's voice drew her to the present. "Yes, of course. Are we stopping and making camp here?"

"No, I have traps farther down the river to check. Are you keeping up all right? Do you need to stop and rest for a bit?"

"No, I'm fine, but thank you for asking." Heather admired how he at least tried to see to her comfort. If she wasn't careful, his kindness might just melt her heart, and then where would she be?

As far back as she could remember, she had prided herself in not losing her head to every man who paid her a compliment. Back in Scotland she had attended private classes taught by famed Edinburgh physician Robert Liston. Most of the students were men. They grumbled at her presence and played cruel jokes on her. Still, she was there to learn and managed to accomplish a great deal by staying strong without falling into despair.

Now here she was, getting all starry-eyed over a tall, dark Frenchman with strong muscles and an even stronger faith in God. But there was more to it than that. He was eager to learn and willing to stand up against injustice even if it cost him. How could she not admire qualities like that?

The mule let out a whinny when Louie placed the hatchet back in the pack. "Are you ready to proceed?" He took the animal's reins.

"Of course." She lifted her heavy wool skirts and picked her way along the trail. She didn't mind when Louie began singing "Amazing Grace" by John Newton. She rather liked the tune and sang along with him. When they finished he taught her "Oh God, Our Help in Ages Past" by Isaac Watts.

An hour later a peace settled over Heather. Maybe there was something to this business of trusting God in times of trial after all. Faith in the Lord had meant everything to Papa and Mama. They had taught her to read from the scriptures. She believed in God too, but her heart was still too sore to trust in Him at this point in her life. Believing in Him yet not trusting in Him confused her.

Christian faith sure made Louie happy. Perhaps she could ask him more about it over dinner that night.

A few steps later and her skin prickled. The sound coming from the river up ahead made her stomach sick. The anguished cries of a wounded animal.

◆—————◆

Louie watched Heather stir a pot hanging over the campfire. Tears stained her cheeks. Remorse and protectiveness wrestled within him. A good man earned an honest living, and sometimes that required stepping on feminine sensibilities.

He shook his head. She was the one who had insisted on coming out to trap animals. If she didn't like how it was done, she could very well go home.

A Bible verse floated into his mind. *"The Son of man came not to be ministered unto, but to minister, and to give his life a ransom for many."* That one was in Matthew. He thought of another one about esteeming others better than himself. He sighed. Best make peace now and finish skinning the beaver later.

"Heather," he said. He heard a sniffle and cast a glance at her. She continued to stir the stew, but at least her tears had dried.

"I saw how distressed you were at the animal's last moments, and still I killed it in your presence. I'm sorry."

"You did what you had to do. I'm just upset that. . .well, I've never seen an innocent creature suffer so much. I suppose you killed the poor thing to end its suffering."

Yes, he'd wanted to put the creature out of its misery. He killed it because it was worth money too. But he wasn't telling her that. His honest nature tugged at him to tell the truth, yet that would cause her more pain. He sighed. The predicaments women put men in.

"Why don't we study some more after dinner? I think I'm getting the hang of some bigger words, especially the verbs," Louie said.

He warmed and felt his muscles relax when a smile played on her lips. She really was a beautiful woman, especially with those strands of auburn hair framing her face. She had an inner strength too, even if she was wrestling with God. He didn't believe she was cantankerous on purpose. She simply had some things to work out with the Lord regarding the loss of her parents. Losses like that would put anyone in a tizzy. He resolved to pray for her more often.

"After we eat, I'll bring out some more advanced books like my copy of the *Edinburgh Dispensary*, maybe even the Bible. It will be a nice way to end such a sad day." Heather ladled venison stew into two bowls and set a fresh biscuit in each one.

"Here you are." She handed him a bowl. Parsnips and carrots swam in the steaming, thick broth. When he inhaled the aroma, his stomach emitted an audible rumble.

"Thank you." Louie folded his hands. He noted a scowl on her face but closed his eyes and voiced his praise anyway.

When he opened his eyes and looked at her, his heart melted. Head bowed, hands folded in prayer, lips moving, she was having a moment with God as well. Perhaps it wouldn't be long before she realized her need for the Almighty. Then, together, they could go after Theodore McGill. With God on their side, who could be against them?

Louie savored a bite of carrot. He swallowed and asked, "Do you know any other trappers who know how to read?"

"Papa read well. He's the one who taught me, but I can't speak for the rest of them. Why do you ask?" Heather stared at him with eyes as green as fresh leaves popping out in the spring.

Logic flew from his mind. His heart skipped like a stone over the water's surface. He cleared his throat so he could regain his thoughts. "My friend Jedediah Smith was a fine scholar, and he knew the Lord. God rest his soul."

"I'm so sorry for your loss, Louie."

"Thank you. You know, it was Jedediah who led me to the Lord. I had too much liquor at a Rendezvous a few years back. Wandered off and couldn't find my tent. Jedediah found me near the creek. He took care of me that night, prayed for me. I never forgot that kindness."

"It sounds like Mr. Smith was a fine man. Papa mentioned him a time or two and spoke very highly of him."

Several locks of her wavy red hair came loose from their pins and blew around her face in the gentle breeze. Louie wished he could run his fingers through them and tell her how beautiful she was, how brave he thought she was.

Louie warmed a few degrees and deemed it best to continue. "Anyhow, I thought it might be prudent to have other trappers join us in our mission to set things right with McGill."

Heather smiled. "That's an intelligent idea. I'll speak with Papa's trapper friends."

"Speaking of intelligence, where did you learn about medicine?" Louie asked.

"I began as a midwife, taught by an old woman who lived in a little town called Bathgate. She had been a midwife for decades. She was a third-generation midwife, and proud of it. I also sat in on some classes taught at the home of a great Scottish physician. I was the only female there, but I learned quickly and earned their respect."

As much as Louie admired her for her skills, he realized how hard it must have been, being a lady among such esteemed gentlemen. But riches and education didn't make a man a gentleman. McGill was proof of that.

Just knowing he and others were being taken advantage of caused his temperature to rise. He reached for a handkerchief and wiped the sweat forming on his forehead and at his temples. The bowl of stew was suddenly heavy.

"Oh Lord, not another fever, not now." He dropped his bowl to the ground with a *thunk* and began to tremble.

"Louie, Louie." Heather rushed to where he sat. "Are you all right?"

"I—I can't get warm." Could she understand him through his chattering teeth?

"Don't you worry one bit. I'll mix up a tonic and have you feeling better in a jiffy."

Louie groaned. "Oh please, Heather, not the stuff you gave McGill."

Heather spun around and stared at him, her green eyes flashing. Without another word, she hurried to where the mule was tied. He watched her fish around in her pack and withdraw several vials. She stoked the fire and added boiling water to his tin cup. Her hands moved quickly for someone unaccustomed to living outdoors.

The air chilled by several degrees in a matter of seconds. His insides seemed to tie themselves in knots, and he shook even more violently.

"Oh please, God," he groaned. "If I'm to die now, let my heart be right with You, and please, protect Heather. Let her eyes be opened to Your love."

Chapter 6

When the first light of dawn colored the sky with ribbons of gold and purple, Heather rose from the cold ground and stretched her aching muscles. The fire needed to be stoked and more water heated for Louie's medicine, dried ground feverfew and peppermint. His fever hadn't broken yet, but it should only be a matter of time. Another dose of the tea would help.

While measuring the ground herbs into his tin cup, she heard him move. She turned to face him and said, "Rest now, Louie, the fever will soon break. I'm mixing more tea for you."

"Thank you," he rasped. Although flushed, he lay back and smiled.

Heather tried not to think of all the Bible verses he'd quoted through the night and the prayers he'd said. Strange, she thought, how he voiced his praise to God even as he tossed and suffered with near delirium. Could it be that God had heard his prayers and in exchange decided to heal him? She didn't think the Lord worked that way, but there was something reverent about the way Louie prayed.

She added hot water to the tea and stirred it, then held the cup to Louie's lips. "Here you are."

Louie gulped down almost half the contents. He must have been thirsty, but then, sometimes fevers did strange things to a person's physical body.

By lunchtime Louie was out of bed. Heather had wrapped her shawl around his shaky shoulders, but he still sporadically trembled with chills. Heather had managed to chop and stack a load of firewood, bring water from the river, and prepare a stew for noonday meal.

"When I was getting water from the river, I checked the traps. I didn't see any more animals caught." What she wouldn't tell him is that while down there she'd made as much noise as possible to frighten off any poor, unsuspecting critters. She'd even tried to wash away some of the beaver gland scent used to lure them into the traps. If she had to listen to another creature crying in agony as it suffered—well, she didn't know what she'd do.

"You should be proud of yourself. You're doing better than most women would in such rugged conditions, without the benefit of any modern conveniences." Another smile spread across Louie's face.

Heather warmed at the praise. How could someone be so kind like that all the time? Mustering her courage, she asked, "Would you like to read some scriptures and maybe explain a few to me? It might be a nice way to pass the time while you recuperate."

She didn't think it was possible, but he smiled bigger and brighter than ever. "That would be lovely."

A measure of joy, with only a hint of trepidation, flowed through her. After all, to risk her heart meant risking it to pain, but the rewards seemed worth it. Rising from her perch, she stepped into her tent and pulled her parents' worn book from her bag. Strolling back to Louie, she sat beside him. Their fingers touched as she flipped through the pages. Heat rushed through her when he placed his calloused hand over hers with such tenderness.

"What is your favorite verse?" he asked.

"Oh, well, I don't know. I've never given it much thought."

"Quite all right. Just tell me which one sticks in your mind and why you think it does so."

For a long moment, she thought about his request. What had her parents always said to each other? She closed her eyes and let the memory of Papa and Mama sitting in front of the fireplace come into focus in her mind. Mama knitting socks for Papa to keep his feet warm while he was out checking traps. Papa reading from the family Bible and assuring Mama how much he appreciated her. Finally, the words came to Heather.

"I like the one that says, 'Let nothing be done through strife or vainglory; but in lowliness of mind—' "

" 'Let each esteem other better than themselves. Look not every man on his own things—' " Louie continued.

" 'But every man also on the things of others.' " Heather finished the verse. "Papa and Mama said that often."

"I believe that's in Philippians, chapter two, verses three through four."

Heather followed along in her Bible as Louie quoted the words. A lightning bolt came out of nowhere and pierced her heart. Had she not made McGill sick for her own selfish ambitions? Oh, she'd tried to convince herself it was for the greater good, but she knew better.

Her motivations were to clear her dear Papa's name, yes, but she wanted to make McGill suffer as well. Not that it mattered to Papa—he was in heaven. But didn't McGill deserve to be humiliated and revealed as the crooked thief he was? Whether he deserved the treatment she'd doled out or not, something about exacting revenge didn't sit well in her heart.

With such a fine line between justice and vengeance, and how blurry it was at times, how could she know where or when she crossed it?

"You seem deep in your thoughts. Mulling things over with the Almighty, I presume?"

"Yes, I suppose I am." Heather chuckled. Some of this Bible stuff was beginning to make sense. She liked it, but for some reason it made her feel vulnerable too.

◆—————◆

After a last dose of Heather's tea, Louie crawled into bed. He slept soundly and rose in the morning filled with energy. After donning his clothes and stuffing his feet into his boots, he stepped from his tent ready to get to work.

Pancakes and frying salt pork sizzled in the cast-iron skillet. The aroma wafted to him and made his mouth water. For a long moment, he allowed his mind to linger on how nice it would be to wake up to a hot breakfast every morning. And how much nicer it would be if Heather were the one cooking it.

Louie ran his fingers through his messy hair to clear the thought from his head. He had a busy day before him and didn't need to be distracted.

"Good morning, Heather. Breakfast smells wonderful."

Heather paused before flipping another pancake. "Good morning, Louie," she said. "Now that you're feeling better, I suppose we'll break camp and head farther upriver."

Louie let out a deep sigh. He'd practiced in his mind what he wanted to say, but not knowing how she'd take it made him worry.

"Actually, Heather, I thought you could stay here and tend camp. There's plenty to be done. I'll check the traps, and you won't have to hear the cries of any animals I have to kill."

She stood and smoothed her apron. He held his breath, hoping she wouldn't be offended. More often than not, he was at a loss for what to say when it came to conversing with women and not upsetting them.

"Fine," she said a bit too crisply. "Will you be back for the noon meal?"

"I'll be doing well if I'm back before dark, but some of your tasty biscuits and salt pork would keep me well fed and happy throughout the day." He hoped he sounded genuine. The last thing he wanted was to make her feel abandoned while he was gone.

"Fine, I'll pack something for you."

Louie decided to pray extra hard over any food she packed. He didn't want to think she'd lace it with what she gave McGill, but one never knew.

"Please don't be upset. I'm not trying to insult you or doubt your abilities to deal with the wilderness. I'm only trying to spare you further heartache."

"You're right, Louie, I'm sorry." She hummed the hymn he'd taught her the other day as she dished up a heaping pile of pancakes and salt pork and handed it to him.

"Thank you," he said.

He watched her place food on her plate. Then she sat on a large boulder, folded her hands, and asked, "Shall we pray first?"

Louie grinned. There was hope. He bowed his head and prayed. When he opened his eyes, he noted her sweet smile and rosy cheeks. A joy that comes from seeing someone draw close to the Lord filled his being. He skewered a piece of salt pork and didn't even try to hide his happiness.

While chewing he tried to assess how many traps he could check that day. He still worried about hurting Heather's feelings and wanted to make sure she would be all right while he was gone.

Between bites he tried to further clear the air. With the progress he felt he'd made, the last thing he wanted was discord to wheedle its way between them. "When you're finished washing the breakfast dishes, why don't you hunt for wild berries growing down by the river. That way you don't have to worry about being bored while I'm gone."

The twinkle in her green eyes and the smile on her face made his stomach flip-flop. "Hmm. . .I wouldn't be bored, and you would get berries for dessert tonight," she said with a laugh.

Louie grinned at her, finished eating, and scraped his tin plate clean. He loaded his gear onto his pack mule while Heather packed a few biscuits, some salt pork, and cheese, and filled his canteen.

"Be safe out there, and don't worry about things here at camp. I'll be all right." She handed him the burlap bag of food.

"You be safe too. I'll pray for you today." Louie meant every word. A part of him hated to leave her. He tried to convince himself it was because she'd be alone at camp, but he knew better. He'd been fighting a growing attraction to her. They stood so close he could touch her cheek, see the longing in her eyes. What he really wanted was to take her in his arms, kiss her, and shield her from all the ills of the world.

Before conversation got too complicated, he cleared his throat and reached for the reins of his mule. As he headed up the trail, he called over his shoulder, "Goodbye."

Heather stood, with her chin held high and waved.

The sun climbed higher and higher into the sky as Louie proceeded along the rocky riverbank. Nearly every trap he'd set had an animal in it. That was good for his pocketbook, but every animal he had to kill and skin took precious time and kept him from getting back to camp, and Heather. He'd hardly had time to stuff a biscuit into his mouth by the time the sun reached its zenith.

The mountain air warmed considerably as the day wore on. Louie steered his mule around a large herd of buffalo grazing in a wide-open field. The temperamental beasts weren't used to humans, and there was no telling how they would react to his presence. Not only that, but a stampede might frighten off any beavers, river otters, or minks he hoped to catch.

All afternoon Louie took the time to reset his traps. Wherever possible he anchored them to a tree as opposed to staking them to the ground. That way the animals couldn't wander off after they were caught. He couldn't afford to lose any of his precious traps.

By the time darkness encroached, he was headed back downriver. The denseness of the forest made it difficult to see the trail. He'd have to trust his instincts to get back. He held the mule's reins and walked ahead of it, rather than ride it.

A noise startled him. The mule hee-hawed and pulled at the reins.

"Hush, you stubborn beast." Pausing for a long minute, he listened. There it was again. Fear barreled into him. Wild animals were already out and could be attacking Heather. He had to get back to her quickly.

Louie's heart pounded in his chest. The Ree Indians had attacked so many of his friends. He prayed that neither he nor Heather would face the same fate. Gasping for breath, Louie tugged on his mule's reins even harder. The poor animal protested, and for a second, Louie considered going on without it.

The third time he heard the noise, he recognized it as human. Quickly he wrapped the reins around a tree branch. Pulling his gun from its leather sheath, he yelled, "Who's there?"

All manner of crazy thoughts assailed Louie's mind. What if McGill was out there intending to harm him and then Heather?

"Identify yourself or I'll shoot!" he called into the brush, much louder this time.

The sound of groaning reached his ears. That was someone in pain. Louie rushed ahead a few paces and tripped over a lump in the path.

"Oof!" He went down with a thud. The gun dropped from his hands but didn't go off. He breathed a prayer of thanks and one for his safety. Fumbling around in the darkness, he located a warm, moaning body.

Buckskin trousers and what felt like a buffalo-hide coat told Louie the person was a man.

"Hey, are you all right?" Louie asked. There was no response. He checked for a pulse and gratefully found one. He ran his hands over the man's chest and then his head. His hands came away sticky with blood.

Chapter 7

Louie wasn't back yet, and Heather wondered if she'd spend the night alone. Slightly worried, she reached for the kettle over the fire and poured some hot water into her tin cup. Should she try to sleep or wait up for Louie? The aroma of rose hips wafted up to her. She breathed deeply, inhaling the warm soothing scent. It wouldn't hurt to be up a few more minutes, just long enough to finish her tea and read some scripture. Something from the book of Psalms might alleviate her anxiety. She traipsed into her tent and retrieved the family Bible from her pack. Then she settled down by the fire and flipped through the chapters.

Scores of notes were written in the margins in both Papa's and Mama's handwriting. The pages of the worn book felt good to the touch. Memories of Papa and Mama sitting by the campfire, reading the thin pages, assailed her. There was nothing between them and the Lord Almighty now—how could she be sad for them? Tears slipped down her cheeks. She missed them so much.

Heather sniffled, and in spite of her tears, she smiled at the recollections that danced in her mind. They wouldn't want her to be bitter and angry with God. She blew out a deep breath and flipped through the book of Romans, searching for their favorite passages.

She hadn't been reading for more than a moment when an image of Louie popped into her mind. She looked up and gazed into his empty tent. She hoped he was safe and on his way back to her. Her lips curled up in a smile. He would be happy to see her reading the Bible.

"Lord, please be with him, and protect him." She basked in her growing attraction for him. There might be time to court later, providing he felt the same way about her. Maybe later, after McGill had been brought to justice. For now she'd be content to study the herbs and roots along the trail.

A noise caused her to jump. She reached for Papa's pistol and quickly loaded it. No pack of wild animals would catch her off guard this time. She was ready for any uninvited creature that ventured near her and posed a threat.

"Who's there?" she called into the darkness. The sound came from the river.

She tore a strip from her petticoat, wrapped it around a dry stick, and held it to the fire to make a torch of sorts. With the loaded pistol in one hand and torch in the other, she snuck a few steps closer to the rushing waters. The sound echoed in the night again, but it was no pack of wolves. This sounded like an animal in trouble.

She picked her way to the river's edge. In the dim light she saw a horse lying on its side, its front hoof scraped and bloodied. The poor thing kicked, threw its head back, and whinnied. Heather took pity on the poor creature.

"There, there, don't worry," she soothed. "I'll be right back to help you." She stuffed the pistol into her pocket and hurried up the embankment. Inside her tent she rummaged through her pack of medical supplies. Among her vials and bottles of herbal tinctures she searched for something that would relieve the animal's pain, and with luck help it sleep. The bottle of laudanum should do it, or so she hoped.

Three steps out of her tent and she lurched to a stop. In her haste to get back to the animal she realized she had forgotten something. Most humans would drink the herbal mixtures she provided although some needed more coaxing than others. Getting a wounded beast to drink the concoction would be quite a challenge.

Heather sprinted back into her tent. Inside her medical bag she found a funnel for pouring mixtures into small glass bottles. She yanked a heavy wool blanket from her cot and headed back to the river.

Out of breath by the time she reached the scene, she took a moment to inspect the rocky river's edge. The horse looked up at her with pleading eyes. She tamped down her trepidation and set to work.

Kneeling beside the horse, she thrust the funnel into its mouth and poured the mixture down its throat. The beast protested by kicking, whinnying, and shaking its head. Some of the medicine dribbled through her hands and onto the ground, but a good portion of it went into the horse.

When the bottle was empty, she brushed her hands through the horse's thick, coarse mane. "There you go. You should rest now, and then I can see how bad you're hurt." Worry nibbled at her mind. The heartbreaking treatment for horses with badly broken legs ended with the animal's demise. Her middle clenched. She hoped that wouldn't be the outcome for the gentle creature before her. While waiting for the medicine to take effect, she prayed for the horse, and for Louie.

Before too long, the horse quieted. Utilizing soothing words and a gentle touch, as she did with most human patients, Heather managed to assess the wounds on the animal's leg. It wasn't broken or bleeding profusely, but it had several nasty scrapes.

She inspected the hoof and found it healthy and uninjured. This gave her hope the animal would make a full recovery. She put the last of her salve on the injured limb and placed a splint on it for good measure. Then she bandaged it.

"Can't have you running off in the night, hurting yourself worse." Heather pushed a stake into the ground and tied the horse's reins to it. She covered the sleeping critter with her wool blanket and decided to turn in for the night.

First she had to take stock of what medical supplies she had left, which at the moment were scattered over her cot. A quick assessment told her there was very little—a small roll of bandages, a few powders, but nothing for pain or fever. She placed what few items she had back into her bag and set it on the ground by her bed.

"Oh Lord," she prayed, "I hope no life-threatening emergencies arise between now and the two days it'll take to get back into town. I have no supplies to treat them."

The excitement was over, and Heather hoped she'd seen the worst the night could offer. She pulled Papa's pistol from her pocket and placed it on her bedroll. Then she wiggled out of her dress and stripped down to nothing but her shimmy. The brisk air made her skin tingle, and she shivered.

"Now, where did I put my nightclothes?" In the commotion of getting supplies for the horse, she'd made a mess of her tent. Now she couldn't find anything. She couldn't very well sleep in her underthings. She'd freeze, especially with her only heavy blanket covering the horse.

Before she had the chance to rectify the situation, a holler pierced the cold night air.

◆—•————•—◆

"Heather!" Louie yelled as loud as he could. The shirt he'd wrapped around the injured man's head was soaked with blood and slipping loose. He had to get him back to camp fast, or he might bleed to death. He didn't know much about medicine, but he knew head wounds were serious business.

"Come on, you stubborn beast." Louie pulled hard on the reins, but he worried the wounded, unconscious man might fall off the pack mule. He yelled again for Heather, hoping—praying she'd have the right medicines to save this poor man's life.

Through the darkness, he spotted the gleam of a campfire. Out of breath, he pushed toward it with strength that had to have come from the Almighty. "Heather!" Breathing heavily from the exertion and all the hollering, he bellowed one more time as loud as his burning lungs could manage.

He staggered into the campsite just as Heather bolted from her tent.

"Who's there?" She wielded her pistol, clad in nothing but her shimmy.

"Don't shoot, it's me." Noticing her scant attire in the dim firelight, Louie blushed from his toenails to his hairline. A coughing fit seized him as he tried to dislodge the lump clogging his throat. He turned away and looked at the sky, the moon, the ground, the trees, the river, anywhere but at her.

"Louie!" Heather yelped. She bolted back into her tent. From behind the tent flap, she called out, "You're back. I wasn't sure if you'd make it tonight."

Louie cleared his throat for the dozenth time and said, "What do you mean? I told you I'd be back by nightfall." Did she really think he'd leave her alone in the wilderness, overnight? She was a strong woman, and he admired her for that, but he was still gentleman enough to look out for her.

A ragged groan drew him back to the moment. The wounded man. Spurred to forget his own plight and focus on the precarious state of another human being, he called, "Heather, I need you to come out here."

"Is something wrong?" she hollered, again from the confines of her tent.

Louie detested having to raise his voice to a female, but the urgent situation required it. "I found a badly injured man on the way back here. He might die."

Heather popped out of her tent and rushed toward him. Louie thanked the Lord, not only because she carried her medical bag, but because she was dressed.

"Where is he?" she asked. Together they pulled the man down from the mule and onto a cot in Louie's tent. Louie lit a lantern for her and then stepped back and watched her work. She unwound his shirt from the man's head and inspected the deep gash on his temple.

"Bring me some hot water, Louie, I need to clean this," she said.

Louie balked. "Shouldn't you stop the bleeding first?"

"In my midwifery training, cleanliness was always stressed, for the benefit of both mother and child. Now get me some hot water, please."

Louie complied. After she cleaned the wound and sewed a few quick stitches, she wrapped a thin bandage around his head and stood.

"There's nothing more I can do for him." She wiped her hands on her apron.

"Is he going to die?" Louie had buried a few trappers in his days with the Rocky Mountain Fur Company, and it wasn't a task he took lightly.

"I—I don't think so. But I have nothing to give him if he develops a fever." She shifted from foot to foot, wrung her hands in her apron, and kept her gaze on the ground.

Louie was puzzled. "You didn't use up all your supplies on me, did you?"

"Not really. . ."

"Then what?" Frustration grew, and Louie was in danger of losing his patience. *Lord, give me strength.*

Heather pointed in the direction of the river. "I used them on a wounded horse down there who needed them badly."

Louie ran down to the riverbank. In the dim lantern light, he saw a horse covered in a blanket, with its leg splinted and bandaged. *No*, he thought, *she couldn't have*. He groaned and kicked a rock for good measure. He jogged back into camp to confront her.

"Are you trying to tell me you used the last of your supplies on a horse?"

"I didn't mean to. Oh Louie, you should have heard the poor thing crying."

Unable to think of anything sweet and kind to say, Louie bent over, set the lantern on the ground, rested his hands on his knees, and kept his mouth shut. The horse likely belonged to the injured man and was worth good money. Yet if Louie had been here, he would have shot the animal and reserved the medical supplies for any humans.

Taking a deep breath, Louie straightened and placed his hands on his hips. Tears glistened in Heather's eyes, and his heart softened.

"I'm sorry, Louie." Heather pursed her lips and then ducked her head. "But how was I to know you'd bring an injured soul back to camp?"

"Have you no idea how many men get hurt out here, or how badly? How many of them die and are never seen again?" Louie bit his lip. He didn't want to hurt her feelings even more, but how could he make her understand how dangerous the wilderness was?

At that moment, the wounded man emitted a raspy groan. "Water," he croaked.

"Praise be to Jesus," Louie said. Here was one man who, if Louie could help it, wouldn't die in the woods.

He pushed what Heather had done to the back of his mind and focused on the situation. He hardly noticed her as she ducked into her tent. Louie grabbed the lantern and hurried to the man's side and knelt beside him. "Don't be frightened, sir. We're going to help you. Can you tell me your name? Or where you're from?"

"Name's Jonah." The poor fellow coughed and licked his lips.

Heather reappeared. "Here, drink this." She lifted Jonah's head and held a tin cup to his lips. He slurped three times, moaned, and laid his head back.

"Can you tell me how you were wounded?" Louie asked.

Jonah stared at him, his blue eyes wide with fear. "Please don't let me die. I know things that will put McGill behind bars."

Chapter 8

By God's grace, Heather had kept Jonah alive through the night. The man was strong and used to rugged conditions, but he still moaned in pain as he slept. Guilt seeped into her. She should never have given all her opium to the wounded horse. But she couldn't allow an animal to suffer without doing something. Her oath to heal demanded that she take action and ease the suffering of all who needed it, human or not.

Heather packed her mortar and pestle into her haversack. This untamed land was proving to be more than she had bargained for. It was no small wonder that Papa refused to take her with him on his trapping expeditions. If her parents looked down from heaven, she hoped they weren't disappointed in her. Yes, she had made some mistakes, but in her heart she wanted to do what was right.

Louie interrupted her thoughts. "We best break camp and get Jonah into town. He needs shelter and rest in a warm bed."

"And proper nutrition," Heather finished. She turned to face Louie. "I'll get the rest of my things packed." She went down to the river and was relieved to see the horse alive and doing well. She untied him, let him drink from the river, and led him up to the campsite. "I guess the horse will have to limp along the best he can."

"A good thing his bones weren't broken. I would've had to shoot him, and then all your medicine would have really gone to waste." Louie chuckled and winked at her.

At his teasing tone, Heather stamped her foot in mock indignation. He was upset about her use of the medicine, but he had gotten past it. He was right though, regarding her uneasiness at killing animals. Papa had shot deer and brought them home for food, and killed hogs and chickens too, but she had never been around for that. Hearing an animal's last cry before it died was much harder than she'd anticipated.

Quiet hung in the air for the hour it took to break camp. It took all her strength to hoist Jonah onto the mule, although Louie did most of the lifting. She helped him strap Jonah to the animal. The mule couldn't carry all their supplies and Jonah too. That left Louie and Heather to haul most of their belongings on their own backs.

Louie didn't seem to mind, but Heather's pack weighed heavy on her. She struggled under the weight. Mercy, how had Papa managed? Or any other trapper for that matter. No wonder so many of them died.

Louie pulled on his mule's reins, guiding him along the trail. With one hand, Heather helped balance a semiconscious Jonah on the pack mule. Holding the wounded horse's reins in her other hand made it difficult to trudge along the rocky, uneven terrain.

"How much farther must we go?" Heather let go of Jonah to wipe the sweat from her forehead with her sleeve.

"Only another five miles till we reach town. We should be there before nightfall, providing we don't run into a pack of wolves, or worse yet, a mama bear and her cubs."

Weariness of body and spirit rolled through Heather. She groaned and then caught herself. Each step she took brought her closer to town. Therefore she chose to view each step as a victory. The beauty of the land had always captivated her. She tried to notice how breathtaking the scenery was, but it was difficult considering the weight she carried.

A scripture floated into her mind, and she meditated on it until she felt some comfort, but a slow realization dawned on her. Papa's debt to the company was a problem too heavy for her to carry, just like the pack on her back. Yet in her impatience and stubbornness, she'd taken the yoke upon her own shoulders and hadn't trusted God with it. She'd allowed anger and bitterness to drive a wedge between her and the Lord, and for that she was truly sorry. A pain pierced her heart. Papa and Mama would be a sight more disappointed in her for being angry with God than they would be for her shortcomings in wilderness living.

"Lord, please forgive me," she said. Her stomach flipped. Humbling herself before the Lord was no easy task. "I'm sorry I've tried to carry all this by myself. Please, give me some peace regarding my circumstances."

"Do you need a rest?" Louie asked.

He stopped under the shade of a large tree, and she paused as well.

"Yes." Heather wrapped the horse's reins around a tree limb, close enough to the creek where he could drink his fill. The poor creature wasn't limping, but he could probably use the rest as well. Then she dropped the pack from her back and plunked down on a nearby rock.

"I'll check on Jonah." Louie tethered his mule and stepped to where Jonah was slumped over the animal's back.

"Please, Lord, let him be all right." Heather gasped as she prayed. Her feet ached, but her back hurt too much for her to lean down and rub them. Her arms and shoulders burned with the exertion of the day. Her parched mouth and throat cried out to be satiated. She reached for the canteen and guzzled the water so fast it dribbled down her chin. She wiped her chin and repinned the loose strands of her hair. Sweat glistened on her temples, but she was grateful they had made it this far.

"Heather." Louie's voice sent a shiver of dread through her.

"What?"

"I can't tell if Jonah is still breathing."

◆—————◆

Panic crept to the edges of Louie's mind.

"What do you mean, he's not breathing?" Heather jumped from the rock with surprising agility and speed for someone who had complained nearly the entire trip back to town.

"Let's get him down," she said. At least it was easier getting him down from the mule than it had been getting him up there.

Worry and fear all but swallowed Louie as he watched Heather work over the now delirious man. If Jonah died, he would take his knowledge of McGill with him to the grave. Even if Jonah spilled his secrets, would the information be credible, given his current state of mind? They had to get back to town, and soon.

"He's still breathing, but he's still bleeding too."

"Shall I get your medical bag for you?" Louie asked. Before she could reply, he scrambled over to her backpack and brought it to her.

"Thanks."

"Can I get you anything else?"

"Water, please,"

At her request, Louie retrieved a canteen of fresh water from the creek. Their fingers touched when he handed it to her, causing his heart to beat faster. But there was no time to dwell on romantic notions. A man's life hung precariously near death's grasp.

Louie helped her unwind the dirty bandage from Jonah's head. Heather poured water over the wound and rewrapped the bandage.

"I wish I had more clean bandages. Until we get to town, all I can do is keep cleaning the wound and pray it doesn't get infected."

Louie agreed. If they could just keep him alive until they arrived in town. Perhaps the doctor would know of some new treatment for head wounds.

Although he was itching to confront McGill, Louie didn't like the idea of Heather seeing the man. Whatever Jonah knew, it couldn't be good for McGill. That meant McGill would probably be as mad and mean as a riled grizzly bear, and lash out with violence like he did with both Jonah and Heather's Papa. Hadn't he heard her voice her suspicions about the man? Louie's heart beat even faster with the revelation. All their lives could very well be in danger. Louie hated the thought of McGill being alone with Heather, and the thought of the man doing bodily harm to her made his ire rise.

Jonah picked that moment to pop his eyes open and become lucid. "There's an old box buried under the cross of Duncan's wife's grave."

Heather gasped.

"What kind of box? What's in it?" Louie asked.

Jonah's head lolled to the side, and his eyes closed.

"Jonah, Jonah," Louie implored. He grasped the man by his shoulders and shook him gently a few times. Jonah remained unconscious.

Louie stared at Heather. "Do you know anything about this?"

"Of course not! Papa told me nothing."

Louie slapped his coonskin cap on his leg. If the contents of the box implicated McGill in something illegal, why hadn't Duncan told him about it? Did Duncan keep it a secret to protect folks? If that was the case, the box had to contain some powerful evidence, but was it incriminating enough to drive McGill to murder Duncan or Jonah? Louie shook his head in disbelief.

Jonah popped his eyes open again and reached for the string around his neck. "Take this key, and the box, to the nearest lawman you can find. And for the love of God, don't let McGill know what you're doing."

Chapter 9

Hours later, after Jonah regained consciousness, Heather and Louie trudged into town. Heather longed for a warm bath, but Jonah needed to be tended to first. Louie guided his mule to the doctor's quarters. After tying the mule's reins to the hitching post, he took the horse's reins from Heather.

"I'll take care of the animals. You fetch the doctor."

"Yes, of course." Heather dropped her heavy pack, hiked up her skirt, and rushed to the front door. At least this gave her another opportunity to work with the doctor. That was something to be grateful for. A hot bath could wait.

She banged on the door several times before the young man, half dressed with hair shooting in all directions, answered.

"Oh," Heather gasped. She saw a scantily clad woman sneaking out the back door. Heat engulfed her, but she decided against saying anything. She knew from experience the man was a skilled enough physician, so who was she to question his morals?

Instead, she stated, "There is a badly injured man out here who needs medical attention."

"Very well," the doctor said, pulling on the rest of his clothing.

Together the doctor and Louie wrestled a semiconscious Jonah to the examining room in the back of the building and onto a cot.

To give the doctor a moment of privacy with the patient, Heather stepped outside and retrieved her medical bag. If she was lucky, the doctor would allow her to replenish her supplies, as long as she gave him some of her ground herbs in return as they had done on other occasions.

Heather glanced up and down the street, praying she wouldn't see McGill. As inconspicuously as possible, she pulled her father's gun from her pack and stuffed it into her pocket. If McGill decided to give her trouble, she would be ready for him.

"Heather, why don't you wait here?" Louie asked. "I'll drop Jonah's wounded horse off with the blacksmith and then check the contents of the box buried by your mother's grave."

"Please be careful, and don't let McGill see you." Heather patted her father's gun in her pocket. After seeing firsthand the taking of a life, even if it was just an animal's, she prayed she wouldn't have to use it. Would she have the wherewithal to pull the trigger? She swallowed hard and wiped sweat from her forehead. That was something she didn't want to think about.

"Don't worry about me. There's at least an hour of daylight left." Louie caressed her cheek with the back of his hand. "You stay here with the doctor and Jonah. Don't go anywhere. And watch out for McGill." He reached down and took her hand in his, gave a gentle squeeze, and left.

Heather watched Louie hurry toward the livery and said a prayer for his safety. Then she stepped back into the doctor's quarters.

"How is Jonah doing?" Heather asked.

"Will you fetch me some hot water and fresh bandages, please?" the doctor called from the back.

"Yes, right away." Heather hurried into the living quarters in the front of the building. She found a teapot simmering on the potbellied stove. She rummaged around the cupboard and located a bowl and two rolls of clean bandages. She poured water into the bowl and carried the items to the doctor.

"Here you are," Heather said. "I brought the teakettle in with me so you'd have fresh water handy."

"Thank you." The man proceeded to undress Jonah to further assess his wounds.

Heather cleared her throat and took her leave. She wandered around the front part of the office observing the newest instruments and medicines. Just how they stacked up compared to her herbal tinctures and poultices she didn't know but would love to find out.

On a shelf sat a bottle of clear liquid marked "Experimental." Curious, she picked it up, undid the stopper, and smelled the contents. Her head spun, and she quickly replaced the cap.

Stepping to the entryway to the back room, Heather asked the doctor, "What is this 'experimental' stuff in the clear glass bottle?"

"Some type of new anesthetic that renders patients unconscious."

"Gracious, what a medical breakthrough. How does it work?" Heather held the bottle up to the light and studied its contents. Clear liquid that looked, to her, like water.

"You put a bit of it onto a cloth and have the patient breathe in the fumes. It was a gift from a Dr. Guthrie when I was in New York a few months ago."

"What a discovery. I bet it's very expensive."

"Yes, it's very valuable. Will you put it back, please?" the doctor said.

"Yes, of course." Heather held the bottle carefully as she headed back to his living quarters. If she broke the bottle and lost the precious medicine, she'd have to replace it, and that was an expense she could ill afford.

"I have to run to the saloon for more liquor to clean some gashes I found on his legs," the doctor called from the examining room. "I'll be right back."

"Okay," she answered. "I'll keep an eye on Jonah."

The doctor stepped out the back door. Heather strolled into the exam room and pulled a blanket over Jonah to keep him warm until the doctor could return. Satisfied that he was resting well, she stepped to the front room to return the bottle to the shelf. But before she could, a voice behind her caused her to whirl around.

"Nice to see you back from the wild. I've missed you."

Heather slipped the bottle into her left pocket since her right pocket held her gun. She thought the medicine might prove useful. If she could somehow make this man breathe a big dose of it, he'd sleep soundly, and then everyone would be safe while they gathered the necessary evidence.

McGill leered at her.

His hand snaked out and grabbed her by the wrist. "If you think I'm going to let that illiterate Frenchman ruin my plans, you're sadly mistaken."

"Let go of me," Heather demanded. The heavy gun bumped against her thigh, but McGill held her right hand, and she couldn't reach her gun with the other. Her gaze darted along the nearest countertop.

If she could just reach one of the doctor's instruments, a surgical saw, a scalpel perhaps, anything to injure him enough that she would have a chance to reach for her gun.

McGill flashed a smile at her. "Don't you worry, Miss Duncan. I'm taking you to my quarters. Louie Renault is there waiting for us. He's been kind enough to go over your father's accounts with me."

Heather shivered but kept her voice steady. "I don't believe you."

McGill threw his head back and laughed. "The accounts read that your father's debt has been paid in full. Matter of fact, he paid more than he owed. So the company actually owes you for your father's overpayment. Louie will tell you it's true. Just come with me, and I'll give you the money."

Heather didn't want to believe him, but what if he was telling the truth? Had Louie found the evidence Jonah spoke of and confronted McGill? She shook her head. Even if that were so, Louie had told her to stay put. He would never send McGill after her.

Jonah emitted a pain-filled groan.

"I need to tend to my patient." Heather squared her shoulders and tried to move toward Jonah. McGill yanked her arm so hard she yelped.

"You're coming with me whether you want to or not."

"I'm not going anywhere with you!" Heather growled.

"Oh yes you are." McGill slapped a hand over her mouth and dragged her from the doctor's quarters. Shocked at the strength he possessed, Heather struggled and kicked, praying the gun wouldn't go off and shoot her in the leg.

Terror washed over her as McGill dragged her down the back alley. She tried to scream through his hand, but there was no one along the deserted streets to hear her pathetic attempts. Nobody emerged from the noisy saloon either. She struggled as he pulled her toward his quarters. The moment he dragged her into his dimly lit living area, she knew she was in serious trouble.

◆◆———◆◆

Louie refused to let exhaustion keep him from finding the truth about McGill. He placed his free hand over the key hanging around his neck. Unsure of what he'd find at the Duncan homestead, he said a prayer for his safekeeping, and Heather's. He hoped she and Jonah were faring well at the doctor's, and that McGill hadn't spotted them yet.

"Come along, boy," he said to Jonah's horse as he tugged the animal into the livery at the end of the street. "I hope the blacksmith can keep you while both you and your owner recuperate."

The blacksmith greeted Louie and guided the animal to a nearby stable. "This horse belongs to a man named Jonah," Louie said. "I don't know his last name. Anyhow, he's resting at the doctor's and will come retrieve the animal and pay you when he's well again."

"Recognize the horse and the name. Won't be a problem." The blacksmith bent down to check the horse's leg.

"I need to rent one of your healthy horses if you have one available. Will two rabbit furs be payment enough?" Louie said.

"Sure, but all I have is a mustang, and he's only half broke. Threw McGill right into a bed of poison ivy the other day." The blacksmith chuckled.

Louie groaned. What other choice did he have? "I'll take him." He helped the blacksmith saddle the animal. Soon he was riding hard for the Duncan homestead. The horse took him there without incident. He didn't seem to have a problem with being only half broke. The problem must have been the rider.

After tying the mustang's reins to a corral post, Louie hurried to the barn and found a shovel. The same implement he'd used to bury his friend. Had that been only two months ago? A pang hit him in the chest. Duncan had been like a father to him. He missed him. He shook his head and strode to the gravesites.

Standing over the plot of Mrs. Duncan, a fine lady by her husband's accounts, Louie felt like he was desecrating the poor woman's resting place. He hoped God, and the Duncans, would forgive him.

"Lord, give me strength," he muttered. Then he removed the cross and dug. A mere foot below the earth's surface he was met with resistance and a loud clang. Louie dropped to his knees and used his hands to unearth a tin box. Hands trembling, he pulled the key from his neck and opened the box.

His skin tingled at a sudden chill that had nothing to do with the cool breeze sweeping through the trees. Inside the box he found what they were looking for. He still couldn't read very well, but he knew enough to comprehend what he was looking at. The missing pages of McGill's ledger.

Louie wasn't sure, of course, but those pages gave what looked like, and what he hoped, was an account of how McGill had swindled the trappers—in McGill's own handwriting! Louie recognized the loopy flourish to the *McG* from the crook's signature on past receipts when he turned in furs.

Accompanying the pages were sworn statements by Jonah and Duncan—at least he thought those signatures at the bottom of the pages were theirs. What a tragedy there were no local sheriffs or deputies on hand. Had Jonah and Duncan sat on their evidence, hoping to hold off until a circuit sheriff arrived in the area? Is that what gave McGill time to commit his evil acts?

Louie shoved the papers back into the tin box. His gaze darted from the trees to the river, to the cabin, praying he wouldn't see McGill. He locked the box and hung the key around his neck again. Their only hope was to carry the papers east to the nearest law enforcement officer and pray that he would press charges against McGill. Louie was sure the Rocky Mountain Fur Company would have their say in the matter and want to press charges as well. He and the other trappers could go to the company owners and request their assistance.

What if McGill left town or went farther west? Or what if the company and the law didn't care to bother with McGill? Louie shuddered. If McGill wasn't stopped, he was sure to seek revenge on those who tried to send him to jail. Then Louie and Heather could be on the run for the rest of their lives. Determination gripped him. He would not allow McGill to harm Heather no matter what he had to do to protect her.

Louie crammed the tin box into his knapsack and cinched it tight. Then he mounted the mustang and rode hard for town.

Night was beginning to fall as he traveled the road into town. He worried about Heather and Jonah. "Please God, let Jonah live, let Heather be all right." He had really grown to care for her in the months he'd worked with her, the months she'd spent teaching him to read. That valuable skill was one that would not only enable him to study the scriptures and deepen his faith but help him better his life too. Gratitude seemed too small a word to express how he felt toward her. He more than owed her. He loved her.

The small community's buildings were just coming into view when he heard a scream followed by a gunshot.

Chapter 10

Within the confines of McGill's living quarters, and after a small scuffle, Heather finally felt as though she could breathe again. She opened her eyes to see if she'd shot McGill, and how badly. The man huddled on the floor, clutching his right leg. Blood flowed from the wound.

"Don't move your leg, Mr. McGill." Heather stuffed the gun back into her pocket and leaped into action. McGill kicked at her and snarled like a beaver caught in a trap. For a second, she felt pity for him. At least he wouldn't suffer the same fate as trapped animals, not if she could help it.

"I told you to lie still, Mr. McGill." She grabbed a bottle of rotgut alcohol from the table and poured it into the man's wound. He cussed so profusely her ears burned at the assault. She tore a strip of cloth from her petticoat and wrapped it around his bleeding leg.

"Mr. McGill, you must stop thrashing around. If the bone has been hit, you could lose your leg." His moving around like this would likely make his injury worse. That must not have mattered to him though. He crawled toward a shotgun resting against the wall.

Heather sat on him. Enraged, he continued to thrash around. He yanked at her skirt and tried to pull her off of him.

They rolled back and forth across the floor.

Her hair came loose from its pins.

The man grabbed a handful of her hair, and she yelped.

She reached for his hair and prayed desperately for the strength to subdue him somehow. With a free hand she reached into her pocket and pulled out Papa's gun again. The barrel made a loud click as she cocked the trigger and held the muzzle to the back of McGill's head.

"Please, Mr. McGill, I don't want to shoot you," Heather cried. Even with all the pain he'd caused, she really didn't want to kill him. "God, please help me," she prayed.

McGill continued to swear.

Heather searched her surroundings for something to tie him up with. She couldn't see any ropes within view or reaching distance. She still had to tend the man's injured leg somehow. She placed her free hand over the bullet hole to staunch the bleeding and held tight. McGill cried out, but at least he was still for the moment.

"Louie will be here any minute, with evidence of your wrongdoing. Jonah is going to live, no thanks to you, and both men are going to testify against you in court."

McGill reached for the nearby fire poker.

Heather gasped. "Oh no you don't." Anger bubbled in her with a fierceness that almost frightened her. Would this man never give up? While keeping the gun aimed at McGill, she managed to tear another piece from her petticoat with her free hand. Next, she pulled the doctor's bottle of experimental liquid from her pocket. The substance had a faintly sweet smell to it, and she held her breath. She poured a small amount on the cloth and held it over McGill's mouth and nose.

The man thrashed harder, but with God's grace and strength, she held on.

Moments later, when his body went limp, Heather stepped back and sucked air into her lungs. Tears brimmed in her eyes. She was safe for the moment. She prayed God would keep her safe from this sick man.

Muscles aching from the exertion, she tore yet another strip from her petticoat and tied his hands behind his back. "Let's see how much squirming you do now. You're going to jail for a very long time." All she had to do now was wait for someone to show up.

"Help," Heather yelled. She glanced around for something to dress the wound on McGill's leg but found nothing. There was no time to search the quarters. A quick assessment revealed no exit wound, which meant the bullet was still in him. The doctor needed to operate and remove the bullet, and soon, or McGill would be in danger of losing the leg.

Heather debated over running for the doctor or the blacksmith. The doctor said the medicine made people sleep, but he didn't say for how long. Heather feared McGill would wake up and try to kill her, or at least escape. That would be bad for all parties, most of all McGill. She decided against leaving him alone.

"What is taking Louie so long to get back?" she asked aloud. She prayed for his swift return and that he'd think to look for her at McGill's quarters. If and when he found her, they could summon the doctor and, when McGill was treated, they could lock him up somewhere. How long would it take for the circuit sheriff to arrive?

Part of her wanted to leave McGill to his own consequences, but her oath to heal made her decide otherwise. Friend or enemy, this man was in desperate need of medical attention. Probing the wound again, she felt for the bone. Lucky for McGill it was still intact. Instinct told her to run for the doctor, but she needed to bandage the wound before he lost too much blood.

Heather untied her petticoat and tore the last remnants into strips. Indignation swept through her as she wrapped the tattered lacy fabric around his leg. With her petticoat ruined, she no longer owned even one piece of pretty feminine clothing.

Louie burst through the door at that moment. "Heather, are you all right?"

She rushed into Louie's arms. He held her close, and she relished his warmth and strength. Without his prayers, patience, and demonstration of the unconditional love of Christ, she might never have found God again. "I was hoping you'd think to look for me here when you didn't find me at the doctor's place. I'm fine, but I shot McGill in the leg. He's sleeping now, but he needs a doctor."

"He's sleeping?" Louie's mouth hung open,

"Yes, I gave him some newfangled concoction to make him sleep, but I don't know how long it'll keep him asleep. We need the doctor, now." Without knowing the proper dosage, she was afraid she'd given him too much. She shivered. What if he never woke up?

"We both can't go. What if he comes to?" Louie said.

"I don't know if he will," Heather said. *Oh Lord, what have I done?*

"What do you mean, you don't know? You didn't kill him, did you?" Louie stared at her, his dark eyes wide.

"No, I mean, I don't know." Panic unfolded in Heather. A sob escaped.

"What exactly did you give him?" Louie held her by the shoulders. The concern in his eyes told her he too was frightened.

"Some experimental medicine I got from the doctor." Heather cried, unable to stop the tears. Why couldn't Louie stop asking questions and just fetch the doctor? The experimental liquid was so new, not even the doctor knew what the effects were.

Fearing the worse, she leaned down and felt for breath under the man's nose. A sigh escaped. "Thank the Lord, he's still alive."

"I don't know what you're up to, but you need to go get the doc, and fast." Louie procured a strip of leather from somewhere and tied McGill's good leg to the potbellied stove. "If he wakes up, this won't hold him for long. I'll get the shackles from the blacksmith. You run for the doctor. Hopefully he's still here, and alive, when we get back."

Heather bolted out the door and to the doctor's quarters. Jonah slept on the cot in back, but the doctor wasn't there. She took a few seconds to make sure

Jonah was all right and then tried to think of where the doctor might be.

Heather groaned and headed for the saloon. There she found him, seated at a card table, holding in his lap the scantily clad woman she'd seen sneaking out the man's back door earlier that evening.

Heather whistled to get the doctor's attention.

The man looked over at her, and his eyes went wide. "Please tell me our patient is still alive?"

"Yes." Heather rolled her eyes at the heavens and saw a gaudy, oversized chandelier hanging from the ceiling. If Papa and Mama could see her there, they'd be aghast. Best get to the point, and quick. "But I shot McGill. He needs your help."

The doctor jumped from his seat and dropped the woman to the floor. She yelped as the doctor stepped over her.

"Show me our next patient," the doctor said.

Saloon patrons didn't rank high on Heather's list of reputable people, but at least this doctor seemed to truly care for the sick and injured.

"Let me get my medical supplies," he said.

Heather waited not so patiently while the doctor sprinted into his quarters and reappeared moments later with his medical bag. She explained the situation to him while dragging him down the street. By the time they reached McGill's office, there was no sign of Louie or the blacksmith, and McGill was gone.

✦━━━━·━━✦

Louie raced to the livery. There stood the mustang tied to the hitching post, but there was no sign of the blacksmith. He grabbed the tin box with the ledger pages and raced around the inside of the hot structure calling out the man's name. No answer. Where could he be?

Still carrying the precious box of evidence, Louie sprinted behind the building and hollered again.

"I'm in the outhouse." The blacksmith's muffled reply made Louie groan.

That figured. Louie stood as close to the privy as his nose allowed and relayed the news about McGill's capture to the man. He took another few moments to explain about the ledgers, the papers in the tin box, and even how Heather had dosed McGill with some strange new medicine. Talking through the outhouse wall made him feel silly, but there was nothing else he could do. Time was of the essence.

The blacksmith finally emerged, hoisting his suspenders over his shoulders. "You get back to McGill's office. I'll head back to my shop, grab the shackles, and meet you there."

Louie was out of breath by the time he ran into McGill's office. He saw

Heather standing off to one side with the doctor. A strip of leather lay on the floor, one end tied to the potbellied stove, the other end sawed through. Louie chastised himself for leaving McGill alone. Why hadn't he thought to check McGill's pockets for a knife? Now he had to deal with the man's escape.

"The ledgers," Heather exclaimed. She rushed into the back room.

The blacksmith burst into the room, hat in one hand, shackles clanging in his other.

"We don't need those just yet." Louie pointed to the iron chains. "McGill's escaped."

The blacksmith let out an expletive and smacked his cap against his leg. "I guess this explains why that half-broke mustang is missing from the hitching post. I bet McGill took off with it."

Louie heard Heather rustling in the back room while he tried to make sense of it all. A few minutes later she reappeared.

"I've searched everywhere for the ledgers," she said. "They're gone, but I found some statements from the company implying there are—were—several pounds of gold coins meant as pay for the trappers. Only I couldn't find any gold coins among McGill's belongings. I bet he stole every bit of it."

Louie noted tears brimming in her eyes. He pulled the ledger pages from the tin box he carried and handed them to Heather.

After taking what seemed like hours to read them, she said, "These pages are sworn statements from Jonah and my father. They give a full account of conversations they had with McGill that implicate him in stealing from the trappers, cheating the company, and pocketing the money for himself."

Although they had the missing ledger pages, those pages wouldn't do anyone any good if they didn't have the ledgers they belonged to. Without a full and accurate record of the men's accounts, they would be stuck paying off debts they didn't owe. He had to find McGill and those ledgers and bring him and the stolen money back.

Louie rushed outside and into full darkness. The thin sliver of moon did little to illuminate his surroundings. In vain they searched by lantern for a blood trail, horse tracks, any sign of McGill, but could see nothing along the deserted streets or around the darkened blacksmith's shop. Louie couldn't climb the trail leading out of town in the dark. Frustration rolled through him. McGill had a head start, but at least he couldn't get far in the dark either. Louie would have to wait.

That night they bedded down in the doctor's quarters. Heather slept in the front room while Louie and the doctor occupied cots in the back examining room. Louie wasn't about to wake Jonah to question him further, but if the man woke of his own accord, he wanted to be there. With so much at stake, he prayed like never before.

The next morning, just before the sun peeked over the horizon, the doctor announced that Jonah would live. The injured man had slept soundly, but the doctor advised against disturbing him.

Louie dressed and stuffed his pockets with some cold biscuits from the doctor's pantry. He packed a few more supplies and headed for the livery.

It was time to find McGill. Louie yawned all the way to the blacksmith's shop. When this was all over, he hoped to sleep for a week.

"I'm sorry, Louie," the blacksmith said. "McGill took off with the only good horse I had, that mustang. Jonah's horse isn't quite ready to travel just yet, and I believe someone borrowed the doctor's pinto."

Louie could ask the doctor who and track the animal down, but that would waste precious time. Resigned to his pack mule, Louie lashed his backpack and bedroll to the tired beast's back.

The blacksmith held out a pair of shackles. "Here. I don't see McGill coming back without a fight."

"Um, thanks," Louie said. His stomach turned, but he added the chains to his pack and then turned and walked away. He had to say goodbye to someone special before he left, and prayed it wasn't forever.

Heather emerged from the doctor's quarters, a heavy Indian blanket wrapped around her shoulders.

"I'm going after him," Louie said to her. Her long hair hung down to her waist. She looked both strong and vulnerable at the same time. He needed to hold her, if just for a moment, before he left to find McGill.

"Louie, please," Heather cried. "Please be safe."

She stared at him with green eyes that captivated him. He pulled her into an embrace. If only he didn't have to let her go, he'd profess his love for her and perhaps steal a kiss. But if he didn't catch McGill, the man would likely move to another town and harm more people. Nobody in the territories would be safe. He'd have to deal with his feelings for Heather later.

"I want you to be safe too, Heather. Promise me you'll stay here until I return."

She bit her lower lip and then said, "Okay, I promise."

In spite of her adventurous personality, he believed she meant it. As an added precaution, he addressed the blacksmith, who stood nearby. "Look out for her, please, until I can return."

The blacksmith nodded and ducked back into his shop.

"Go," she said.

Her weak smile told him she understood. The image of her face pressed into his memory. Leading his mule back to the blacksmith's shop, Louie found what he had hoped for.

A blood trail and horse tracks leading out of town.

It was a start. Louie climbed on his mule. It might take days to catch up with McGill, if ever, and yet he was not deterred. The drive to bring this man to justice prodded Louie forward. Louie followed the trail out of town. From there the tracks led up the rolling foothills. To his right, he could see nothing but the face of steep rock reaching higher and higher up the mountain. To his left, the trail dropped off, creating a vast precipice. The sun moved higher in the sky as Louie made slow time up the steep, narrow trail.

Hunger gnawed at him. He stuffed a cold, dry biscuit into his mouth. Hours later there was still no sign of McGill.

Then a horse whinnied. The blacksmith's stolen mustang galloped down the trail and straight toward him. Frightened, Louie steered his mule to hug the side of the cliff and begged for God's protection as the mustang ran past him.

When he caught his breath, he realized McGill must now be on foot. Louie nudged the sides of his mule to hurry it along.

Snow spotted the landscape, and Louie struggled to climb farther up the side of the cliff. How far could this man go with such a severe leg wound? Louie emitted an exasperated sigh.

A cry pierced the air, followed by a gunshot. Louie spotted McGill. The man was crazy enough to fire a gun at these heights. Would the noise and ricocheting bullet cause a rockslide? Louie slowly eased off his mule and wrapped the reins around an outcropping of rocks.

"Stay back, I tell you, or I'll drop the money and the ledgers over the side, into the river," McGill sneered.

Louie watched as the man reloaded his pistol and fired again. He ducked behind his frightened mule. The bullets missed Louie and, thankfully, the mule, but ricocheted off the loose rocks not more than two feet over his head. Small rocks tumbled down the face of the mountain, pelting both Louie and his frightened mule.

"Lord, please help me talk some sense into this man." They needed those ledgers to prove McGill had swindled them all. If they didn't have proof, dozens of trappers would be financially ruined. And how would such a loss affect the company? It was almost too much for Louie to consider at that moment.

"McGill," Louie pleaded. "Let's go back to town. That money isn't worth dying for, and I'm sure you're sorry." Louie believed McGill swindled folks because he was greedy, but now wasn't the time to debate motive or the possibility of the man repenting.

McGill snarled and limped backward while rubbing his bloody leg. If Louie could get close enough to grab McGill's pack, then at least the evidence would be safe.

Louie had almost reached McGill, but then the man held the pack over the side of the cliff. Louie sucked in a breath. The wild look in the criminal's eyes made the hair on Louie's arms prickle. He held his hands up. "No, McGill, don't!"

"I should have found a way to kill you like I did Old Man Duncan, like I thought I did with Jonah." McGill growled. "Then that little Scottish wench would have no choice but to marry me. Now get back, or I'm dropping this."

Angered, Louie sprang forward and knocked McGill to the ground.

McGill kicked Louie in the belly and yelled, "Get away from me, or I'll take us both over the edge."

"I don't want to kill you, McGill, but I'm not letting you get away with this pack either." Louie had his hands on the pack and begged God for help.

McGill landed a punch that made Louie go dizzy for a few seconds.

Fear-crazed strength drove Louie forward, and he wrestled the pack away from McGill. Then Louie stood to his feet and wiped blood from his chin.

McGill pulled a horn of powder from his belt and prepared to reload his weapon.

Louie dropped the pack and took the opportunity to spring onto McGill. He managed to grab McGill's wrist and bang his hand on a rock.

The gun slipped from McGill's hand and tumbled over the edge of the cliff.

McGill yelled, rose to his feet, and stumbled farther up the trail, cussing. Louie scanned the ground for the pack containing the ledgers and money, praying it hadn't gone over the edge along with the gun.

⊷•——•⊶

"Miss Duncan!" the blacksmith exclaimed. "You can't go out there alone. You could be attacked by Indians or animals, or both."

"McGill is badly injured and needs medical attention, and I intend to give it." Heather climbed onto the doctor's recently returned pinto. The doctor had rented it to one of his trapper friends and was fortunate enough to get the animal back when he'd asked for it, claiming it was for a good cause.

She picked up the reins. Louie had a few hours head start, and the injured McGill couldn't be far ahead of him. But with the doctor's fast horse, she was sure she could catch up with them.

The blacksmith crossed his arms over his chest. "I stood right here and heard you tell Louie you'd stay put and wait for him to come back."

"I changed my mind."

"Fine. Good luck." He threw his hands in the air and walked away.

Heather led the animal out of town and up the steep mountain. The horse seemed familiar with the surroundings and picked his way along the trail with little difficulty. They moved quickly, and for that she was grateful. Seeds of fear threatened to burrow into her, but this time she rebuked them and cried out to God for help.

She hadn't gone far when her horse whinnied. His ears twitched, and he skittered sideways, away from the edge.

"Whoa, boy, whoa!" Heather gripped the saddle horn to keep from toppling off. A twisting in her middle told her something was wrong. For a minute, she feared something awful had happened to Louie. Her breath came in quick gasps. Sweat broke out on her forehead.

A galloping sound up ahead caught her attention. Someone was coming down the trail. The pinto whinnied again. She spoke to calm the animal and steered away from the edge, praying that whatever was coming wouldn't send them plummeting down to the river below.

The blacksmith's mustang, minus a rider, shot past so close it was a wonder they all didn't fall over the cliff.

Her heart thudded and she took a deep breath. "Thank You, Lord, for Your divine protection." She nudged the horse onward. Louie and McGill couldn't be far ahead. She prayed again that Louie would be safe and have things under control.

The sun was crawling toward the horizon by the time she spotted them. Elation and relief surged through her when she saw Louie lumbering toward her. He was safe, and he held McGill's haversack. She didn't see McGill.

She dismounted and tied the horse to a tree branch, then ran to help him. Several rocks fell from above, but she dodged them.

"Heather," Louie said. "What are you doing here?"

"I came to help bring McGill back to town."

Louie harrumphed and pointed at McGill, who was walking away from them.

Heather jolted into action. She rushed to Louie and placed her arm around his waist. The poor man breathed heavily. Swelling on his bruised cheek made her heart convulse. A few groans escaped as he walked. She helped him stagger to his mule and tied the haversack on its back. Blood oozed from Louie's arms and chin.

She turned to see McGill limping away from them up the trail so fast it surprised her. She knew he must have lost a lot of blood. If he didn't get help soon, she feared he would pass out.

"Wait," Heather called. "Mr. McGill, you could die from your wounds. Come back to town with us and turn yourself in. Yes, you'll go to jail, but at least you'll be alive."

McGill turned to face her and walked backward up the trail. "You ungrateful wench, stay away from me!"

Heather wondered if he cared whether or not he died. It turned her stomach enough seeing an animal die—she couldn't watch that happen to McGill too. Rage and vengeance seemed to consume him, and it saddened her to think how twisted his mind must be.

Hoping to calm him, she took a few steps forward and spoke to him as if he were one of her patients.

"Mr. McGill, I'm so sorry for anything I've done to hurt you," she said. Sometimes some folks were so frightened they couldn't think straight. If she could convey a tone of gentleness, perhaps he would settle down and let her help him.

To her horror, the man slipped on the loose rocks and tumbled to the ground. He landed on his wounded leg, screamed, and rolled over the edge of the cliff.

"Oh," Heather gasped. "Mr. McGill, no!"

McGill held on to a few loose rocks, but his legs dangled precariously over the precipice.

"Hang on, McGill," Louie shouted. "We'll pull you back up."

Louie raced past her and threw himself so close to the cliff's edge, Heather screamed. She hiked up her skirts and ran to help. She loved Louie, and if he went over the side with McGill, her heart would be sliced to ribbons.

"Take my hand." Louie stretched, reaching for McGill.

Heather sprawled on the ground beside Louie and also tried to grab McGill. Louie cried, "Heather, get back!"

With one hand, Louie grabbed her bodice and held tight. Dear Louie, trying to protect her, as he did when they were trapping together. Heather peered over the cliff at the man who had caused her, and so many trappers, pain, the thief who had stolen not just money, but hope. Yet if Jesus could forgive a thief on the cross, who was she to do any less? The anger brimming in McGill's eyes should have frightened her, but all she felt was pity.

"You will never see me in jail," McGill growled.

"That's what you think!" Heather lunged forward and grasped McGill by the hair. She pulled with all her might. The man bellowed and swatted at her and Louie, but they managed to wrangle him back up and onto stable ground.

"I borrowed some shackles from the blacksmith. Go get them out of my pack," Louie instructed.

Heather sprinted to his mule, retrieved the heavy chains, and hurried back to

Louie. The rattling of the irons caused her heart to squeeze.

McGill had passed out from blood loss and probably defeat. Worry enveloped her. She hurried to the pinto and yanked her medical bag off the saddle. The man may be a skunk, but he was still a human being. She poured every bit of whiskey she had into his wound.

"I hope this takes care of infection, but I can't make any promises." Heather cast a glance at Louie, who sat on a nearby boulder, holding his bandanna to his bloody chin. At least the man she loved wouldn't be financially ruined or constantly looking over his shoulder for McGill. That was something to be grateful for.

Turning her focus to the more injured man, she pulled several strips of muslin from her bag and rebandaged his leg. The bullet was still in McGill's leg, but the side of a cliff was no place for surgery.

When McGill's wrists were chained and he was on the pinto, Heather allowed the tears to fall. It was over. Justice would be served and Papa's debt paid. She marveled at how God had been with her all along, even when she wandered from Him. Somehow she knew He understood.

"Heather, thank the Lord you're safe." Louie wrapped her in a tender embrace and buried his face in her hair.

"Oh Louie," Heather cried. "I was afraid McGill would pull you over the cliff with him. The thought of living the rest of my life without you was more than I could bear."

"Heather Duncan, I never want to leave you. I love you." Louie pulled her close and nuzzled her neck.

The sun began its descent into the vast blue-gold horizon, and Heather felt every bit of its warmth. Her heart thumped in her chest at being so close to Louie. Propriety was forgotten as he ran his fingers through her hair. She leaned into his embrace and stared into his ebony-colored eyes.

He said no words but placed a tender kiss on her lips. She swam in the heady feelings that swept over her. When he pulled away, she struggled to catch her breath. She laid her head against his solid chest until her legs felt strong enough to support her once again.

After a moment, she said, "I'm so glad we have the evidence to clear Papa's name."

"Let's get back to town and get this whole ledger mess straightened out and handed off to the law," Louie said. He took her hand, and they headed down the mountainside and into a new life together.

Epilogue

Early June 1833
The Rendezvous, Ham's Fork, Wyoming

Heather sat on a rock to rest her tired feet and warm herself in the summer sunshine.

"Afternoon, Mrs. Renault," Red Feathers said.

"Afternoon," Heather said. "I hear you and Louie are doing well in your lessons on reading and arithmetic."

"Yes, we are. I believe being able to read and write the white man's language will help my people." Red Feathers straightened his spine and gave her a wide smile.

The assortment of copper necklaces hanging from the Shoshone Indian's neck shimmered in the afternoon sunlight. The beaded pieces of jewelry adorning the man's wrists gave off a rainbow of colors.

"I'm proud of both you and Louie. Reading is a wonderful ability, one I hope brings you great joy, and knowledge too."

Red Feather's dark skin didn't mask the blush that colored his cheeks. "I must go now." He smiled and nodded. He then wandered to the circle where one of the men was telling another outlandish tale.

The past year hadn't been without sadness, at least for McGill. She and Louie had gotten him back to town alive, but he had lost his leg due to infection. Last she had heard, he had been moved to an asylum in New York. She extended her sympathies to the man by means of praying for him often.

Heather's blessings were so abundant she could hardly count them. Louie and three men from the Rocky Mountain Fur Company had read statements from Papa and listened to Jonah's testimony. It took months for them to meticulously go over the entire batch of ledgers. In the end, the company had settled the accounts, and each trapper's record was as straight as a Shoshone arrow. With money in his pocket, Louie had proposed, and she had accepted.

After their marriage, they moved into Papa and Mama's homestead. Fur trapping was a dying trade, so Louie and Heather farmed the land. Louie had traded his furs for two ax-heads, horse tack, and plenty of ammunition. As a special gift for Heather, he'd gotten yards and yards of calico and flannel, and a twenty-five-pound barrel of sugar. Red Feathers had given a rattle to her and Louie for their soon-to-be-born baby. They weren't wealthy by any means, but they were happy.

The child in Heather's womb made its presence known with a hearty kick. She massaged her rounding belly. She could hardly wait for September, when the baby was due.

Music erupted from the circle of men. A bearded red-haired man played a squeeze box, and another joined him on a tambourine. The rest sang a boisterous song Heather didn't know the words to.

Heather felt tears tingling in her eyes, and a smile spread across her face. What happy, carefree days with cherished friends. No wonder Papa loved these events so much. If only they could go on forever.

"May I have this dance?"

Heather gazed up at her husband. "Of course." Louie took her in his arms as the child kicked again within her. She was part of a family again, not just an earthly one, but a heavenly one as well. She couldn't have been more content.

Debby Lee was raised in the cozy little town of Toledo, Washington. She has been writing since she was a small child and has written several novels but never forgets home. Debby enjoys being a part of the Northwest Christian Writers Association and Romance Writers of America. As a self-professed nature lover and an avid listener of 1960s folk music, Debby can't help but feel like a hippie child who wasn't born soon enough to attend Woodstock. She wishes she could run barefoot all year long but often does anyway in the grass and on the beaches in her hamlet in cold and rainy southwest Washington. During football season, Debby cheers on the Seattle Seahawks along with legions of other devoted fans. She is also filled with wanderlust and dreams of visiting Denmark, Italy, and Morocco someday. Debby loves connecting with her readers through her website at www.booksbydebbylee.com.

MissTaken Identity

by Kimberley Woodhouse

Dedication

To Mom and Dad,

I know there were many times you didn't know what to do with your youngest child, whose love for music and all things creative kept you on your toes. But thanks for pushing me to work hard and aim high. Thank you for all the chauffeuring to piano and voice lessons, competitions, concerts, play practices, and everything else. I know it wasn't easy—or cheap!— but I hope you know the sacrifice was and is greatly appreciated. The love of books was a gift from you both and shaped me into the writer I am today. It brings me so much joy to know that you read my books now too. Thank you. Thank you for modeling how to walk in God's grace and love. Being your daughter is a joy and a privilege.

Therefore, since we are surrounded by so great a cloud of witnesses, let us also lay aside every weight, and sin which clings so closely, and let us run with endurance the race that is set before us, looking to Jesus, the founder and perfecter of our faith, who for the joy that was set before him endured the cross, despising the shame, and is seated at the right hand of the throne of God.
HEBREWS 12:1–2 ESV

Chapter 1

"But Miss Abigail, this has got to be the craziest idea you've had."

Abigail Monroe raised her eyebrows at her maid. At twenty-four years old, she was used to hearing that her servants called her crazy behind her back—because, let's face it, in the past she'd done some crazy things—but she was older now, and none of them had been bold enough to say it to her face since her parents' passing. "It is not crazy. It is simply. . .eccentric." She held up a pair of brown leather chaps and eyed them for size.

"Bah." Sally crossed her arms over her ample chest. "If your sweet mama were still alive—"

"Don't you dare bring Mama into this. She and Daddy have been gone for more than two years, and you know how much it crushed me." Abigail skirted the bed and knocked over the boots she'd placed on the floor. Catching herself before she fell down on her bustle, Abigail took a deep breath. She'd definitely have to work on not knocking things over if this was going to work.

"You know I do, miss, but I can't say they would approve of"—she waved her hand around the room—"this."

Putting her hands on her hips, Abigail sighed. Sally knew her better than anyone else. "Well. . .*this*. . .is what I need to do." She looked at the other clothes laid about before plopping onto the bed in a very unladylike sit. "Do you have any idea how difficult it is to be a wealthy, single woman landowner?" Knowing full well that Sally understood, Abigail needed to vent anyway. She waved a hand at the door. "How many proposals a month am I getting? Five. . .six? And not a single one of them wants anything to do with me. They want my land. They want my money. They want my cattle. But none of them want *me*." Tears sprang to her eyes.

"Oh, you know that's not true. You're beautiful, and all them gents have remarked about how nice it would be to have a pretty wife on their arm."

"Pretty wife. On their arm." Abigail groaned and brushed at the tears. "Exactly. They don't know a thing about me. They don't care about what I like or dislike. They *really* don't care about my work with the Woman's Christian

Temperance Union. They just want an ornament for their arm and all my money and land. Land that Daddy poured himself into. And I'm not about to get married just so one of those gold diggers can get their hands on my ranch."

Sally huffed. "That's still no reason for you to take off on whatever crazy idea you have to who knows where—"

"It's called an adventure, Sally. But rest assured, when I return, I'm going to have to do some serious thinking on what I'm looking for in a husband. He will definitely need to respect my beliefs about abstinence from alcohol—because we all know it leads to immorality—and I refuse to marry a man who doesn't have the same faith in God. But I'm not too proud to admit that I will need some help running this place." She sighed. "For now, I need—or I guess I should say, I *want*—to explore the frontier. Everyone expects me to settle down, and I'm sure I will, but I need to do some exploring on my own. To see more of the world than just this little spot in Coleman County, Texas. Don't you understand that?"

"You and your adventures." Sally shook her head and clucked her tongue at Abigail. "All you've ever wanted is something new and exciting. Whatever's out of reach. What's wrong with finding that right here? It wouldn't hurt you to have an *adventure* or two here learning about the runnings of this place. Your daddy wanted you to be able to run it by yourself if need be."

Abigail felt scolded. She put her hands on her hips. Who was in charge here? "Sally, you've always spoken your mind with me and given me guidance over the years, but you need to remember that I'm old enough to make my own decisions."

"Old enough to have children too—but that doesn't mean you need be acting like one." Her maid's words were muttered, but Abigail heard them anyway. The older woman had been taking her in hand for more than twenty years. Abigail imagined Sally would still be scolding her thirty years from now.

"While I appreciate your sage advice, I don't believe I'm acting like a child." She lifted her chin. "I'm sure there will be plenty of adventure for me here as the years go on. Raymond's got things under control, and there's lots of time for me to learn the workings when I return. Haven't *you* ever wanted to get out of your regular routine and try something new?" As much as she pleaded and hoped to have an affirmative answer, she knew how Sally would respond.

"No. I haven't."

The look on her maid's face made Abigail laugh. "Of course not." She stood up and went back to figuring out her new wardrobe. It wasn't as if she'd ever be able to convince Sally that her idea was a good one.

"This is my home. Your family has been very good to me." The maid's brown eyes snapped with conviction.

"This is my home too. And it will be our home for the rest of our lives."
Abigail wasn't sure what she could say next. The woman in front of her was like
a beloved aunt. Even though she worked for Abigail, there wasn't anyone she
respected more. Even when they disagreed. Which was a lot. "I guess I simply
wanted to figure out a little more of my life. Besides, your husband will keep it
all running while I'm gone."

"Child, you have a stubborn streak a mile wide. I just wish you'd listen to reason." Sally sighed. "But I guess I shouldn't expect things to change. You've never
been too good at listening." She waved her hand at Abigail in dismissal. "Mark
my words: you're gonna end up in a heap of trouble over this one."

"Me? In trouble? Your imagination is running wild, Sally."

It was the older woman's turn to laugh. "Would you like me to start listing
all the pinches you've gotten yourself into over the years? And all the times my
Raymond had to come rescue you when your Daddy wasn't around?"

Abigail shook her head. "That was when I was young and naive. I've got a
plan this time."

"A plan?" Sally pointed to the clothes on the bed. "Your idea of a plan is to
dress like a man? You don't know the first thing about how to act like a man!"

"Of course I do! I've been surrounded by men my whole life."

"Oh child." She started folding the trousers Abigail had set aside for fitting.
"This *is* going to be a disaster."

Abigail laughed it off. Sally always did preach doom and gloom. Always to
try and convince her *not* to do something.

"It won't be a disaster. Everything will be fine. You'll see."

"Mm hmm." The sarcastic affirmation reinforced that Sally thought she was
going to fail. "Remember what your Mama always said. . . ."

The inference to Abigail's tendency in the past to be accident prone made
her lift her chin. Well, she would just have to prove her maid wrong. She was
older now and hadn't had a mishap for quite some time.

The smell of baking bread made her mouth water. A change of subject was
in order. "That bread smells delicious, Sally."

"I need to check it. But this discussion isn't over. I'll be back to help you
finish packing." Sally turned to the door and then looked over her shoulder.
"Have you thought about your undergarments? Exactly how are you planning to
lace your corsets? And don't tell me you're going to ban them like some of those
ridiculous other temperance-shouting women. Unless of course you're planning
on wearing men's underthings as well? I'm trying to picture you in a union suit."
Her hearty laughter followed her out of the room.

Abigail cringed. No, she hadn't thought on that. There was not a chance in the world she would wear men's underwear. Not. Ever. The thought of wearing a union suit was repulsive. A shiver raced up her spine. She might be posing as a man to take this trip, but she was a lady, after all. She'd just have to wear her corset and bloomers underneath the baggy men's clothing. But that still didn't solve the problem of how she would dress herself. Guess she'd just have to get good at tying her own laces. If that was even possible. They were in the back. Stretching her arms behind her, she tried to see how difficult it would be. With her dress covering her for now, she couldn't really tell, but maybe she could do it as long as they didn't have to be too tight. It was awkward and painful to hold her arms that way for long, but she'd give it a go.

Scanning the room, she pursed her lips. Traveling light seemed to be her biggest problem now. After all, she'd never done much traveling, but when she had, she'd taken multiple trunks.

That would be a problem. Regular, ordinary men didn't travel with trunks. In fact, this whole idea started last week when she'd seen a man get off the stage carrying one simple bag. The smile on his face as he hefted it over his shoulder and sauntered over to the hotel made Abigail long to do the same. And her so-called crazy idea had been birthed.

She longed to do something exciting. And she was so tired of the proposals and men who implied that she shouldn't be running the ranch alone. Not that she did much of the running of it. At least not yet. She was also tired of the way people treated her now that her folks were gone. While she knew that her parents had overlooked and covered up a lot of her shortcomings when she was younger, it still didn't make sense to her that people didn't like her outspoken ways. Why didn't they all speak up for social reform, women's suffrage, and the evils of alcohol like she did?

Everyone had seemed supportive and compassionate for the first six months or so after Mama and Daddy died. But after the grieving period was over, she'd received more than one critical comment about being too opinionated, about expecting her daddy's name to open doors for her, and about her inexperience. Apparently people had been willing to listen to her spout her causes as long as her father was alive to sanction them. Grace had been given to her until she was on her own. Now she'd have to find some way to earn people's respect like her father had.

Another reason why she wanted to do this now. It might not be her most well-thought-out plan, but how hard could it be? Men were allowed to travel alone and make their own decisions and have adventures. She just wanted a taste of it. Nothing grand or extreme. A simple few weeks on the road by herself where she could do some exploring and see the frontier. And get away from all the demands of life here.

Abigail sighed. Looking around the room, she once again admired the details that Daddy had put into this massive house. The wood floors covered in lush carpets he'd ordered from all over the world. The wainscoting throughout. Bold, hand-painted wallpapers, and then the ornate crown molding he'd had carved by hand. Every space was expansive—including the closets—with a fireplace in each room. Each bedroom even had an attached bathing chamber. All this had been to please Mama since he'd said more than once that he'd dragged her out to the middle of nowhere. The thought made Abigail smile. Mama had loved it here and didn't mind one bit that they had left the city. That was all before *she* had come along. But Mama made sure that Abigail was dressed in the finest things and had the manners of the wealthiest socialite. Even though they lived in the country, Mama had insisted.

As memories of her upbringing washed over her, a tiny twinge of longing pricked Abigail's chest. One day she hoped to pass it all on to her own children. But would that ever happen? Not if all the men she encountered were only interested in money. She wanted a marriage like her parents'. One based on love and faith. Why did that seem so impossible?

The thought made her sigh. Shaking off the negativity, she focused on the task at hand. The pile in front of her would surely fit into the bag. Right?

She packed the leather bag with underthings, pants, shirts, an extra pair of boots, an extra set of chaps, and a few miscellaneous items. She lifted it to gauge the weight. She wouldn't be able to carry it far, but she could manage. Hopefully.

She sat on her bed again and thought about where she might go. Colorado was supposed to be really pretty country. Wonder how long it would take to get there?

Shrugging, she figured she'd check the train schedule in the morning.

A smile lifted her lips. This was it. She was about to go on an adventure. Just what she needed.

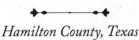

Hamilton County, Texas

Someone needed to teach those sheepherders a lesson. There wasn't enough room for them here in Texas.

Texas was cattle country. Not stupid sheep country. Whoever had thought it would be a good idea had another think coming.

Taking the last swig out of his glass, Leroy nodded at the barkeep and dropped another coin on the wood counter as he grabbed the bottle and took it with him.

What he needed was a diversion. Something to keep the Rangers off his scent while he got rid of the sheep farmers for good.

He bet he could be rid of them all by the end of the month.

Now wouldn't that be fun?

He chuckled to himself. Boss would be happy and would pay him for solving the problem.

What could be easier than that?

Chapter 2

Jim Williams knelt down by another fence. It didn't take a lengthy investigation to know the barbed wire had been cut and the culprit didn't leave a trail. It was the tenth one this week. None of them had any clues other than the cut wire. Any footprints had been smoothed over. Whoever it was had dragged what appeared to be a flat rock or possibly even a brick over the surrounding ground to cover their tracks.

Standing back up, he took his Stetson from his head and let out a long breath. This battle between the sheepherders and the cattlemen was making his job as a Texas Ranger a miserable one.

Fences had been springing up everywhere since barbed wire came on the market for anyone and everyone to buy. In a matter of just a few years, you couldn't go far in Texas without seeing a barbed-wire fence. The problem was, too many people were putting up fences on land they didn't own in an attempt to keep their competitors away from shared grazing lands and water. Between the large cattle ranchers who owned thousands of acres, the small cattlemen who didn't own any, and the surge of sheepherders who had flooded into Texas, there was no way to know who the culprits were. But he'd find out.

This would stop on his watch. It was why he'd been sent here. And he'd ensure everyone in the county knew that the Rangers wouldn't put up with these shenanigans.

Before it all turned more violent. Which was the fear that kept niggling at the back of his mind. Trouble started with the fence cutting, which led to the brawls, which could all too easily escalate into a shootout over who was right and who was wrong.

At thirty years old, Jim had been thinking a lot the last few months about getting out of the Rangers. The work definitely took a toll on the body and mind, and frankly, he was sick of not having a home to return to. Sick of spending more time with bad guys than anyone else. When was the last time he'd been able to even go to church without being called out to work?

It'd been too long.

Everyone thought the life of a Texas Ranger was filled with excitement and adventure. That might be so. He did love his job, and he was awfully good at it. But truth be told, he was tired of it. Tired of the constant traveling to new stations and assignments. Tired of living in jails, shacks, and shanties. And definitely tired of his bedroll—especially when he had to use it on the ground.

All of it had been a sacrifice he'd been willing to make for the past ten years. But being a hero all the time didn't leave any room for friendships, much less family.

At some point, a man had to realize that he might be getting too old for the rigors of the job and want to settle down. Days like today were a reminder of that. He'd already broken up two fistfights between ranchers and had taken a punch to the gut and one to the face. All because the men were arguing about the grazing needs of sheep versus cattle.

Sure, he knew several Rangers who were happily married. But they spent too much time apart from their families, and Jim knew it took its toll. The job of a Texas Ranger sapped every ounce of a man's life. Oh sure, it was all right for a time, but the long term? No, best get out while he still had something to offer a woman.

Standing back up, he shook his head to clear his thoughts and looked around for more clues in the area. But there weren't any. The only tracks were that of his own horse and the ranch owner's. When the man had spotted the fence, he'd gone to the jail—the Rangers' temporary office—to find Jim.

Now that he was out here, his gut told him he was dealing with someone who'd planned all these cuttings. They weren't just randomly cutting the fences out of aggravation.

He looked around and tried to picture all the locations he'd visited this week. Even though a pattern didn't seem to be in play, his instincts felt even more right.

This was premeditated. And Jim couldn't help but feel like there might be something much more sinister behind it all.

◆━•━━•━◆

That blasted Ranger was getting too close.

But there were ways to fix that.

The plan was working; it just needed some tweaking. A trip was in order. A trip to find the perfect man. Once he took care of that, it should be smooth sailing.

The Ranger would be happy.

He'd be happy.

Boss would be happy.

If he had to eliminate a few problems along the way, he could do that. He wasn't afraid of getting his hands a little dirty. Besides, a message needed to be sent. Sheepherders weren't welcome here.

It didn't matter if they'd bought their land legally. They weren't going to be allowed to stay.

Let 'em go whining to the Rangers that someone was cutting all their fences.

That wasn't his problem.

And they'd realize that fence cutting was the *least* of their problems if they decided to fight back.

+-------+

Tuesday, June 5, 1883
Hamilton County, Texas

The stage rocked and rolled all over the place. Add that to the rain and muddy roads, and Abigail was weary of travel already.

It hadn't helped that she'd boarded the wrong stage this morning. Instead of heading to Abilene to catch the train that would take her on her journey to Colorado, she'd gotten on the one headed the opposite direction. Tomorrow she'd have to take another stage to Gatesville just so she could catch the train and go back around to Abilene. Oh well, it would be another part of her adventure. A part she'd definitely leave out of her letter to Sally.

She'd promised to write her trusted maid about all the wonderful things she saw and did, but leaving out a mishap here and there wouldn't be a crime.

One thing was certain, her rear end ached and the stench inside this stage was enough to make her want to hold her nose. Who knew men could smell so bad?

The stage hit another hole, and she wished for the umpteenth time there was something to hold on to. Every bone-jarring bump and jolt made her corset cut into her. Maybe she should take it off at the next stop. She felt herself turning red just thinking about it. She'd probably feel naked, but the two men traveling in the stage with her sat much more comfortably. They were able to slouch and lean back to catch some sleep. Which she envied at the moment. *Shut-eye* was the term one of them used. She'd have to add that to her cowboy vocabulary she wrote down in a little book. Not only did men talk differently and sit differently, but they in general did *everything* differently. Something she was just now coming to realize. Why hadn't she noticed any of this before? She could almost hear Sally's *I told you so* in her ears.

Abigail had tried to chat with the other passengers at the beginning of the journey, but apparently they had little use for her information on the perils of drinking alcohol and didn't care much for her ideas on social reform.

Originally she'd thought that as she met people—men especially—she could have a greater impact for the WCTU. Posing as a man, she could have intelligent conversations with others of the male species and garner more support for her cause. Wouldn't it be wonderful to help strengthen their stance!

But so far she hadn't had much luck. Maybe Sally's warning had a little more weight to it than Abigail wanted to admit. Or maybe she just needed to keep at it and try a different tactic. Shifting on her seat, she decided to get some sleep herself. At least she could try. The two men sat across from her, which gave her the whole seat on her side of the stage to herself. Positioning her bag as a large, lumpy pillow, she leaned over as much as her corset would allow under the loose and bulky clothing.

◆━━━━━◆

Something was shaking her. "Hey Miller. . .get up."

With a deep breath, she lifted her heavy eyelids open a crack. Why did it feel like grit had taken up permanent residence in her eyes? Rubbing at them, she looked up and saw the stage driver leaning over her. Why had he called her Miller? In an instant, everything rushed over her. She was dressed like a man and called herself Chuck Miller.

She was on a stage. That's right. With a glance around him, she realized the other passengers had left. Abigail cleared her throat. "Thanks." Even though she tried to sound husky, her voice ended on a squeak.

She sat up and stretched her limbs, then leaned down to get her bag off the floor. Wait. How had it gotten on the floor? Hadn't she laid down on it?

The stage driver exited ahead of her, and she extended her hand like she expected someone to help her. Realizing her flub, she pretended to swat a fly and had to manage the steps on her own. Because that's what men did.

But it still puzzled her that her bag hadn't been under her head when she woke up. Maybe she'd tired of the lumps at some point and put it on the floor. Shrugging, she realized she wouldn't be able to figure that one out.

The stage left and rumbled down the street as she got her bearings. In front of her sat the Hamilton General Store. She turned and looked at everything in sight. There wasn't much, but she spotted a hotel down the street. At least she could get a room and hopefully a bath. She'd have to choose her garments more carefully tomorrow. Maybe if she wore multiple chemises, she could get away without the corset. Then she could slump with the rest of the men. For some reason, that thought made her giggle.

Covering her mouth so her girlish laughter wouldn't be heard, she tossed her bag over her shoulder like she'd seen the other men do and tried to walk like a man.

It was harder than it looked. She glanced over at a man on the boardwalk by the bank. His stance was wide and his stride was long.

She stopped and pretended to shake her leg like there was something in her boot. Deep breath. She started again. Why, oh why, hadn't she thought of all this before the trip? Once again, she should have listened to Sally. Not that she wanted to admit that to her maid. Abigail was well out of the realm of her expertise. But she could learn, and she would.

As she took longer steps than normal down the street, her spurs clinked and she felt pretty awkward. But as long as she didn't look like a lady, she was probably all right.

The bag she carried over her shoulder like a sack of potatoes grew heavier by the second. The hotel hadn't seemed that far, but goodness, she'd almost prefer to drag the wretched thing than to keep it up where it was.

Leaning over to handle the weight, her steps felt bunglesome, but at this point she didn't care. She just had to make it to the hotel. Then maybe someone would carry her bag to her room for her.

Oh wait. Ordinary men didn't ask for help carrying their bags.

Dagnabbit. What had she gotten herself into?

Heat filled her face with shame for thinking such a term. Even if it was only in her mind. Spending all day in a stagecoach with two crusty men must have had an influence.

Lord, please forgive me. I'll do better, I promise.

Heavy footsteps sounded behind her. Whoever they were, they just needed to pass her up and leave her to her burden. She focused on the hotel. Maybe fifty more steps. She could do this.

The footsteps were beside her now. By this point, she was hunkered down pretty good under her burden. Whoever it was, he was tall, because she couldn't see much higher than his chest as she looked to her side. The Stetson on her head was too big—so it could contain her mass of hair and she could keep it pulled low over her forehead—and it hindered her view. Oh well. The person just needed to move along.

"Chuck Miller?"

Abigail stopped in her tracks and dropped her bag. No one knew her alias other than the stagecoach driver and the man who'd sold her the ticket. She swallowed and kept her voice pitched low. "Yeah?"

"You're coming with me." A tough yank on her arm pulled her to the side as the man picked up her bag. Thank goodness she wouldn't have to carry it anymore. But where were they going?

"Wait. . . . What?" There was that squeak in her voice again.

"You're under arrest for fence cutting."

Chapter 3

Jim walked to the jail hoping he could get some answers out of Miller today. Last night had been a mess. After he'd locked the scrawny man up in the jail, he'd gotten called out on another brawl between ranchers almost immediately and had left the man alone all night. The incident had taken a lot longer than usual because he'd had to drag the two troublemakers to the doctor. Shaking his head, he wondered what it was going to take to get these ranchers to see eye to eye and stop fighting like a bunch of schoolboys.

Now he had to deal with the man he'd arrested. Hopefully the night in jail calmed him down and would make him talk. Was it too much to ask for?

He unlocked the door to the small jail and walked to the back where the cells were housed.

His prisoner was at the bars with a scowl on his face. "You left me in here all night without food or water. That's inexcusable!" The voice was strange, like a young boy's cracking as he got older.

Jim raised his eyebrows. The guy was educated, that was for certain. He couldn't recall when he'd last heard a criminal use a word like *inexcusable.* "I had duties to attend to." Jim crossed his arms over his chest. Not that he needed to explain himself. But it didn't appear that a good night's sleep had calmed the man. "Now why don't you tell me all about your fence cutting, and I'll talk to the judge about maybe some leniency since you're so young." It had to just be a kid in front of him. Small in stature, face without whiskers, constantly changing voice. All the clues added up to that. Besides. . .there was something just a bit too. . .*sweet* about the kid's face. Even with the dirt smudged all over it. Chuck Miller was a puzzle. One Jim would figure out soon enough. Of that he was certain.

"I have no idea what you are talking about." Miller crossed his arms too. "I don't know anything about any fence cutting. And how do you know my name?"

Spunky kid too. "It's my job to know everyone who comes into this little town."

"I don't know who you are, but that sounds suspicious to me."

That made him chuckle. "I'm a Texas Ranger. Jim Williams is my name. And the stagecoach driver always gives me a list of the passengers. Is that better?"

The scowl deepened. "Well, I don't know. How do I know you're really a Ranger?"

Jim pulled his jacket aside, revealing his badge.

Miller huffed and grunted. "Fine. But it's completely insufferable to hold an innocent person and not even feed them."

"My apologies. I'll have something brought over for you as soon as you tell me about the fence cutting."

Miller stomped his foot. "I told you. I don't know anything about any fence cutting." The man wiggled in a strange way that Jim had never seen in a man. What was going on with this kid? "And I must insist that you take me to the outhouse. It should be considered abuse to keep a person like this."

If this case weren't so dang serious, Jim would have laughed out loud at the man before him. Who talked like that? Jim went to grab the keys and came back to the cell. "You do realize that you will be escorted the whole way?"

"I'm not an imbecile." A soft grunt came from Miller as he shifted to his other foot again.

"Good, I'm glad to hear it." Jim opened the cell door, grabbed the man's hands, and put handcuffs on him.

"What are these for?"

"To keep you from running."

"How am I supposed to. . ."

"I'm sure you'll figure it out."

A bunch of unintelligible words came out of his prisoner's mouth.

As they exited the building and walked the few yards to the outhouse, Jim watched the young man out of the corner of his eye. Something wasn't right here. He just needed to put his finger on it.

They made it to the outhouse, and Jim opened the door and propped it open with his foot. "Go ahead. . ."

Miller gasped. His face turned red. "Nope. Not until you close the door and move away."

"I don't trust you."

"You think I'm going to escape with my hands in these things?" He held up his wrists. "And I don't trust you either." Miller jutted his chin out. "This is inhumane."

Jim couldn't help but laugh. The kid's vocabulary was quite good. "All right. But no funny business. I'll be standing directly outside." He stepped back and closed the door.

A thud echoed after him. Probably the kid kicking the door. Jim hoped he could get this guy to 'fess up. Then another thought hit him. There must be a ringleader somewhere. There was no way this young man was planning all this on his own.

Thinking back through the different incidents of fence cutting in his mind, Jim knew they all had to be done by the same person. What little facts he did have were the same for each one. But who was behind them? How could he find out unless the kid talked?

Shaking his head, he paced outside the outhouse. Miller was the key. Jim was just going to have to get him to cooperate before the judge came back to town.

Another thud made Jim turn around. The kid had kicked the door open. It was almost comical how his shirt was meticulously tucked in. Not easy to accomplish in those cuffs. He walked over to the prisoner and grabbed his arm. Way too thin for a seasoned felon drenched in a life of crime. Another fact that made Jim confident there was a mastermind behind this somewhere. "Let's go."

Miller jerked when Jim pulled on him and used his leg to slam the door shut. A splintering sound made Jim stop in his tracks. As he turned and looked at the outhouse, he shook his head. The door had cracked and hung on only one hinge. Not that it was the most sound building—a good wind could probably knock it over—and it was old. But still. Obviously the kid had a temper. Great. "You do realize I'm going to have to fix that now."

"Good." Miller gave him a disgusted smirk.

"Well, I guess you'll just have to wait to be fed until I do it then."

Miller's faced clouded and a strange growling noise came out of his mouth.

"Maybe that will give you some time to think. About all that you want to tell me."

◆━━━●━━━◆

Abigail squirmed in her cell. Her head itched from the blasted hat, but it wasn't like she could take it off. If she did and the Ranger was around, he'd see her hair for sure and figure out she wasn't who she said she was or even *what* she said she was.

But wait. . .didn't she want him to know? It would get her out of this scrape if she just confided in him. And he might treat her better too.

No. Then he'd have to contact Raymond and Sally at the ranch and she'd have to go home with them knowing her humiliation. She hadn't even been gone a day before catastrophe found her, for Pete's sake.

She shook her head. No. She was going to see this through. Besides, she didn't do anything wrong. There was no way the Ranger was going to prove that she did anything, because she'd never cut a fence in her life. She'd never even been to this area before. As soon as he figured that out, she'd be free to go on her way. This wasn't going to be the end of her adventure. It couldn't end when she hadn't even really gone anywhere yet. Hamilton County didn't count. She wasn't even supposed to be here!

One thing was certain, she didn't like Hamilton County and couldn't care less if she never set foot here again.

Footsteps sounded down the hall. Ranger Jim must be back.

As he walked toward her, she noticed his broad shoulders and his lean frame. She liked the way his eyes seemed to take in everything around him. If she hadn't been sitting in a cell posing as a man, she might have even said he was handsome. Which he was. But she couldn't admit that acting as Chuck Miller. And she shouldn't be thinking that anyway. He was the reason she was in this cell. Which meant she was mad at him.

"Good afternoon, Mr. Miller. Any chance you've reconsidered?"

She lowered her brows and crossed her arms over her chest. "Reconsidered what?"

"Telling me about whoever put you up to all the fence cutting." He stood in front of the cell in an easy stance. It portrayed confidence and yet seemed relaxed at the same time.

"There's nothing to tell, because I haven't done any fence cutting."

"Are you sure you want to continue lying to me?" Jim raised one eyebrow. His gaze was penetrating.

For a moment, Abigail felt caught. Technically, she *was* lying to him. But not about the fence cutting. She was simply lying to him about who she was. God would forgive her for that, wouldn't He? "I'm going to say it again. I. Didn't. Cut. Any. Fences." Her voice cracked on the last word, her throat sore from trying to disguise her voice.

"Are you sure you want to stick with that story? Because I've got two eyewitnesses coming in. It'd be best if you were honest before they identified you. Make it a lot easier with the judge."

"Eyewitnesses? Good. They'll be able to tell you I didn't do anything."

"Pretty certain are you?"

"Definitely." Abigail nodded. "I haven't committed any crimes." Unless dressing as a man and creating a false identity was one. She prayed it wasn't. "When will the judge be here?"

"Oh, he should be back sometime next week."

"Next week?" she squeaked. "You can't hold me a whole week can you?"

"Of course I can. Until the judge rules, I can hold you as long as I want."

Tears pricked her eyes. Standing up, she ducked her head for a moment and got control of her emotions. Trying to put on a steely look—like the one Ranger Jim Williams shot at her when she'd first arrived—she walked to the bars. "I have never even been in Hamilton County until the stage brought me on Tuesday."

"Is that so?"

"Yes." She stomped her foot.

"How do I know you're not lying?" He stepped closer to her.

She moved until her face was up against the bars, her hat smashed up on her forehead. "I'm not lying—I've never been here before." She raised her right hand. "I swear."

The handsome Ranger stared at her. As their eyes connected, Abigail felt like an electrical current passed between them. The man was powerful attractive. His blue eyes piercing.

Several seconds passed before he blinked. Then he squinted and stepped back. "I need to go for a walk. I'll be back in a few minutes with your dinner."

Chapter 4

Jim walked out the door and paced in front of the jail. While he'd only had Chuck Miller as a prisoner for a day, he thought he'd watched and examined the man enough to have it all figured out.

And then he'd gotten close to the prisoner just now. *Real* close. And after staring into those green eyes. . .Jim knew he was in trouble.

Chuck wasn't a man.

On top of Chuck being a woman—he. . .she—was a pretty woman. Very pretty.

And she smelled good too. Even camouflaged in all those baggy clothes.

No wonder she'd demanded he close the outhouse door.

How had she fooled him? It didn't make any sense.

All he had was the tip that Chuck Miller was aboard the stage and was probably the fence cutter. Two eyewitnesses had written up testimonies. They'd happened to see the fence cutting and then watched the culprit climb on the stage. They would be here tomorrow to verify that Jim had arrested the right man.

How had this happened?

Chuck—or whoever she was—was adamant that she was innocent. Of course, if she lied about who she was, then she was probably guilty. But it still didn't make sense. She couldn't be doing this of her own accord. He was right to have thought there was a mastermind behind it all. Probably someone who had a lot of money to lose.

Maybe he could still rescue her from a life of crime if he could just earn her trust.

The question still remained. Who was behind these crimes? Who had forced that pretty little thing into dressing like a man and going around cutting fences?

One of the ranchers?

Jim aimed his steps for the hotel. He at least needed to bring her something to eat. He hadn't done the best job of taking care of his prisoner, but then again, he'd thought she was a man. No wonder he thought the boy's face was too sweet. It hadn't belonged to a boy.

It probably shouldn't change things, but Jim was raised to be kinder to the fairer sex. He had to be a gentleman. Even if she didn't know that he knew. Maybe he should just confront her on it. No. She already didn't trust him. Why would she confide in him?

Maybe he could appeal to her emotions, tell her that Chuck Miller would be facing a long jail sentence if "he" didn't tell the truth. And then, if she still refused to talk, he would just play along with her little charade. It would be interesting to see how long her stubborn streak would last. Maybe another day or two in the cell would break her.

All in all, what really mattered was getting to the truth. He needed to crack this case and stop any more fence cutting before the ranchers started taking the law into their own hands. If that happened, Jim would have a much bigger mess to deal with. Tensions were high all over the place. He didn't need that here.

After getting a couple plates of food, Jim headed back to the jailhouse. A new plan had formed. He walked back to the cells. "Chuck? Are you hungry?"

"Of course I'm hungry, you merciless Ranger. I haven't had anything to eat since breakfast." The snippy answer echoed in the small area.

Jim scratched his head. Was it true? Had he forgotten to feed her? After he'd fixed the outhouse door, he'd thrown a couple of biscuits at her—when he still thought she was a man—and then he'd had to tend to other Ranger business. Several different cases. He'd been gone the whole rest of the day.

Yep. He'd forgotten to feed her. . .er. . .Chuck. Good grief, he had too much going on and needed to do a better job. "Sorry about that. I've been busy all day."

"I noticed." She came to the bars. "Can I have some food now?" Her tone was clipped, but Jim knew it was his fault. She was probably starving.

"Here you go." He opened the cell and handed her the plate. Now that he knew Chuck was a woman, he noticed it in every movement she made. He must have been really tired to have missed it. Which created another problem. Continuing to call her Chuck. It seemed wrong—especially the longer he knew, which made it that much harder—but as his brain wrapped around the conundrum, the harsh reality hit him.

He'd have to work on his acting skills because *Chuck* it would have to be until he learned the truth about the fence cutting. A new idea formed. He went back to his desk and picked up the chair and his plate. Bringing them into the cell, he plopped himself in front of the door. "Would you like me to say the blessing?" Maybe he could get her to trust him. Sooner rather than later.

Head bent low over the plate, Chuck's gaze lifted a bit. "That would be nice. Thank you."

As Jim prayed for their meal, he sent a silent prayer heavenward for wisdom.

This was a lot more complicated than he'd anticipated.

"Tell me about yourself." Jim tried a friendly approach.

"I'd rather not." Chuck stayed focused on the food but took small bites. Another confirmation that she was a woman. Although she did eat quite fast. Probably because he'd starved her.

"What about your family? I bet they're wondering where you are."

"There's nothing to tell. And no, they're not." She still wouldn't look at him as she scraped the last few bites off the plate.

Maybe this tactic wasn't going to work after all. She seemed determined not to share. "How about a drink then?"

"A drink? Are you referring to alcohol, Mr. Williams? Because if you are, I think it's my duty to inform you of all the horrid things that strong drink causes." She looked up now and squinted at him. "Wait a moment. Why on earth would you be offering a prisoner a drink?" She leaned back and tilted her head as she scrutinized him even further. Then she gasped. "You're hoping to get me drunk so I will admit to the dastardly deeds you accuse me of!" She stood and her tin plate plummeted to the floor. Her fork slid across the cell. "How dare you! Why. . .I. . ." She huffed and paced and then pointed a finger at him. "I should report you to the authorities."

Jim held up his hands in surrender. "I was offering you water, but I'm glad to see that you aren't tempted by alcohol."

Her bluster came to an end and she reached up to straighten her hat. That was another clue he should have picked up on. She never took off the hat. Even to sleep. At that moment, his thoughts went off the investigation and onto the color of her hair. Blond? Brown?

"Ranger Williams." Chuck stood there with her hands on her hips.

He shook his head. "Yes?"

"Could I get that glass of water now?"

"Of course. I'm sorry." Jim picked up her plate, closed the cell door, and went back to his desk. He filled a cup with water and brought it to the prisoner.

She reached through the bars and took it. "Thank you."

"You're welcome." He watched her walk to the bunk and sit down. Underneath that large Stetson, leather coat, chaps, and the boots with spurs was a woman. With deep green eyes and a feisty temper. The mystery around her needed to be solved.

"I'd like to be alone now." Chuck lay down on the bunk.

Jim walked away.

Maybe tomorrow he could find out more about Chuck Miller and who'd put her up to cutting fences.

Abigail listened to Jim's steps as he walked away. This was turning out to be wretched. She'd tried to stay mad at him, but for some reason she found herself liking the man. Too much.

Good grief. She hardly knew Jim Williams. But she couldn't deny that every time he came near, her heart picked up its pace. She liked how he looked. She liked how he walked. She even liked that he was a Texas Ranger. Even though he'd locked her up.

It would be just her luck that the first man she was really attracted to had arrested her and locked her in a cell. And he thought she was a man. Of course.

Sally was right. It was a disaster.

Let's face it, at this rate she never had a chance of settling down. Trouble always seemed to find her. Mama always used to say she was accident prone. And now the only men who wanted her were after her money.

Maybe tomorrow she should just come clean and ask the Ranger to send a telegram for her to the ranch.

But then she'd have to tell him that she wasn't a man—and then she might get into trouble for trying to deceive a lawman. And did she really want Jim to "meet" her that way? Couldn't she just die of embarrassment in her cell and when they took her out to bury her, she could run away and come back as Abigail Monroe?

If only that would work. But it was ridiculous.

If she sent a telegram, then she was essentially giving up. Sally and Raymond would come and Sally would give her the *I told you so* lecture. Of course that also meant that Abigail would have to admit that her plan had failed.

Admitting failure wasn't her strong suit.

Yes, she hadn't thought her plan through. Yes, she'd ended up in jail. But in her defense, she wasn't guilty.

No. She couldn't do it. Asking for help would be the easy way out. She needed to get out of this scrape on her own. And if that meant spending a few days in jail, she could do it. She could.

Once the eyewitnesses got there, they'd have to vouch for her, because she wasn't the person they'd seen. She wasn't the fence cutter. She took a deep breath and pulled the blanket up over her. It smelled musty, and she pulled it away from her nose.

Maybe that was her problem. She was spoiled. Everything had come to her too easily. Maybe she needed to learn the hard knocks of life on her own.

It would all work out. It had to. God had a plan in all this—she was sure of it.

She just wished He'd give her a few hints about what it was.

Shifting on the uncomfortable and miserable excuse for a bed, Abigail tried not to think about her soft, warm bed at home. Even better would be a long soak in her bathtub. She wasn't sure how men accomplished it, but wearing these clothes was downright irritating to the skin. Of course, she hadn't planned on wearing them around the clock, but she didn't exactly have a choice at the moment.

Jim conveniently kept her bag outside the cell. Of course he probably thought Chuck Miller had a weapon in there, but truth be told, it was far worse. Beneath the assortment of men's clothes she'd brought, there were corsets and bloomers. Things she didn't want the handsome Ranger to find.

Thankfully, he hadn't even touched her bag since he'd put her in the cell. Abigail prayed that he wouldn't ever want to.

Her only hope now was those eyewitnesses. Once they testified that she wasn't the fence cutter, she could be on her merry way and forget she'd ever met Jim Williams.

Yes, that was what she wanted.

◆—•——•—◆

It hadn't gone as planned. At least not yet.

But as his ma used to say, there was more than one way to skin a cat. And he was getting paid a lot of money to make this problem go away. So he'd have to find another way to skin that feline.

Soon.

But at least now he had a scapegoat. It was all quite convenient too. If he could just figure out how to make it work to his benefit. And to keep the plan in place.

Too many people were counting on him to follow through.

He'd just have to wait and watch. . . . The perfect opportunity was bound to come his way.

Chapter 5

The howl of a coyote woke Jim up. He tossed and turned on his bedroll he'd placed on the floor behind his desk. But he couldn't go back to sleep. Something had him on edge. Probably the fact that the two witnesses were coming in today. The more he thought about it, the more he questioned the validity of the tip he'd received.

It all seemed too. . .convenient.

Too many questions plagued him. One: If "Chuck" was the fence cutter, why was she on the stage coming *back* into town? Two: Where had she gone and why? Three: How did the two eyewitnesses know that she was on that stage? Four: Why hadn't those men just come to him in the first place?

As he went through all the details, more questions piled up.

Jim flopped onto his back and put his hands behind his head. Huffing out a sigh, he let the questions spin and churn. A good Ranger had to look at a crime from every angle to find the truth.

There *was* the slim possibility that Chuck—or whoever she was—was actually telling the truth and had nothing to do with the fence cutting. But that created a whole 'nother slew of problems.

No. He shook his head. Just because he found the little spitfire interesting and, if he admitted to himself, *wanted* her to be innocent, that didn't mean she was. The fact of the matter was that whoever was sleeping in that cell was most likely forced into this life. She probably needed to be rescued from whatever it was that held her. And rescuing was what Rangers did best.

He sat up, got to his feet, and stretched. The day before him was probably going to be long—might as well get some coffee started.

But the cell in the back called to him.

Still in his socks, Jim was able to walk without making a sound. The lantern in the small walkway put off a soft glow. As he crept up to the cell, he noticed Chuck's hat was askew. Blond hair fell over the side of her face.

He watched her for a few seconds and thought about how beautiful she was in the soft light. Even though she was dressed in men's clothes, he couldn't deny that he felt attracted to her.

Alarms went off in his mind. Shaking his head, Jim rubbed a hand down his face and walked back to his desk. That was not something he needed to be voicing or even thinking about, for that matter. She was his prisoner, for goodness' sake.

After he finished making the coffee, he started on his first cup and pulled out his Bible. The only direction he needed came from the Good Book, and there was no better way to start his day.

He read through the book of 1 John, and two words stood out to him. *Light* and *fellowship*. Going back to chapter 1, he spent a little more time reading it through. Several verses stood out.

> *And these things write we unto you, that your joy may be full.*
>
> *This then is the message which we have heard of him, and declare unto you, that God is light, and in him is no darkness at all.*
>
> *If we say that we have fellowship with him, and walk in darkness, we lie, and do not the truth:*
>
> *But if we walk in the light, as he is in the light, we have fellowship one with another, and the blood of Jesus Christ his Son cleanseth us from all sin.*
>
> *If we say that we have no sin, we deceive ourselves, and the truth is not in us.*

The comparisons of God with light and sin with darkness were pretty simple to understand. But Jim longed for more fellowship—both with God and with other believers. Something he missed a lot because he was always on the road chasing criminals.

More than anything, he wanted to walk in the light—God's light—and shine that light so others could see it. In the pitch black of the jail cell, Jim kept one lantern lit whenever there was a prisoner. That tiny little flicker of light held the dark at bay. Even though they lived in a dark world that was filled with sin and sinners, if all believers would just shine their light, it would be glorious to see. And the darkness could be chased away.

Jim spent some time praying for guidance—not just about all the things he needed to handle as a Ranger, but also for the future. Did he need to stay in this job? To shine His light in the dark places?

Movement from the back caught his attention. *Lord, help me know how to handle this situation as well.*

Tucking his Bible back into his saddlebag, Jim poured another cup of coffee and picked up the keys to the cell. He walked back and put on a smile. "Good morning, Mr. Miller. Would you like a cup of coffee?"

With her hat covering all her hair again, Chuck looked up. "That would be very nice, thank you. But could we take a trip to the privy first?"

Jim nodded and unlocked the cell. He wondered what her real voice sounded like. All he'd heard was the constant clearing of her throat and the low, raspy way she'd forced her words. Maybe he should tell her he knew she was a woman, and then she wouldn't have to fake it anymore. The thought made him smile. But unfortunately, that wouldn't help the situation any. He needed her to think that her ruse was working.

Chuck held out her wrists to be handcuffed. Jim set down the tin cup next to the lantern and placed the cuffs on her tiny wrists. He wasn't about to tell her, but she could probably wiggle her way out of them.

As they walked to the outhouse, he whistled a hymn.

Chuck turned toward him with a slight smile on her lips. " 'Sweet Hour of Prayer'?"

He furrowed his brow. "You know it?"

"Of course I do. It's one of my favorites."

She entered the privy and shut the door, leaving Jim to be even more perplexed by this case. He hadn't run into too many criminals in his experience who actually knew hymns—much less had a favorite.

Once again his theories about his prisoner ran wild. She could have been raised going to church and then been forced into this life of crime. That fit with what he knew about her so far. Or she could be telling the truth and could be innocent. An idea that had taken root and that he tended to lean toward. But if she was innocent, why on earth was she on a stagecoach dressed as a man? Jim shook his head again. He couldn't allow himself to be swayed by emotions. Just because he felt sorry for her didn't mean his judgment should be clouded by that.

When she came out, they walked back to the jailhouse. An awkward silence built between them.

Chuck tripped on a rock and went down face first. Jim leaned down to help her up, and in the process, she spit out a mouthful of dirt all over his boots.

"Sorry." She swiped at her mouth with her restrained hands and found traction with her feet again. "Don't you believe in allowing prisoners to wash up?"

With a frown, he realized once again his neglect of a prisoner's needs. But in his defense, this was the first time a prisoner had ever asked to "wash up."

Bringing Chuck back inside, Jim led her over to the washbasin he used. "Go ahead. I can get fresh water if you need it."

"This is fine." She splashed water on her face with her handcuffed hands.

The water turned a dirty brown. She'd collected quite a bit of dirt when she fell. Grabbing the rag beside the bowl, she wiped her face dry.

Jim tried not to stare. With all the dirt washed away, her fair complexion was a striking complement to her green eyes. As he stepped closer, he noticed that light freckles dotted her nose. Quite fetching. He shook his head. Those were thoughts he shouldn't be having right now. Especially since she still thought *he* thought she was Chuck—a man.

"Thank you. That is much better." She held out her small hands. The handcuffs dwarfed them, but she must have been examining them for cleanliness. With a sigh, she let them drop back in front of her. "Any chance I could have that coffee now? I'm fairly famished."

"Of course." Jim led her back to the cell and took the cuffs off her and then handed her the cup. "I hope it's not cold."

"At this point, I don't care." She plopped down on the bunk and looked up at him. "What? No interrogation this morning? Or have you realized that you've arrested the wrong person?"

"I figure you might be more cooperative after you've eaten, so I'll get you some breakfast." He sent her a small smile.

A corner of her lips lifted. "Don't count on it, Ranger."

Locking the door behind him, he shook his head again at her spunk and headed down to the hotel. He'd forgotten about feeding her again. What was wrong with him?

When he brought the plate back, he'd barely delivered it to her when he heard noise at the front door. "I'll be back for that interrogation."

"I can't wait." The sarcasm dripped from her words.

At the front door stood two rather shady-looking characters. Jim squinted his eyes. "What can I do for you fellas?"

"We're here to be witnesses. Against Chuck Miller." A short, stocky man missing several of his front teeth puffed out his chest.

"Yeah." The taller one shoved his hands into his pockets.

Jim stepped closer and got a whiff of them. It made his eyes water. "All right. Tell me what you know."

"We saw him."

"Yeah, we saw him."

Jim looked between the two men. "What exactly did you see him do?"

"Cut them fences. That's what." Shorty was obviously the spokesperson, and the other guy was the echo.

"You saw him cut all the fences? How fortunate for you to be in all the locations at the same time. That's quite a coincidence."

"Nah. We didn't see all of 'em." Shorty laughed. "But we saw him do one the other day."

Jim sat at his desk and pulled out paper and a pencil. He'd have to record everything they said and see if it lined up. "All right. So walk me through what you saw. What did he do?"

Shorty sighed and rolled his eyes. "He cut the wire fence, that's what he did. Then he took a brick and dragged it along the ground to get rid of his footprints."

"Yeah, he dragged a brick. Tied to a rope." Echo nodded.

"Why can't you just let us identify him? Isn't that all you need?" Shorty looked a bit disgusted. "We got places to be."

Jim pasted on a smile. "I'm sure you do. But to answer your questions, no, that's not all I need. I'll need your names for my report." He looked both of them in the eye.

The two men looked at each other.

Shorty spoke first. "Name's Smith. John Smith."

Jim raised his eyebrows.

"Write it down." Shorty pointed to the paper.

"All right. John. . .Smith." Even as Jim wrote down the name, he knew the man was lying. He looked to Echo. "And you are?"

"Um. . .I'm Tom Smith."

Of course he was. Jim scribbled down that name too. "All right, can you describe the man you saw cutting the fence?"

"Uh. . .can't we just see him? Why ain't that good enough?"

Jim's hunch was right. These guys weren't eyewitnesses to anything. Something else was at play here. "No, I'm sorry to say, I need your description first. Anything that could help identify him would be useful. Colors often help."

Shorty huffed at him. "Fine. He was about this tall." He held a hand in the air close to his own head. "And was wearing a black hat with a brown coat and brown pants and brown boots."

Well, at least he got some colors in there. "How about color of his hair? Color of his eyes? Mustache? Beard?"

Echo laughed. "Nah, he was too far away to see any of that."

"But you still think you can identify him?"

"Of course!" Shorty jutted out his chin. "But you don't have to just take our word for it. We saw him stick his wire cutters and that brick in his bag he was carrying."

"Oh really?" Now Jim was intrigued. Evidence was always a good thing.

"Look. We got to get back. Do you want us to identify the guy or not?" Shorty squinted at Jim.

Jim stood. "Let's go on back and see if you think the guy I have is the same one you saw."

The two men nodded.

Leading them down the hall, Jim stopped in front of the cell.

"That's him! That's the guy we saw." Shorty pointed.

Chuck stood and put her hands on her hips. "No, I'm not!"

"Yeah, you are!" Echo shouted and pointed too.

"I most certainly am not, because I haven't cut any fences. I wasn't even in this county!"

"Yeah, you were. We saw ya." Shorty spat on the floor. "Check his bag, Ranger. I bet you'll find exactly what we told ya you'd find." He crossed his arms over his abundant midsection.

"This is ridiculous!" Chuck came closer and put a hand to her nose and then stepped back. "You are mistaken."

Jim looked back and forth between the two so-called eyewitnesses and the lady he knew only as Chuck. The only way to get this over and done with was to open her bag and show that she didn't have the items Shorty and Echo said. He felt wrong about opening a woman's bag. But then, nobody else knew that *he* knew that she was a woman.

He sighed. Why did this have to be so stinkin' complicated? Why couldn't she just admit who she was?

He crouched by the leather bag he'd carried over when Chuck Miller dropped it in the street. As he lifted the heavy flap, his heart sank.

Right there on top sat a pair of wire cutters and a brick with a rope tied around it.

Jim looked up at Chuck's face.

She'd gone ashen. "Those aren't mine. I've never seen them before."

Chapter 6

Looking up at the sun, Leroy figured that by now the ranger had put all the pieces of his case together. Witnesses, evidence, and a prisoner. That was good enough to hang people in the past, so it should be enough to keep the man distracted now.

Then if anything else came up. . . Well, there were other ways to get rid of pesky problems. Leroy wasn't afraid of using any of his other methods.

In fact, he looked forward to it.

◆━━━━━◆

Abigail paced the floor in the cell and wondered what on earth would happen to her now. Those two nasty men had accused her of fence cutting. She thought for sure Jim hadn't believed them. . .until he'd opened her bag. Then his face had twisted into an angry scowl and turned red, and he had ushered the men out. He'd been gone a good while now, and Abigail was pretty sure her goose was cooked. How had those things gotten into her bag? She'd had it with her on the stage, and then it was carried here. The only times it had been out of her sight was when she went to the privy.

Dread and fear made their way through her mind and body. But there had to be an explanation.

There had to be a way to exonerate Chuck Miller's name—since she'd made him up, after all—and still get out of this without revealing who she really was.

Her spurs clanked on something. Looking down, she found the fork that had flown off her plate last night. Had that really just been yesterday?

She picked it up. A new idea struck. Perhaps she could pick the cell lock. Maybe she could escape—well, Chuck could. After all, he was the one under investigation for fence cutting, not her—and then he could disappear and she could go back to being Abigail. No one would be the wiser. Chuck would be gone, and she could forget all about this ridiculous fiasco of being locked in a jail cell in Hamilton County, Texas.

She plopped onto the bunk and shook her head. Why did things like this happen to her? She'd never known anyone who got arrested—much less for a crime they didn't commit—and then when they were dressed up and using a fake name! Chuck Miller was a figment of her imagination.

It just wasn't normal for a person to have this much trouble. Was it? Thinking back on how Mama had described her. . . Well, Abigail was beginning to think that "accident prone" was too tame. Sally would probably say she was *disaster* prone. Abigail was about ready to agree with that.

She knew she couldn't just sit here and do nothing. In all her years, she never would have believed she'd be accused and identified as a fence cutter. Those men were lying.

Which wasn't all that surprising since they stunk to high heaven. Anyone who smelled that bad couldn't be an honest person. The same thought she'd had on the stage the other day.

Oh no. The stage. She'd slept on the stage and found her bag on the floor and not underneath her.

And the two men with her had smelled just as rank.

Could they be involved somehow? They had to be. She started pacing again and tapped the fork against her leg as she walked. The only problem was, the two men on the stage were not the same two men that had come to the jail as witnesses.

She needed to tell Jim. He had to listen; he was a Ranger. And she was pretty sure that he didn't think those men were telling the truth. Until he'd seen the evidence in her bag. She sighed. The more she thought about it, all the more she realized how much trouble she was in.

She tapped the fork against her leg again and looked down at it. She might as well try to escape. If she got caught. . . Well, if she was going to sit in this cell, it might as well be for something she actually did.

Abigail jabbed the fork in the lock and tried to move it around. Of course she had no idea what she was doing, but she had to at least try. After wiggling and bending it around with no results, she pulled it out and stuck in the other end. Still nothing happened.

Yanking it out of the lock, she stomped her foot. "Ugh!"

It was hopeless.

Her thoughts raced back and forth. What could she do? With a sigh, she thought of the handsome Ranger she'd spent the past couple of days with. He seemed like a fair man. Someone she'd really like to spend time with as *Abigail*. Her only real hope now. . . She'd just have to somehow earn Jim's trust.

Thoughts of home swelled. Why had she left in the first place? To have an adventure. She plopped back down on her bunk. This didn't feel very adventure-like.

In fact, now that she let herself really think about her situation, the fear and dread she felt earlier came rushing back.

She lifted her chin, and her stubbornness took over. "No. I have nothing to fear because I didn't do anything wrong. Fear is not of the Lord, and I am innocent. Chuck Miller is innocent."

The sound of the front door opening made her sit up straight and put the mangled fork behind her back.

Slow, steady footsteps approached.

Abigail lowered her head and bit her lip. If that was Jim, she wasn't sure what she could say to make this better.

"Mr. Miller." Jim's voice no longer held anything like a friendly tone. "I'm trying to figure out how a man who constantly talks of being innocent could possibly expect me to believe that now."

She raised her head and looked at him. "Because it's true."

His laugh was dry and lacked any humor. "And you think that just because you say that, it makes it so? I found the evidence in your bag."

"I told you, I've never seen either of those things before." She narrowed her eyes. Why did he have to be so antagonistic toward her?

"That doesn't mean anything to me when the facts say otherwise." He stepped closer to the bars. "Why don't you just tell me the truth. Perhaps there's something I can do to help you."

For a moment, she wanted to tell him everything. It almost felt like she needed to. But where would that put her? Especially with the cutters and brick found in her bag. If she told him who she was, then would Abigail Monroe be arrested instead of Chuck Miller? Would she have to go on trial? She couldn't risk losing everything her parents had built. Especially not from something that happened because of her own stupidity.

Jim took a deep breath and pulled out his keys. As he unlocked the door, he mumbled something under his breath she didn't catch. Within seconds, he'd opened the door and stepped inside. "Look. I don't know what kind of trouble you're in, but you really should just drop the lies and tell me the truth."

His nearness did funny things to her insides. He stepped closer to her.

She stepped back. "I told you. Those things aren't mine. I've never been here before. I haven't cut any fences." There. That was all truth. No lies.

He crossed his arms over his chest and inched closer. "Tell me who you really are."

Oh no. What did he suspect? She felt her face heat.

"If you've been forced to do this, just tell me the truth. Help me put the ringleader behind bars, and no one will get hurt. We can stop this. Together."

For a moment, his concern touched her.

"I can see it on your face. I'm on the right track, aren't I?" He moved even closer. "All you have to do is admit your crimes and point in the direction of whoever put you up to this, and then I can help you."

Abigail narrowed her eyes at him. So he still thought she did it. She really was in trouble. If Jim didn't believe there was a possibility she hadn't done the fence cutting, then there probably wasn't any hope of anyone else believing her.

Abigail swung her hands up in exasperation at the very same moment that Jim put his hands forward.

"Ow!"

Now she'd done it.

"What did you. . . ?" He looked at his hand.

Covering her mouth, she stepped back. She'd stabbed the Ranger with the fork. They should just keep her in jail forever. She took her hands down. Her bent fork was sticking out of the palm of his hand. "I'm sorry. I didn't mean to!"

"You didn't mean to? Well, that was awfully coincidental." He stared at the embedded utensil and then put his other hand on it and yanked. Blood oozed out of the holes the tines made. "I'll be back. This isn't over." His narrowed eyes told her he meant business.

All at once, she realized she was no longer innocent. She'd lied to a Texas Ranger, and now she'd stabbed him. Sitting back down on the bunk, she wondered how much jail time she would have to serve.

He came back with a rag wrapped around his hand.

"How bad is it?" Oops. For a moment, she'd forgotten to change her voice. Hopefully he hadn't noticed and would just think she was nervous.

"I'll live." He entered the cell again, an odd look on his face. "Do you have any other weapons in here, or do I need to search for myself?"

She felt her eyes widen and shook her head vigorously.

"Good." He crossed his arms in front of him. "Now, I believe we were at the juncture where you were about to tell me the truth."

"But I did—"

"No. . .you stabbed me with a fork, remember?"

Footsteps ran toward them. "Who stabbed you, Ranger?"

Abigail gasped and tried to cover it with a cough as Jim turned to face the visitor. She knew that man. He was a reporter. He'd done an article on her parents after they'd died. No. No. No. This was very bad. She tugged her hat lower and ducked her head. She couldn't let the man see her. If he recognized her, she'd be ruined.

Jim walked out of the cell. "Who are you?"

"Paul Glover, Ranger Williams. I'm a reporter for the *Herald*. I heard you had arrested the fence cutter, and I was going to do a story—"

"You will do no such thing, Mr. Glover." Jim stood tall and towered over the scrawny reporter. "Not until I get to the bottom of this. I don't need the paper to be full of speculation that gets people all up in arms."

"But it won't be speculation, because I'm getting the story from you." The reporter smiled, his pencil poised above a small pad of paper.

Jim shut the door to the cell and locked it. Grabbing the man's arm, he dragged him away from the cell and told him in no uncertain terms that a story would not be printed until the truth came out. As they walked away, Abigail couldn't hear the rest of their conversation. Jim must have escorted the man outside.

She let out a sigh of relief. The reporter hadn't seemed to take much notice of her, which was a good thing. But this only meant that she couldn't let anyone know who she really was. If she did, the best-case scenario she could see was that she'd be acquitted for fence cutting, but she'd be a laughingstock back home as soon as word got out. Her father's name would carry the embarrassment of her actions. The worst-case scenario was she could tell them who she was and still get convicted of being a fence cutter and spend the rest of her life in jail. Her ranch would be sold and all the beloved people who worked for her would lose their jobs and their homes and be run out of town.

Neither option held any appeal. Of course, sitting in this cell dressed as a man held no appeal either. But at least for now, her real identity was protected. The people she loved at home were protected.

Footsteps came back toward her.

She cleared her throat and lifted her chin. She was innocent; she just had to remember that.

Jim stopped in front of the cell and crossed his arms over his chest again. An act that made him even handsomer. And more fearsome.

Abigail swallowed.

"I'm not leaving until we get to the bottom of this." He held her gaze and paced in front of the cell. "Now, I'm a reasonable man. And I'm guessing you're caught up in something that has you scared to tell me the truth."

If he only knew.

"So let's start back at the beginning." He raised his eyebrows.

She blinked at him. What else could she tell him? She'd already told him everything. Wait. No she hadn't. "You know, while you were gone, I had some time to contemplate my circumstances. I was trying to figure out how those things got put in my bag when it's been in my sight the whole time. Except when you take me to the privy. . .and when I'm *asleep*."

He huffed at her. "Are you grasping, here? No one has been in this jailhouse while you were asleep."

Stepping to the bars, she grabbed them with both hands. "No. I'm not talking about here. On the stage. There were two exceedingly smelly men who sat across from me who I thought were asleep the whole time. My bag was on the seat next to me until I lay down to sleep myself. I used it as a makeshift pillow, but when we arrived here, the stagecoach driver woke me, and my bag was on the floor."

He dropped his arms to his side. "And you're sure when you fell asleep you were lying on top of it?"

"Yes. And those men were gone when I awoke."

Chapter 7

I should be back by supper." Jim looked to Dusty—the man who often helped him out by watching a prisoner while he went back out on the trail—and hoped the day would bring answers. "Mr. Miller shouldn't give you any trouble." Oh, how he hoped that were true.

He put his foot in the stirrup and swung up onto his horse. If there was any chance Chuck was telling the truth, he needed to find that out. And not just for her sake. Even though the tug he felt toward the lady dressed up as a man did prod him on. But the real criminals needed to be the ones behind bars. He just couldn't think of her as a criminal. Something in his gut told him he had to be correct on that.

As he urged Star into a gallop, Jim knew he needed to do something about these feelings. Whoever she was, she had gotten under his skin. That was very unusual for him. But if she refused to tell him the truth, he couldn't allow himself to feel anything toward her. He was a man of the law and couldn't tolerate someone who held no respect for it.

His only lead right now was from Harry at the General Store. He'd identified the two men who had been on the stage with Miss. . . Well, whoever she was. *Chuck*. He had to stop thinking of her as anyone other than Chuck Miller. Otherwise, he could make a mistake. Right now he needed to focus on finding the culprits.

Hours later he wasn't any closer to the truth than he'd been that morning. The two men on the stage with Chuck had disappeared. At least for now.

He swiped a hand down his face and headed back to the jail. He needed more information before the judge arrived.

As he rode up the street, he saw smoke spiraling into the air. Pressing his knees into Star's flanks, he urged his horse faster. Dread sat in the pit of his stomach.

And for good reason. The jail was on fire!

A bucket brigade had started outside, but Jim couldn't see Dusty or the prisoner. They must still be inside. "Did you get everyone out?"

"We didn't know anyone was in there, Ranger." One of the men threw a bucket of water at the flames.

Pushing through the crowd, Jim ran into the smoldering building. "Dusty!"

No answer.

"Chuck!"

Still no answer. Jim put his kerchief over his nose and mouth and headed to the cell. The smoke was getting worse and flames licked the walls.

He had to get down on his hands and knees to be able to see anything. As he crawled, he heard a moan. Behind the bars were two prone forms.

Jim looked around and then scrambled back to the desk. The keys were gone.

Returning to the cell, he saw Chuck move. "Chuck!"

She sat up, and her eyes went wide with fear. "Help me!" Her hat fell off her head, and blond hair spilled all over her shoulders. She grabbed for the hat and put it back in place. Crawling toward the door, she found Dusty and shook him. "Wake up!"

The man didn't move.

Jim grabbed the bars of the door and shook them. Without a key, there was little hope of getting them out in time.

Chuck came close to the bars, tears streaming down her face. "I didn't do it. I promise. I'm innocent. Please believe me. I don't want to die a criminal."

"You're not going to die." Jim ran back for his shotgun. The only hope now was to shoot the hinges off. When he came back to the cell, Chuck was on the floor coughing and gasping for breath. "Get away from the door."

She moved and put her arms over her hat-covered head.

Jim shot the hinges, and thankfully they came loose. He pried the door away from the wall, took hold of Chuck's arm, and dragged her out the back door.

Coughing and sputtering, she lay on the ground and breathed deeply.

He'd just have to take the chance that she wouldn't run off. Jim went back inside for Dusty and dragged the unconscious man out. Then he went back in for his guns, notebooks of evidence, and the few personal effects he had. He tripped over Chuck's bag on the way out. Might as well save that too.

As he exited the building, Chuck was still on the ground coughing and Dusty was still unconscious.

"What happened?" Everything surrounding Chuck Miller seemed to spell chaos. And now there was no jail. He glanced back at the building and saw the bucket brigade still sloshing water on it, but he doubted it would do much good at this point.

"I don't know. . ." Chuck's voice was raspy and hoarse from the smoke.

"Dusty took me to the privy, and I accidentally knocked over the lantern when we came in."

"Accidentally?"

"Well, I definitely didn't do it on purpose!" Another coughing fit overtook her. "Next thing I know, someone knocked me over the head and I woke up to smoke and fire everywhere."

So it *was* intentional. That's how Dusty had gotten in the cell, and it also explained the missing keys.

The only thing that made sense now was that someone must be framing Chuck for the fence-cutting crimes. And they'd just tried to kill two people and get rid of all the evidence.

Jim eyed Chuck Miller. There was more to this story than he first thought. A whole lot more.

◆━━━━◆

Saturday, June 9, 1883
Hamilton County

The early morning light from the sun cast long, golden rays across his bedroll. Jim hadn't slept much during the night. He had too many things to think through. He sat up and looked across the campfire. Chuck appeared asleep with her back to him, the poor hat she'd worn day and night smashed around her head.

The woman was a complete mystery. Why was she dressed as a man? If she wasn't caught up in the fence cutting, what could be the reason? And why on God's green earth was she so determined not to let him know who she really was? Especially if she was innocent. It didn't make any sense to him. But he wouldn't rest until it did.

The fire had been very disconcerting. Dusty was at Doc's with quite a bump on the head and a burn on his leg. When Dusty woke up, Jim would have to question him more about what he remembered.

Whoever had been at the jail and locked them in had done it on purpose. And tried to prevent there from being any witnesses. And no evidence. . .

The thought hit him square in the face.

The evidence.

Jim went over to Chuck's bag and lifted the flap. Just what he'd suspected.

No brick. No wire cutters.

He dug deeper just to make sure, praying that she would forgive him for digging around in her bag.

One thing was certain, no man would travel with an extra pair of chaps, an extra pair of boots, four pairs of pants, and eight shirts. That was excessive. Not to mention the two corsets, two chemises, and two pairs of bloomers in the bottom of the bag.

At least he knew he was correct. Chuck definitely *wasn't* a man.

But even more of it didn't add up. The extra items made Jim think this was no ordinary woman. She was a woman of means. That would explain her speech and vocabulary.

He repacked the bag the best he could and sat back on his bedroll. It seemed even more shocking to him that a lady of her social status would pose as a man.

He tried to dismiss the thoughts. None of it made sense, and unless she started telling him the truth, he wouldn't be able to help her.

Since the hour was so early, hopefully she'd sleep a bit longer. Besides, he needed to clear his head without her as a distraction. Taking a quick bath in the creek might not help him solve the case, but at least he'd get rid of the smoky smell seared into his nose and lungs. It would have to do for now.

Abigail woke up on the ground facing a tree. What had happened?

She blinked several times and tried to swallow. Her throat and her eyes burned.

The fire. It all came back to her. Someone had tried to kill her.

She sat up straight and looked down. Her hands were cuffed together. Guess it was too much to ask for the Ranger to believe her. Of course, if the roles were reversed, she wouldn't trust her—er, Chuck—either.

Pulling her knees to her chest, she felt hot tears skim down her cheeks. Things had gone from bad to worse, and now she really was afraid. With no hope in sight. What would her parents think if they were alive? They'd think she'd failed them. That's what.

All because she was stubborn and strong willed and so stupid to go after adventure. She should have known better. Sally had warned her. Multiple times.

It didn't matter now that she was innocent. Someone was out to kill her. It was possible she wouldn't even make it out of this horrible situation alive.

Glancing around her, she saw a makeshift camp but no sign of anyone else. Had Jim just left her here? Too disgusted with her to do anything other than just let her face her fate. A fate that truly did seem to spell disaster.

She needed to use the privy, and she also needed a bath. Every inch of her was covered in soot, and she smelled like smoke. The odor made her feel like the flames were still chasing her in the jail. Which only made the tears come in earnest. She never should have left home. If she'd simply stayed there and married one of the gold diggers, she'd at least be safe right now.

The thought made her chuckle through the tears. No. She never would have done that—it simply wasn't in her. But she really had come to her wit's end this time. The predicament she now found herself in was much worse than anything she'd ever experienced. And she didn't know what to do. She should probably wait and see if Jim returned for her and what he would do with her next.

At this point, she was ready to give up.

Lord, I've gotten myself into quite a pickle this time. I don't know what to do. I don't know where to turn. I'm sorry I haven't consulted You more on this trip. . . .

Goodness, she realized she hadn't even brought her Bible along. What kind of heathen was she?

Forgive me for where I've failed You. And if You would. . .could You help me out of this mess? I promise to behave myself from now on.

A promise she intended to keep. As soon as she got out of this.

Chuck Miller would have to be her name until this whole fiasco was over. Jim could surely find the real criminals, and then he'd have to let her go. Taking a deep breath, she tugged her misshapen hat down lower on her head. She'd overcome lots of obstacles in the past by being positive. She just needed to keep her chin up. She could do this.

Closing her eyes for a brief moment, she pictured Jim's face. Wouldn't it be nice to meet him under different circumstances? She could be Abigail, and he wouldn't look at her like she'd grown horns every time she spoke.

Oomph. Landing hard on the ground, she tried to scream, but something—or someone—had plowed into her and knocked the wind out of her. Before she could pull in a breath, a blanket or coat was thrown over her face. Rocks cut into her back and legs, and she couldn't see. The person on top of her pushed.

Kicking and flinging her arms as much as she could, she still couldn't dislodge the person on top of her. All the air was smothered out of the space around her. The black covering pressed harder, and she couldn't inhale.

Lungs burning from lack of air, she could barely lift her limbs anymore. Tiny dots of light pricked her sight behind her eyelids. Her ears started to ring.

Gasping for all she was worth, Abigail let her limbs fall to the ground. This was it. God had seen fit to answer her prayers by taking her home. Sally and Raymond and the rest of her staff would wonder what happened to her. But it was better this way. Both Abigail Monroe and Chuck Miller would die in Hamilton County, Texas.

Chapter 8

Being clean felt good, but Jim couldn't wait to get back to Chuck. He'd had several revelations at the creek that he hoped would crack this case. And hopefully get her to open up to him. He'd have to do some investigating on the trail, but he'd just have to bring her with him, for two reasons. One was for her safety, and the other. . . Well, it wasn't like he had a place to keep her locked up anymore.

He crested the hill where they'd made camp and saw a dark figure struggling with someone on the ground.

Running as fast as he could, Jim pulled out his revolver. "Put your hands up!"

The figure lifted his head. He had a kerchief over the bottom half of his face. He jumped up and ran in the other direction.

Jim chased him until the man jumped on his horse and took off like a bolt of lightning. Jim aimed his gun and fired.

The masked man skirted behind a tree and disappeared.

Catching his breath, Jim lowered his gun. If only he had caught the guy. Chuck!

He ran back to their little camp and found her lying as still as death. A blanket covered the upper half of her body. Jim knelt down and lifted it off of her. Patting her face, he prayed he wasn't too late. "Chuck. Can you hear me?"

A moan escaped her pretty pink lips. How he'd ever thought this was a man was beyond his reasoning.

"Chuck?"

Her eyelids fluttered. Then she jerked up to a sitting position and gasped for air. "Jim!" Her eyes were wide. "He. . .he. . .he. . .tried to kill me."

"I know. I chased him, but he got away. Are you all right?"

She nodded, and hair fell into her face. Reaching up with her cuffed hands, she must have realized her hat was missing. Twisting from side to side, she seemed frantic.

"Don't bother with the hat. . .*miss*." He emphasized the last word for good measure.

She closed her eyes and groaned.

Jim sat back on his haunches. "Are you sure you're all right?"

Still breathing heavily, she frowned at him. "I thought for sure I was dead. But yes, I think I'm all right."

"Good." His heart needed to find its normal rhythm again. He went to the fire and put some space between them. "Why don't you tell me the truth now while I make us some breakfast?"

"Um. . .could you let me take care of some business first?"

"What business could you possibly need to take care of?" What was she up to this time?

She raised her eyebrows and gave him a look. "Personal business. As in the privy kind of business."

He rubbed his neck. Well, he should have at least thought of that. Maybe she wasn't changing the subject after all. "Of course. Just scoot behind that tree there. I won't look, I promise." On second thought, someone had just tried to kill her. Again. "Actually, I'd better stay close."

"As awkward and inappropriate as that sounds, I was going to ask that you accompany me." She held out a hand. "But I expect you to be a gentleman and look away."

"Of course."

When they came back, Jim warmed some leftover biscuits in a skillet.

She sat across from him and pulled her knees up to her chest. "I see you got cleaned up. Is there a creek around here? I'd really like to get rid of the smoke smell." Now that she wasn't trying to disguise her voice anymore, Jim found it had a soothing lilt to it.

"I tell you what. . . You tell me what you know and who you are, and I'll let you take a bath in the creek while I stand guard. It's not any accident that someone is trying to kill you. You also have to promise not to run away."

"Where am I going to go?" She held up her wrists. "I'm a prisoner, remember? Besides, why would I want to run away? You just saved my life."

"Do we have a deal?" He raised an eyebrow at her. She was wily. And had answered with more questions.

Chuck jutted out her chin. "How do I know I can trust you?"

"I'm a Ranger. Why wouldn't you be able to trust me?"

"Have you seen everything that has happened to me since I set foot in your county? Granted, again, you've saved my life. Twice now. But it hasn't exactly been a stroll through the flower garden."

Her sarcasm made him laugh. At least she still had a sense of humor. "Okay, well, let's start simple. Why don't you give me a name to call you other than Chuck."

She shook her head. "I'm more comfortable remaining Chuck right now."

"Even though you know *I* know you're not a man?"

"Of course. And it's safer this way. You're the only one who can know. You have to admit, I had you fooled for a long time."

"No, you didn't. I've known since. . ." He let the words drop. He wasn't sure he wanted to admit when he'd realized it.

"Since when? You've been calling me Chuck for days."

Shaking his head, he cleared his throat. "It doesn't matter."

She tried to cross her arms and grunted at the handcuffs. "So, do you actually believe me now?"

"Believe you about what?"

"That I'm not a fence cutter."

Jim took a deep breath and then handed her a warm biscuit. "I'm not sure about that. Since you seem to be unwilling to tell me the truth."

"Ugh!" She kicked the dirt with her spurs and then jumped to her feet. "You are so pigheaded. I've told you the truth about everything you need to know."

"Pigheaded? Who's the pigheaded one here? I don't think I've ever met anyone as stubborn as you! Insisting on being called Chuck when you are *clearly* not a man. What is it that you're hiding?" Standing up too, he towered over her.

"You bet I'm stubborn! I have to be to put up with *you*." She inched closer, and they were only a breath apart. "And for your information, the *only* thing I'm hiding is my identity." Her face was flushed. "Maybe I just don't want you to know it!"

At that moment, the only thing Jim wanted to do was pull her into his arms and kiss her. As soon as the thought ran through his mind, he stepped back in shock.

Taking several deep breaths, he forced his mind back to the case. His Ranger training kicked into gear. With a calm voice, he sat back down and spoke. "I apologize for being so difficult to deal with." The sarcasm slipped out. He held up his hands in surrender. "I'm sorry. Why is it that you don't want me to know who you are?"

He'd obviously diffused the situation, because he saw her hands tremble.

Her eyes sparkled with unshed tears. "I don't know. I'm sorry too." Collapsing back into a heap on the ground, she sniffed. "This has been the longest and most exhausting week of my life."

"No stroll through the flower garden, huh?"

She swiped at a rogue tear that made its way down her cheek and laughed softly. "More like thorns and thistles up to my neck."

"I'm sorry." He took a deep breath, hoping they were on better footing again. "I need you to know that my job is serious, okay? And this is for your protection. So please, let's start over, shall we?" Jim couldn't allow his thoughts to go back to the place where he'd wanted to kiss her. It had been a long time since he'd let down his guard. "Start from the beginning—that is, when you first became Chuck."

"All right." She sat up a little straighter and sighed. "Tuesday morning, I—"

"Hold on." He held up a hand. "I'm sorry to interrupt, but when you say Tuesday, do you mean this past Tuesday? The day I arrested you Tuesday?"

She looked at him funny. "Yes. What other Tuesday would I be referring to?"

"Never mind. Please continue." Apparently Chuck had come into being a lot later than Jim thought.

"As I was saying. . .Tuesday morning I boarded the stage in Coleman after two men got off. Then two different men got on." She lifted her hands to gesture, but with them cuffed together, it appeared to distract her. She looked back up at him, her green eyes clear and bright. "The two men that got on, I'm pretty sure were in cahoots with the two that came in as witnesses. Same horrible smell. I'd recognize that stench anywhere."

"Where were you headed?"

"To Colorado."

"Wait a minute. You were headed to Colorado but took a stage south and east? Isn't that the wrong direction?"

She rolled her eyes. "I got on the wrong stage."

The more she talked, the more it puzzled him. "So you weren't even supposed to be on the stage that came here?"

"No. I wasn't planning on coming anywhere near Hamilton County. But here I am." Pink tinged her cheeks. "My mother used to say I'm accident prone. So I'm *accidentally* here."

It made a bit more sense now. Just like her knocking over the lantern in the jail, breaking the outhouse door, and stabbing him with a fork.

The facts seemed clear though. She really wasn't a fence cutter. Which greatly relieved him. But there was still the concern about why she was concealing her identity. "Chuck, I have to ask this: Why are you traveling as a man? Are you in trouble with the law somewhere else?"

She straightened and gave him a glare. "Of course not. I've never been in trouble with the law."

"Until now."

"Well, yes, until now." Another glare was shot his way.

"Well, that still doesn't explain it—"

"Fine!" She looked down at her boots. "I wanted to have the freedom of traveling by myself, so I dressed up as a man and bought my ticket as Chuck Miller."

"What?" He'd never heard anything so ridiculous in his life. "You can't be trying to tell me that you did all this. . .simply to travel by yourself? That's crazy."

"So I've been told." She looked at him and attempted to cross her arms again. That fire in her eyes was back, and it was aimed at *him*.

For the moment, he had nothing more to say. He blinked and stared at her. Every instinct in him said she was being framed. But by whom? And why? Especially if she wasn't even supposed to be here. Watching her, he was fascinated with her spunk and spirit. She wasn't like any other woman he'd ever met.

Of course, every other woman he'd met had been dressed like a woman.

Jim shook his head. What had he gotten himself into?

One thing was for certain. There hadn't been any other complaints about fence cutting since he'd arrested her. So whoever was behind this was being careful.

"I need to tell you something." He stood up again.

"What is it?"

"I went through your bag."

She jumped to her feet. "What?" Her face blushed crimson. "Did you—?"

He held up his hands, hoping to calm her fears, but there was no delicate way to say it. "Yes, I saw some. . .things. . . . But let me tell you what I *didn't* find."

"What?" Her voice squeaked.

"The brick and the wire cutters."

She gasped. "That means that whoever knocked us out in the jail. . ." Her eyes grew wider as she let the words trail off.

"Exactly. Whoever knocked you and Dusty out planned for you two to die in the fire. They took the tools they'd planted in your bag, because they belonged to them and they wanted them back."

"So you just need to find whoever did that to us."

He shrugged. If he could do it before the judge arrived, he might be able to keep her from humiliating herself in front of the court.

"What are we waiting for? Let's go find them!"

❖━━━•━❖

Chuck Miller proved harder to kill than he'd imagined. How could one insignificant, scrawny man give him so much grief?

The only thing Leroy had to worry about was being identified. And Chuck Miller was the only one who could do it.

Leroy's men were supposed to make the prisoner disappear, but so far they hadn't done their job.

Time to move things along and get rid of the man once and for all.

Chapter 9

Sunday, June 10, 1883
Somewhere in Hamilton County

The trail had not been kind to Abigail. Or her backside.

After they'd gone back to the jail and examined the tracks outside the back door, Jim had mumbled something about checking another lead. For hour upon hour, they'd trekked back and forth between ranches, farms, and a couple of small towns. She sat on her horse while Jim did whatever a Ranger did in these things. Once he gave her a piece of jerky and a swig from his canteen. And twice he'd stopped for her to relieve herself. Other than that, she'd had plenty of conversations with her horse.

A horse she'd named Sir Theophilus since Jim didn't even know if the horse had a proper name.

Sir Theophilus ended up being quite a good listener and a much better trail companion than a certain Texas Ranger. Apparently Mr. Williams was good at his job, because he was completely engrossed in it.

But Sir Theophilus would whinny at her every once in a while and snuffle after she rubbed his nose. It was better than nothing.

She was still handcuffed—which Jim said was because they had to keep up the appearance of her being the number one suspect—and she still hadn't had a bath. Which greatly irritated her the more she thought about it.

The evening sky began to show signs of sunset, and Abigail found she couldn't wait to get off the trail, even if she did have to sleep on the ground. Again.

Sir Theophilus plodded along behind Star and his master.

Several minutes passed, and the sky darkened a bit more as clouds rolled in and covered up the last rays of the sun.

Then the deluge began.

Abigail pulled Sir Theophilus to a halt and let the rain wash over her. At this point, it was the best bath she was going to get, so she might as well relish it.

But soon the rumbling started and lightning struck off in the distance. Her mount sidestepped and shook his mane. It wasn't ever good to be atop an animal that sensed trouble in a storm.

Jim turned around and rode toward her. The rain came down so hard now, he had to shout over it. "We're going to need shelter."

She nodded at the obvious statement, and a shiver raced up her spine. The temperature had dropped considerably in the last few minutes.

"Here, take my coat, and follow closely." He wrapped his long oilskin duster around her shoulders. Then, with a flick of his fingers, he had her out of the handcuffs.

"How'd you do that?" Had she known all this time that she could have whisked them off so easily, she would have readily done it. Especially when trying to use the necessary.

He shrugged and gave her a smile. "Follow close, got it?" As rain dripped off his Stetson, her heart did that little jolt thing again. Ranger Williams was a very handsome man, and the way he'd looked at her the past couple days made her feel very special. Even if he had basically ignored her while he investigated.

Abigail slid her arms into the sleeves of the massive coat and urged her horse to follow Star.

The rain turned into a full-blown Texas gully washer. She could barely see Star in front of her, and Sir Theophilus was clearly not happy with the slippery slope he was climbing.

She leaned over and patted his withers, getting her voice as close to his ear as she could. "You're doing great, just a little bit farther."

They plodded on for what seemed like forever, and Abigail began to feel like a drowned puppy dog. Wrapping Jim's coat tighter around her, she tucked her chin to her chest and prayed for their safety. If the storm didn't let up soon, she wasn't sure what they would do.

A bolt of lightning struck a tree only about twenty feet away from them, and both the horses reared. Abigail felt herself sliding off Theophilus, but she couldn't grab anything fast enough.

Her scream split the air as she tumbled and slid faster and faster down the incline slick with mud. The river of rain carried her along with her screams until everything went black.

◆•———•◆

Jim tied up the horses as fast as he could and chased after Chuck, her screams subdued by the thunder and rain. Then all of a sudden she was silent. No!

He slid his way down the hill until he saw a bluff and the drop-off. Clawing for all he was worth, he slowed his descent. *Lord, please don't let her have gone over the side. Please. Help me find her.*

Coming to a stop near the edge, Jim peered through the mud and the rain. He couldn't see anything. He moved a few feet to the west and looked again.

When he couldn't see anything, he moved another few feet and tried again and then again.

His heart cramped at the thought of not protecting her during the storm. Why had he kept pushing and pushing? They should have stopped hours ago. But he'd been so determined to solve the case and exonerate her that he'd ignored the changing conditions around them.

Jim pushed his way down the ledge through the mud and kept looking. He had to find her. He just had to.

Several excruciating minutes passed. No sign of the lady he knew only as Chuck Miller.

Another bolt of lightning lit up the sky and Jim counted it as a gift from God because he saw what appeared to be a person hanging off a rock ledge.

"Chuck!"

No movement.

Jim worked his way down to the ledge. "Chuck! Can you hear me? Don't move, I'm coming to get you."

Still nothing.

When he reached her, he noticed a trail of blood from her head down the side of her face. She must have hit something that knocked her out. Lifting her up, he saw that his slicker was snagged. As hard as he tried, he couldn't get her free, so he eased her arms out of the coat and lifted her into his arms.

He took a deep breath and put his ear up against her face. Praise God! At least she was breathing.

Now if he could just get them out of here alive.

◆— · —◆

Monday, June 11, 1883

Something pounded on her head. Like a hammer on a tabletop. There were voices around her, but it all just sounded like noise, nothing intelligible.

Abigail lifted her hands to her head and squeezed. Whatever was beating it needed to stop. And fast.

Her eyelids were so heavy. Trying to lift them felt like carrying that horrid bag off the stage.

"Chuck? Can you hear me?" Someone's words broke through the pounding.

Using all the strength she had, she worked at opening her eyes.

"Chuck. I need you to look at me." That voice. She knew that voice. And she really wanted to listen to it.

A moan escaped her lips as she tried. Then a slit of light pierced her eyes. There.

Someone was with her. Leaning over her.

"Hey. Good to see you opening your eyes." It was Jim. He was standing over her. And she was in a soft bed. How did she get here?

"Wha. . .what happened?" She blinked and opened her eyes a little wider.

He crossed his arms over his chest—a stance she'd come to admire—and smiled at her. "You ruined my coat, that's what happened."

"I did?" She furrowed her brow. "I don't remember that."

"It's probably a good thing you don't remember. Sliding off that bluff was not something I would have recommended."

All of a sudden, she remembered the storm and getting reared off the horse. How far did she fall? "Are you all right?" He seemed to be in one piece.

He nodded and sat down next to her.

"Am *I* all right?"

"You're pretty banged up and bruised, and you've got a pretty good bump on your head, but I think my coat took the worst of it. You slid over the edge, and a rock sliced up the back of the leather but thankfully caught you like a fish on a hook. I don't know how long you could have hung there, but I'm glad I found you when I did."

As the fog cleared in her mind, she couldn't believe that he'd risked his life to rescue her. "Thank you."

He leaned closer and smiled. "You're welcome."

Abigail tried to scoot herself up in the bed. "Jim. . .I hate to ask this, but do you think this is almost over?"

His smile faded and his brow turned serious. "The case?"

Nodding, she bit her lip.

"Well, we just received word that the judge will be here Wednesday. I'm going to leave you here with Dusty and his wife. Rosa will take good care of you, and Dusty will keep you safe. Hopefully I'll be able to put it all together by then."

"And if you don't?"

"Don't you worry about that. I always get my man." He patted her arm and reached over to the table where a checkerboard sat. "Dusty will make sure you get to the courthouse on time, and if I don't see you before then, I'll be there. I promise."

Somehow it didn't sound as reassuring as he probably intended. "I need to clear Chuck's name."

He looked at her oddly. "But I thought you made Chuck up?"

"I did. But he's still innocent."

"I see. Are you really that stubborn, or did you just hit your head too hard?"

Abigail smiled. "Both."

He smiled back and set the checkerboard on the bed next to her. "How are you at checkers?"

"Not bad."

"Dusty said he would help you practice so that when I get back you'll be ready for the challenge of playing a seasoned champion." He wiggled his eyebrows as he pointed to himself. Then he stood. "I'd better get on the trail if I'm going to be back for the judge."

"All right."

"I'll see you in two days."

She knew her eyes were shining at him. "Thank you, Jim. For saving my life."

He stood there for a minute and just stared at her. Then he leaned down and kissed her on the forehead. Without another word, he walked away.

Chapter 10

Wednesday, June 13, 1883
Hamilton County Courthouse

L ooking around, Jim felt sure they were ready. Guards were stationed around the room. Even though they always had guards to protect the judges, Jim had brought in two extra, just in case. But he wasn't worried about the judge as much as he was about Chuck. Someone had tried to kill her.

More than once.

But the past two days had been very successful. He'd arrested the two so-called eyewitnesses, and they in turn had squealed on their employer to save their own hides. Even though they'd been hired to plant the evidence and to falsely identify Chuck Miller as the fence cutter, the more serious crimes had been committed by one Leroy Toomes.

A man who was wanted in just about every county in Texas and numerous states. But nobody had ever been able to catch him.

As far as Jim could gather, Leroy had been hired to get rid of the sheepherders who were encroaching on some of the cattle ranches. In fact, Jim had two of them here as witnesses to testify about the man who'd run them off. But those testimonies were only good if he could bring in the man himself.

His only hope now was the trap they'd set for him.

It had actually been the judge's idea, but Jim had been hesitant because it put Chuck right in the middle of it all.

Like bait on a hook.

At this point though, he couldn't do anything else other than follow through with the plan and hope that Chuck would still talk to him after it was all said and done.

Abigail sat in the back of the wagon with a new hat pulled down low over her head. Dusty had instructed her not to talk and to stay out of sight as much as possible. No one wanted another attempt on her life.

Rosa sat next to her and chatted about random things as they drove over the long, winding road into town.

But all Abigail could think about was Jim. Had he caught the culprits? Was he safe? The thought of anything happening to him made her sick to her stomach.

Mama's words washed over her from the day Abigail had asked her when she would know she was in love. *"When you can't think of anything else and you worry about his safety more than your own. . . When he irritates you to high heaven and yet you can't wait to see him again. . . When you want him to be happy and are willing to sacrifice your own happiness to make that happen. . . And when you can't imagine life without him. . .that's when you know you're in love."*

Thinking through each of those things, Abigail knew they were true about her feelings for Jim. But he didn't even know who she was. He didn't even know her name!

Maybe if things had started in a different time at a different place. . .where they could be Abigail and Jim.

But no. That's not how it worked.

And it definitely wasn't where they were today.

She let out a long sigh, just wanting this all to be over. If she was allowed to go free, she would go home and put off the persona of Chuck Miller forever. Then maybe in a few weeks she could return to Hamilton County with Sally and introduce herself proper-like to Ranger Jim Williams.

If he would have her. She prayed that he would.

The wagon hit a bump, and she bounced along with it.

A shot rang out, and she ducked into the bed of the wagon.

Then another one. The wagon's side splintered only a few feet from her head.

"Stay down." She heard Dusty's voice over the cacophony around her.

As she stayed hunkered in the back with Rosa, she heard horses' hooves. Lots of them. Were those the good guys or the bad guys?

She heard Dusty urge the team on and felt them going faster and faster over the uneven ground.

More shots.

"We're almost there." Rosa's voice comforted her.

But it couldn't keep her heart from pounding in her chest. She'd had a hunch they would use her as bait if they hadn't caught the ringleader. Dusty had alluded to as much when he'd shared that the two liars had been arrested. But it was one thing to know it—quite another to live it.

Another shattering of wood beside her as the echo of another shot rang in the air. She tried to make herself as small as possible, hoping she hadn't put more people in danger.

Abigail just wanted it all to be over. Even if the reporter was in the court-house. Even if she had to tell the truth in front of the entire town. She was tired of it all and just wanted to be done.

The wagon came to a stop, and Abigail hit her head on the front of the wagon bed.

"Come on. Let's get you inside." Dusty grabbed her arm and practically tossed her out of the wagon. "Hurry."

She looked around and saw horses and dust and several men struggling on the ground in the distance. "Did they hurt anyone?"

Rosa shook her head. "I don't think so. It seems they were aiming for you." She pointed back toward the wagon.

Abigail took a quick glance and saw two large holes in the wagon's side mere inches from where she'd been huddled. Her heart raced. *Lord, help this to end soon. Please. And please keep Jim safe.*

When they walked into the room that served as the courthouse, Abigail recognized the two men who'd come to the jail to identify her alongside two other shady-looking men—the ones from the stage! They were in handcuffs and looking quite sour. Jim must have arrested them too.

Then a scuffle at the back of the room drew everyone's attention. Jim sported a swollen eye that would probably turn some lovely colors later and a cut on his cheek. But the other man looked a lot worse. He was tall and muscular but obviously hadn't been a match for a Texas Ranger.

As they walked by her, the prisoner spit at her boots.

She frowned and wondered what that was all about. Unless. . .that was the man who had tried to kill her.

The next half hour was filled with chaos. The judge heard testimony from sheepherders who'd been forced off their own property by that man—Leroy Toomes—and the two men who'd worked for him. They admitted to falsely accusing Chuck and to planting evidence in Mr. Miller's bag but swore they had nothing to do with any attempts on his life. Then a parade of men came through who were witnesses about other crimes in other counties.

It all overwhelmed Abigail. She'd never been in a court proceeding before, and she couldn't believe that one man could do so many horrible things.

Then the judge asked Jim to come forward.

The Ranger she'd spent so much time with the past week talked about the trap they'd laid for Mr. Toomes today.

Jim looked at her, a bit of remorse on his face. After all, he'd had to use her for the trap—because Toomes wanted her dead. But she still didn't know why. She'd never met or even heard of Leroy Toomes.

Then the judge called Chuck Miller.

Abigail sat there for a moment, trying to take it all in.

"Mr. Miller." The judge pounded on his desk.

She stepped forward.

The judge looked down at her from his seat at the bench. "You are released and absolved of any involvement in any of the aforementioned crimes."

"Thank you." She went back to her seat. Was it really over?

The judge said something else to Mr. Toomes that she didn't understand, and then the man was escorted away by several Texas Rangers.

Lots of conversations went on around her, and the chaos was a bit much. Dusty leaned toward her and patted her shoulder. "Glad you're all right."

"Thank you, Dusty." She turned to Rosa. "And thank you too."

"It was our pleasure." Rosa leaned over and gave her a hug. She whispered into Abigail's ear. "And one day I want to hear about why you dress as a man."

Abigail gave her new friend a smile. Maybe one day this story would be a good one to tell. One day. To her grandchildren. But right now she hoped no one ever heard it.

Searching through the crowd, she'd hoped to be able to speak with Jim, but he was with the judge. They looked to be in deep conversation.

Maybe it was better this way. If she just left on the next stage, she wouldn't have to face the embarrassment of saying goodbye to the man she loved, who didn't even know who she was.

"Dusty, is my bag still in the wagon?"

He nodded. "Would you like me to get it?"

"No. I'll grab it. But thank you."

◆—————◆

The judge explained to Jim and his fellow Rangers everything that would need to take place to finalize the case. Each man's report, including Dusty's, would be needed that day. The judge couldn't seem to stop the smile that slid onto his face when he rehashed to the court reporter about how his plan worked. While Jim was just as happy that it was all over, he couldn't wait to get to Chuck and tell her all about the rest of the story. But the judge was in charge and didn't seem in any hurry to wrap things up.

As Jim's thoughts kept shifting to her, he hoped that she would finally tell him her real name. The thought made him smile.

Finally dismissed from the bench, Jim looked around the room, but he couldn't see her anywhere.

Maybe Dusty and Rosa had taken her home.

But then he spotted the couple. Without Chuck.

"Where did she go?"

Dusty slapped his back. "She asked for her bag and said she was going to the stage."

Without even saying goodbye? Jim couldn't allow that to happen. He had no idea who she was and how to find her again.

He couldn't let her leave without telling her how he felt.

Running out of the building, he headed down to the general store, hoping the afternoon stage hadn't come through yet.

When he got there, Chuck was sitting on the bench out front, her hat pulled low over her eyes. But he'd recognize her anywhere.

Using his booming Ranger voice, he put his hands on his hips. "Mr. Miller, might I have a word?"

Her head popped up.

Several people stopped and stared.

Grabbing her bag, she came down the sidewalk to meet him. She glanced around and spoke in a hushed tone. "I thought I was released to go."

He stepped closer. "You are."

She let out a long breath. "Good. For a minute there, I thought you were going to arrest me again."

"Well, if that's what it takes to keep you here, I just might have to do that."

Her eyes lit up. "And why exactly do you want to keep me here, Ranger Williams?"

"Perhaps it's simply to learn your name."

She shrugged. "That doesn't sound like a very good reason."

"What if I wanted to tell you about what happened with Toomes?"

"I'd be interested in hearing about that." She toed the dirt in front of her and then looked back up at him.

"It seems that he thought you were someone else entirely." Jim got a chuckle out of the irony.

"Oh really?"

"Yep. He thought you'd witnessed him killing one of the sheep ranchers. That witness was small like you, and when they followed him, they saw him buy a ticket. That's why Leroy had his men on the stage with you and tried to frame you for the fence cuttings. Only the man on the stage wasn't the witness. It was *you*. You weren't even supposed to be on that stage. He only went after Chuck Miller because that's whose name the stage driver gave them."

"Oh." Her pink lips rounded. "And the real witness?"

"Testified before the judge this morning."

"I see."

"Since Toomes thought you'd witnessed him killing someone, he made up his own witnesses and sent the note to me. It was an easy way to keep you locked up where he could then dispose of you."

"Huh. Well, at least he's the one locked up now." She bit her lip.

Jim stepped even closer to her. "You know what fascinates me the most?"

"What?" She looked up at him with those green eyes that he loved.

"He thought Chuck Miller was your real identity."

She laughed at that. "So he still thinks I'm Mr. Miller?"

"Yes, ma'am."

"But I'm not."

Jim's heart picked up speed. "I'm glad to hear that."

She pulled off her Stetson and let her hair fall down her back. Several gasps were heard from people gathered around the store.

But the rest of the world seemed to disappear for Jim. He only had eyes for the woman in front of him. Even if she *was* dressed like a man.

She inched closer until the toes of her boots touched his. "My name is Abigail."

He took off his own hat and wrapped his arms around her. "It's nice to meet you, Abigail." And then, right there in the middle of the street, he covered her lips with his own.

Epilogue

December 28, 1883
Coleman County, Texas

Abigail Monroe floated down the stairs of her family's home like she was on a cloud. Today was the day. The day she'd become Mrs. Jim Williams. For months they'd been planning and dreaming. With quite a few heated spats mixed in there too. But Abigail was learning to listen, and Jim was learning what it meant to be engaged to an outspoken woman who was part of the Woman's Christian Temperance Union. They were both stubborn, and Abigail found that made things quite interesting.

She'd even told Jim yesterday that he'd never be bored. To which he heartily agreed.

The biggest hurdle had been his job as a Ranger. While Abigail assured him that she was perfectly willing to live with him on the road wherever the job took him, Jim wasn't so sure that was the best idea. Especially after she volunteered to dress up as Chuck again.

But after a lot of prayer and seeking the Lord's guidance, Jim had decided to take a job as a local sheriff rather than a Texas Ranger so that he could help her run the ranch if she needed him. He said one day he might even take up fishing. Just for the fun of it.

As Abigail looked around the house—all prepared for their wedding guests—her heart swelled. Six months she'd been waiting to marry this man. It had only taken days for her to fall in love with him and to know he was the one God had for her, but the past few months had shown her how truly beautiful God's grace was in their lives. To be given such a gift as Jim made her want to shout praises from the rooftop.

Sally barreled around the corner from the kitchen. "Miss Abigail, what are you doing down here? We need to get you in your dress."

"I was just checking on things."

Her maid shoved her toward the stairs. "There's absolutely nothing for you to be checking on. It's all taken care of."

That made Abigail giggle. "Well, I know it's all taken care of, but I wanted to see for myself."

Sally shook her head at her, and they walked up the stairs. "Still as stubborn as ever, I see."

"Yes I am."

"We need to get you up those stairs before you have some sort of crazy accident."

"Oh hush. I refuse to have a mishap today. It's my wedding day." Abigail lifted her chin and laughed.

"I'm glad Mr. Jim knows what he's getting into." Her tone grew serious. "He's a good man. Your daddy and mama would be proud."

Abigail hugged the woman who'd been there for her through thick and thin. "Thank you, Sally. That means the world to me."

◆━━━━━◆

Jim stood in the massive room in front of the fireplace with all their guests staring at him. He slid a finger beneath his collar. If it got much tighter, he wouldn't be able to say his vows.

But then Mr. Collins started to play his violin.

Jim snapped his attention to the double doorway. There stood Abigail. His bride.

He'd never seen anyone more beautiful in all his days. Her blond hair was piled on top of her head in a mountain of curls. Her dress was covered in ivory lace that shimmered in the candlelight.

This woman was his.

Swallowing past the lump in his throat, he sent a quick prayer heavenward as she started her walk toward him. They wouldn't be here today had God not brought the two of them together under the strangest of circumstances. But he thanked God every day that he'd had the chance to meet Chuck Miller. And thus. . .his Abigail.

As the violin crescendos brought her closer, he heard an unmistakable sound that made him smile. She must be wearing the boots she'd worn the day they met. Spurs and all. Staring into Abigail's green eyes, he noticed the laughter and joy in them.

She reached him and took his hands. Looking up at him, she whispered, "I had to bring Chuck with me."

The pastor frowned and leaned forward. "Who's Chuck? Is there something I need to know?"

Jim and Abigail both laughed aloud at that one.

Abigail covered her mirth with her hand and then looked back to the pastor with a smile. "Please, continue."

The next few minutes passed in a blur as they repeated holy vows to one another and made a covenant under God in front of their friends.

Tears shimmered in Abigail's eyes as she promised to love and honor him for as long as she lived.

The service ended so quickly, Jim had to take a steadying breath. He was married!

The pastor asked everyone to stand. "What therefore God hath joined together, let not man put asunder. Jim, you may kiss your bride."

Cheers surrounded them, and he brought his new wife into his arms. As his lips captured hers, he didn't think he'd ever want to stop.

The pastor cleared his throat.

Laughter filled the room.

The pastor leaned in again. "So who wants to explain who Chuck is?"

Jim laughed and pulled his wife close again. "Don't worry, Pastor. It was just a case of *miss*taken identity."

Acknowledgments

After umpteen published books, my heart overflows each day with gratitude to everyone who helps to make this happen. You all know who you are. Thank you.

To God, who gave me this journey to travel, thank You.

Jeremy—the love of my life—thank you for twenty-seven amazing years. I'm looking forward to at least twenty-seven more.

Thank you to my crit group who cheers me on and holds my toes to the fire: Becca Whitham, Darcie Gudger, Kayla Woodhouse.

And to my readers—I'm so blessed by you. Thank you for journeying with me again.

Kimberley Woodhouse is an award-winning and bestselling author of more than fifteen fiction and nonfiction books. A popular speaker and teacher, she has shared her theme of "Joy through Trials" with more than half a million people across the country at more than two thousand events. Kim and her incredible husband of twenty-seven years have two adult children. She's passionate about music and Bible study and loves the gift of story.

You can connect with Kimberley at www.kimberleywoodhouse.com and www.facebook.com/KimberleyWoodhouseAuthor.

Lesson of Love

by Cynthia Hickey

Chapter 1

1885
Ozark Mountains

As the sun kissed the top of the mountain, it became obvious to Leah Ellison that she had been forgotten. She clutched her satchel, lifted her chin, and marched to the stagecoach office. Not that she'd arrived in a stagecoach, exactly—more like a wagon. Every bone in her body ached from the jostling. She much preferred the soot of the train over the jolt of the wagon.

She pushed through the door to the mercantile/post office/stagecoach office as the sign proudly pointed out and approached the man wearing a white apron. She cleared her throat several times before he looked up from his ledger.

"Excuse me, sir, but I'm wondering where I might hire a driver to take me to Possum Hollow."

He looked her up and down and laughed. "Who might you be, in ruffles and bows?"

She lifted her chin higher. "I am the new schoolteacher, Miss Ellison. Someone was supposed to have picked me up."

"Do you see anyone out there?"

"I do not."

"Then your hopes of hiring a driver are next to nothin'." He went back to writing numbers in columns.

"Then what, pray tell, am I to do?"

"Start walking." He pointed behind him. "That way. Can't miss it. It's the only cluster of buildings up there."

Walk? Up a mountain? Leah stared at the man with wide eyes. Surely she'd heard him wrong.

"Best get a move on. It gets dark fast up there," he said without looking up.

"But. . .my trunks."

"You can probably get someone to come back in the morning. No one will bother them if you slide them inside the mercantile."

Graduating from a fine ladies college and accepting her first teaching job was fast losing its appeal. Perhaps a position in a larger city, as Mother had suggested, might have been best after all.

By the time she pushed her three trunks inside the store, her hair was falling from its bun and her arms were trembling with fatigue. She was close to tears as she stared at the road angling upward. Standing there staring wasn't going to get her off her feet. She took a deep shuddering breath and started up the incline.

She hadn't gone far before she stopped to rest on a log by the side of what could barely be called a road. At least not the type of road Leah was used to. Filled with rocks and potholes, it was a wonder the road hadn't tripped her and caused a sprained ankle. She removed her boot and rubbed her aching feet. Ah, that felt wonderful.

A twig snapped behind her.

Leah bolted to her feet. An animal? "Hello?" When no answer came and she wasn't attacked by a wild beast, she resumed her seat and removed the other boot. She lifted her perspiring face to the kiss of a soft breeze.

Well, she'd wanted an adventure. This was shaping up to be more of a misadventure, but Leah Ellison did not back down from a challenge.

A louder snap from behind her had her hurtling up the road, boots in her hands and hair quickly releasing from its bun entirely. Leah might be adventurous, but bravery didn't seem to be included in her personality strengths.

She rounded a sharp corner in the road and barreled head first over a man hunched next to a wagon. The breath escaped her in a whoosh. She blinked several times and stared at the night sky. "Wow. I didn't think the stars could be that bright. Diamonds against black velvet."

"Miss?" A man, his face in shadow, bent over her. "Did you hit your head?"

"No, I don't think so. Help me up."

He grasped her hand and hauled her to her feet. "What were you running from?"

"A fearsome beast." She fussed with her gown. "I've torn a bit of lace on my best traveling suit."

The man grabbed a weapon from the wagon bed and stared in the direction Leah had come. "I don't see anything. Most animals are more afraid of you than you are of them."

"Then that animal is petrified with fright. What in the name of Josiah were you doing? If you hadn't been squatting in the—"

"I wasn't squatting. I was trying to fix the wagon wheel. You wouldn't happen to be Miss Ellison, would you?" He tilted his head.

"I am. Are you my driver?"

"I don't know about that. I'm Luke Canfield, cotton farmer, who just happened to be headed to the mercantile to pick up supplies and offered to pick up the new teacher."

"Which you failed to do." She hopped on the wagon bed and put her boots on over her tattered stockings and dirty feet. "But, since the wheel is broken, I guess—"

"It's fixed now."

"Wonderful. Let's fetch my trunks and head home."

"Mercantile is closed now. We'll have to go back in the morning."

She groaned. "Very well. I'll arrive in town looking like a homeless orphan."

"Not much of a town, Miss Ellison." He jumped into the driver's seat, clicked his tongue at the horses, and almost unseated Leah as the wagon lurched forward.

She squealed and grabbed the side. Nothing had gone as planned. She allowed herself one minute of tears and not a second more. She swiped them away with a handkerchief pulled from inside her sleeve and vowed to be the best teacher the "not much of a town, cluster of buildings, Possum Hollow" had ever seen.

◆━━━◆

Luke chuckled as the new teacher almost fell off the wagon. Even through the dirt, she was the cutest thing he'd seen in a very long time. He'd thought her a bit loony when she'd started talking about the stars and velvet but figured out pretty quick that was just her fanciful way of talking. He laughed harder, imagining how the fancy little thing was going to respond when she laid eyes on her cabin and the schoolhouse. Neither could come close to comparing to what she'd most likely left behind.

"May I inquire what is so humorous?" She leaned over the seat, giving him a whiff of something flowery. . .like sunshine and roses. His heart flipped.

"Just thinking."

"How much farther?"

"Couple miles."

"Gracious, and that wretched man expected me to walk the entire distance. Help me into the seat." She swung one leg over and landed in a heap of fabric and lace in his lap. "My apologies."

"My pleasure. Although that type of maneuver could cause us to wreck." Luke had a feeling Possum Hollow was in for a surprise with their new teacher.

"Tell me about Possum Hollow." She settled onto the seat next to him. "It will help to pass the time."

"All right. I'm Luke Canfield, as I've said, and I own the cotton gin around these parts. Mr. Watson, the mercantile owner, lives behind his shop and has no wife or children. Let me see. . ." He rubbed his chin. "Other than that, there isn't much in Possum Hollow but the families of your students. The school doubles as a church whenever a traveling preacher makes his way to us or I've the time. I've been known to give the occasional sermon."

"No regular church? I can't imagine. Tell me about my students."

"I'll try, but I don't run into them much and don't know their names, so I'll just mention surnames." He talked until the first building came into view. "This is it. This is the schoolhouse. Behind it is your cabin. I'll light the lantern for you." He wanted to see her in the light and to make sure no critters had taken up residence since he'd checked the place the day before.

"That is very generous of you."

He lifted her down from the wagon, his hands lingering a bit too long on her waist to be completely proper, but she sure was pretty. "Not a problem, Miss Ellison."

He led her to the small one-room cabin. "The mothers of your students made sure you had the necessities." He pushed open the door.

A mouse squeaked and darted past them.

Miss Ellison crumpled to the ground in a dead faint.

She sure was a strange little thing. Luke scooped her into his arms and deposited her on top of the single bed before lighting the lantern. He held the lantern over her and studied her features to his heart's content until her ridiculously long eyelashes fluttered open and he stared into eyes the color of freshly mowed grass. Long hair the color of an acorn fanned out around her.

"You all right?"

"Heavens. I hadn't expected to find someone so handsome up here."

He stepped back. "Excuse me? Are you always this blunt?"

"Unfortunately." She sat up, then seeming to realize she was on her bed and jumped to her feet. "I tend to fall quickly for good-looking men and hoped I wouldn't find anyone I would fancy up here. I don't need the notion of romance and marriage to distract me from my career."

Marriage? Romance? "I think you hit your head."

"I did not." She grabbed a bucket from the washboard. "Please direct me to the pump."

"Are you sure you don't need me to save you from mice?" He raised his eyebrows. "Miss Ellison, I must tell you that there are all sorts of critters on this mountain. Most will not hurt you. Like a mouse. All you got to worry about is cougars, bears, hogs. . . ." He scratched his chin. "Wild dogs, coyotes. . ."

"Oh, is that all?" Her eyes widened. "Hardly anything." Her breathing quickened. "You will pick me up in the morning to fetch my things, right?"

"Daylight. Let's fill this bucket." He took it from her and led her out back to where a pump served both her and the school. "Fresh, ice-cold water." He pulled up the well bucket and filled hers. "See you bright and early." He headed for the wagon, grinning like a fool as her feet thudded behind him.

She'd wasted no time in running for the safety of her cabin. "Wait, Mr. Canfield. There's no lock on this door."

"Prop a chair against it, Miss Ellison. You're safe enough." Whistling, he climbed into the wagon and set off for his own home half a mile down the road.

He cared for the horse, then entered the house and sat in his favorite chair, which he'd made from the hide of a bull that had gored his favorite horse. He sank into its comfort and toed off his boots. Marriage. He snorted. What kind of woman openly admitted she had a weakness for handsome men?

It might behoove him to avoid the little minx. *Drat.* He tugged his boots back on and headed for the barn. After hitching the horse back to the wagon, he set off down the mountain toward the mercantile. Old Man Watson could just get his grumpy self out of bed and let Luke load up the teacher's things. He didn't need to be driving her to town in the morning.

Another hour spent in her company was another hour too many.

Chapter 2

Leah cried tears of relief to see her trunks piled by the door the next morning. After her outrageous comment about how handsome the dark-haired Luke was, she couldn't imagine facing him. And those eyes! Dark and decadent, like the finest chocolate.

Oh pooh. She opened the first trunk and started carrying things into the house. Soon the trunks served as storage and extra seats. Not that the cabin was large enough for much entertaining.

Leah separated her personal things from the school supplies. By the time she finished, perspiration ran down her back. She wiped her dusty hands on the apron she wore and headed for the schoolhouse. The telegram she'd sent said school would commence on Monday. Today was Saturday. She had very little time to prepare.

She climbed the five steps to the cute white building and pushed open the door. Not nearly as cute inside, but once she cleaned it, set out the things she'd brought, and pushed the desks in some type of order, it would suffice.

◆━━ · ━━◆

By Monday morning, Leah was as ready as she could be. She straightened her white shirtwaist, ran her hands down her navy wool skirt, and waited on the school steps for her students to arrive. At precisely eight o'clock, she reached up and rang the bell.

Children of all ages scurried from the woods and up the road like mice. Their eager expressions brought tears to Leah's eyes. They seemed as pleased for school to start as she was. Except for the three older boys shuffling up the road. Heavens, they looked too old to be in school.

"Gentlemen, may I help you?"

"We're here to go to school. Our Pa said we had to. I'm Mark Haywell, and this is Matthew." The boy pointed to an identical version of himself, right down to the carrottop hair and freckles. "We're fifteen. Too old to go to school, I say. This is our younger brother, Amos. He wants to come."

The belligerent look in Mark's eyes sent prickles of alarm down Leah's spine.

She forced a smile. "I'm pleased to meet you. Please come in and take a seat at the back of the room. That's where the older students will sit."

Clasping her hands in front of her, Leah made her way to the front of the classroom and wrote "Miss Ellison" on the blackboard. "I am so grateful for the opportunity to be your teacher. I'd like the primary grades in the front, the older in the back. As the days pass, we'll know more about your education level and will assign seating accordingly."

The morning passed with her getting to know the students and putting faces with names. When lunch rolled around, she was as eager to step outside as the children were. She sat on the steps and nibbled on an apple.

A buckboard rumbled up the road. The noonday sun glistened off the dark hair of Mr. Canfield. Leah raised a hand in a wave, relieved when he reciprocated. Wonderful. Time would pass, and he would forget her silly words. Perhaps the two of them could be friends.

"That's Mr. Canfield," Lucy Smithson said, sitting down next to Leah. "He's the richest man around these parts other than Mr. Watson."

"Really?" Leah watched him drive away. "He doesn't strike me as wealthy."

"He is." The ten-year-old nodded. "All the girls of marrying age like to cozy up to him, but he don't seem interested."

"He doesn't seem interested."

"No ma'am, he don't."

Leah sighed. "We mustn't gossip."

"Then how else will news get spread?" Lucy flashed a grin and raced off to play jump rope with a couple of other girls.

After the lunch break, Leah again stood at the front of the room. "Please tell your parents that I will be visiting each of your homes in order to meet them." Once she found a way to get around anyway. She wanted to see how each family fared and offer help and advice where needed so her students could thrive.

The Haywell boys spent the afternoon pushing, shoving, and making ribald comments to each other until Leah wanted to pull out her hair. "Boys, please inform your parents that I will be visiting them this evening or tomorrow."

"Just our pa. Ma died five years ago from influenza," Matthew said.

"Don't lie," Mark said, punching him. "It was rabies."

Amos shook his head. "She run off with some fancy fella passing through. Don't listen to them, Miss Ellison."

"Thank you, Amos." She narrowed her eyes at the two older boys. "Lucy, where does Mr. Canfield live?"

"Thataway. Big house with a big porch and a big red barn out back. He keeps his land cleared, so you can't miss it."

Leah was going to take the chance that Mr. Canfield would disregard her earlier behavior and give her a ride out to the Haywell place. Perhaps he could also direct her to someone with a horse to sell or rent. Her parents had made sure she had funds for such expenses. She would become self-sufficient just as soon as she had everything she needed.

When school was over and the last student out of sight, Leah closed the schoolhouse door behind her and set out to find the house with the big red barn. Lucy couldn't have been more correct. Mr. Canfield's land stretched far. A sprawling cabin sat at the forefront, assorted outbuildings behind the log structure. Fields of cotton dotted the landscape with balls of white—a very pretty sight.

"Miss Ellison?"

She turned to greet Mr. Canfield as he approached. "Good afternoon."

He wiped his hands on a piece of red flannel. "How may I help you?"

"Two things, actually. I need a ride to the Haywell place, and I need to know where to rent or purchase a horse."

"I can help you with both of those. Follow me."

"Thank you." She almost had to run to keep up with his long-legged pace. "But if you've a horse to sell, there is no need for you to accompany me to the Haywell place."

He frowned. "Miss Ellison. If you show up at the Haywell place unaccompanied, Horace will think you are there to get hitched. It's no secret the man is actively looking for a mother for his boys."

◆◦——◦◆

Miss Ellison paled. "Surely, if I were to explain my reason for visiting—"

"Nope. The man's as obstinate as a mule. As head of the school board—"

"Oh, you're *that* Mr. Canfield."

"Yes." He closed his eyes and prayed for patience. "As head of the school board, I can put emphasis on the fact that the schoolteacher of Possum Hollow is to remain unmarried as long as she is employed here. After I spread the word, feel free to visit anyone you choose." He led her into the barn and straight to Molly.

"She's beautiful." Miss Ellison reached out and let the horse nuzzle her hand. "Are you sure you want to sell her?"

"More than sure. The horse is a menace. Her spirit is as dark as her hair." He jumped back as Molly tried to bite him. "She only likes women. I think her previous owner, a man, mistreated her."

"She's perfect, aren't you, my ebony beauty?" Miss Ellison leaned her forehead against the horse's forehead. "We'll get along splendidly. How much?"

"Consider her a perk of the job. I'm glad to be rid of her." That was the gospel truth. He'd bought the horse at an auction and bore a scar on his leg that testified to the reason she was sold.

The teacher thought for a moment, then nodded. "Although she is worth much more, I will accept her in exchange for my first month's salary." She thrust out her small hand.

Luke grinned and returned the shake. "Deal. Shall we saddle up?"

A short time later, they rode further up the mountain. Miss Ellison was uncharacteristically silent, at least in Luke's experience with her. Not that he would complain. The sound of the wind rustling the leaves and the birds chirping in the trees made the prettiest sounds he'd ever heard.

"It's like a grand cathedral," Miss Ellison whispered. "See how the sun's rays break through the branches and dapple the path with gold? This is God's true church."

"I couldn't agree more." In fact, she'd just given him the subject for his next sermon—taking time to bask in the beauty of God's creation. "You do have a way with words, Miss Ellison."

"I am an educated woman, after all."

He grinned and admired the way she sat on her horse. The woman could ride. With barely a flick of the reins, Molly did as instructed. Luke quite enjoyed riding behind the teacher. She was attractive no matter which angle he gazed on her from.

He'd sworn a long time ago that life was too full for a wife and family, but that thought was challenged with the arrival of Miss Ellison. Not that he wanted her to speak of marriage and romance again, not at all. Nor would he forget that she could not marry while employed as teacher. He rather liked that fact. Perhaps he could enjoy her company without the pressure of romance.

"Hold up, Miss Ellison. You don't ride up on anyone's home out here without calling out." He pulled alongside her as they emerged from the trees. "Hello, the house!"

"Who is it?" An answering call came.

"Luke Canfield and the new teacher."

"Come on up."

Miss Ellison glanced at Luke. "He sounds quite gruff."

"You'll never meet a more grizzly man who seems to have an aversion to water." He urged his horse forward.

He dismounted and looped the reins around the porch railing as Horace Haywell stepped out of the house. Before Luke could move to help Miss Ellison down, she'd already slid to the ground and secured Molly.

Rather than approach the door as Luke expected her to, she moved to his side. "I'll let you make the introductions. I must admit the man is a bit frightening."

Luke leaned close to her ear. "I'll protect you." With his hand on the small of her back, he guided her up the steps. "Horace Haywell, this is Miss Ellison."

"Pleased." The man's teeth flashed through his bushy, dark beard. "Yore a pretty little thing. My boys didn't lie about that."

She held out her hand. "It's nice to meet you, sir."

He tugged her toward the door. "Come on in."

"Prepare yourself," Luke warned quietly.

She glanced over her shoulder, apprehension written across her face, then squared her shoulders and let Horace pull her inside.

Luke followed and did his best to take small breaths through his mouth. The odor of unwashed clothes and bodies slapped him in the face. The three boys sprawled on the floor in front of the unlit fireplace and smoked foul cigars.

"See, Canfield? This is why you need to get rid of that stipulation saying female teachers can't marry." Horace crossed his arms. "The only single women you bring to town are teachers."

"Now, Horace, Miss Ellison isn't here to talk about your marriage problems. She's here to meet you and discuss your boys."

"What about my boys?" He scowled.

"Well," Miss Ellison said. "They're a bit old for school. Other than Amos, no other student comes close to their age. Plus, they sit in the back of the room and roughhouse, which distracts everyone else."

"They can't read. They're probably bored. Did you try takin' 'em out to the woodshed for a whoopin'? Want me to do that for you?"

Spots of color appeared high on her cheeks. "Definitely not!"

"Then I reckon you'll have to keep them in school and do what you were hired to do. Teach. If not, then quit and we can get hitched. Either way my boys come out the winners."

"Sir." Miss Ellison stomped her foot. Her mouth opened and closed a few times, then with a swish of her skirts, she stormed out of the house and straight to her horse.

Luke and Horace watched through the front door. "She's kinda feisty, ain't she?" Horace asked.

"Yep. I'll talk to her." Luke clapped a hand on the other man's shoulder. "Talk to your boys about behaving. Oh, and if you really want to win over a woman, I'd spend some time cleaning the house and yourselves."

Chapter 3

The next day was pretty much like the day before. The Haywell boys cut up in the back. The only one of them who seemed interested in learning was the youngest. When one of the twins put a toad down the back of the dress of the girl who sat in front of them, Leah had had enough.

She snapped her pointer stick across her desk. "Mark and Matthew, you will stay after school and clean the chalkboard and stack wood. This behavior has to stop."

"What are you gonna do about it?" One of them—she really needed to find a way to tell them apart—crossed his arms and glared. "You ain't big enough to do a thing."

Refusing to be intimidated, Leah marched to the last row, grabbed the young man by the ear, and dragged him, howling, outside. "How's that, Mr. Haywell? You sit on those steps and think about your behavior. If you move one inch, I'll be speaking with your father." She brushed her hands together and stepped back into the classroom.

She cut the other twin a sharp look and continued to the front of the class. "If you would all pull out your readers, we will continue."

By the end of the day, Leah felt as if she'd walked up the mountain with a load on her back. She smiled and waved as the last student headed down the road, then sagged against the wall. She still had families to visit. No help for it. She'd said she would, and Leah Ellison was a woman of her word.

After making sure the schoolroom was set to rights, she mounted Molly and headed for the furthest home on her list. According to her student, Willy Williams, it was five miles straight thataway.

No child could walk that far back and forth every day, so Leah figured it must be more like one or two miles. Regardless, she'd stop at the first house, pay a visit, then ask for directions to Willy's.

The first home happened to belong to young Lucy. Leah couldn't be happier, as the little redhead had captured her heart from the first moment Leah had set eyes on her.

She stopped at the edge of the cleared land. "Hello, the house!"

"It's Miss Ellison." Lucy sprinted down the steps and danced around Molly's legs until Leah feared for the child's safety.

"Get back here, child." A pretty woman with red hair like Lucy's and wearing a faded calico dress stepped onto the porch. "Hitch the horse up right here, miss, and come inside for a sip of tea."

Leah stepped into a cabin that held little more than the bare necessities. Four children younger than Lucy stared from where they sat on crates around a table propped up with rocks. She'd never suspected this type of poverty from the clean but patched clothes Lucy wore. She couldn't impose on what little they had.

"I appreciate the gesture, Miss Smithson, but I can't stay long. I've other homes to visit." She smiled down at Lucy. "I just want you to know what a pleasure it is to have Lucy in my class. Is Mr. Smithson around? I'd like to meet him too."

"My husband died two years ago, Miss Ellison, but he'd be right proud of your words regarding Lucy."

Leah turned to go. Her gaze fell on a quilt draped over a crude rocking chair. "How beautiful. Did you make this?"

The woman stepped forward. "From the clothes my babies wore, at least as much of them as was usable when they were finished with them."

"Have you considered selling quilts? The women in the cities would pay good money for something as fine as this. It would help your. . .straits."

Pain flickered across the woman's face. "I don't have the time, Miss Ellison, or the fabric."

Leah's smile widened. "I can help with that. We can organize a quilting bee at the school. I've leftover fabric from some of my own dresses."

"Charity?" She shook her head. "No, ma'am. None of the folks around these parts have the time for social get-togethers outside of the occasional church meeting. Thank you for your concern." She opened the door.

Dismissed, and knowing she'd said something wrong but not knowing what exactly, Leah left and headed to the next house. *Rats.* She'd forgotten to ask for directions to Willy's.

She continued to insult the folks of Possum Hollow by offering ideas and suggestions wherever she stopped. At the last house, which happened to be Willy's, as the boy had said, Leah suggested to his widower father that they should hold a craft bazaar where folks could sell their wares. She'd never seen so much talent among so few people.

Instead of being grateful for her concern, the people were riled and upset.

She wasn't offering them charity, other than. . . Oh, perhaps she shouldn't have offered to pay for the advertisement in the city paper.

Her shoulders slumped. As the newcomer, she should have taken things more slowly. Instead of moving forward in getting to know the local folks, she'd taken two steps backward. Mother always said Leah spoke before thinking. She'd again proven her mother correct.

By the time she reached her cabin, she'd spent well over an hour berating herself for her outspokenness and could barely hold in the tears. She dismounted and led Molly to the simple structure behind her cabin that served as a single-stall barn.

Leah laid her head against the horse's neck and breathed deep of animal and the rich Ozark clay. "Oh Molly, I'm a fool."

◆—————◆

"As head of the school board, Luke, you have to talk to the woman." Mr. Williams glared down from his horse. "She's overstepping her boundaries. No one here has time to spend making crafts to sell. Why, it took me months to carve that bear head, and she thinks I can whip one up in two shakes of a cow's tail."

"She means well, Hank." Luke sighed. "But I'll have a word with her."

"I suggest you head over before it gets too dark. Lots of folks are upset." He jerked the reins and trotted away.

So much for trying to keep his distance from Miss Ellison. He should have known better, being head of the school board and all. The last teacher had been quite a bit older and a whole lot homelier. All teachers should be just the right side of ugly in order to stay unmarried or a temptation.

The sky was tinged with rose and pumpkin by the time he arrived at Miss Ellison's. He rapped sharply on the door and stepped back.

It took a few minutes for the door to open, but when it did it was quite clear that the teacher had been crying. "Are you all right?"

"Not in the slightest." She stepped close and wrapped her arms around his waist. "The people of Possum Hollow hate me."

"Oh, uh." What did a man do in this situation? He wasn't skilled in comforting women. He awkwardly patted her on the back. Why did she have to smell so sweet and feel so good despite the tears soaking his shirt? "They'll get used to you."

She peered up at him. "I need your help. Sit here, since it won't be proper for you to come in after dark, and I'll bring out coffee." She pulled back and hurried away.

More improper than her throwing herself into his arms? He shook his head. He shouldn't be surprised. Miss Ellison had shown from the first moment he met her that she wasn't like other people.

It wasn't that her ideas for helping the community were bad. Far from it, in fact. She just went about it the wrong way.

"All right." Miss Ellison handed him a porcelain mug. "Tell me how to fix this." She sat down next to him, her skirts billowing around her and covering half his lap.

"You need to find a way to make the idea theirs."

"How?" She turned her head to gaze into his face.

"The people around here are busy, but not too busy, as they seem to think they are." He took a sip of his drink. "You need to find a way to have them think they are helping someone else."

"How would that improve their own lot?" She pulled up her knees and folded her arms on top of them. "I've never seen such poverty, or such pride. With their talents, they could live so much easier. Mrs. Smithson barely has a roof over her head, and five little mouths to feed. It is my Christian duty to help her, and I know she will not accept charity." She turned to face him. "Anonymous gift?"

His eyes widened. "Do you have so much that you can leave gifts at all these homes?"

"No." She groaned, then tapped her forefinger against her lips. "I know. We can use some of the proceeds from the craft fair to build a church and hire a full-time preacher. Say, half of the proceeds will go to those making the items and half to the building, not to mention that the school could also use some repairs and supplies."

"It might work, but I don't know how you would get them to accept any of the proceeds."

"Help me, Luke. May I call you Luke? I feel as if you are the only friend I have here." She gripped his arm. "Perhaps you could offer your support to my idea and the others would follow? Oh, and please call me Leah."

A first-name basis with the prettiest gal on the mountain? Luke was doomed. "I'll think on it. . .Leah." He stood. "It's late, and you've students to teach in the morning. If I come up with a solution, I'll let you know."

"Thank you." Her grin sent his heart racing. "You are the kindest man I've ever met."

He gave a curt nod, not knowing a single thing to say to that, and almost ran to his horse. He swung up into the saddle and raced away as if Leah had proposed marriage.

Once out of sight of the house, he slowed. He had no idea how to convince folks to spend time making items to sell. Unless. . . He smiled. After putting up his horse, he headed for the cotton gin and the pile of lumber and scrap metal he had piled in the back.

It had been ages since he'd created a sculpture, but perhaps if he made something and the others saw the worth of homemade goods, they'd want to do the same. He'd place the sculpture in the schoolyard and have Mrs. Smithson do a sketch of it. He'd tell her she was helping him sell it by drawing a picture for an advertisement in the paper. The woman was as good with a pencil as she was with a needle. He'd pay her for the drawing, admit to needing money from the sale if that's what it took to get her to unknowingly allow him to help her. God would forgive him for the falsehood. Hopefully word would spread.

He cut and welded far into the night, more grateful for his father teaching him the blacksmith trade than he'd ever been before. While it wasn't the path Luke had chosen, the skill came in handy.

Hours later he swiped his forearm across his forehead. He'd finish in the morning. The teacher wasn't the only one who needed sleep. A cotton farm didn't run itself.

Luke tried to fall asleep wondering how, exactly, the pleas of a pretty woman had caused him to work far later than usual. He laughed. He knew exactly how. From the moment the frightened woman, hair streaming down her back, had fallen over him and talked about diamonds on black velvet, he'd been smitten.

Chapter 4

The week passed, and Leah hadn't gotten a peek of Luke. She'd probably frightened him off by her improper behavior. Her traitorous mind wouldn't allow her to forget how wonderful she'd felt in his arms and how kind he'd been to let her weep like a foolish woman. Still, she should have known better than to throw herself at a man.

Since it was Saturday, she had the day free to plan lessons, do laundry, and ride to the mercantile for foodstuffs. She saddled Molly and set off at a leisurely pace.

The morning sun warmed her back. A soft breeze kept the humidity at bay. By the time Leah reached the mercantile, her spirits had lifted. She looped Molly's reins over the hitching post and skipped into the store.

"Good morning, Mr. Watson." She leaned against the counter and slid a list to him.

"What's so good about it?"

"The sun is shining, and God is in His heaven. What could be more glorious?"

"For you not to be so chipper." The corner of his mouth twitched.

"You can smile, you know. Your face won't crack, I assure you."

"Perhaps not." He scanned her list. "I have these things." He lifted his gaze. "I hear you're causing trouble up on that mountain."

Her smile faded. "Not intentionally."

"Look, girlie, maybe it's none of my business, but why don't you lead by example?"

"How so?" She straightened and fingered a bit of lace on a ready-made dress. Could the people of Possum Hollow afford such a thing?

"What skills do you have?"

"None." She stiffened. "I've just realized I don't have a single creative bone in my body."

"All right." He twisted his lips. "There went my idea." He turned to the shelves of cans behind him.

"You're giving up, just like that?"

"It's your problem, not mine."

She opened her mouth to retort but snapped it shut when Mr. Haywell entered, his three boys trailing behind. Leah suddenly had an intense interest in the wanted posters hanging near the mail window.

"I see you, Miss Ellison." Mr. Haywell tapped her on the shoulder. "My boy said you kicked him out of school."

She took a deep breath to compose herself and turned. "Only for misbehavior. He sat outside for twenty minutes, sir, and was then allowed back in."

"He said you hurt his ear."

"He said I was too small to do anything." She crossed her arms and glared into his bearded face.

The man stared for a moment, then burst into laughter. "Yep, you are a mighty little bird. I might just make you one of my carved birds to put in that shop of yours."

She frowned. "I'm not opening a shop." Is that what people thought? Did they think *she* wanted part of their proceeds? "I'm saying to have a craft fair, invite folks from miles around to purchase your items, and help all of you at the same time."

He shrugged. "I reckon I might have misunderstood. Watson, I need some tobacco. Put it on my credit."

"I cannot extend you any more credit after today, sir. You'll have to pay off your debt." Mr. Watson handed him a tin.

Haywell exhaled sharply out of his nose. "Yep. I got to make me some bird carvings. Good day, Miss Ellison."

Moments after he left, a smiling Mrs. Smithson entered. "Good morning. I'd like some sugar, coffee, and flour, please."

Mr. Watson flushed. "I can't handle two chipper women at once. Do you have cash, Mrs. Smithson? Your credit—"

"Yes, sir, I do." She slapped money on the counter. "Mr. Canfield hired me to do a drawing of his sculpture." She glanced at Leah. "Said he's going to sell it and needs a drawing for the paper."

"That's wonderful." Leah clapped. He didn't hate her, after all. The opposite was true, in fact. Luke was going forward with her idea. "Perhaps Mr. Watson will allow you to put a flier in the window offering your drawing skill to others. Mr. Haywell said he'll carve some birds."

She smiled. "Perhaps I was wrong in thinking you snooty, Miss Ellison. Some of the folk will come around. Others. . . Well, Mr. Williams is quite irate. I'd watch out for him. May I put up a flier, Mr. Watson?"

"If it will help you pay your debts on time." He handed her a sheet of paper and a short pencil before focusing on Leah. "If Williams is upset with you, Miss Ellison, others will be too. This woman is right. Watch yourself."

"I will." She gathered her things and put them in a fabric bag to loop over her saddle horn. She tossed a wave to the Smithson children and headed home to prepare the next week's lessons.

A shadow passed over the sun, and Leah shuddered. Not only had the day grown cooler with an approaching storm, but her good mood had dissipated. Every noise in the trees along the road caused her to jump. If not for the placid behavior of Molly, she'd be making a mad dash for home.

A horse and buggy approached from the other direction. As if the conversation in the mercantile had caused the man to appear, Mr. Williams rode toward her. They passed without speaking. His hard glare sent a prickle down Leah's spine and she physically recoiled from the hostility reflected on his face.

She urged Molly to move faster, wanting to put as much distance between herself and the man as possible. Maybe when he arrived at the mercantile, if that was indeed where he was going, he would hear from Mr. Watson that some of the area's folks were warming to the idea of making a bit of cash.

Instead of going straight home, Leah decided a thank-you was in order and turned Molly's head toward Luke's.

❖━━━━❖

Luke pounded the bit of steel into the straight shape required and plunged it into a barrel of water. Steam rose with a hiss. A shadow fell across the doorway of the barn. He glanced up and grabbed for his shirt.

A wide-eyed, open-mouthed Leah stood there, frozen as if she'd never seen a shirtless man before. Maybe she hadn't. It was inconvenient that he was her first.

"Your chest," she whispered.

Scar tissue from a fire ten years ago had left his chest puckered and an unhealthy white. Luke turned and buttoned up his shirt before facing her. "What is it now, Leah?" He hated his boorish tone the moment it left his mouth, but he couldn't pull it back.

"I wanted to thank you." She turned to go.

"Wait. I'm sorry." He hurried forward and placed a hand on her arm. "I'm overly sensitive about my scars, I know."

"Does it hurt?" Tears filled her eyes.

He smiled. "Not anymore. Come out where it's cooler and say what you came to say."

"Oh, that's right. Thank you very much for convincing Mrs. Smithson. . . ."

Wait, that's not right. Thank you for hiring Mrs. Smithson so that—"

"You're adorable when you're flustered."

"I'm not flustered." She stiffened. "I simply have a lot on my mind." She took a deep breath. "Thank you again. I need to get home before the storm comes."

Dark clouds roiled. "I don't think you'll make it."

"I'll make it. Molly is fast." She grinned and swung into the saddle. Before he could blink, she was off, the horse's hooves kicking up dust and obscuring Leah from his view.

Luke watched the rain come across the field in front of his house. It carried a biting chill, and Leah's shriek rang out as the first drops hit her. Soon her hair flew loose from its bun. She bent low over Molly's neck, her hair mingling with the horse's mane. A beautiful sight.

Once she was too far down the road to see her through the pouring rain, he turned and went back to work. The rain stopped and the air grew still. A sound like a rushing train sent a shiver down Luke's spine. He banked his fire and stepped outside.

A twister roared, cutting a path between his land and Leah's home. *Lord, please have let her made it home.* Not that she had a safe place to go once she got there. Luke whirled and sprinted to the barn.

Moments later he rode hard down the path of destruction left by the tornado and prayed harder than he'd ever prayed before. Leah had to be all right. She just had to.

He was off his horse in her yard before coming to a complete stop. The house and school still stood, but branches and loose boards stuck out from one side of the cabin like quills on a porcupine. Her front door hung sideways on a broken hinge.

"Leah!" He burst into the cabin. Since the only hiding place was under the narrow bed and she wasn't there, he raced for the small barn. Empty. Molly wasn't even there to bare her teeth at him. He darted up the steps of the schoolhouse. "Leah?"

She poked her head up from under her desk. "How bad is it?"

He blinked a few times. "Uh, nothing that can't be fixed. How are you?" He moved slowly toward her.

She stood and brushed bits of wood chips from her skirt. "I wasn't too terribly frightened until the roof lifted. I've never seen such a thing before. It lifted up and sat right back down." Her eyes rolled back in her head and she crumpled into a pile on the floor.

Rushing forward, he lifted her into his arms and took her to the cabin. Propriety could fly away. He laid her on her bed and went to fetch a pail of water.

When he returned and laid a cool cloth against her forehead, her eyes fluttered open.

"Good heavens, I'm a ninny."

He smiled. "Have you been through a twister before?"

"Is that what that was? It sounded like a train. Before I could look outside to see what was going on, the roof rose right into the air. I dove under my desk right away." She sat up and took the glass of water he offered her.

"Did you hit your head?"

She took a sip, then handed back the glass. "You ask me that question a lot."

"It might have something to do with the fact that you say strange things after falling down."

"But the roof did rise up, Luke." She narrowed her eyes. "Molly." She slid off the bed and dashed outside. "She's gone."

"She'll come back. Most horses have more sense than people when disaster strikes." He took her by the arm. "Let's take a stroll around the property and see exactly what needs to be done."

"The one side of my cabin will look like a giant woodpecker had a field day when those boards are removed. Imagine the force required to do that." Her eyes widened.

"Imagine." His heart had finally slowed to a normal rhythm, and he found himself enjoying the extra time spent with Leah despite the circumstances.

They circled back to the schoolhouse. "I'll get some men over here tomorrow to secure the roof. You shouldn't hold school until it's fixed."

"We can learn outside. We'll have a science lesson." She grinned and placed her small hand on his arm. "Thank you for coming to check on me. You're a good friend, Luke Canfield."

"Just being neighborly."

She stopped and stared up at him. "It's more than that. You care about me. Not as a man cares for a woman, but as a buddy." She gave a definitive nod. "Yes, a buddy."

The more time he spent with her the less he wanted to be just her "buddy." He was in a heap of trouble for sure. Trouble with meadow-green eyes, a bit of improper behavior at times that was charming rather than scandalous, all wrapped up in a tiny package that barely reached his chin.

Deep, deep trouble, and he didn't have a shovel big enough to dig himself out.

Chapter 5

"My pa doesn't seem to like you much." Willy pointed to the edge of the woods where his father leaned against a tree and glared at the school-house. "Why do you think that is, Miss Ellison? I like you right fine."

"I have no idea, Willy, but thank you very much." Leah rested a hand on the boy's head. The more important question was, why didn't the man help the others work on the schoolhouse roof? She stood her ground and did her best not to fidget as she returned his stare.

Mr. Williams narrowed his eyes, then stepped back out of sight.

Leah shuddered and turned her attention to the task at hand, teaching her students arithmetic. Outdoor schooling was difficult, and they could only study leaves and insects for so long. Reading, writing, and arithmetic were as import-ant. She'd been amazed at the knowledge the children had about their world. She'd promised another trek into the woods after their lessons.

Now the afternoon was upon them and her cabin still looked like a pincush-ion. She hadn't slept a wink last night.

"My ma says folks don't like teacher 'cause she's uppity," one of the younger girls said. "Wants to change our ways to what she thinks is better."

"Why, that's not what I want at all, Sara. I only want to help."

"Folks around here don't want help unless they ask for it," another student said.

Leah had a strong feeling very few asked for help of any kind.

Willy spoke up. "Well, my pa says that having a sale for doodads will only bring people to our hollow that don't belong."

"Oh yeah?" Lucy got to her feet and planted fists on her skinny hips. "My ma says there ain't nothin' wrong with wantin' a little more cash to put sugar in her coffee. Iffen we have coffee. She says if it's okay for Mr. Canfield, then it's okay for the rest of us."

Bless Mrs. Smithson's heart. Maybe Luke wasn't the only friend she had in Possum Hollow.

A loud argument soon ensued among her students as to who was right—those opposed to Leah's plan for improvement or those for it. Mercy, she hadn't meant to cause such a ruckus. "That's enough, children. Everyone is entitled to their own opinion."

"Not if it goes against what we believe," Mark—or was it Matthew?—said. "Our pa is all for makin' more money iffen it's legal. After his run-in with the law over moonshine, he says it's time to walk the straight and narrow iffen he wants to find a wife." He grinned at Leah.

Gracious. She fiddled with the lace at her throat and directed her attention to the schoolhouse.

Luke walked the eave, arms held out for balance. He caught her looking and faltered a bit, stealing her breath for fear he'd fall. But he righted himself and tossed her a wink before continuing to the other side of the roof.

Her heart rate returned to normal. "Who is ready to teach me more about the local foliage?"

Every hand raised except for the twins'. "Pa said we have to help with the repairs when we finish the school day," one said. They packed up their slates and lunch pails and headed for the schoolhouse, leaving Amos behind.

From the grin on the youngest brother's face, he was more than pleased. "I'd like to be the leader for this, Miss Ellison. I want to go to college someday and study botany. Then I can come back here and make lives better, just like you're trying to do."

She hoped he had a better reception than she did. Most likely, being a native, and not a foreigner as she'd heard someone call her when the men arrived to repair the roof, he'd be well received. "I think that's a wonderful idea. You may definitely lead us." With one more glance to where Luke moved across the roof like a nimble goat, she followed her students.

"Watch for snakes," she called out as they raced down the path ahead of her. "Bring me anything you might not be familiar with."

"What's this?" A few moments later Lucy handed her a green plant with spikey leaves.

"That's poison ivy, dunderhead." Amos slapped it out of Leah's hand. "Don't touch any part of your skin, Miss Ellison. Not until you wash up real good."

"I'll head down to the creek right this instant. You students stay together, and Amos, please let the others know of any more bothersome plants in the area." She hitched her skirts and rushed to the babbling brook.

Would the plant wash off without soap? There were too many things she didn't know about this mountain and its people.

A bird shot from a nearby tree with a loud squawk.

Leah jerked to her feet and spun to face the threat.

Mr. Williams leaned against the tree, a small twig in his mouth. He studied her for a moment, then pushed away from the oak and approached her. He stopped a foot from her. One side of his mouth twitched.

Leah would not be intimidated. She lifted her chin. "Good afternoon, Mr. Williams."

"Teacher."

After a few more minutes of silence, Leah sighed. "Is there something you want, sir?"

"I want you to stop this fool notion of a bazaar."

"Half the community agrees it will be a fine thing."

"Half this community is as idiotic as you are." He yanked the twig from his mouth and tossed it to the ground. "I ain't one to threaten women on a normal occasion, but in this instance. . . Well, you should seriously consider reconsidering."

"Or what? Surely you are not serious." She shook her head. "Mr. Williams, if you do not want the bazaar, then simply do not attend." She swished her skirt and went to move past him.

He grabbed her arm and leaned close enough for her to smell the whiskey on his breath. "I am not one to make idle threats, woman!"

"Let go of me or I shall scream, and ten men will come running." She kicked the man as hard as she could in the shin.

He cursed and gave her arm a strong jerk.

"All you need is one." Luke stepped from behind a tree. "Take your hands off her."

Mr. Williams released her and held up his hands. "Just getting acquainted, Canfield. No need to get your dander up." He gave Leah a thin-lipped smile and headed across the creek.

Leah hurried to Luke's side. "He actually promised me harm if I didn't stop the plans for the fair. Why is he so against it?" She blinked in an attempt to hold back tears and swiped a hand across her face. "How did you know I needed you?"

"The students said they went looking for you and saw Williams grab your arm. They've all gone home now." He ran his hands down her arms. "Are you all right?"

"I'm always all right when you're by me."

❖━━•━━•━━❖

His heart danced at her words. "I got worried when the students told me you were alone with him." More than worried, actually. He'd been concerned for her safety. "Why did you walk off alone?"

"Poison ivy."

"Ah. That's what the red splotch on your face is. You need soap to get rid of that."

"I've some in the cabin." She pulled away.

"Too late. Perhaps some cream to take away the itching?"

Her shoulders slumped. "I'm not sure I have anything."

"Do you have baking soda?"

"Yes, but only a little."

"Follow me." He led her to her cabin. "I need a bowl and some water along with the baking soda." Soon he had a thick paste made. "Sit there, Leah."

She perched on a hard wooden chair and peered into the bowl. "I'm starting to itch something fierce."

"This will help. You must not scratch." He leaned over and spread the paste on the spots appearing on her pale skin. She smelled like flowers, always. If he moved his head just a bit closer, he could capture her lips with his. Instead, he raised his eyes and locked his gaze with hers. "I could get lost in your eyes," he whispered.

"I think they're my finest feature, unlike my nose. It's rather large for my face, don't you think?"

He laughed, relieved that she'd broken the connection, and dabbed some of the soda concoction on said nose. "It's perfect for you since you're always putting it where it doesn't belong and getting others upset."

"My parents have accused me of that my entire life." She drew in a breath when he took one of her hands in his and started spreading the paste on her palms.

Her parents were a safe topic to keep his thoughts from straying where they shouldn't. "Tell me about them."

"Mother can be more than a little strict." She rubbed the palm of her other hand on her skirt. "She was very opposed to my coming here. She'd much prefer I teach in a city school. Father was more inclined to let me stretch my wings. I did have to agree to a trial period though. Come spring, if I haven't been accepted, I'll head home."

"I accept you, Leah. Faults and all. Don't wipe that off." He set down one hand and picked up the other. "The people will come around. Winter is hard this high in the mountains. They'll be more inclined to slow down and listen to what you have to say when they don't have to work in their fields."

"Do the students still come to school?"

"They rarely miss." He grinned. "They'd rather go to school than pitch hay or shovel manure."

She giggled. "I can understand that." She reached for her face.

"No, ma'am." He pushed her hand away. "I said don't touch." He straightened and set the bowl on the table. "I'm going to saw off those boards on the side of the cabin. I'd thought to pull them out, but leaving them in will patch the holes. I'll fill in around the chunks with clay."

She stood and followed him outside. "Thank you, Luke. You always know just what to do."

Not always. He lay awake at night wondering whether he could give up the bachelor life and wed a chatterbox like Leah. As long as he could remember, he'd craved solitude. Her arrival changed all that. He rubbed his chest, feeling the scars through his shirt.

Being alone had its advantages. His family had died in the fire that gave him the scars. A fire he'd started. Oh, not on purpose, but he was at fault all the same. Being alone meant he couldn't be responsible for harm coming to anyone but himself.

He took up the saw he'd brought and sawed at the boards. When he finished, he tossed them on the woodpile, noticing how low the pile had gotten, and went to dig clay. The men were supposed to take turns keeping Leah supplied with wood for her stove. It looked like that task would also fall on him.

For a man who didn't want to be responsible for another, he sure did a lot for her. When he had the clay, he slapped it against the side of the cabin, taking out his frustration on the job. There. Finished. He arched his back, wincing at the pops along his spine.

He opened his eyes. Laughter burst from him.

Standing with a tray in front of her was a white-faced Leah. She'd applied so much of the paste she looked like a ghost. Every inch of face and hands were covered.

She narrowed her eyes. "What? It itches."

"Absolutely nothing. Is that coffee for me?" He grabbed a mug, unmindful of his dirty hands, and took a gulp. Fire burned the roof of his mouth.

"Careful, it's hot."

"Now you tell me." He took another look at her and laughed again. "Life is never boring around you, is it?"

"So I've been told." She set the tray on the edge of the porch and marched back inside the cabin, her nose in the air.

Chapter 6

Leah moved the table away from in front of her door, then stepped out onto the porch. Ever since her encounter with Mr. Williams, she'd slept fitfully and moved as many things between her and the entrance to her cabin as possible. She could only pray her home would never catch fire with her inside.

Stretching, she gazed to where the schoolhouse stood. It would be the church today. A traveling preacher was coming. Leah missed regular church attendance, and while Luke had said he sometimes spoke, she had yet to witness it. Still, she would see him today in one of her good dresses she'd brought from home.

Would he think her pretty? Oh, why had she brought attention to her nose? She touched the offending part of her face. When would she learn to think before she spoke?

She sighed and headed back into the cabin to start water boiling for coffee and oatmeal. She glanced to where a crate sat. One that had arrived from her parents just the day before. Opening it gave her something to look forward to that afternoon after church. A day she'd promised just for herself. No lesson plans, no stacking wood—what an abominable chore—no ironing. . . Nothing but leisure.

The rumble of wagon wheels drew her outside an hour or so later. She grabbed her Bible and went to join the arriving churchgoers.

"Good morning." She smiled and waved to so many people. Most smiled back. A few scowled. Luke was right. It would take awhile for some of these people's hearts to mellow toward her.

One woman glared at the perky hat on Leah's head, then ran her scornful gaze down the peacock-blue dress. She wrinkled her nose. "Snooty." With a purse of her lips, she headed into the building.

Tears stung Leah's eyes. She'd overdressed. Back home the women always wore their best to church. She assumed they did here too, only their best wasn't much better than their daily garments. Swiping a gloved hand across her wet cheeks, she headed back to her cabin to change.

By the time she slipped into one of the back desks of the schoolhouse/ church, the singing of the hymns had just ended. She'd missed her favorite part and didn't see signs of a preacher. The day was nothing like she'd hoped.

Mrs. Smithson, Mae as she suggested Leah call her, slid into the seat next to her. "Luke is speaking today."

The day got brighter. "Why doesn't he teach every Sunday?"

"The man is busy, Leah."

Of course. "Do you consider yourself my friend?"

"Most definitely."

"Then may I ask you a favor after church?" She lowered her voice as Luke started to speak.

Mae nodded and patted Leah's hand. "I'd best knock my oldest in the head. Lucy said she'd watch the young'uns." She moved to the seats opposite Leah and settled in between her squirming children.

Leah sat riveted through the sermon as the most wonderful man in the country raised her opinion of him. Something she hadn't thought possible. He started off speaking of the wonders of God's creation and moved right into how spectacular it was that He'd provided such diversity, not only in His plants and animals, but in His people also.

"Think how boring our world would be if we all had the same shade of hair, color of eyes, thoughts, and beliefs." He grinned. "Who would we debate with then? God has called us to love all of His children. Those from the mountains, the lowlands, by the sea. Rich or poor. Remember the childhood song 'Jesus Loves the Little Children' as you go your separate ways today. Let us pray." He bowed his head. "Lord, we come to You as little ones and ask that You open our eyes and our hearts to the wonderful variation of Your creation. Let us set aside our prejudices and welcome the foreigner into our midst as You have asked. Amen." He raised his head and winked in Leah's direction.

She smiled through her tears. The realization that Luke might be more than just a friend in her heart slammed her with the force of the twister that had roared through the hollow. She stood and darted outside before someone saw her being a ninny.

"Leah?" Mae, a baby propped on her hip, hurried after her.

"I'm being a silly little girl." She forced a trembling smile and clasped her hands in front of her. "The favor I'd like to ask of you is whether you would consider tutoring me in the ways of Possum Hollow. I seem to make mistakes every time I turn around. Will you stay and join me for lunch?"

"I most certainly will, to both requests. Mr. Canfield's sermon today will have changed a lot of folks' minds, at least until tomorrow. Perhaps you should enjoy the hospitality while it lasts." She grinned and stepped back as several of her students' parents approached.

Leah shook hands and grinned until she thought her face would split and her arm fall off. A few people still glared in her direction as they headed on their way, but as Mae had said, most expressed apologies for the way they'd acted.

Finally, the last person left in front of her was Luke. "You rushed out so fast," he said, "I feared I wouldn't get to talk with you."

"Stay for lunch." She had no idea what she could serve such a group. "The Smithsons are staying, and you are more than welcome. It's small payment for your sermon."

He took her hands in his. "I pray it helps you."

"It already has. More than you know. Please, will you stay?"

"It's the best offer I've had."

"No one else invited you, did they?"

"Nope."

She laughed and pulled him toward the Smithson clan. "Luke is staying also. He will watch the little ones with Lucy while Mae and I figure out what to serve." Opening her crate could wait.

Leah pointed to her food shelf. "That is what I have. What can I make enough of?"

"Chicken and dumplings." Mae pulled a can of chicken stock from the shelf. "I've always wondered if this tastes the same as homemade."

"A bit saltier but quite delicious. I've got canned chicken too." Leah took another can from the shelf. "I've plenty of flour if you will show me how to make dumplings."

"Consider it part of your highland lesson."

◆—•———•—◆

"Teacher's on fire, Mr. Canfield." Lucy Smithson pointed through the open door of the cabin.

Luke stopped playing marbles with the other children, scooped them into his pocket to prevent the baby from putting one in his mouth, and raced for the cabin. Leah danced up and down patting at her apron. He grabbed a bucket of water from beside the door and tossed it over her head.

She shrieked as if he'd stung her. "Land sakes, Luke! You've ruined my hair and my dress."

He must have resembled an owl in that moment, eyes wide. "You were on fire, Leah."

"I was handling the situation." She stomped her foot. "I got too close to the stove is all."

Mae covered her mouth with one hand to stifle a giggle. "You make my soul laugh, Leah. It's been a long time." She glanced at Luke, her eyes dancing. "She isn't much of a cook, even with canned goods."

"Good to know." He handed Leah a towel. "Stuff your hair under a kerchief and you'll be fine."

"My dress?" Her eyes snapped.

"It'll dry."

"You're incorrigible. Please leave the cabin and close the door so I can change my clothes. Mae will make the biscuits." She stretched out an arm and pointed to the door.

Luke skedaddled and closed the door. He wasn't fool enough to mess with a riled-up woman.

"I've never seen teacher so mad," Lucy said. "Not even when the Haywell boys misbehave."

"She is a force to be reckoned with." He sat on the porch step. The Smithson children stared up at him with black-button eyes. "We'll be eating shortly."

Shortly turned out to be an hour because Mae was determined that Leah master the art of making biscuits. Still, Luke wasn't positive that what sat before him was indeed a biscuit.

"It's a dumpling," Leah said, slapping a bowl in front of him. "Dip it in the broth."

"Aren't dumplings usually already in the broth?"

"Seriously, Luke, I'm strung tight, and out of patience. I'm a lousy cook. There. I've said it." She plopped across the table from him.

Leah sat on an unopened crate while the children gathered in front of the fire. "It's mighty tasty," Leah said after tasting the broth. "There's bits of chicken in it. I suppose that makes it more like chicken soup and biscuits than what we'd originally planned."

"May I ask what you've been eating, Leah?" If she couldn't cook, then what was she living on?

"Oatmeal and other canned foods," she said softly. "We've a chef at home."

"Didn't you hear the sermon this morning?" Mae asked. "Remember God's diversity. We can't all be good cooks, same as we can't all be teachers."

Leah gave Luke a soft look that sent his stomach tumbling. "Yes, I remember."

"Then, all right." Mae clapped her hands. "This crate I'm sitting on is big enough for two people. I know for a fact Mr. Haywell carted it up here two days ago. Why ain't you opened it?"

"I intended to after lunch." Leah smiled, her bad mood seeming to have dissipated. "So, why not now? I do believe there is something inside for you."

Other than moving the crate to the center of the small room, Luke was banished to sit against the wall while Leah pried the top open. Once she had, she set the top aside. "The crate is the perfect bench. I asked for it to be built sturdy for that purpose."

"Very resourceful of you," he said, smiling.

"I am resourceful." She grinned at him, then pulled out a sketch pad and colored pencils. "For you, Mae, so you can sketch the things people want to sell."

"Oh no, miss. I can't take that."

"I insist you take it as payment for sketching my portrait. My parents begged me to ask you."

Luke coughed to cover a laugh. Leah was the world's worst liar. "You get a tic next to your left eye when you're telling a falsehood, Miss Ellison," Mae said.

"Oh pooh. They do want a portrait, Mae, that's the truth. The lie was the tablet being payment for the drawing. I planned on also giving you money."

"The tablet is payment enough. Thank you." She took the sketch pad and ran her hand over it with a feather's touch. "I've never had such a thing before."

"You deserve it." Leah then pulled out a bolt of maroon and navy fabric. "Oh goodness. I ordered enough for a dress. It seems there will be some leftover. Would Lucy like a new dress?"

Mae laughed. "You, Leah, are a sneaky one, asking that question in front of my daughter."

Luke laughed along with them, enjoying the things pulled from the crate as much as the others. Not everything was for Mae. The crate contained school supplies such as books, chalk, and slates. Enough for every student to have their own.

The afternoon grew late before the Smithsons left, chattering about the pictures their mother would sketch. Luke stood in front of the cabin with Leah. "When you love, you love with all your heart."

"I do." She leaned her head against his shoulder. "That's why it hurts so much that some of the mountain folk resent me. I love my students so much."

"Perhaps you'll be a lesson of love to these people." As she was to him. He turned and planted a kiss on her forehead. "Thank you for a wonderful day, Leah."

He strolled toward home, taking one glance over his shoulder before turning on the road.

Leah stood watching him.

Chapter 7

As the weather started to cool down, preparations for the craft fair were in full swing. Mae sat in the back of the classroom during the day, her little ones at her feet, and sketched the crafts brought into the building by the students. Each one was so very proud to hand her what their parents had made. Mae may not always be paid with cash for her drawings, but she'd told Leah her shelves were full of food, and that was often better.

Leah was very careful to write the item and its selling price into a ledger. It seemed she might very well be manning the fair herself. No one stepped forward to volunteer. The weight of her undertaking bore down on her shoulders daily.

A letter from her parents assured her the congregation of the church they attended would attend the fair with funds ready to spend. They wanted to know whether the children would be in attendance.

Leah scanned her classroom. In no way did she want these dear children to be spectacles on display. Rather, she wanted the city folk to see the pride and determination in their faces. How hard most of their parents worked. How intelligent the little ones were despite spotty schooling.

While her students practiced their letters or spelling words, Leah approached Mae. "Since I'm still rather ignorant of mountain ways, I'm wondering if I would be stepping over any boundaries if the children were to perform at the craft fair."

"That would be one way to get the parents there. We love to watch our children shine."

Leah clapped. "Wonderful. We'll have recitations, a spelling bee, a singing . . ." The children could do almost anything. With less than a month before the event, they would need to get started.

She stood at the front of the room and waited for the children to quiet and focus their attention on her. It took quite awhile with the shenanigans of the Haywell twins. "I had rather hoped you would have finished your assigned lesson before we moved on to something much more fun." She narrowed her eyes at the twins. Those two needed something to keep them busy since they had absolutely no desire to learn.

"Matthew and Mark, will you approach my desk, please?"

"You're in trouble," someone sang out. The rest of the class giggled.

"That's enough, students." Leah squared her shoulders as the sullen-faced boys approached. She didn't speak until they started to squirm. "I have a question for you."

"Yes'm?" Matthew tilted his head.

"Are you interested in learning, or in developing a trade?"

"What's that mean?" he asked, glancing at Mark.

"You don't seem to care much about reading or arithmetic."

"Nope. We're too old to be in this stupid classroom."

"How are you at carpentry?"

"What's that?"

She smiled. "If you cared more about learning you would know that it is building things out of wood."

"Like carving?" Mark asked.

"More like building furniture and such. Interested?"

"I reckon we are," Matthew answered. "What do you want us to build?"

"A stage for a student performance and booths in which to sell our crafts. After school, I'll ask Mr. Canfield to supervise and guide you, but I expect the two of you to do the majority of the work. I'm sure you'll do a fine job."

The two boys stood a little taller at her words. "I reckon we will at that," Mark said. "Does that mean no more schooling?"

"If you can get your pa to agree to that, then yes. Of course, you'll find Mr. Canfield to be a very smart man. You might change your mind after working with him." Leah hoped so. Despite their rascally ways, they had good minds. "Take your seats. While the others work, you can formulate a list of supplies you think you might need. You'll need measurements for every structure. The booths need to be large enough for a couple of shelves and for an adult to stand behind."

They grinned and rushed back to their seats.

Wonderful. She hoped her sneaky way of getting them to use their brains would work.

By the end of the day, each student had been assigned a part in the program. Excited voices rang across the schoolyard as they dashed toward home.

Leah smiled. It might be difficult to settle them down in the morning, but the promise of rehearsal at the end of the day might spur them toward behaving. She went through her routine of closing up the school, then set off for Luke's. She couldn't wait to tell him of her plans.

She swung her arms as she walked, reveling in the leaves beginning to turn to vibrant shades of daffodil, crimson, and pumpkin. A crisp bite to the air chilled her cheeks. The notion that the mountain people were actually coming to accept her, or most of them anyway, warmed her heart. Nothing could ruin her fine mood.

Nothing except the man leaning against a tree ahead of her. Refusing to be daunted, Leah lifted her chin and marched past him with purpose in her step.

Mr. Williams's eyes narrowed. He gave her a curt nod but didn't speak.

Leah glanced back before turning to Luke's. The man was gone. She huffed. All he wanted was to frighten her. Well, it wouldn't work. She was doing nothing wrong.

She stepped onto Luke's porch and raised her hand to knock. A woman giggled from inside. It appeared Mae had arrived to give Luke the news.

Leah pressed her ear to the door to hear the children. The room had grown quiet. Her throat clogged. Of course Mae would be interested in a man like Luke. What woman wouldn't be? The pretty widow needed a good man to love her and her little ones.

Before Leah could straighten, the door opened and she tumbled inside.

◆—————◆

"What in tarnation?" Mae rolled from under Leah. "Why didn't you knock?"

"I was about to." She glared up at Luke.

He crossed his arms. "Were you eavesdropping?"

"Do I have any reason to?"

What had her dander up? He offered one hand to her and the other to Mae. With a tug, he pulled them to their feet. "Mae and I were discussing the craft fair."

Her eyes flashed. "That's why I'm here, but please, don't let me interrupt."

Interrupt what? She was acting stranger than usual. "Is there something you needed?"

"Yes. I'm hoping you will agree to supervise and guide the Haywell twins in a few construction projects. It's the only way I can think of to get them to learn anything." She cut a glance at Mae from under lowered lashes. "I know you're a busy man, but if you could spare a few hours every day—"

"Of course I can." He was between seasons. "I'll be over every afternoon after lunch. Will that work?"

She gave him a strained smile. "That will be just fine. They are to have a list of supplies they think they will need for a raised stage and booths. I'm sure they'll be off a bit, but you can help with that. Please have them do the thinking as much as possible. Thank you." She turned and marched out the door, leaving him and Mae staring at each other.

Mae put a hand over her mouth and giggled. "She thinks I'm chasing after you."

"For what?"

The incredulous look at his stupidity told him all he needed to know. "You mean she's jealous?" He grinned.

"Perhaps. Why don't you walk her home? I'd best be getting home. It isn't good to leave the little ones with a neighbor for too long. I'll get started on that project right away."

"Thank you." He dashed after Leah.

Luke spotted Mr. Williams watching Leah from behind a tree at the same time he saw her. The other man drew back. Luke took another glance at Leah, then followed Williams. It couldn't be a good thing that the man had been watching her. Her safety was more important than his questions about whether she was jealous of Mae or not. He could ask her another time.

Williams didn't seem in a hurry as he meandered along a weed-filled trail. He whistled a tuneless melody, occasionally picking up a rock and tossing it into the brush. Where was he going at such a slow pace?

Luke peered up through the trees. Night would fall soon, even earlier in the thick woods. The last thing he wanted was to be caught in the dark with a man like Williams.

Just as he'd decided to turn and head back, the brush ahead opened onto a clearing. Luke ducked and peered through the branches.

Williams strolled up to a moonshine still. The man didn't expect to get caught. His animosity toward outsiders coming to the hollow now made sense. He was afraid someone would stumble across his still. Men had died for less in Possum Hollow.

Luke slowly crept backward. He'd have to keep a closer eye on Leah until after the fair.

By the time he emerged back on the road, night had fallen. It was too late to visit with Leah.

At home, he lay on his bed and stared at the ceiling, hopeful that Mae was correct in her assumption that Leah was jealous. He also hoped she would enjoy the surprise he had planned for her.

The next morning he wolfed down a couple of biscuits and headed to his forge to complete the final details on his sculpture. While he planned for this one to sit outside the schoolhouse, he'd be more than happy to take orders for others like it. The large wooden book on the metal platform would last for years.

It wasn't until his stomach growled that he remembered the time. He washed up, grabbed his wooden toolbox and an apple and a chunk of cheese from his cupboard, then hurried for the school. Leah was just ushering the students back inside after recess when he arrived.

She said something to the twins, who turned and dashed to Luke's side. One of them—Luke supposed he'd have to learn the difference if he were to work with them—waved a sheet of paper in his face.

"We've got figures."

"Well then, let me take a look." Luke flashed a grin over the boy's shoulder at Leah, but she'd already stepped inside. The day lost some of its appeal.

Apparently she still thought his interest lay elsewhere. He'd set her right soon enough.

He glanced over the numbers and drawings on the paper. "This is good, boys, but we'll need twice this much. Let me show you how to figure out the amount of wood you'll need." He pulled out a measuring tape. "Let's use the front of the school as an example."

He showed them how to measure, then told them to figure out how many feet the booths and platform should be. Once he felt as if someone were watching him and glanced up at the schoolhouse window. He thought a shadow passed in front of it but couldn't be sure.

"Is Miss Ellison feeling poorly today?" he asked.

"Nope." One of the boys, pencil behind his ear, tongue hanging out of his mouth, paused a second in his measuring. "She acts the same as always. Bossy."

Luke chuckled. "Ready to head to the sawmill?"

"How are we supposed to pay for these things?" one of them asked, frowning.

"I'm head of the school board, so you let me worry about that." He didn't have any qualms paying for the supplies, although he'd have a fight on his hands once Leah found out. She'd been stubborn enough before, but now, being angry with him, she'd fight like a cougar over who would pay.

Chapter 8

Leah barely spoke two words to Luke over the next few days. He'd come to work with the twins in the afternoons, then disappear into the woods. Not that it was his fault. If she saw him coming her way, she suddenly had something to do with one of the students.

What could she say to him? That she was happy for him and Mae? That Mae was perfect for him. She couldn't question her friend either. According to Lucy, several of the younger Smithson children were down with colds.

Time ticked toward the date of the craft fair with increasing speed. Leah sighed and returned to writing spelling words on the chalkboard. Students would arrive in a few minutes, and she was running behind.

The rumble of a wagon pulling into the schoolyard drew her away from her task. She stepped outside and clapped. The lumber for the booths and stage had arrived.

Clutching her skirt in one hand so as not to trip, she dashed down the steps. "Oh, thank you. How much do I owe you?"

"Mr. Canfield already paid, ma'am." The man motioned to a younger version of himself. "Where do you want this stacked?"

"Over there out of the way." She pointed toward the outhouse. *Pooh.* She'd have to speak with Luke about payment. Her traitorous heart leaped at the thought. She missed him something terribly and would have to work on remaining friends as long as Mae didn't mind.

She pasted on a smile as the children started arriving. When they realized what the wood was for, their excitement bubbled up and spilled over like a creek after too much rain. It took longer than usual for them to settle down for lessons. The Haywell twins didn't bother entering the building. They insisted they had to verify delivery and count each piece of wood.

By the noon hour, Leah's head pounded from the boys' yelling and hammering. She'd insisted they wait for Luke, but they were convinced they could handle the job. While the other students ate lunch and played, Leah sat at her desk and rubbed her temples.

"Feelin' poorly, Miss Ellison?" Willy peered up at her. "Want my bread?"

"No, sweetie, you eat that." The wonderful little boy wanted to give her what was probably the only thing in his battered lunch pail. "Actually, I am feeling poorly and don't have much of an appetite. I've a sandwich smeared with canned meat. Will you half it with me?"

His eyes sparkled. "Meat in a can. Wowie. Yes, ma'am, I reckon I'd like to try that."

The doorway darkened with Luke's form. His gaze flickered to Willy. While his smile didn't fade, his eyes narrowed a bit. He gave Leah a nod, then headed back out. Soon his voice joined the Haywell boys'.

Willy wolfed down his half of the sandwich, declared it mighty good, and raced outside to play. Leah propped her elbows on the desktop and rested her chin in her hands. It wouldn't hurt to close her eyes, just for a moment.

"Leah?"

She raised her head to see Luke and her students staring down at her. She wiped her mouth and fumbled for something to say. "Oh, I . . ." She sighed.

Luke reached to touch her face. "Are you feverish?"

"Just a headache." She pulled back.

He leaned forward and placed the back of his hand on her forehead. "You feel hot to me. You'd best go home, Leah. You've been working too hard."

His tender gesture brought tears to her eyes. "I have students to teach."

"They can go home early. Come on." He held out his hand.

She eyed it, then placed her hand in his. His mere touch warmed her more than any illness. "Class is dismissed."

The room rang with cheers, then the thundering of feet as the children sprinted outside. Leah smiled. "I didn't sleep well the last few nights. A nap will do me good."

His eyes clouded with concern. "Would you like me to walk you home?"

"No, that's quite all right. I'll take a nap, then work on finalizing plans for the fair. You're needed here, Luke." She focused on gathering her things.

"Leah, look at me." When she didn't, he used his forefinger to turn her head toward him. "Dare I hope that you are jealous?"

"Of whom?"

"Mae Smithson."

"Whatever for?" She turned away. "You're being ridiculous. We'd have to be courting for me to have a reason."

"Would you allow—"

"Teacher! Mr. Canfield, come quick!"

Leah darted a look at Luke, then sprinted out the door and around the building with him. She covered her mouth with her hand. The wood had shifted and fallen, knocking one of the twins to the ground and partially burying him.

Leah knelt on the ground next to him. "Which one is he?"

"That's Matthew, ma'am."

"Help me move these boards, Mark." Luke grabbed the end of one long plank. "Leah, is he breathing?"

She turned her head and felt a slight breath on her cheek. "Yes, barely. I think the boards are crushing his chest." She glanced at his brother. "Mark, run and fetch a doctor, then your pa. Mr. Canfield and I will take Matthew to my cabin. Hurry now." Headache forgotten, Leah waited while Luke fetched his horse and wagon.

When he returned, Leah grabbed Matthew's feet while Luke gripped under his arms. "Very carefully," he said. "We don't know the extent of his injuries."

Although she could see her cabin from the front steps of the school, it was safer for Matthew to lie flat in the back of the wagon. While Luke drove the boy slowly across the yard, Leah dashed for her home and prepared her bed. Moments later, Luke carried the young man inside and laid him on top of the quilt.

"There's a medical journal that belonged to my uncle in the crate by the chair. Father thought it might be useful up here. Would you fetch it, please?"

Luke hurried away, returning with the leather-bound book. "What shall I look up?"

Leah unbuttoned the boy's shirt. "Abdominal bruising." This was all her fault. She should never have let the boys tackle such a large project. Tears stung her eyes and her headache started anew.

◆━━━━━━━◆

"He could be bleeding inside, Leah." Luke had never felt more helpless. The doctor who serviced the folks in the hollow could be hours away. "We should check for broken ribs. One might be puncturing something."

"How do we do that?" High spots of color burned on her cheeks.

Luke felt her face again. "Leah, you're burning up. I'll take care of Matthew. You go sit in that chair."

"I'll take the journal and see what I can find." To his surprise, she shuffled to the chair and fell into it.

Luke felt as helpless as a newborn kitten. When Lucy Smithson appeared in the doorway to request a cup of sugar, he couldn't have been more relieved. "I need you to tell your mother to come quick. There's been an accident, and Miss Ellison is ill. Hurry now."

Lucy nodded and darted away.

It would be at least thirty minutes before help arrived. To his surprise, Mae made it in twenty. She leaned in the doorway and panted. "Who's that?"

"Matthew Haywell. He got trapped under some falling lumber. Leah has a fever. It feels rather high to me." He got to his feet. "I have no idea what to do."

Mae seemed to immediately shake off her tiredness. "Start a fire, for one." She grabbed a folded quilt from the foot of the bed and covered Leah. She placed her lips against Leah's forehead. "Yep." She then moved to Matthew and stared down at his black and blue stomach. "I've seen this before. It'd be darker if he was bleedin' inside. Find me some strips of cloth to bind his ribs. See that little indentation? He has at least one broken rib."

Luke had just thought the boy overly skinny. He started opening trunks until he found a bolt of muslin material. "How many strips?"

"About five that will wrap twice around this boy, then some smaller ones to bathe Leah's face with cool water. When you're finished with the strips, fetch some well water and lay rags on her forehead and neck."

"Should I be worried?"

She nodded without looking away from Matthew. "My babies were sick, but they weren't as feverish as Leah. Fevers can be dangerous to adults."

An icy fist gripped his heart as he set to tearing the muslin with a strength born of fear. He couldn't allow anything to happen to Leah. He couldn't. He still hadn't told her how much he cared for her or how she had no reason to be jealous. There was no other woman in the world for him but her.

He dropped the bundle of fabric strips next to Mae, then grabbed the bucket and made a dash for the well. He'd failed to save his family from a fire he'd started. Accidentally or not, he'd been at fault. He couldn't fail again. He'd filled the bucket and turned back to the house when Horace and Mark arrived.

"Where's my boy?"

"He's inside. Mae Smithson is with him. Miss Ellison is sick, so it might be best if Mark stay out here and watch the little ones." He motioned his head to where Lucy and her siblings drew in the dirt with sticks. "It would be a big help."

"I can do that, Pa." Mark sat cross-legged on the ground and rested his chin in his hands.

Night had fallen before the doctor arrived. Matthew's eyes were open, but Leah's fever still raged. After poking and prodding, the doctor declared Matthew a lucky young man and said he could go home and take it easy for a few days to give his ribs time to heal. His prognosis for Leah wasn't as cheery. He examined her as the Haywells left.

"She doesn't appear to have influenza. Her lungs sound clear. My best prognosis is exhaustion, pure and simple. Put this young woman to bed, try to keep her fever down, and let her sleep. If she isn't better by morning, hunt me down."

Luke shook the doctor's hand. "Thank you. What do I owe you?"

"How about ginning my small bit of cotton for free when the time comes?"

"That's a deal." Luke shook his hand again, then turned back to Leah as the doctor left.

"You can't stay here, Luke. It isn't proper." Mae stood in front of him.

"Then leave Lucy with me, because I'm not going anywhere."

"You silly man." She patted his cheek. "You've fallen quite hard. All right, I'll leave Lucy here until morning."

"Thank you." Luke turned to find Leah staring at them with wide eyes. Then her eyelids fluttered closed again."

"Carry her to the bed, and I'll put her in her nightclothes. Then I'll take my babies home."

Soon Leah lay comfortably in the bed Matthew had vacated. Lucy snored quietly on a pallet on the floor. Luke tucked the quilt up around Leah's shoulders and started the act of laying cool rags on her face and neck for what seemed like the hundredth time.

As he worked to bring her fever down, he prayed.

Awhile later he jolted upright, dismayed he'd fallen asleep. His hand covered Leah's, and the quilt was rumpled where his head had lain. He rubbed his thumb over the top of her hand, then looked up into her eyes.

"You're awake."

She frowned. "You're still here."

"Where else would I be?" He raised her hand to his lips, overjoyed to find the skin cool.

"But. . .Mae."

"Mae is home where she belongs, same as I am."

Confusion flickered in her eyes. "I thought you and she—"

"Nope. I have my sights set on a little bitty minute of a gal who speaks impulsively, acts improperly, and loves with all her heart."

She'd fallen asleep again. He had no idea whether she'd heard him or not.

Chapter 9

After a week of lying around, then another of frantically preparing for the craft fair, Leah pinned up her hair and set off at a brisk pace to the already bustling schoolyard. Luke and Mark Haywell plopped bales of hay at strategic places around the grounds and in front of the stage for seating. Ribbons fluttered from the booths with bright gaiety to attract attention to the wares displayed there.

Leah's gaze scanned those milling around for sign of her parents. They hadn't arrived. The only ones present were those selling or performing. Leah felt like a lollygagger. Even her students had arrived before her.

"Good morning, Matthew," she said on her way to the schoolhouse. "Should you be up and about?"

"Fine as frog hair, Miss Ellison. I promise not to lift anything heavy." He grinned. "I couldn't miss the day we've worked so hard for."

She stopped and stared at an enormous book carved from wood. The book sat on an iron pedestal. She smiled. Luke's doing, she guessed.

Luke glanced up from final preparations on the stage and tossed a wink her way. Leah's face warmed. She'd thought of little else over the last weeks but him and the fair, and in that order. "Good morning, Mr. Canfield. It's beautiful."

"Good morning, Miss Ellison. Thank you. A good teacher deserves a tribute."

She read the inscription on the book's wooden page. " 'To Miss Ellison, the teacher who taught us how to love.' "

Head ducked to hide a face-splitting grin, Leah opened the door to the schoolhouse. Cheers rose from her students the moment she entered the room. Their joy and excitement were contagious.

"All right, children. One more run-through of our program—"

Cries of a different sort rang out.

Leah laughed. "Very well. I don't suppose you can do better than perfect, and that's exactly how yesterday's rehearsal went. Go ahead and explore the booths, but remember to be back in here at exactly ten o'clock."

They thundered outside like a herd of wild horses, almost knocking over the couple trying to enter. "Goodness," the woman said.

"Mother." Leah rushed forward. "Father." She stepped into their arms and immediately felt as if she were back home.

"You look good, daughter," Father said, holding her at arm's length. "Over your bout of exhaustion?"

"That was so silly of me. I think I was more worked up over this craft fair than my students." She clutched their hands. "What do you think of our setup?"

"It's quaint." Mother glanced around the room. "You've put our donations to good use."

"Wait until you hear the children recite the things they've learned. I've fallen in love with each and every one of them." And a certain part-time preacher, but she didn't believe her parents were ready to hear about a man in her life. Not that Luke was in her life as more than a friend, but he had tended to her during her time of weakness. Surely he felt something for her other than mere friendship. But she'd seen Mae caress his face.

"You look confused, dear." Mother tilted her head. "Would you like to talk about it?"

"Yes, but later. I've too much to do to fill you in at the moment." She planted a quick kiss on her mother's cheek. "Enjoy yourselves." She hurried outside, overjoyed at the number of visitors perusing items at the booths. From the smiles on the people of Possum Hollow, she could tell they felt the same.

"Oh Leah, you did a wonderful job." Mae beamed from behind a table filled with baked goods for sale. All proceeds from the food would go to the building of a church and the hiring of a full-time preacher. The monies from the handmade goods would go to the ones who'd made them. "City folk aren't as snobbish as I'd thought."

Leah laughed. "No, they aren't. May I ask you a question?"

"Of course."

"Are you and Luke courting?"

"Heavens no. The man loves you." Mae smiled and shook her head. "You'd have to be blind not to see the light in his eyes when he looks at you."

Leah turned to locate him. She hadn't imagined his declaration of love then. She'd thought it merely a figment of her fever-ravaged mind. Not seeing him in the crowd, Leah hurried around the building to where she'd spotted him last.

"Excuse me," she said to a man standing there. "Perhaps you've seen—"

The man turned and snarled at her. Mr. Williams. "You think you're mighty somethin', don't you, Teacher? Now these woods are full of nosy Nellies." He pulled a knife from his pocket. "I warned you."

"I will scream if you take one step forward." Leah turned to run.

The man grabbed her and clamped his hand over her mouth before she could blink. "You do that, and I'll have to cut your mama. Now, you gonna come easylike?"

Fear clogged her throat. She nodded.

Mr. Williams took his hand from her mouth. "Now walk toward that stand of trees real casual-like and smile like you're having the time of your life."

Leah pasted on a grimace and glanced at the window of the schoolhouse. Her mother stared out with wide eyes, then gave Leah a curt nod. Good. Help would come.

It came almost immediately. Luke and a man wearing a shiny star on his shirt strode around the opposite corner of the building. Luke glanced up, surprise on his face, then narrowed his eyes. "Let her go, Williams. It's over."

The other man stepped forward. "I'm Sheriff Dalton. Now, normally I wouldn't haul you to jail for moonshine, but threats and kidnapping is a whole other story."

Williams held his knife against Leah's throat again.

She swallowed, afraid to move.

"I'm taking this little gal with me. Once I'm free of this place, I'll let her go, iffen she don't aggravate me too much. Take care of Willy. He's the only good thing on this mountain." He dragged Leah backward into the trees.

Leah spotted the sheriff through the branches of a juniper bush. He aimed a gun in their direction. She brought the heel of her boot down hard on her captor's foot and fell to the ground.

A shot rang out. Mr. Williams fell.

The sheriff dashed toward the fallen man, and Luke gathered Leah into his arms.

He cupped her face. "Are you all right?"

"More than all right." She peered into his eyes. "Mae told me you love me."

He smiled. "I do."

"Then I reckon you need to change the rule about teachers being married, because I'm marrying you in a week's time."

◆━━━━◆

He pulled her close. "Oh, you are, are you?"

"Yes."

"I'm Mr. Ellison, Leah's father." A man in a fine-tailored suit stood in front of them.

"Oh." Leah scrambled to her feet. "Luke, these are my parents. Mother, Father, this is Luke Canfield, the man I'm going to marry."

Luke couldn't wipe the grin from his face, but extended his hand. "I am very pleased to meet you, sir." He cut a quick glance to where the sheriff dragged away a cursing Williams. The man bled from a wound in his side. It looked as if he'd live to spend time in a cell.

Mr. Ellison returned his handshake. "We'll talk more later. I'm much obliged for your part in rescuing my daughter."

Leah wrapped her arms around Luke's waist. "He wouldn't think to do anything else. That's how he is."

Mrs. Ellison cleared her throat and raised her eyebrows. "Leah."

With a sigh, Leah straightened. "What time is it?"

"Ten past ten," her father said.

"Oh mercy!" She darted away.

"You'd think I'd be used to her impulsiveness by now," Mrs. Ellison said.

"I wouldn't change a thing about her." Luke motioned his head toward the school building. "Shall we?"

It took every ounce of willpower he had to act as if seeing the woman he loved being held with a knife to her throat didn't cause his heart to freeze. Her parents didn't need to fret; rather, they should focus on their daughter's hard work with the children of Possum Hollow. Luke, and they, if it was their nature, could fall apart later.

He seated the Ellisons on a front-row hay bale, then stood at the back, leaving the seats to the guests. His gaze scanned the line of students approaching the stage.

Little Willy's eyes searched the crowd. His smile faded a bit, then brightened.

Luke glanced over his shoulder. The sheriff and Mr. Williams stood a few yards away. From the way the man's arms were behind him, he wore handcuffs. From somewhere, they'd found a jacket in which to hide the fact he was injured. The sheriff was a good man. It meant a lot to the children to see their parents at the performance, and Willy was no exception.

The children recited poetry, sang songs, and gave readings to the enjoyment of all watching. Claps and cheers rang out with abandon when each student finished. Leah's smile broadened with each one. Occasionally her gaze would wander to where the sheriff and his charge stood, but she braved on. Once the program ended and the students were released into their parents' capable hands, Leah made a beeline for the schoolhouse.

Mr. and Mrs. Ellison started to follow but stopped as Luke did the same. "You go," Mr. Ellison said. "My daughter is most likely falling apart from her ordeal. She'll want you. Mrs. Ellison and I will browse the booths."

"Thank you, sir." Luke bounded up the steps and through the open door.

Leah's arms were folded on her desk, her face hidden in them. Her shoulders shook with sobs.

"Darling." He raced forward and knelt beside her. "It's going to be all right."

"What about Willy?" She raised a tear-streaked face. "Who will care for him?"

"We will. My house is plenty big enough." He pulled a handkerchief from his pocket. "I hope to fill it with children. I thought you were crying from the kidnapping."

"Oh pooh, that didn't last long enough to cause me too much distress." She took the hankie and blew her nose, then attempted to hand it back.

"You keep it."

She smiled. "I apologize for my rash proposal in the woods. I got carried away."

He blinked, feeling very much like an owl. "You didn't mean it? You don't want to marry me?"

"Oh, I do, very much." She took his hands in hers. "But it's a man's place to do the proposing."

Relief flooded through him. "Since when do you do what's normal? Since I'm already on my knees, will you marry me?"

"Yes." She flung her arms around his neck. "Next Saturday."

"All right." He stood, pulling her up with him. "If you're certain you're going to be fine, your parents are waiting, as is every parent of your students. You're the belle of the ball, Miss Ellison."

Hand in hand they stepped out of the building. Applause thundered. Shrill whistles ripped through the crowd.

"They like me now," she whispered.

Luke squeezed her hand and smiled down at her. "You gave everyone here a lesson in love."

"They taught me far more than I taught them."

Catching sight of Willy, and no longer seeing the boy's father or the sheriff, Luke slipped his hand free of Leah's. "Go enjoy your moment. I've a little boy to talk to."

He approached where Willy sat on one of the hay bales, looking more forlorn than any child should. Luke sat next to him and put an arm around his shoulder.

"My pa is gone for a while," Willy said.

"Yes, he is. He made some bad choices. How would you like to come and stay with me until he returns?"

"I'd like that right well." With the flash of a grin, he darted away and joined a group of boys tossing handfuls of hay at each other.

Leah took the boy's place and leaned her head on Luke's shoulder. "I don't care if I'm behaving properly or not. I'm exhausted."

"I think everyone is used to your spontaneous shows of affection." He rested his cheek on top of her head. "You mother, on the other hand, is giving me the stink eye."

"She'll understand when we tell her we're getting married next week. Then again, maybe not. She'll be upset there's only a week to plan and I want to be married right here."

"Let's give everyone something big to talk about." He tilted her face and kissed her.

Chapter 10

I'm completely flabbergasted that we managed to put together a wedding in a week." Leah's mother shook her head, tucking a strand of hair into Leah's upswept hairstyle. "But then again, this wedding is nothing like I imagined my only child would have."

"This place is nothing like you're used to, but it's perfect to me." Leah smiled at her mother's reflection in the mirror. "I've never been happier. God has taught me so much through these people. Pride in oneself, perseverance—the list goes on and on."

"You've grown up without me." Her mother placed a simple lace veil on Leah's head. "Your father and I are very proud of you."

Tears stung Leah's eyes. She couldn't remember ever being so emotional. "That means the world to me." She turned and hugged her mother. "As has spending this last week with you. I trust you were comfortable at Luke's?"

"The house is very sufficient, although it lacks a woman's touch." She smiled. "Are you ready to become Mrs. Canfield?"

"I've been ready from the moment I laid eyes on him."

"That very hairy man is waiting outside with a wagon." Her mother shuddered. "He's quite different, isn't he?"

Remembering how Mr. Haywell had once said he intended to marry the new teacher, she nodded. "He has a good heart." She linked her arm with her mother's and headed downstairs to the waiting buggy.

"About time," Mr. Haywell said. "My beard was growing longer standing here. You sure look pretty, Teacher."

"Thank you." She allowed him to help her into the wagon. He then assisted her mother onto the seat beside her.

As the wagon rumbled toward the school, folks fell into step behind it. Leah waved over her shoulder. "Is this a custom I don't know about?"

"Just them wishing you luck. Everyone thinks highly of you and your groom," Mr. Haywell said. "We know how to throw a regular shindig around here."

The man's secretive smile made Leah uneasy. What was he planning?

Her father waited for her on the steps of the schoolhouse. "It's standing room only inside, daughter. I think everyone on the mountain is here."

From inside, a fiddle started playing. This was it. Leah was about to marry the most wonderful man. She couldn't be happier than she was right at that moment. With gaze forward, she stepped through the doors.

Those in attendance stood and smiled, but Leah could only see the man waiting at the front of the room. His face lit up with a grin as she made her way toward him.

Thankfully, someone had been able to locate the traveling preacher, and the man now beamed down at them from behind Leah's desk. "Dearly beloved. . ."

Leah heard very little. She obviously responded when appropriate because the words she'd been waiting for were said. "I now pronounce you husband and wife. You may kiss your bride."

Luke lifted her veil, then dipped her over his arm and kissed her breathless to whoops and hollers from those watching. When he righted her, her face flamed and she stared up at him through blurry eyes.

"I love you," he whispered, resting his forehead against hers.

"I love you." She slipped her hand into his. Together they turned to face their friends and family.

Outside, tables had been set up and piled with food. Mae had baked a chocolate cake, and from the way Mr. Haywell gazed on her when he had a piece, Leah predicted another wedding in the future.

After a couple of hours, Luke took her by the hand and helped her into the wagon. "It'll be dark before we get home. Let's go."

Home. With her husband. Could there be a better place on earth? Her parents had agreed to spend the night in her cabin and now waved them off. Her mother's cheeks shined with tears. Leah's students ran after the wagon until the pace of Luke's horse got to be too much for them.

"I never intended to marry," Luke said. "I didn't want the responsibility."

"I'm glad you changed your mind." She leaned against him. "May I ask why?"

"Why I changed my mind, or why I didn't want to marry?"

She smiled. "Both."

"You saw the scars on my chest." He turned the horse's head into their yard. "I was fourteen and learning to be a farrier, my father's trade. It was a windy day, and my father told me not to work on a project I wanted to finish."

Leah's heart stuttered. This story couldn't end well.

"Needless to say, I snuck out after the others were in bed. A gust of wind blew sparks into a haystack. The barn went up faster than I'd ever imagined anything could. I was trapped under a falling timber. When I woke, everything around me was gone. Including my family."

"It wasn't your fault, Luke. You were a boy."

He shrugged. "I changed my mind about getting married when a pretty little minute of a woman tumbled over me in the dark and started spouting nonsense." He gave her a crooked smile. "I can't thank you enough for that. I was a mighty lonely man."

He probably should have told her long before their "I do" in case she wanted to cancel the wedding. Instead, she leaned over and placed a gentle kiss on his cheek. "I don't deserve you," he said.

"I do believe it's the other way around, but thank you for saying so." Her teeth flashed in the moonlight.

He hopped from the wagon and lifted her down. "I have a surprise for you. It's what Mae and I were working on the day you got so jealous."

"The wooden book isn't the surprise?"

"Nope." He took her by the hand, and they dashed up the porch. He swung her into his arms and carried her across the threshold. When he sat her on her feet, he turned her toward a picture hanging on the wall.

"Oh Luke." Tears coursed down her face. She ran a finger lightly over a drawing of her falling over Luke's back as he changed a wagon wheel. Mae had rendered a drawing of Leah's first encounter with Luke on the day she had collided with him as she ran up the mountain. "It's incredible. Mae is very talented."

"I don't want you to ever stop being my reckless Leah." He stepped behind her and wrapped his arms around her waist. "Think of the story we have to tell our children about how we met."

"Because I thought I heard something and got frightened."

"Because I broke a wheel."

"Because I fell over you."

"Because you spouted nonsense." He chuckled. "It's quite the story."

"Like no other." She turned and wrapped her arms around his neck. "Kiss me, husband."

He obliged. "It's getting late. Head upstairs and get ready." He knew what might be coming and didn't want her in the way. The coming celebration might frighten her. He almost wished he'd taken her away for the night, but the wagon ride to the city would have taken more than a day, and he didn't want them to spend their first night as husband and wife on the cold ground or in the back of a hard wagon. "I'll be up in a bit."

She hadn't been upstairs long before he heard the arriving wagon and readied himself for what was to come.

Leah prepared herself for bed while Luke waited downstairs. A ruckus outside drew her to the window. Minutes later a group of men with bags over their heads dragged a struggling Luke out of the house, put a sack over his head, and dumped him into the back of a wagon.

She pounded on the window. "Hey!"

The wagon drove away.

Hitching her nightclothes up, she dashed down the stairs. "Luke!" She stopped in the middle of the road, shoulders slumped. What was happening? She thought long and hard about a mountain wedding custom she might have forgotten.

Shivaree. She laughed. Luke would be home as soon as he found his way. She grabbed a blanket from inside the house and curled up in a rocker on the porch to wait.

Luke's hands were untied, and he was rolled out of the wagon bed by a booted foot placed against his back. The fall to the ground knocked the breath out of him. He groaned and got to his knees. Some customs deserved to die. This was one of them.

"Have fun finding your way back," someone taunted.

Luke pulled the bag from his head and glanced around him, trying to find out where he was in relation to his home. Ah, he recognized the lightning-struck tree. He had three miles to walk due east. Grateful that he'd suspected the shivaree and kept his shoes on, and that the moon was full, he started walking.

Was Leah worried about him, or had she figured out what happened? If she'd been able to recognize the ringleader, Horace Haywell, she wouldn't have worried too much.

He kept his mind off how tired he was from the long day and on his wife. How he loved that word. He grinned like a fool and increased his pace.

The moon sat high in the inky sky by the time he saw the glow of a lantern in the window of his house. He spotted a bundled-up Leah on the porch. It was too cold for such nonsense. "Leah," he called out, not wanting to frighten her.

"Luke." She bolted upright and down the stairs. She sprinted toward him in her bare feet and into his outstretched arms. "You're home."

"Right where I belong." He lifted her and carried her into the house.

Cynthia Hickey grew up in a family of storytellers and moved around the country a lot as an army brat. Her desire is to write about real, flawed characters in a wholesome way that her seven children and five grandchildren can all be proud of. She and her husband live in Arizona where Cynthia is a full-time writer.

Maddy's Llamas

by Marjorie Vawter

Dedication

To my daughter, Kathy.
Like your mother, you've had to learn the truth of Psalm 19:14.
And you have done well. I love you more than life itself,
and I constantly pray God's best for you each day.

Let the words of my mouth, and the meditation of my heart,
be acceptable in thy sight, O LORD, my strength, and my redeemer.
PSALM 19:14

Chapter 1

1898
Colorado

Maddy Williams stepped into Spencers' General Store holding her dripping umbrella away from her. Seeing another umbrella drip-drying on the floor to the left of the door, she reopened hers and set it down next to it. Then she tried to straighten her dress, though why she bothered when her skirts were soaked below her knees she had no idea. Drat the convention that expected her to wear skirts when walking to town. She'd be much more comfortable in her usual trousers. Especially on wet days like today.

No one had come from the back in response to the bell that tinkled when she shut the door, so she pulled the scrap of paper from her damp reticule and started down the aisle with the canned goods stacked on the shelves. She didn't really need the list. It was a repeat of most of her biweekly walks to town.

Setting three cans each of green beans and corn on the counter, she looked at her list. Flour. Sugar. Corn meal. For those, she'd have to wait for Mrs. Spencer. As stationmaster, Mr. Spencer was sure to be at the train station—getting the mail and making sure there was enough water and coal on board to get them back to the next station at Nederland.

Maddy looked down at her list. Where was that dratted woman? She wanted—no, needed—to get back to her sweet Betta. Chewing her lower lip, she pondered the last item.

Healing salve, with three question marks after it.

The sore on Betta's right front shoulder hadn't responded well to Maddy's herbal home remedies. But would some newfangled ointment do any better?

A quick glance at the curtain that covered the door to the back of the building—the Spencers' sitting room—confirmed that no one was coming to help her right away. She turned and walked toward the shelf on the wall to the left of the counter. It held a variety of medical supplies.

She pulled down a jar of carbolic acid. A quick read-through of the directions for use caused Maddy to frown. This was obviously for human use, but would it work on animals? On Betta?

A rustle of fabric and a scent of lilacs alerted Maddy to Mrs. Spencer's entrance. She turned.

"Oh, it's you, Miss Williams."

Was there the slightest bit of emphasis on "Miss"? Maddy shrugged it off. There would always be those who disapproved of her choice of staying single.

"Good morning, Mrs. Spencer." The carbolic acid still in hand, Maddy walked to the counter and set it down beside the other items she'd selected.

Mrs. Spencer nodded. "Sorry to keep you waiting. I didn't hear the bell." She pulled Maddy's items to her side of the counter before ducking down behind it, presumably for packing materials. But not before Maddy saw blotching on her neck and cheeks.

What on earth could the woman be doing that caused her to blush like that? Maddy shrugged the thought away, thankful her llamas were much easier to read than people.

"If you're looking for packing materials, Mrs. Spencer, don't bother. I've brought my bag." She held up her brightly colored shoulder bag as Mrs. Spencer stood upright. Only a hint of color remained in her cheeks.

"Oh yes. How could I forget that outlandish bag?" The corners of her lips tightened as though she would smile, and she reached for the bag.

"Outlandish?" Maddy studied her bag. What could possibly offend the woman?

Mrs. Spencer glanced over her shoulder at the slightly billowing curtain. Was someone back there? Someone she didn't want Maddy to know about? According to town gossip, Mrs. Spencer entertained several miners when they were in town. Right under her unsuspecting husband's nose.

"What do you mean, outlandish?"

Mrs. Spencer pinched her lips as she put Maddy's canned goods in the bag. "Oh you know. These colors." She held the bag open between the tips of her forefinger and thumb, as if it were contaminated with some awful disease.

Maddy started to roll her eyes but cut the action short. "It's only a bag, Mrs. Spencer. From Peru." She strove to keep her voice level. Goodness, but it was hard!

Let the words of my mouth be acceptable in Your sight, Lord.

But really, how quick people were to judge a culture foreign to their own.

Mrs. Spencer let the fabric opening drop close. "Oh, that reminds me. You have a letter."

Her heart jumped. "From Peru?"

"No, from Denver. The zoo."

This time Maddy did roll her eyes. Not another attempt to take her livelihood away from her, not to mention her best friends.

Mrs. Spencer pulled an envelope out of one of the slots in the wall cabinet they used for the mail. "Do you need anything else?"

Maddy took the envelope from Mrs. Spencer and slipped it into her skirt pocket. It would wait. "A pound each of flour, sugar, and corn meal."

"Aren't you going to read it?" Mrs. Spencer set the small parcels in Maddy's bag. "That letter's been sitting here for nearly a week."

Busybody. "I'm sure it will keep." And no doubt be useful in getting her stove lit tomorrow morning.

Maddy handed the woman money to cover her purchases and picked up her bag, slinging it over her shoulders in the way her Quechua Indian friends in Peru did.

◆—◆　　◆—◆

Harrison Collier stepped off the train onto the tiny platform at the Eldora station and inhaled a huge breath of pure mountain air. Recent rain had sharpened the piney tang that filled his nostrils and had also swelled the roaring stream next to the tracks. He reveled in the glorious majesty of the Rocky Mountains.

No matter what tricks or strategies his father employed to lure him back to the family ranch in south Texas, nothing could induce him to move away from these mountains. Here he was at home. If only he could live up here. But his job at the Denver Zoo kept him firmly rooted in the small city.

Today he would enjoy himself to the fullest extent. It wasn't often he could combine both his loves—zoology and mountains. When Mr. Graham approached him with the plan to meet with the "old biddy"—his boss's words, not his—who consistently ignored the letters requesting her to share the llamas she raised with the people of Denver, Harry jumped at the chance. After all, he knew he could turn up his charm and the old woman would do whatever he asked. After he accomplished that task, he was free to do whatever he liked the rest of the day before taking the several-hour train ride back to Denver later in the day.

Harry looked around him. Surely there was someone who could direct him to Miss Williams's llama ranch. But the place looked deserted. Amazing for a place that boasted several mines as well as a resort. But maybe it was too early in the season for many tourists.

He spotted a sign hanging on a porch down the road to the west of the depot. He squinted a little, trying to read it. He'd have to break down one of these days and get some spectacles. The sign finally came into focus, and he murmured as he read: SPENCERS' GENERAL STORE AND ELDORA US POST OFFICE.

Certain that someone at the post office could give him directions, Harry spotted the steps that would get him off the platform. As he started down the stairs, a man with a fringe of gray hair bristling around a bald head put his foot on the bottom tread.

"Are you needing help, sir? We don't get too many strangers around here. Leastways not until the resort opens."

Harry returned the man's grin, descending the last couple of steps to stand beside him. He took the man's outstretched hand. "Harrison Collier, sir. With the Denver Zoo."

"I'm Peter Spencer." His grip was firm.

Harry's dad always said you could tell a man's character by the way he shook hands. Dad would say that Mr. Spencer was a fine, upstanding man.

Harry nodded toward the store. "That you?"

Spencer followed his gaze. "Yep. Supply master, stationmaster, and postmaster—all standing right next to you, Mr. Collier." He grinned and ran his hand over his bald spot. "Looking for anyone in particular?"

"Yes, sir. A Miss Magdalene Williams. Raises llamas."

Spencer's eyebrows shot halfway up his forehead. "Really?"

Harry hesitated. The man looked so surprised, shocked even. "Is there something wrong? She does live near here, right?"

Spencer shook his head. "No. I mean yes. I mean. . ." He took a deep breath. "No, there's nothing wrong, if you don't mind eccentricity." He grimaced as though he did mind. "Yes, she lives here, if you don't mind a little bit of a hike."

"I don't mind. Just point me in the right direction."

Spencer pointed at the road crossing the tracks on the opposite side of the depot. "Just follow that road a mile or so to the east. You'll see it on your left. Can't miss it. The llamas are in a paddock right next to the road." He scrutinized Harry. "Does she know you're coming?"

Harry shrugged. "She should. I wrote her over a week ago, setting an appointment for today."

"Ah yes. That would explain it."

"Explain what?" The heaviness in the pit of his stomach increased the longer he talked to Mr. Spencer.

Spencer shook his head. "Nothing to concern you, young man. My wife said she picked up the letter yesterday but didn't read it." He smiled. "She doesn't get many letters, and my wife was surprised that she didn't open it right away. I'm sure you'll enjoy your visit with Miss Williams. She's an interesting. . .um, unusual lady."

Now what did that mean? Harry wondered what the man was keeping back from him. The only other time he'd encountered someone who looked as guilty as Spencer did was just before he paid a surprise visit to Melinda, his so-called fiancée back in Texas. He knew she wasn't expecting him to show up, but the man giving him directions held back the information that a celebration was to take place that day at her parents' house—Melinda's wedding.

Harry blocked the memory. He wasn't facing the same kind of situation here. The only thing he knew about this woman was that she was a spinster, an older woman, doing a man's job. Not that he didn't think a woman capable of running a ranch, but she wouldn't appeal to him even if she were a young woman.

After making sure of the return train time, Harry took off on the wagon road that would take him to his destination. The train must have passed the ranch on the way into town. He dodged puddles left by the rain, and thankful for his sturdy boots, he trudged through the mud alongside the train rails.

Twenty minutes later, Harry spotted the llamas—exotic-looking animals— on his left, their paddock and barn backing up against the mountain. He walked up the path toward the cabin nestled in a copse of trees across from the paddock, expecting to find Miss Williams taking her midday meal.

But then he spotted a man in the paddock next to the barn, doing something with one of the llamas. As he got closer, he saw the wound on the llama's left shoulder. Looked like a graze that had gotten infected.

He cleared his throat before speaking, loud enough to catch the attention of the animal, if not the man tending to the wound. "Excuse me, sir. I'm looking for Miss Magdalena Williams. Could you tell me where to find her?"

To his horror, the man startled, bumping into the llama's sore shoulder and letting out a high-pitched shriek. The llama put her head down and butted the man hard enough to send him head over heels.

Chapter 2

Maddy's chest tightened as she struggled to get a breath. Not only had Betta butted her in the diaphragm, but she had bowled her over. She could feel the wet earth of the paddock seeping through her overalls and shirt. Her cap, holding her wealth of chestnut-colored curls, had flown off, and water and mud now tickled her scalp as well.

If only she could get a breath. Dark spots floated in front of her eyes, and through the haze she saw the intruder bending over her holding out a hand. Why on earth was he doing that?

Breathe, Maddy, breathe. The words screamed through her mind, and she closed her eyes, blocking out the abhorrent man above her before her lungs finally kicked back in and allowed a deep breath to enter them.

As from a long way off, she heard a man's voice—a very nice mellow but tinged-with-alarm baritone—gabbling above her. Focusing her gaze, she looked up into velvety brown eyes projecting alarm and concern. Then she saw a second pair of eyes above a long furry nose also staring down at her. Only Betta's did not reflect concern; they looked at her with contempt.

Contempt? Betta had never looked at her like that before. The contempt must be for the man now holding a hand above her. She grabbed it and pulled herself up out of the slimy mess on the ground.

As soon as she was upright, she dropped the hand and turned her back on him. She hadn't invited him, she didn't know him, and she wasn't about to listen to his garbled apologies. Maybe he would give up and go away. Why was he here on her property anyway?

She reached a hand out to Betta. But the crazy animal literally walked away from her and reached around Maddy's shoulder to cuddle up to the strange man. Cuddle up? It was the only word she could think of for the outrageous behavior her favorite llama exhibited at the moment.

Then, to crown all the other indignities, Betta began to hum when the man reached out his hand and scratched the animal behind her ears.

"Who *are* you?" Maddy's indignation burst out as she whirled to face the stranger.

"Harrison Collier—call me Harry—um, ma'am." He stretched out his hand as if he expected her to shake it.

She supposed it was the friendly thing to do, but she wasn't capitulating that quickly. She took a step back, brushing a slimy tendril of hair from her cheek. His name sounded vaguely familiar, but she couldn't place it.

The velvet in his eyes disappeared as he took in her overalls, flannel shirt, and muddy hair spilling over her shoulders and down her back. His brown eyes were as hard as mahogany.

"And why are you here, Mr. Collier? Upsetting my animals?"

The man had the audacity to laugh, and the velvet returned to his eyes. "You call a llama humming upset?"

"What do you know about llamas?" She thought she could be pretty sure the man had never been to South America, and as far as she knew, her llamas comprised the largest herd in North America. Maybe the only herd. She had a hard time convincing people to use her llamas rather than donkeys or horses when they needed to move supplies. And while they were distant cousins to camels, llamas were unique.

"Didn't you get my letter, ma'am?"

Letter? The only letter she'd gotten was from some yahoo at the Denver Zoo, wanting her to give up her precious animals to strangers. But his name wasn't Collier, was it?

Her heart sinking, she pulled the now damp and slightly muddy envelope out of her back pocket and studied the return address. Oh no! She slammed her eyes shut, as if it would help her block out the name now burned into her brain. *Mr. Harrison Collier.* If her pride sank any further, she wouldn't be able to dig it back out of the mud puddle at her feet.

Without a word, she turned her back on her visitor and ran to her cabin, slamming the door shut behind her.

◆——•——◆

Harrison stared at the cabin where the young woman had disappeared. He absently stroked the still-humming llama's neck. What had he said?

He'd seen that the letter she'd pulled from her back pocket hadn't been opened. Even though it looked a little worse for wear, he recognized it as his own. But the young woman couldn't possibly be Magdalene Williams. Miss Williams was a much older woman. Maybe she'd forgotten to tell Miss Williams about her letter and the lady would appear any moment.

But at that thought, Harry knew he didn't want to meet Miss Williams. The younger woman was much more intriguing. It was all he could do to keep from laughing as he saw her upended in the mud puddle and heard her horror when the llama came to him humming.

No young woman had ever intrigued him as much as this one. Not even Melinda, though he couldn't even begin to put Melinda in overalls and tending to a horse, let alone a strange creature like the one he continued to pet.

The llama butted her head into his shoulder, reminding him of the sore on her shoulder. He bent down to inspect it and then looked around for the jar he'd seen the woman holding before he startled her.

There. By the mud puddle.

He quickly moved into the paddock and picked up the brown jar, squinting in the now bright sun to read the label. Camphor. Well, she'd gotten the best on the market for wound care. He looked around for a rag to dab the medicine onto the wound and found one draped over the top rail of the fence. Thankful it had missed the dunking in the mud puddle, he found a clean portion of the rag and poured the camphor onto it. Then he dabbed it on the llama's wound.

She stopped humming.

Harry looked into her eyes and saw pain, as well as something undefinable. Like she was measuring his expertise in animal care.

How had the wound started? It looked a little like a rope burn but deeper.

Behind him, he heard the cabin door slam shut, and he turned. Surely this would be Miss Williams.

He narrowed his eyes when he saw the young woman, now dressed in a clean pair of overalls, her hair hanging in damp burnished curls down her back, walking toward him. The llama next to him started humming again, but this time she directed her contentedness to the girl.

The girl walked to the fence, putting her hand up to caress the long nose of the llama, a wry smile on her face.

"I guess we'd better start over, getting the introductions out of the way."

Her voice was a sweet alto, low and clear. Much better than the strident tones she'd used earlier.

She held out her hand. "I'm Maddy Williams."

She was Miss Williams? All his misconceptions crumbled to ashes as he grabbed her hand and gave it a brisk shake before letting it go as if it were a red-hot branding iron.

"And you're Mr. Collier, as you said." She cleared her throat and refused to look him in the eye. "I'm so sorry for what I said earlier. I am really working. . . . Well, no, if I'm honest, Aunt Susie and the Lord are working, but I—"

Laughter bubbled up his throat before he could stop it. She stared at him before her lips quirked upward.

"Now it's my turn to apologize," he finally managed to blurt out.

But she shook her head, still grinning. "Aunt Susie keeps telling me I'll live to regret my hasty words. But I can't seem to regret them as much as she thinks I should. Maybe that's why it's so hard"—laughter bubbled up in response to his—"to. . .to change."

"Who's Aunt Susie?" Harry managed to ask between spurts of laughter he couldn't keep in. "Does she live with you?"

"No." Miss Williams pointed a little to the northwest. "She lives on her own place, over there."

She walked into the paddock and took the bottle of camphor and the rag from him. Then she walked into the small stable and set them on the workbench just inside the door.

"She's not really my aunt, but I call her that." Miss Williams cleared her throat again and met his gaze. "She's the closest person to family I have." She shrugged. "Well, at least on this continent."

"On this continent? What do you mean?" Harry couldn't imagine what she was talking about. One didn't usually talk about their loved ones who had died as living on another continent, did they? This girl sure was eccentric. And she wasn't even old.

Miss Williams turned and led the way back out into the paddock. "My parents are missionaries in Peru. They sent me home with Betta and Arturo five years ago."

"Why?" The question burst out of him before he could think to hold it back. He held his breath, waiting for her to refuse to answer the impertinence.

Instead, Miss Williams sighed. "They didn't want me to marry a 'native.'" She put a lot of bitterness into the last word. "In reality, they don't want me there. They consider me a nuisance."

Harry's heart wrenched, recalling Mr. Spencer's comment that she rarely received letters. "But they write you, don't they?"

"Oh, maybe two or three times a year." She waved her hand before her eyes as she turned away from him. "I always get their Christmas letter—the one they send to all their financial and prayer supporters."

Harry didn't know what to say. He sure wasn't going to tell her of the long, newsy letters he received from his family weekly. Even when he knew he was a disappointment to his father.

Before he could think of a suitable response, she turned back to him. "So your letter says you have a proposition for me." Color flooded her face as she realized what she'd said. "I mean, uh. . ."

He put up his hand to stop her, suppressing the smile that threatened to break through. "I know what you meant. Yes, my boss, Alexander J. Graham, the head zookeeper at the Denver Zoo, sent me. He would like to have a few of your splendid llamas for an exhibit at the zoo. . . ." He faltered and stopped at the set expression on her face.

"Go on." Her words hit him like rocks thrown up from a horse's galloping hooves.

"Well, um, you may know from his previous letters that we're trying to emulate Mr. Carl Hagenbeck's zoological ideas at his zoo in Germany. The animals we acquire will have their own environmental settings rather than encaging them within large iron-barred rooms. So with the llamas, we want to design an area that emulates the Andean mountain range and have the animals live there."

Miss Williams drew herself to stand as straight and tall as her five-foot-and-some-inch frame would let her. "None of my animals will ever be part of an exhibition where people can come and stare at them. Not ever. So goodbye, Mr. Collier. I never want to see you or anyone else from the Denver Zoo ever again."

Chapter 3

I've met a man, Aunt Susie." Maddy pushed the door to Aunt Susie's cabin closed behind her, shutting out the latest snowstorm, and then turned to face her feisty older friend. "Oh whoa! What did I say?"

Aunt Susie's face exhibited surprise and shock as Maddy thought about what she'd said. But her eyes also held a glint of amusement. What had she said?

"You met a man?" Aunt Susie visibly struggled to remove the shock that held her frozen in place.

"Well, what's so surprising about that?" Maddy shed her coat and propped her umbrella next to the door. "In this place the men outnumber the women at least two to one, maybe more, with all the miners without their families."

"It's not what you said, sweet girl, but how you said it that surprised me." Aunt Susie turned back to the stove and set down the pan of cookies she'd just taken out of the oven. "Put your wet coat over the back of a chair and sit yourself down. Would you like some tea?"

Maddy followed Aunt Susie's instructions. "Yes, please. It's still so chilly out there, in spite of it being the end of May."

Aunt Susie busied herself making a pot of tea and getting out the rest of her tea things from the cabinet near the stove. Maddy looked around the tiny cabin. It was only one room, but Aunt Susie had placed everything so precisely that it made the space seem much larger. The bed stood in a back corner, opposite the wood-burning stove, and as far away from the door as possible. A round oak table was in the middle of the room, surrounded by four oak chairs.

Aunt Susie placed the teapot, cups and saucers, and sugar bowl in front of Maddy. Then she turned back to the stove, put the cookies on a plate, and set them next to the tea things before sitting down next to Maddy.

She waited while Maddy poured her a cup of tea and pushed the sugar bowl nearer. "So. . .this remarkable man." Her lips quirked into a mischievous smile. "What's so special about him?"

Maddy took her time pouring her own tea and picking out a cookie. Why had that unfortunate choice of words popped out of her mouth the moment she saw Aunt Susie? She shook her head and took a sip of the hot beverage before answering. "Who said he was remarkable? He's just like any other man."

Aunt Susie said nothing, but she quirked an eyebrow.

"You know. He doesn't like the way I'm dressed." She set down her cup. "In fact, he doesn't even like the idea of my raising llamas."

"Did he say so?"

Maddy savored her first bite of the warm ginger cookie. Then she snorted. "Of course not! He's too much of a *gentleman* to say so. But of course I could tell."

Aunt Susie's silence got to her. She didn't believe her. Maddy stood abruptly, nearly knocking her chair on its back. But she caught it, set it in place, and paced the floor.

"I got some medicine to put on Betta's shoulder. You know, the place she rubbed raw because Crazy Ernie didn't put her pack on right last time he had her out. So I'm putting it on, and this city gent meanders up the path to the paddock. He startled us both when he cleared his throat and addressed me as 'sir.' Betta butted me in the stomach, knocking me into a mud puddle." She grinned. "You should have seen his face when my hair came tumbling out of the cap."

Aunt Susie laughed. "I've seen plenty of other men's faces when they realized you're a young woman, not the boy they thought you were. Go on."

Maddy resumed pacing. "Well, I got mad. Told him off. He just stood there with a silly grin on his face."

"He left you sitting in the mud all the while?" Aunt Susie's eyes had that mischievous look again. "I thought you said he was a gentleman."

Maddy snorted again. "Oh yes. In his natty city attire." She shrugged. "No, he didn't leave me sitting in the mud. He helped me up. But do you know what that traitor Betta did? She took one look at him and started humming!" Her voice cracked.

Aunt Susie laughed.

Maddy stared at her erstwhile friend. How did she dare to laugh? Well, she didn't have to put up with it. She stomped to her coat and attempted to put it on, but she couldn't find the second sleeve.

Aunt Susie stood up, swallowing her laugh. "I'm sorry, Maddy-girl. I couldn't help but laugh at the outrage in your words." A little giggle escaped her. "Take that coat off. You're not leaving until you tell me the whole story." Aunt Susie grabbed the loose sleeve and pulled Maddy around to face her. "Truly, I want to hear it."

Maddy's anger dissolved, and allowing Susie to take her coat, she sat down and took another swallow of her cooling tea. Why was she so upset? Plenty of other men had mistaken her for a man. Plenty of them didn't approve of her choice of occupation. And plenty of them had tried to make an honest woman of her by offering marriage.

But none of her llamas had *ever* hummed at the sight of a man before.

After Aunt Susie freshened the teapot with hot water, she took her seat next to Maddy again. "You are upset because Betta hummed at this paragon of a city gent?"

Maddy squirmed. "Well, yes. She's never done that for anyone else. In spite of the fact she's my favorite, she rarely does it for me." She could hear the whine in her voice. This was ridiculous. Whining over a dumb animal for humming in the presence of a man.

Her lips quirked up as she saw the humor in the situation. Trust Aunt Susie to see it first.

Maddy looked her friend in the eye and shrugged. "Oh well. He won't be back."

"How can you be so sure? Who is he anyway?"

"Harrison 'Call Me Harry' Collier." Maddy stuffed another cookie in her mouth. "He *says* he's a zoologist with the Denver Zoo. They sent him up to see if he could talk me into giving my llamas to the zoo for a new exhibit."

"You told him no?" Aunt Susie's gaze held hers.

"Of course! I told you, he won't be back."

✦•——•✦

"How did your visit to the old biddy go?"

Harry looked up from his reading to see his boss standing in the doorway to his office and sighed. "She told me in no uncertain terms never to come back." Why did that put an ache in his heart? "And she's not so old either, Mr. Graham."

Mr. Graham's heavy, dark eyebrows shot up his forehead as he moved into Harry's office and sat down on a chair in front of Harry's battered desk. There really wasn't much room in the cramped office space, especially for two grown men. "Do tell, Harry."

Harry eyed Mr. Graham. Like a child, his boss liked to think everyone saw life the same way he did, and he expected everyone else to fit his expectations. When they didn't, Harry never knew which way the man would go. Lose his temper, write the person out of his life, or readjust his thinking on the situation.

"Miss Williams is closer to twenty than thirty. And she dresses like a man." Harry grimaced, remembering his first verbal faux pas with the lady in question. "I called her 'sir' and got a blistering response in return."

Mr. Graham's laughter barked out of him, drowning anything else Harry had to say.

A wry grin worked its way onto Harry's lips as he too saw the humor in the situation. Only it hadn't felt that way yesterday. The best thing that happened then was Betta's humming. It had really upset Maddy Williams. And brought satisfaction to him, relieving him of some of the sting of Maddy's definite refusal even to consider his proposal of bringing some of her llamas down to the zoo.

When Mr. Graham finally brought his laughter under control, he wiped his streaming eyes. "Oh, the picture that conjures up in my mind! I wish I'd been there."

Harry didn't remind him of his pushing the unpleasant task onto his zoologist. If he returned—and he was pretty sure he would—he didn't want Mr. Graham poking his large, red nose into Maddy's paddock. She was his project now, and Mr. Graham could go find another.

Mr. Graham set his elbows on the chair's armrests and steepled his fingers in front of his face. He whistled softly as he contemplated. . .what? His next move? Harry's next move? Harry didn't dare ask, afraid he might be given an assignment for something that was doomed to failure.

Finally, Mr. Graham lowered his arms and looked at Harry. "What exactly did she say about loaning some of her llamas for exhibition at the zoo?"

Harry frowned in concentration, not wanting to lose any of the inflections Maddy had put into her refusal. "She said, 'None of my animals will ever be part of an exhibition where people can come and stare at them. Not ever. So goodbye, Mr. Collier. I never want to see you or anyone else from the Denver Zoo again.' And she turned away from me and stalked into the stable."

Mr. Graham grinned appreciatively at Harry's imitation of Maddy's voice. "Will that stop you from trying again?"

Harry didn't have to think that one through. He'd come to his decision within three minutes of leaving Maddy's ranch. "No sir. I'm going back next week."

"Good." Mr. Graham stood and strode to the door. "And don't come back until she says yes."

Chapter 4

Maddy hummed her favorite hymn as she tightened the girth strap on Betta's pack. Every once in a while she'd burst out into full song, but the llamas didn't seem to appreciate her singing.

"Great is thy faithfulness, great is thy faithfulness, morning by morning new mercies I see. All I have needed—"

Betta put her head down and butted Maddy.

Sitting on the ground brought back the memory of the last time Betta had butted her. The time that uppity city gent Harrison Collier witnessed the event. Her cheeks warmed with embarrassment as she thought about her uncontrolled words. She had hoped he wouldn't take her seriously when she told him never to come back. But it had been three weeks since that memorable visit.

She didn't blame him. Who would want to face a crazy woman who couldn't keep her tongue under control?

Maddy stood, muttering, "Let the words of my mouth, and the meditation of my heart, be acceptable in Thy sight, O Lord, my strength, and my redeemer. Let the words of my mouth—"

"Is that Betta's favorite occupation?"

Maddy whirled around, shading her eyes from the early morning sun just popping over the mountains to the east. Harrison Collier was standing on the other side of the fence. Smiling. At her. Behind her Betta hummed and walked toward him.

"Well? Did the head butt affect your speech?" He laughed.

He laughed! Evidently he was easily amused.

Maddy turned her back on him, refusing to answer. Here she'd been remorseful about what she'd said and the tone of voice she'd used. How dare he laugh at her?

She hoisted another heavy pack onto Arturo's back and started tying the straps that would hold it on. She needed to get these animals loaded and started on the way to the mines above Lost Lake. The miners needed their supplies and didn't like taking time out from their work to come back down to Eldora to get them.

Mr. Collier's brown eyes, still shining with mirth, gazed at her across Arturo's back. "Need some help?"

"If you want, sure." Maddy tried to shrug off how her heart leaped at his offer. She hadn't mistaken the warmth she'd seen in his eyes in her dreams either. It wasn't good to look into his eyes, she reminded herself. She'd never get on the road if she did.

But she couldn't stop the warmth rising into her cheeks at the pleasure that he'd returned. She didn't even care if he pursued the subject of making an exhibit of her precious llamas. Not that he would get his way. But he didn't know that.

Yet.

"So, does Betta make a habit of butting into you?" Mr. Collier picked up another pack and started strapping it onto Carla's back.

Maddy grunted as she hoisted the last pack onto another of the llamas. "No. Believe it or not, she only does it when you're around." The admission made her lips quirk. What was it about Mr. Collier that made Betta act that way with her? It was almost as if she were jealous.

Mr. Collier's deep chuckle sounded in her ear as he came over to help her tighten the last of the straps. Betta was on his heels.

He looked around the paddock. "Is this all?"

"For this trip. Yes." Maddy busied herself with making sure the halters were secured on the four animal's heads. The llamas would be fine once they got on the trail up to the mines, but until then she would have to lead them. Betta would help with that task. Besides being Maddy's favorite, Betta was the best lead animal in the herd.

Though with Betta's behavior toward Mr. Collier being what it was, she might need to rely on Arturo or Martin today.

Unless Mr. Collier would consent to go with her.

The thought jumped unbidden into her mind, and she tried to reject it. She couldn't ask him to go along. She didn't want to hear his refusal to be seen with her in her "men's clothing." And she certainly didn't want him to take her animals without her.

Her cabin door slammed shut, and Maddy looked to see Aunt Susie hurrying toward her, carrying a packet that she knew contained sandwiches and fresh cookies. Aunt Susie always helped out with food for these trips, and she did the chores for the llamas left behind. Frankly, Maddy wondered if her business would survive if it weren't for the help and support Aunt Susie gave her.

"Ahhhhh." The word stretched out as Aunt Susie gave Mr. Collier the once-over.

Maddy took the package from Aunt Susie and tucked it into the top of

Betta's pack. "What does 'ah' mean?"

Aunt Susie grinned and turned back to Mr. Collier. "I assume you are the young man Maddy met a few weeks ago? The man from the zoo."

He started to answer, but Aunt Susie wasn't done. "I must say, I thought you'd be a little older. Well, maybe a lot older, from the letters she received."

Maddy bit her cheek to keep from laughing out loud as the red rose up Mr. Collier's neck and bled into his cheeks.

"Well, yes, ma'am, but—"

"The young man who evidently didn't listen to Maddy when she told you never to come back?"

Aunt Susie was on a roll now, and Maddy's own cheeks grew warm. She ducked down behind Arturo, making sure his straps were tight and wouldn't rub a sore while carrying the pack.

Then Aunt Susie took pity on Mr. Collier. She bestowed her best sweet smile and held out a ginger cookie. "You must be Mr. Harrison Collier, yes?"

"Yes, ma'am. My boss—the one who wrote the first letters—insisted I come back after I told him. . ."

Maddy stared at him. She didn't think his cheeks could get any redder without breaking out into flame. What had he told his boss?

"That you had no intention of paying attention to Maddy's refusal?" Aunt Susie grinned and gave a little hop when his shoulders slumped and he dropped his gaze. "Ha! I knew it. You're a good man, Mr. Collier. Shake. I'm Aunt Susie." She held out her hand to take his and gave it a brisk shake before dropping it.

Maddy decided she needed to step in. Mr. Collier and Aunt Susie could carry on without her. "Are you done, Aunt Susie? I need to get going, or I'll be spending the night up there." She gestured to the west.

"Well, you're not going alone! Mr. Collier, I'm sure, would love to go with you." Aunt Susie faced Maddy, turning her back on Mr. Collier. "Besides, it would give him an opportunity to see the llamas in action, right?"

Maddy narrowed her eyes. "What are you getting at, Aunt Susie?"

Aunt Susie let out a little giggle, and Maddy stared. She'd never seen Aunt Susie behave this way.

"Why nothing, sweet girl. Just that Mr. Collier might want to see the llamas doing what they're best suited for—packing great loads on steep mountain trails." One of her eyelids dipped in a wink. "Not in an exhibit for city folk to stare at."

Maddy's heart dropped into her stomach and then jumped into her throat. Was Aunt Susie matchmaking? Or did she think she was helping Maddy get rid of Mr. Collier?

"I'd love a day hiking with you, Miss Williams."

"But I thought he'd stay with you, Aunt Susie."

They spoke at the same time, and Aunt Susie clapped her hands and laughed, adding to Maddy's confusion. Her friend was acting like a child.

Shaking her head, Maddy turned to Mr. Collier. "Are you sure you're up to a hike? I mean, it's about five miles up to the mines on some pretty steep climbs. And we'd need to be back before dark."

"Then why waste time? I'm ready."

❖━━━━━━━━━❖

Harry fell into step with Maddy, who led Betta with her hand on the halter. The other llamas fell into line behind Betta.

"Thanks for letting me come along." Harry knew she hadn't "let" him, that it was all Aunt Susie's doing. He didn't know what the old lady was up to, but so far he liked her strategy. His heart smiled, but butterflies were doing a number in his stomach.

Maddy gave him a look before upping her pace. Did she want to get rid of him? She'd have a hard time doing that. But he gave her credit for not believing the "letting me come along" comment.

Mr. Graham might have a long wait in front of him. He didn't think Maddy would give in easily to letting the zoo have some of her llamas. If she ever did.

"How did you get here so early?" Maddy didn't even give him a glance to indicate she'd spoken.

But since no one else was around, he assumed she was talking to him. At least it wouldn't be a silent hike. At least not right away.

"I came up yesterday on the train and got a room at the Goldminer Hotel."

That earned a look from her. "Isn't it terribly expensive?"

He shrugged. "The room is small, but it suffices. And no, it isn't particularly expensive. Besides, the zoo is paying for it."

He grinned at her disgusted "humph." He would be camping out if it weren't for the zoo's paying for a room at the hotel. It was only a year old, but in spite of its usual clientele of miners—not always with the best reputation of being clean and sober—it retained its air of "newness."

"So why are you delivering goods to the miners?" He wanted to keep her talking, and he hoped this was a topic to which she would respond.

She waved at Peter Spencer standing on the porch outside his general store. "Peter pays me and the llamas to take supplies up to the miners every couple of weeks. The miners pay extra for the service, but in the long run it saves money. They don't have to leave their mines to spend a day getting supplies."

"As they say, 'time is money,' " Harry quipped.

"In my pocket, which is most important." Maddy's gorgeous smile made a brief appearance.

When they reached the other side of town, the road wound upward, following the stream back into the mountains. "Isn't there another supply town around? I thought I read something about it before I came up the first time." Harry couldn't remember the name of the town, though he was sure one had been mentioned in the article.

"Hessie." Maddy led Betta around a large mud puddle in the middle of the wagon road, and the rest of the llamas followed.

"Pardon?" Sounded like she'd sneezed. But maybe not. He had fallen behind to make sure the llamas all followed their leader.

"The town's name is Hessie."

Harry frowned and caught up to Maddy. "Isn't that a lady's name?"

Maddy grinned. "Yes. The town is named for the postmaster's wife. Nice lady. She runs the inn there."

Was she teasing him? He decided he liked it, whatever she was doing. Her tone was almost playful. "Okay. But why?"

"Why Hessie? I'm sure you've heard of the multiple name changes for Eldora."

"Um, no." Harry's breath was getting shorter with the climb. "I must have missed that." He suspected Maddy was practically running on purpose. To get rid of him?

She cut a glance at him, giving a "cat that swallowed the canary" smile. Probably thinking the "city gent" couldn't keep up. "So what about the name changes?"

She pulled Betta to the side of the road and pulled out a small flask. "Would you like some tea? Aunt Susie made it."

He accepted a tin cup half full of a clear brown liquid and quirked an eyebrow at her.

"Well, the first settlers named this valley Happy Valley, and that's what they were going to call the town. But when gold was found, they decided they needed a better name, so then it became El Dorado or the El Dorado Camp." She took a swallow of tea. "But then the mail kept going to California and El Dorado, California's, mail came here. It caused a lot of problems with pay records and packets, and added to the headaches of keeping several mines open." She pulled a cookie out of the packet of sandwiches Aunt Susie made and offered it to him.

He shook his head. Maybe later. The ginger aroma was enticing, but he wasn't really hungry. Yet.

"So finally they shortened the name to Eldora, and it's stuck."

He handed the tin cup back to Maddy, and she stored it in the pack with her cup and the flask. "Were you here through all the name changes?"

Maddy shook her head. "No, but I got here before the last name change." She pulled on Betta's halter. "A lot of people still call the area Happy Valley. I guess it is, kind of."

"A happy valley? Yeah, I suppose the miners who've hit gold would think so."

It was good to share a laugh with Maddy. Her spontaneous, gutsy laugh heartened him.

After another mile or so, the road came near the stream, and he pointed to a large rock. The spring runoff was loud, making it difficult to talk. She understood his gesture for rest but shook her head no, pointing up the road.

Harry shrugged and followed her. Around a bend in the road, he understood why. The little town of Hessie lay spread out in a clearing. At the inn, Maddy tied the llamas to the hitching post and sat down on the steps leading into the building.

"Nice town." Harry could see the entire settlement laid out before him. Several more cabins sat on the mountainside behind the inn.

Maddy nodded. "I love it here. But there's not enough room for my llamas."

"Which is why you chose the valley outside Eldora?"

"Partly. Even that doesn't really have the room I need to grow my own hay." She caught his eye. "But I'm making do. For now."

For now. Did that mean she *might* consider moving some of her llamas to the zoo?

Chapter 5

Maddy allowed herself a huge sigh of relief as she and Mr. Collier turned to the downward slope. Their deliveries to the miners done, all they had to do was get themselves and the llamas back home. Before dark.

But with a quick glance at the sky, Maddy wasn't sure they would meet their deadline. They could at least get to Hessie before dark, she decided.

"What do you think? Will we make it home before dark?"

Maddy glanced at Mr. Collier, who was also studying the sky. She looked again at the clouds forming over Devil's Thumb Pass on the Continental Divide and shook her head. "Not hardly. We'll be fortunate to make it to Hessie before dark, and that's if we can beat the storm."

Mr. Collier's face reflected his concern, and he nodded. "That's what I thought." Then he looked at the four llamas strung out behind them. "Can't we ride them?"

Maddy snorted. "I'd like to see you try." She shook her head and glanced back at Betta. She'd almost stopped, and Maddy gave her a tug. "See? Even Betta understood your question, Mr. Collier."

"Harry, please, Miss Williams." He put his hand over hers on the leading rein and helped her tug. "Sorry, Betta. I didn't mean to insult you. Come on, girl."

To Maddy's surprise, Betta not only got moving again, but she started to hum. Maddy shook her head, and Harry dropped her hand. "What did you do to bewitch her?" She cut a quick glance at Harry before starting down the wagon road again. "Only if you call me Maddy."

Catching up to her, Harry grinned. "Okay, Maddy. I'm as flummoxed as you are by Betta's behavior. Love at first sight, maybe?"

"Ha!" Maddy grinned at Harry. "Don't believe in it. Do you?"

A rock rolled under her foot, and she stumbled. Harry put his hand on her elbow to steady her, but once she was stable again, he didn't let go. Her skin tingled at his touch through her shirt sleeve. She needed to keep her gaze down at the path or she would fall and hurt herself. Not what she needed right now.

They didn't speak until they'd passed Lost Lake and started down toward the road that would take them to Hessie.

Harry glanced back toward the lake, which was no longer visible. "What did you say the name of that lake was?"

"Lost Lake." Maddy kept her eyes down. "I think you can figure out why."

Harry chuckled. "Yes, most appropriate. You don't see it until you're practically in it."

Maddy risked a quick look at the sky again. "That storm is moving in real fast. We'd better notch up the pace a bit, unless you really want to get soaked."

Harry didn't reply, just increased his pace to keep abreast of her, though he did release her elbow in order to help his own balance. Maddy shrugged away the feeling of abandonment. What was the matter with her? Normally she would have disdained even that little offer of help. She was as bad as Betta. Or would be if she allowed herself to fall for the man.

"Tell me a little about the zoo. I never really heard of it until a couple of years ago." Maddy wanted to keep him talking, partly because she liked his mellow baritone, but mostly to block out thoughts of the storm building up behind them.

"The zoo only got its start two years ago. Mayor Speer had a bear cub given to him, and he didn't know what to do with it. So he tasked Mr. Graham to open a zoo, and Billy Bryan became the first exhibit."

Maddy had heard about Billy Bryan but thought the animal was apocryphal. "So Billy Bryan is real? Was he really named for William Jennings Bryan?"

Harry laughed. "He's real. And yes, the mayor named him after Bryan."

"Are there more animals there? I mean, it wouldn't be much of a zoo if there's only one black bear to see."

"Sure there are more animals. But it takes more time to build a natural environment for them, which is what Mr. Graham has committed the zoo to do. Since Billy, we've added an eagle, deer, elk, and bison. We'll continue to add as we can build exhibits—mostly for animals and birds that are native to our state."

Maddy's lips quirked. "Of course those would be the easiest exhibits to build. So then why do you want my llamas? They aren't indigenous to this area."

Harry raised his eyes to hers. "No, but they are indigenous to a mountain environment."

"Okay, but why llamas? Couldn't you go after an elephant or something else? Like a giraffe or zebra?" Maddy tried to keep the desperation out of her voice. She didn't want to give up *any* of her herd. They were hers, and each one was an individual. It was like selling her children to even think of parting ways with them.

She could feel Harry's gaze on her, but she refused to look back at him. She was sure all she'd see was false compassion. He didn't care. Nor did his boss. Bringing him along today was a waste of time, just as she had expected.

"We don't want to buy them from you." Harry touched her free hand briefly as he moved forward to walk beside her. "We want them on loan. Besides, you've already adapted them to this climate and terrain."

On loan or buying them—what was the difference? She'd still have a depleted herd.

Harry finally turned his gaze from her. "We'll eventually get an elephant and giraffe and many other animals and birds from Africa, but Mr. Graham thought we should start our out-of-state exhibits with animals from our side of the world." He shrugged.

The defeat in his voice brought her eyes to his face. Did getting some of her herd really mean that much to him?

"But Harry. It feels like I'm selling my own children, even if it's only a loan. How can you ask—"

The stone she'd put her foot on rolled. Maddy lost her balance, but she still had the presence of mind to let go of the leading rein as she tumbled down the mountainside.

❖━━━━━❖

Without regard for his own safety, Harry ran down the mountain, hoping against hope to catch Maddy before she could fall too far. But she rolled to a stop against a large boulder before he could reach her.

Gasping for breath, he skidded to a stop and knelt down at her side. Her eyes were closed, and she didn't respond to his repeated use of her name.

He glanced up the road to where Betta and the other llamas stood, confused and startled. Thankfully, Betta wouldn't let the others move without her, even though her leading rein lay directionless on the ground in front of her. But as soon as Betta caught Harry's eye, she started down toward him.

With another glance at Maddy, he stood and waited until Betta joined him, bringing the others with her. "Good girl, Betta." He reached to touch her neck and scratch behind her ears. "Now to figure out how to get Maddy out of here."

He knelt at Maddy's side again and reached out to brush the hair from her forehead. Other than bruises and a few cuts from her tumble down the mountain, he couldn't see any other injuries. He raised her head and felt the back of it. His hand came away sticky with her blood. She'd hit her head at least once, which would explain her unconscious state.

Should he move her? Try to get her on Betta's back? Surely the loyal animal would allow that, even if she didn't normally like riders. After all, packing loads was inbred, wasn't it?

But would Betta consider an unconscious Maddy a pack load?

Harry shook his head. He didn't know. In fact, there was an awful lot about the breed he didn't know. But Maddy did. He thought back to what she was saying just before she fell. Couldn't she see he wouldn't take the animals on loan without her? She knew them so much better than he ever would. But how would he get Mr. Graham to agree to another employee? A woman too.

Maddy stirred and groaned a little, and then, just as Betta stroked her cheek with her nose, she opened her velvet-brown eyes. "What?" She brushed at Betta's long nose to push her back, and sat up. "Ouch." She winced at the pain of her cuts and then felt the lump at the back of her head.

Harry reached to pull her hands into his. She didn't need to poke at all her bruises and cuts, even if she could stand the pain. "Don't, you'll just make them hurt worse." He let her hands go. "Can you stand?"

She placed one hand on the boulder next to her and placed her other hand in his for support and tried to lever herself to an upright position.

Relief poured through his muscles, giving them strength to pull her up. At least she didn't have any broken bones.

But as soon as she took a step toward Betta, Maddy gasped and collapsed against him.

"What's wrong?" Harry struggled to hold her upright, but she kept one foot hanging just above the ground.

"My ankle." She gasped, then grimaced with pain. "Let me. . ." She motioned with her free hand to the boulder.

Harry helped her to sit on the big rock and then knelt down to examine her ankle. "Is it broken?"

She shook her head and swallowed hard. "I. . .I don't know. I don't think so." She took a deep breath and closed her eyes. "I think it's the one that rolled on the rock. Up there." She motioned up the mountainside to where she'd taken her tumble.

Harry took her foot in his hands. The swelling around the top of her boot was already evident. His fingers fumbled with the buttons on the side of her boot, releasing its hold on her foot. He couldn't see any discoloration through her cotton stocking, but he didn't need to in order to determine that broken or sprained, it needed attention.

"Where's the stream?" He could hear it but couldn't tell how far away it was.

She motioned to her right. "Over there, through the trees." Her words were coming in quick gasps. "But it will be awfully cold."

Without asking permission, he scooped her in his arms and carried her in the direction she'd pointed. Not able to see his footing, he stumbled a little, thankful for the aspen grove that held him upright. He sure didn't need to hurt himself now that Maddy needed him.

The swollen stream came into view, and Harry stopped, looking for a dry place close to the edge where he could set Maddy down. She needed to get that ankle into the water. Unable to hear above the noise of the water falling over the boulders in the stream, he saw Maddy's lips move as she motioned downstream. He followed her arm movements and finally saw what she'd pointed to.

A large rock, large enough for both of them to sit side by side. Dry on top, but with the water flowing just a few inches below the edge nearest the stream. Harry set her gently down, scrambled to seat himself next to her, and found that she'd already placed her leg up to her calf in the freezing water.

Her hold tightened on his arm, and she closed her eyes against the shock of the cold. With a gasp, she brought her leg out of the water, letting it dangle above the stream. He realized then she'd been holding her breath.

"It–it's c–c–cold."

Harry nodded his understanding and gently pushed her leg down into the water again. He kept his hand on her knee for half a minute and then drew her leg out of the water again. He didn't want to risk damaging the skin because of the freezing water, but she needed the cold to help bring down the swelling.

Just as the first raindrops speckled the water, he felt a cold nose touch the back of his neck. He turned to see Betta and the others standing right behind their rock. He grinned.

Betta was offering to help.

Chapter 6

Maddy sat on her front porch and watched Betta gambol around the paddock where Harry worked with the llamas. One would think that Betta was still a very young animal. Only Maddy knew better. Betta was the matriarch of the herd, but she sure wasn't acting like it these days.

What a week! Ever since her fall, Harry had come every day to do the chores for the llamas. As far as she knew, he was still at the Goldminer Hotel in Eldora. That could get expensive, but every time she suggested an alternative, he told her not to worry, the zoo was paying for his lodging.

She shifted in her chair and tried to find a better position for her foot on the stool Harry had placed before her after he carried her out to the porch. The days were definitely warming up, though most afternoons brought a rain shower or two. As she did most days—well, when she thought of it—she thanked the Lord again for the previous owner of her cabin. He had built it well, and more important, he had covered the porch so she could sit there rain or shine. Only if the wind picked up did she have to retreat inside.

She didn't know how long Harry would continue to stick around and work with the animals each day. Surely not the full six weeks the town's doctor had told her to stay off her severely sprained ankle. Maddy sighed and shifted once more. A sure sign she was bored. If only she'd controlled her mouth a little longer on the supply run she and Harry had made. At least until they'd gotten to a less steep portion of the trail.

But no! That tongue of hers was determined to get her into trouble whenever Harry was around, though he'd assured her he didn't blame her tongue. All she'd been doing was revealing her heart for her llamas. The trouble was that she liked having him around. He was fun to talk to. A good companion—one with whom she didn't feel she had to carry on a conversation at all times. He was companionable even in the quiet. And he was really good with the llamas.

And therein lay her problem. She didn't *want* her llamas to get too used to having him around. Next thing she knew, they'd want to follow him down to Denver. Especially Betta. It was uncanny. She'd never, ever have dreamed that

Betta would fall for a human—a man, no less—like she'd obviously fallen for Harry. Even to the point of allowing him to put Maddy on her back to carry her home.

She certainly understood why the llamas did so well packing heavy loads in mountainous terrain. They were as surefooted as deer. Maybe even more so, since they carried heavy loads and deer weren't created for that chore.

"A penny for your thoughts."

Maddy's hands stilled in her lap, and she raised her eyes to meet Harry's as he strode from the paddock toward her. Betta followed him with no lead line or anything to tether her.

Maddy chuckled. "You've got a shadow."

Harry grinned as he sat in the chair beside her. "She isn't happy unless I let her follow me around. So. . ." He shrugged.

"You let her." Maddy shook her head. "You're pretty sure she won't run off, aren't you?"

This time he laughed out loud. Maddy's stomach jerked, and she could almost feel her heart melt. That was happening now every time she heard him laugh. She'd quit trying to understand the why behind it.

"Not when I almost have to tie her inside the stable in order to leave each evening."

Maddy let the silence of the late morning fall between them. She wanted to ask him how long he planned to stay, but she didn't want to seem ungrateful. Not when she was trying to make her thoughts and words pleasing to the Lord. Plus, every time she let up on being vigilant over her tongue, she was the one who had to pay. She figured that was punishment enough.

Why was it so hard to watch her mouth and the vitriol that spewed from it whenever she let down her guard? And why would Harry stick around for yet another eruption from Mount Maddy?

She sighed and then wished she hadn't. Harry turned his warm brown eyes to her. She felt he could read her soul with those eyes. If she'd let him. She braced herself against his gaze, trying to stare him down. But she couldn't hold the stare.

Then Harry's eyes softened. "What's up, Maddy-girl?"

He'd started using Aunt Susie's endearment the past couple of days. She wished she could tell him not to, but she had to admit she liked it.

"Bored?"

She squirmed a little in her chair and tried to find another position for her foot. "A little." She knew the words were building in her, looking for an outlet.

Let the words of my mouth, and the meditation of my heart, be acceptable in Thy sight, O Lord.

The corners of Harry's mouth twitched. "Come on, Maddy. You might as well let it out. I can see you need to say something." He put his hand over his mouth to hide a smile, but Maddy could see the smile in his eyes.

She looked away. To be honest, if she said what she was thinking, his smile would disappear. And even if in a way Harry was laughing at her, she loved his smile and what it did to her insides. Oh, she didn't really blame Betta for following him everywhere he went. Humming. She too wanted to break out humming whenever he was around.

Mentally, she shook herself. Identifying with a dumb animal! What was the world coming to after all? And what would her parents say if they knew about Harry?

That thought sobered her. Not that they would find out about him. What would she tell them anyway? This silliness about the man was just in her mind. If he knew what she was thinking, he'd be halfway to Denver before she and Betta could get off her porch to go after him.

"Well? Are you going to spit it out?"

Maddy forced herself to meet his gaze. "No." She gave him a half-smile when his eyebrows rose in disbelief. "Believe it or not, I am trying to control my tongue."

Harry stood and looked down at her for a long moment. Then he held out his hand. "Come. I want to show you something."

◆—————◆

Harry held his breath as Maddy contemplated his outstretched hand. He didn't blame her for being bored. He knew he'd be bored if he were in her situation. But would she accept his invitation?

After what seemed like an eternity, though it was only a few seconds, he released his breath as she reached out her hand and levered herself to an upright position. She let the bare toes of her right foot barely graze the porch while she still gripped his hand.

"I can't walk very far," she cautioned him.

A surge of affection hit his heart as he realized how much trust she put in him. She was willing to go with him just because he'd asked.

He released her hand and put his arm around her waist, her sore foot between them, lifting her enough to guide her down the steps of the porch.

"We're not going far," Harry assured her. "Just to the stream." He tightened his hold around her waist. His heart beat faster, but it was because he was practically carrying her. Her proximity to him, the fresh-air smell of her hair, couldn't possibly be the cause.

Maddy stopped. "Wait." She placed her arm around his waist, making his breath catch tight in his throat. She gripped his belt and hopped forward on her good leg. "That's better."

Her grin, so close to his face as he leaned over her, brought a desire to kiss her lovely lips.

Harry forced himself to stand upright. This wouldn't do at all. It was a distraction, but there was no way he could fall for her. *Remember the overalls.* He was thankful she'd put on a dress now that she couldn't work with the llamas, but he had to admit she looked great even in those baggy overalls with a man's shirt tucked under them. Those overalls would make an appearance as soon as she could walk on her own again.

They took another three steps forward—her steps were really hops, since she kept her sore foot up under the hem of her skirt—before she stopped again to get her breath. Maybe this wasn't such a good idea. It was hard enough to think straight when he picked her up in his arms and carried her to the porch each morning and back into the cabin each evening. But she didn't put her arms around him then. Not like now.

Gratefully, he finally got her to a flat rock near the still-swollen stream and helped her sit down. If she wanted, she could scoot forward and place her ankle in the cold water. Better than putting it in a basin of cool water on the porch.

Harry sat on another rock nearby. "Now isn't this a little better?"

She smiled, her brown eyes a velvety chocolate color, and nodded an assent. Then she scooted forward, hitched up her skirt, and placed her ankle gingerly into the cold water. The tight lines around her mouth relaxed a little as the rushing water soothed the pain of her sprained ankle.

He watched Maddy relax but knew he couldn't let her keep her ankle in the water for too long. Just as the words to caution her started to his lips, she drew her leg out and gingerly dried it with the hem of her skirt. Then, pulling both feet under her skirt, she settled herself against the aspen trunk just behind the rock and said, "What did you want to show me?"

Harry cocked an eyebrow at her. But she just smiled. "Don't try to tell me there isn't anything you want to talk about." She glanced back at the little cabin she called home, sitting above the stream, well away from any floodwaters. "Trying to get me to talk was only a ruse. So spill it."

She knew him a lot better than he first thought. Of course, this last week and their close proximity day in and day out had brought about a knowledge of each other they couldn't ignore. And the more he knew about her, the more he wanted to spend more time with her.

He knew his grin was a little sheepish. He still wasn't sure how he felt about the letter he'd gotten yesterday. But he knew he wanted to share it with her and get her opinion about it. He reached his hand into his shirt pocket and pulled out the letter.

"This was waiting for me at the Goldminer when I got back last night. Mrs. Given put it on my bed so I would get it as soon as I got in."

Maddy rolled her eyes at his mention of Mrs. Given, the manager of the Goldminer. He knew what her opinion of Mrs. Given was, but he didn't agree. She'd always been kind to him but never the flirt Maddy and Aunt Susie had made veiled references to. Maddy had shared some stories involving Mrs. Given's special favors to the more disreputable men who sometimes stayed at the hotel. They were all hearsay, as far as he was concerned, with no real facts to back them up.

"Who's the letter from?"

Harry frowned down at the folded paper in his hand and sighed. He would read it out loud. Maybe it would help him get a better grip on what it said. "My boss, Mr. Graham."

Chapter 7

Maddy shifted a little on her rock, trying to find a better position. She was thankful Harry had walked her down here. Her sore ankle was numb from dunking it in the stream.

She glanced at Harry, who was still perusing his letter with a frown line between his eyes. What could his boss have said to upset him? It was the first time she'd seen him ruffled. She considered asking him but decided against it. Let him come to it in his own time. After all, he was the one who showed her the letter in the first place.

The silence lengthened. Maybe he regretted bringing it up in the first place. Maybe he'd gotten fired because he'd taken too much time off. Or maybe he was trying to decide which parts to read to her. Maddy forced herself to stop pleating her skirt. Why was she getting upset?

Harry cleared his throat and finally met her eyes. His hard mahogany eyes bored into her, and the frown lines remained in place. "Right." He cleared his throat again and looked at the paper in his hand. "I'll read you the relevant parts. 'Dear Mr. Collier—' "

"He calls you Mr. Collier?" Maddy's eyebrows soared into her hairline. "He's really that formal?"

"No, of course not." Harry's eyes now laughed at her. "It's just how he writes letters. You know, formal and all that."

Maddy's cheeks prickled with heat. She wasn't sure why Mr. Graham's formality surprised her. His letters to her were always addressed to Miss Williams. But Mr. Graham didn't know her from Eve. From what Harry had told her, Mr. Graham knew him a whole lot better. She shook her head and mumbled, "Sorry. Go on."

With a grin that Maddy took to be an acceptance of her apology for interrupting, he looked back at the paper he held so tightly. "Um. . . This first part is personal. Then he says, 'I want to inform you of a new position opening up that you might be interested in, especially as you are still pursuing Miss Williams and her llamas. The zoo has bought a ranch west of Arvada, and we need someone to manage it. We'd like to place our more feeble acquisitions there in order to bring them back to health so they can be exhibited later. It also has the capacity to house animals and birds while we build native habitats for them.' " He folded the paper and put it back in his pocket. "That's it."

"That's it?" Maddy's voice was shocked, even to her ears. "What exactly would the manager be expected to do? Sit there and watch others do the work, or do all the work himself? Where is the mention of a salary? Is there a place to live on that ranch?" She shook her head. She was sure she'd come up with more questions the more she thought about it.

But one look at Harry snapped her mouth shut. She was doing it again— allowing her mouth to spew without control.

Let the words of my mouth. She ducked her head down and rested it on her drawn-up knees.

And the meditation of my heart. Her arms tightened around her legs to steady them as she moved. Her ankle twinged. Rats! She'd have to put it back in the water soon.

Be acceptable in Your sight. She grimaced and refused to look at Harry. What must he think of her? Why, oh why, couldn't she remember to watch her words?

Finally, Maddy knew she had to break the silence. She took a deep breath, sat up, and squared her shoulders before looking directly into Harry's eyes. "I'm so sorry. I shouldn't have spouted off like that."

Harry grinned, halfheartedly it seemed to Maddy. It didn't last long, and he broke the tenuous connection between their eyes. "It's okay. I was expecting something like that from you."

Maddy dropped her legs flat on the rock, sending a jolt of pain up her injured leg. She winced and began moving herself to the edge of the rock. Time to put that ankle back in the water. Did he really think that badly of her? Chagrin roiled in her stomach, and she bit back a groan.

Gingerly lowering her leg into the water, she tried to relax. But every muscle in her body seemed to have tensed up in anticipation of the cold. Too bad! Her ankle needed this. She gritted her teeth and began to count the seconds before she could take her leg out of the water.

Harry slid over to her rock, placing himself at her back. As if reading her mind, he placed his hands gently on her shoulders and began to knead her tight muscles. Oh, it felt so good! She wished he would go on working out the knots in her shoulders, but he dropped his hands way too soon for her liking.

"You'd better get that leg out of the water." Harry's voice held a hint of amusement. "Then we can talk about what Mr. Graham didn't say in his letter."

Maddy pulled her leg up and wiped it down with the hem of her dress. But she couldn't move back to her former position because Harry still shared her rock. What was he doing? Her heart banged so hard against her ribs at his closeness that she was sure he could see it.

However, it didn't seem to affect him. He helped her back against the tree, then squeezed in beside her. "You don't mind, do you? It's easier to talk over the stream noise this way."

She couldn't speak, so she just shook her head. She hoped her heart would settle down soon. He was sitting so close, surely he could feel it against his arm.

"First of all"—Harry took her hand, asking permission with his raised eyebrows—"I've seen this ranch and knew the zoo was pursuing the ideas of its use mentioned in the letter." He took a deep breath.

Maybe their proximity to one another was affecting him. Maddy eyed him closely, but he looked composed enough.

"The duties of a manager include caring for all the animals that are placed there. Plus overlooking the kinds of habitat they need at the zoo and supervising the workers there. With my training as a zoologist, it's perfect."

"But would you like that kind of hands-on care of the animals?" Maddy knew he was good with the llamas, but as the manager of such a facility, he would be expected to care for all sorts of animals. She wasn't sure what his training in zoology involved.

He grinned. "You bet! My father raises beef cattle in Texas. Longhorns included. And they can be mighty temperamental."

❖─────❖

Maddy's eyebrows rose and her eyes grew wide. "Longhorns?" Her voice squeaked. "Have you ever gotten caught on one of those horns?"

Harry patted the top of Maddy's hand nestled in his. He liked the way it fit—as if it were made for his. "Nope. Believe me, when one of those animals lowers its head, I know to run for cover. Pronto!"

"Pronto?" She gave it the Spanish pronunciation while his had been in his heaviest Texas accent.

"It means—"

She waved her free hand at him, like she was batting away his words. "I know what it means! I was just making sure we were talking about the same thing." She grinned cheekily at him.

Of course! She probably knew Spanish a whole lot better than he did. He only had the occasional phrase. He remembered one of their conversations when she told him about her parents being missionaries. She'd lived in a Spanish-speaking country ever since she was born.

Sobering, she asked, "Is this what you want? To run a ranch adjunct to the zoo?"

"It's better than a desk job like I've got now." Her face was easier to read than a book at times. This was one of those times. He grinned. "Yes. I took the job at the zoo thinking it would be more hands-on than it is. Mr. Graham knew that, but there isn't room for keeping animals we receive without having an environment ready for them.

"Oh, the job still requires me to spend time at a desk most days, but I also get to take care of the animals. That's the reason I've enjoyed coming up here to see the llamas. To talk you into—" He broke off and tried to control his facial muscles. Idiot!

But Maddy finished his sentence. "Sending my llamas to the zoo."

Whoa! Maybe he was finally getting through to her and she could see herself loaning some of the younger animals to them. Especially now that she'd seen him interacting with them.

"Well, since we now have the land and the ranch, they would be much closer to the zoo there. It wouldn't be so much of a change in their environment."

She hesitated. "No, not too much of a change." Her tone was grudging and she shook her head. "Not that getting this ranch changes anything about my llamas." She started to ease her hand from his grasp.

He tightened his hold. "Maddy." He stopped. He hadn't expected to sound like a whiny child. He took a steadying breath and tried again. "Maddy. What I meant to say was that *I* will be much closer now. And there's plenty of land with the ranch. I can provide you with homegrown hay."

Eying him with those deep chocolate-brown eyes—he could almost drown in that chocolate—she finally gave him a quick nod. Agreeing with him? He resolved to make good on his promise of hay for her llamas whether he got the job or not.

He changed direction. "So, do you think I should pursue the job?"

She watched the water as it rushed past their rock. Had she heard him? Should he repeat the question? He didn't know why it was so important to him to have her answer, but he found himself holding his breath in anticipation.

Then she gave another slight nod. "Tell me more about your father's ranch." She pulled her hand out of his. "But on the porch. Not here."

Chapter 8

"Look what I brought you." Aunt Susie puffed her way up the three steps to Maddy's porch, waving two letters in the air.

If Maddy's leg were better, she'd have grabbed them out of her elderly friend's hand by now. But it wasn't, so she waited until Aunt Susie dumped them in her lap and situated herself in the chair Harry usually sat in when he finished the chores with the llamas.

"Thanks. You didn't have to go to town before coming out here." Maddy eyed Aunt Susie with concern. "Did you walk all the way?"

Aunt Susie rested her head on the back of the chair, her hand on her heaving chest, and shook her head. "No, I rode Charlie."

"Good." Maddy looked at the paddock. Aunt Susie's horse, almost as old as his mistress, basked under the ministrations of Harry. "Still. You didn't have to—"

Aunt Susie's hands made a shooing motion at Maddy, cutting her off. "Of course I did. I needed groceries, so while I was checking my mail, I had Mrs. Spencer give me yours." She grimaced. "She acted as though I had asked her to break the law, but in the end I won. I wonder why she's always so grumpy."

Sheer orneriness, Maddy thought, but she kept her mouth shut. Picking up the envelopes, she saw that her parents had finally written her. It was a thin envelope. Probably only one page. A little unusual. Their letters were usually full of news about their work in Peru or a lengthy condemnation of their daughter. She sighed and looked at the other letter. No surprise there. It was from Mr. Graham, Harry's boss at the zoo.

Since Harry had read his letter from Mr. Graham out loud three days ago, she suspected she knew her letter's contents. She opened it first and skimmed it before reading it aloud to Aunt Susie.

Dear Miss Williams,

I have heard from young Mr. Collier that he told you of the contents of my letter to him. He mentioned you had some valid questions, so I am writing to answer your concerns.

The zoo board has approved our buying a ranch nestled in the foothills west of Arvada. We plan to grow hay and other crops so we can feed the animals both at the zoo and the ranch. It is our hope to have enough to sell to other ranchers. Mr. Collier has told me that you don't have enough land to provide for your own animals. So we would like to put you at the top of the list of ranchers needing extra supplies. You can let either Mr. Collier or myself know if you agree to this.

We also plan to house all our newest acquisitions at the ranch to get them acclimated to our environment before moving them to an exhibit at the zoo. Of course this is all for long-term planning, as the zoo is only two years old and we haven't that many animals yet.

The reason we would like Mr. Collier to take the management of the ranch is because of his childhood experience of helping his father on their ranch and because he is highly qualified with his college training in zoology. We would like to have the loan of some or all of your llamas as our first animals at the ranch and later at the zoo. Mr. Collier is fully informed of the details that arrangement entails.

Finally, I was sorry to hear about your accident. It is my prayer that you are healing quickly while taking advantage of the skills Mr. Collier possesses. He has my full authorization to stay in Eldora as long as you need him.

Most sincerely,
Alexander Graham

Silence greeted the end of Maddy's reading, and she looked over at Aunt Susie. "Well?"

"Well what, child? Has anything changed since the last time we talked?"

"No." Maddy shook her head. She had told Aunt Susie about the ranch and Harry's interest in it two days ago. And she knew that while Aunt Susie liked Mr. Graham's proposal, she fully supported Maddy's intentions of keeping her animals where they were. "I wondered if Mr. Graham's letter"—she held up the page she still held—"changed your advice in the matter."

Maddy waited while Aunt Susie thought it over. She knew Harry had meant well when he mentioned her concerns to his boss, but she couldn't help her resentment that he had done so without telling her.

Finally, Aunt Susie shifted in her chair and spoke. "Not if your resolve is still the same."

Maddy's frustration rose, tightening her vocal chords and squeezing tears from her eyes. She batted them away. "That's the problem. I keep thinking I'm being selfish. But every time I try to tell Harry how I feel about loaning them any of my llamas, I can't. Or I say too much of the wrong thing and end up pay-ing the consequences."

Maddy lifted her injured foot and ankle out of the now tepid water in the bucket at her feet and reached for the towel on the porch floor beside it. Harry had filled the bucket earlier with very hot water before heading out to do the chores. When he came in, he'd fill it with cold water from the stream. This method of soaking had helped the swelling, but the bruises were multicolored and plentiful. This particular consequence of letting her mouth run away she wouldn't be forgetting soon.

Aunt Susie grinned, and the mischievous gleam in her eyes sparkled. "I, for one, am still finding laughter in your 'consequences.'"

Maddy glared at her but not for long. Her lips quirked and she let out a chuckle. "Yes, I can see the funny side of it. And Harry certainly sees it. I'm sure he laughs every time he fills this bucket." She pulled the bucket to one side and gingerly set her bruised leg on the footstool that Harry had thoughtfully put behind it.

Aunt Susie reached out and plucked the other envelope from Maddy's lap. "You have another letter here you'd better read. Don't you want to know what your parents think of Harry? You did tell them, right?"

"Not really, no. I told them a man from the zoo had come to see me. I'm hoping they've included lots of news, not a diatribe about my choice of friends." Maddy took the letter from Aunt Susie and tore open the envelope. "Want me to read it to you?"

"Only if you want me to hear it." Aunt Susie's voice was gentler than usual.

Maddy skimmed this letter also and winced. "There are no secrets between us, Aunt Susie. Maybe it won't hurt as much if I share it with you outright." It was worth a try anyway.

Dear Magdalene,

We are writing immediately after receiving a letter from Mrs. Spencer at the general store in Eldora, telling us of your behavior with a young man. As usual, you are impulsive and eager to follow every whim. We despair of your ever learning how to comport yourself as a Christian should.

We have never approved of your chosen means of living and working a man's job. We have long regretted allowing you to take Betta and Arturo home with you. And now Mrs. Spencer tells us of the Denver Zoo's proposal to take your animals. We believe this is the means God is using to take you out of your disgraceful lifestyle. Our prayer is that you will have already given over all the animals, including Betta.

Maddy stopped reading, noting that all was underlined three times in heavy black lines. Indignation engulfed her whole body, stiffening her limbs and tightening her voice. How did Mrs. Spencer dare to complain of her behavior when she was no better than Mrs. Given at the hotel? She forced a swallow past the lump in her throat before reading the rest of the letter.

As for Mr. Harrison Collier, stay away from him. He sounds like the devil, trying to worm his way into your good graces with flattery and other charming ways. Another Enrique, in our opinion. After all, Satan loves to appear as an angel of light. You don't seem to know if Mr. Collier is a Christian. This is something you should have established from his first stepping on your land.

If we hear either that you have turned down Mr. Graham's proposal or that you are seeing more of Mr. Collier, we may have to come home to take care of these matters ourselves.

Your loving parents,
Maude and Clarence Williams

Loving parents? Harry bit back a snort that threatened to break into the silence that followed Maddy's reading. If that letter was loving. . .Harry failed to imagine how the Williams would rate his relationship with his parents. They expected their children to toe the line, but never, ever had he heard his parents speak to any of their five children the way Maddy's parents did to her.

He sat down hard on the top step, forgetting he'd not announced his presence to the ladies engrossed in the letter Maddy read. But one glance at Maddy assured Harry his presence still hadn't registered. Tears streamed down her cheeks, even with her eyes scrunched tight against them. He couldn't begin to imagine the heart pain she must have endured over the years. No wonder she'd held him off at arm's length. She had had no example of true loving.

His heart ached for her, and he longed to take her into his arms and tell her how much he loved her. No matter that she was making a living in a man's world. No matter that she dressed like a man when she did the chores. No matter what she said, unguarded and straightforward.

Reaching out, he put his hand on Maddy's knee. Aunt Susie did the same from the other side. Maddy's eyes opened wide in surprise. And then her tears fell faster than ever. She laid her hands on top of theirs, accepting their unspoken support in the gesture.

Finally, she broke the silence. "Thank you both." Her voice cracked. Then she looked directly into Harry's eyes. He felt her eyes bore into his soul. He wondered if she read what he hadn't been able to say until now. He held her gaze until she lowered her own to her hand covering his.

Her chuckle was wry. "Well, too bad Mother and Father aren't here, or I'd give them a piece of my mind right now. In spite of Psalm 19:14. Give up Betta? What are they thinking?"

"They obviously aren't thinking."

Harry's words made Maddy's eyebrows rise. He smiled. "I mean that."

She studied his face. "I do believe you do mean it." Then she sobered. "Did you hear what they said about you?"

He nodded and moved closer to her chair, scooting along the edge of the porch. His lips quirked into a mischievous grin, and he waggled his eyebrows up and down. "But the only opinion that means anything to me is yours. Who do you think I am?" He didn't even care that Aunt Susie was there, avidly and openly listening to every word.

Harry turned his hand upward and clasped Maddy's in his. When she didn't say anything, he leaned a little closer. "Well?"

Her cheeks turned a beautiful shade of rose, but she held his gaze. "Mother and Father haven't met you yet. So we can ignore what they write. But when they do meet you—and I don't believe you'll have to wait long for that—they won't be able to *not* love you as I do."

She loves me! Harry's heart soared.

"I mean"—she snatched her hand from his, her cheeks glowing like a fire—"um, I *meant*, I love you like I love Aunt Susie. Or. . .no, not really." She covered her burning face with her hands. "There I go again! My mouth." She moaned. "My stupid mouth."

Harry's heart plummeted to his toes. She loved him, he didn't doubt that. But how did she love him? Like a family member? As a friend? Or as a trusted work partner?

Could he ever hope she'd love him enough to marry him?

Aunt Susie burst out laughing. Tears streamed down her face, and she grasped her middle, trying to control her giggles.

Harry and Maddy stared at her.

That only made Aunt Susie giggle harder. What on earth was so funny? Harry couldn't grasp how he'd gone from being appalled at the words Maddy's parents had written to wanting to laugh with Aunt Susie for the pure pleasure of laughing. He'd heard of contagious laughter but until now hadn't really believed in it.

Maddy turned her gaze to him, but he could only shrug and smile weakly.

Somehow he needed to find the words to tell her he needed to leave. To go back to Denver. Decide whether he wanted the job at the ranch without her at his side. She was doing a little better in that she could put a little weight on her injured ankle. She wouldn't be able to do all the chores he'd been doing, but she could do the basics until he got back. Maybe Aunt Susie would stay with Maddy until she could get around on her own. Harry didn't think he would be gone long, maybe a day or two.

Aunt Susie's laughter finally died away in a huge hiccup, and she leaned back in her chair, still gasping for air. Maddy stared at her friend, her hand over her heart. "Are you all right, Aunt Susie?" She'd asked the same question several times, but this time Harry heard it. So did Aunt Susie.

She patted Maddy's hand. "Yes. . .dear girl." She took another deep, steadying breath. "But the looks on both your faces"—she motioned to Harry—"were priceless." She chuckled. "I've never heard such a garbled declaration of. . .love."

Harry pushed himself off the porch, planting his feet on the ground below. Turning to face the ladies on the porch, he tried to keep from showing his heart. "I must go." He smiled and gave them a wave of his hand. "I should be back in a couple of days."

Chapter 9

M addy stood, ignoring the pain in her ankle, and watched Harry practically run down the drive to the road. She couldn't blame him, not after hearing—how much of it had he heard?—that awful letter from her parents. If she'd known it would be that bad, she never would have read it aloud for anyone to hear, let alone Harry.

In spite of the pain of putting a little weight on her ankle, she kept standing until Harry disappeared in the direction of town. Then she sank back down to her chair, but she didn't elevate her ankle again. She leaned over and picked up the letter that had fallen to the porch floor.

Where was he going? Probably home. She wouldn't blame him after hearing what her parents thought of him. She bit back a snort. Satan, indeed.

Maddy pushed the letter, and hopefully the unloving thoughts it aroused in her, into her pocket. She would see if the adage "out of sight out of mind" was true. She didn't expect to see Harry ever again.

She grabbed the bodice of her dress as her heart wrenched. Maybe if he stayed out of sight long enough, she would forget him. But everywhere she looked, she was reminded of him. Reminded of his love for animals and the special care he gave her llamas. Reminded of his strong arms, so willing to carry her out to the porch each morning and back into the cabin each evening. Reminded of his cheerful whistling as he went about his work, even when it included the womanly chores of cooking meals.

Maddy startled when a black nose nudged her hands. Betta nuzzled in closer. Harry must have left the gate to the paddock unlocked. She put her hands on the arms of her chair, preparatory to standing. She'd have to check the gate and return Betta to captivity before the rest of the llamas followed her into freedom.

"Stay down." Aunt Susie's voice was firm. At least her laughter was under control again. Maddy had never heard anything quite like it, and it unnerved her a little.

Maddy stood, gingerly putting weight on her sore foot. "I was just going to put Betta back and make sure the gate is secure. You stay where you are."

But Aunt Susie ignored her, chirruping to Betta to follow her. Betta gave Maddy a questioning look and then followed Aunt Susie. Thank goodness for that.

Truth to tell, she wasn't sure she'd be able to walk as far as the corral. And she wondered how on earth she would get the chores done now that Harry had left her in the lurch.

Well, not really in the lurch, Maddy's heart amended. Sure felt like it though, no matter how her heart wanted to convince her otherwise.

She'd have to hire a boy to take care of the llamas, fetch water from the stream for her and the animals, and do other little chores. Surely there was someone in Eldora to fill her need for help. At least until her ankle healed.

Aunt Susie walked back to the porch. But instead of climbing the stairs, she walked over to stand in front of Maddy. "The gate wasn't latching. I wonder if Harry noticed and if he'll bring back a part so he can fix it."

Maddy shook her head. "He's not coming back." She didn't think her heart could sink much lower than the porch floor, but with her statement of truth she felt it plummet down between the boards. "I'll check with Mr. Spencer and see if he has what we need."

Aunt Susie gave her an odd look but didn't contradict her. She pointed at Arturo on a leading rein behind her. "I'm taking him to my place to get some things. I'll be back before supper." She turned to go.

"I'm perfectly fine by myself." She was, she told her doubts, hoping they would flee before her spoken word.

But Aunt Susie ignored her and walked toward her place without another word. Maddy shrugged. She suspected her inner doubts listened about as well as Aunt Susie.

Maddy put her head back and closed her eyes, trying to put the letter from her parents, Harry's reaction to her mouth's betrayal of her thoughts, and Aunt Susie's uncontrolled laughter out of her mind. But she couldn't. The longer she sat there, the more her thoughts taunted her.

The letter from her parents was the worst she'd ever received from them. She knew they didn't like her chosen profession. But they had sent her home so she couldn't be an embarrassment to them by marrying a "native." No matter that he was one of their strongest believers. She knew they rarely approved of anyone she befriended, especially men. So why had she told them about Harry, even as an afterthought?

And to think she'd fallen for Harry. And practically told him so too. She groaned. No wonder he ran away. He wouldn't be back. She was sure of that. His love—if she could call it that—came with conditions, just like her parents'. He didn't like her being a "rancheress"—a word she'd made up when she decided to raise her own herd of llamas as a means to support herself while helping others. He didn't like the way she dressed when working the ranch. And he didn't like her running supplies up to the miners every couple of weeks by herself.

Her cheeks burned with the fire of embarrassment. How had she ever deceived herself into thinking he returned her affection? Just because he felt obligated to help her out when she was injured didn't mean he was doing it out of love. No, once he got back to Denver, he'd never be back for her. He would know he was well out of the situation. The letter from Mr. Graham today would be the last she received from the zoo.

Maddy finally dozed off. She dreamed that she watched Betta nose the latch on the gate to the corral until it let go. Betta, with her eye on Maddy a short distance away, eased herself out of the corral and headed down the approach to the cabin toward the road and disappeared just as Harry had done a few hours before.

She jerked awake when a train whistle sounded from across the valley. It was headed down the mountain. With the dream still vivid in her mind, she stood, stretched, and gazed into the corral. She limped down the stairs, trying to count the llamas that were visible to her. Though her ankle protested, she could at least put a little weight on it, but it wouldn't let her move quickly as the panic rose in her chest.

Her breath coming in short puffs, she finally reached the gate. She knew as soon as she saw the unlatched gate.

Betta was gone.

✦•——•✦

Five days later, Harry stepped off the train at the Eldora depot and took in a deep breath of rain-sharpened air. So refreshing. Anticipation of seeing Maddy rose in his chest, swelling his lungs.

He had hoped he could take care of business and be back within a couple of days, but to his disappointment, he'd been held up. But now that all the red tape had been worked through and the papers to the ranch signed, he could have something solid to offer Maddy.

"Mr. Collier."

Harry turned to see Mr. Spencer trotting along the depot platform. "Hello, Mr. Spencer. It's good to see you again."

Mr. Spencer shook Harry's outstretched hand and tried to get his breath back. "Glad I caught you. We have something of yours we thought you'd like to take with you. That is, if you're going out to Miss Williams's place."

Puzzled, Harry turned to where Mr. Spencer pointed. In a small paddock,

Betta stood facing him, humming loudly enough for everyone in the train yard to hear.

"Betta!" Harry sprinted down the stairs and over to the paddock. "How? What?" Words failed him. Had she been here all the time he'd been gone? Did Maddy know? If not, she'd be frantic. He reached up and patted Betta's neck.

"She came into the depot just as the train to Boulder was pulling out the day you left. Couldn't have missed you by more than three minutes. But it was too late to stop the train. So we put her here."

"What about Maddy? Didn't you let her know?"

"Um, no." Mr. Spencer shifted his weight from one leg to another. "The missus said it would be a waste of time to go out to her ranch to let her know. Especially as she left soon after you did."

Harry, his hand on Betta's neck, knew the shock of Mr. Spencer's statement showed. "What. . .what are you talking about? Maddy wasn't going anywhere. She can hardly walk on that ankle of hers."

Mr. Spencer was decidedly uncomfortable under Harry's scrutiny. He shrugged but wouldn't meet Harry's gaze. "I don't know about that. The missus said she was shamming the pain in order to keep you waiting hand and foot on her. In fact, it was the missus who told me she'd left. Heard all about it from the boy who's been tending the animals, she did."

Harry remembered some of Mrs. Spencer's comments when he stopped in to get medical supplies for Maddy's ankle and wondered that Mr. Spencer hadn't seen through his wife's dislike of everything about Maddy. He shook his head. Mrs. Spencer had obviously lied to her husband, and it wasn't his place to question Mr. Spencer's gullibility. At least not right now. He needed to get to Maddy and settle her fears first.

Turning away from the stationmaster, Harry searched for the gate. Finding it, he strode to it, Betta following him on her side of the fence. He didn't need a rope to tie to her halter as a leading rein. She stayed as close as she could without stepping on the back of his foot. He didn't take the time to secure a room at the hotel, knowing that Maddy would be anxious about Betta.

It probably had never occurred to Maddy that Betta would follow him into town. And if she didn't have a reason to come to town herself—or send Aunt Susie—she couldn't know that Betta was safe. He shuddered to think of the dark days Maddy had had to endure, all because of him. He'd wanted to have everything in place and just right—his plans for the future—before coming to Maddy to declare his love. With Betta gone, he was sure she believed him a thief and wouldn't want to see him.

Harry's mind went into his quick-thinking mode. He needed to come up with a plan to return Betta to Maddy without turning her against him. He shook his head, trying to clear it. He thought about the ring in his pocket—the ring he hoped Maddy would accept as a token of his love and desire to make her his wife. Could he attach it somewhere on Betta where she would see it and wonder? Could he send Betta without him down the path to Maddy's house?

Would she go alone?

By the way she was following him so close, he wasn't sure.

Was there a way to get to Maddy's house without her seeing him? He wondered if the spring runoff had slowed enough to allow him to cross the stream without getting his feet wet. He hadn't been paying attention to the stream when he rode into Eldora on the train.

Harry stopped and listened. When he'd left five days ago, he could easily hear the stream from anywhere in the valley. But now all he heard was the chirping of birds and small animals, a breeze rattling the aspen leaves. . .and a faint roar in the distance. That was the stream.

"Come, Betta," he urged. He headed across the valley out of sight of Maddy's cabin. The noise of the stream muffled any sounds he and Betta made as they wound their way alongside the stream to the back of Maddy's house. It was definitely down from a week ago, and they crossed the stream west of the cabin.

Harry stopped near the rock where Maddy had put her ankle in the water. He reached into his jacket pocket and pulled out the diamond and sapphire ring he'd bought, hoping that Maddy would say yes to his marriage proposal. Maybe if Betta came to her with the ring, she'd be quicker to say yes. At least he hoped so.

He secured the ring to Betta's halter strap, praying Maddy would see it. Then he whispered instructions into the llama's ear before slapping her rump to send her on her way.

Chapter 10

Maddy limped the last few steps from the paddock to her cabin porch before she allowed herself to sink down into her chair and lay her head against the back. The last few days had been some of the most difficult of her life. In some ways worse than when her parents had sent her home to the States. Even then, there was the silver lining—no matter how much they regretted allowing her to take Arturo and Betta with her, they had still let her.

Now she couldn't even see a silver lining. Yesterday she'd sent Aunt Susie home. She wanted to be alone. Might as well get used to it. After all, she'd been successful in sending Harry away. For good. And she'd thought he was different from all the others.

She shifted her weight in the chair. She should get up and get the two buckets she now used to soak her ankle in hot and freezing cold water. She'd had Aunt Susie pick up some Epsom salts from Spencers, which had allowed the swelling to go down enough to hobble to the barn to take care of the llamas.

A rustling in the grass at the side of the cabin opened her eyes wide. All she needed with an injured foot was a snake. Praying silently for the snake to disappear—but wouldn't that be worse, not knowing where it was?—she looked around the porch for something with which to fend it off. Leaning against the support beam on the other side of the steps was her walking stick—one she had fashioned out of a cottonwood branch she found down by the stream.

Rising gingerly from her chair, she tried to move soundlessly the few steps required to reach the stout stick. But instead of startling the snake into silence, she seemed to be making it more frantic to reach her perch above the ground. The rustling grew louder. But now she heard another sound.

What was it? If she didn't know better, she might think it was a llama. The new sound was like their hoofbeats. She cast a quick glance at the paddock. But all her llamas were in there. Except Betta, of course. The traitorous girl!

Five days ago, Maddy cried when Betta followed Harry into Eldora. She was past tears now, but she still couldn't forgive him for beguiling her first and best friend from the herd. He was probably sitting in his comfortable office at the zoo right now, planning how to lure the rest of her animals away from her.

Harry had told her he'd be back in a couple of days. Well, nearly a week later, her eyes were opened to his true character. Her parents were right. She couldn't trust any man. Not even those with warm mahogany-colored eyes.

The rustling had stopped. But Maddy waited, holding her breath. If it was a snake, maybe it had found a warm spot in the sun. She must have imagined the hoofbeats.

Slowly, she lowered her arm, but she kept a firm grip on the stick. Maddy wasn't in the mood to care who or what she ripped into, which was why she'd sent Aunt Susie to Eldora to pick up some supplies the day before. She didn't want Mount Maddy to spew all over the general store owner or his busybody wife. How had the woman dared to write Maddy's parents?

Easing herself another step closer to her chair, Maddy hoped the snake would lose interest. But no sooner had she sat down than the rustling started to life again. When would this end?

The stealthy movements steadily moved closer. And closer. And—

Maddy squelched a scream when Betta's face eased around the cabin corner. "Betta!" Her treacherous heart leaped into her throat. Had Harry come with her?

Struggling to a stand, Maddy watched Betta come closer, until she stood right in front of her. Maddy threw her arms around Betta's neck, laughing and crying at the same time. "What are you doing here, Betta? I thought for sure you'd followed Harry." She ran her hand over Betta's roughened coat. Harry would have taken better care of Betta than her rough fur indicated. She knew that. No matter that he'd obviously spurned her, he would never let an animal like Betta go a day without grooming. Yet. . .

Her fingers caught in a tangle of Betta's fur. What was this? Talking in an undertone full of endearments, Maddy tried to loosen the knot. But something hard kept getting in the way.

"Oh Betta. Betta. I thought I'd never see you again. I thought you'd followed that traitorous Harry, and that he got you onto that train."

Her fingers fumbled again around whatever was holding Betta's fur in a knot. "But how did you get into this state of. . .um. . ."

Maddy's voice trailed off as she saw a flash of blue next to her right index finger on Betta's neck. What on earth? She fumbled in the clump of fur, and finally a silver ring tumbled into her hand. Was that a sapphire? Her favorite semiprecious stone. And a diamond.

She stared at the beautiful ring. How had it gotten tangled into Betta's fur? These were polished jewels, not some stray find in one of the mines.

"Harry?"

Why had his name jumped to her lips? Betta could have picked it up from anyone if she'd truly been wandering the mountains looking for Harry. Maddy had no doubt he'd been the one Betta had followed. But what could possibly make Maddy think he was responsible for the ring in Betta's fur?

Betta turned away from Maddy, humming.

It had to be Harry. She never hummed for anyone else.

Maddy started down the stairs after Betta, her hand still closed around the ring. "Harry?" Just wait until she had that traitor in front of her! She'd give him a piece of her mind.

Then she stomped off the bottom step with her right foot. Pain shot up her leg as she crumpled to the ground. Before she could cry out, she felt strong arms around her, lifting her up.

"Maddy." His voice was tender, kind, warm—loving.

Every emotion stirred a similar one deep within her heart, and she buried her face in his chest. Tears streamed down her cheeks and soaked into his flannel shirt. Taking in a shuddering breath, she smelled his familiar woodsy cologne.

"Oh Harry. I thought you'd forgotten me, that you didn't want to come back."

His arms tightened around her. "How could I forget you in five days?" He took a deep breath. "Every day that kept me from coming back, I thought of you. Everything I did, I thought of you."

He pushed her back from him. His hold on her shoulders was firm, and he looked at her, adoration shining in his eyes. "Maddy, I love you. I want to spend every day of the rest of my life with you."

He loved her! Every word of condemnation she had thought of in the past few days melted away in the surge of joy that accompanied his words of love.

For the first time in her life, Maddy had no words.

❖━━━━•━━•❖

Harry carried Maddy up the steps to the porch and settled her in her chair. Then he went inside to get some warm water for soaking her reinjured ankle. His heart banged against his ribs, but he knew it was anticipation of the days, months, years that she, in her silence, had granted him to love her and cherish her.

He stirred in the Epsom salts he found sitting next to the pail before taking it out to the porch. After getting her comfortable, he sank into the chair beside her and reached for her hand.

But it was clasped tightly over something she held.

He put his hand over her tightly clasped hand in her lap. "Want to show me what you found?"

She gazed at his soul through her eyes. He felt as though he would drown in the deep brown velvet.

"Did you mean it? You really, truly love me?" Her voice was soft, even a little scratchy, as though she hadn't spoken in a very long time.

He gazed back at her, matching her intensity. "I really, truly love *you*."

"But why?" She grimaced. "My parents don't, even though they say they do."

He sent a quick prayer up for help. He'd known they would have to cross this bridge, and he prayed for the right words. "I don't know your parents, and I don't know why they don't seem to love you. But I do know that *I* love you. And nothing will ever change that."

"Not my overalls? Not my desire to continue working with my llamas? Not even the words I can't seem to control?" Her eyes reflected the incredulity in her voice.

He shook his head. "Not what you choose to wear. Not what you choose to do. Nor what you choose to say at any time will change my love for you."

She looked down at his hand covering hers. "You say that now, but how do you know that won't change in the future?"

He reached with his free hand and tucked a finger under her chin, pulling it up until she met his gaze. He knew deep down in his gut that his reply meant everything to his future with her. "I don't know that in myself I could guarantee that it wouldn't change in the future. But I believe with all my heart that God has given me this love for you, and I'm going to do all I can, with His help, to show you what true love is for the rest of your life."

She gazed at him for what seemed like an eternity, and then she nodded. Just once. But it was enough. He let go of her chin as her hand under his in her lap stirred.

Slowly she released her grip on the ring, allowing it to rest in the palm of her hand. But still she said nothing.

"What do you think? Do you like it?"

"It's so beautiful." She took a deep breath. "How did you know that sapphire is my favorite stone?"

Harry's breath released in a whoosh. "I didn't know. But it is mine. And I wanted you to be able to wear this ring forever, as a symbol of my love for you."

She gazed at it a little longer before looking up. A mischievous light twinkled in her eyes now. "Don't you think you'd better put it on my finger then?"

He knelt on the floor beside her as he took the ring and held it above her left hand. "Will you marry me, sweetheart?"

Tears leaked out of the corners of her eyes as she gazed at him. "Oh yes! I love you, Harry, my dearest."

He slipped the ring onto her finger, and their lips met in a sweet kiss of surrender to one another.

Epilogue

A year later

Maddy sat on the spacious front porch of the ranch house, watching Harry tend to the new family of elephants they had welcomed a week before. His faithful shadow, Betta, followed him. They hadn't been sure how the elephants would react to the llamas, but they seemed to take Betta in stride and were now using their long trunks to smell her thick wool. It would soon be time to sheer her wool. The days were growing long and warm. Too warm for a thick coat of wool.

Maddy's fingers itched to get deep into the wool, cleaning it, then brushing it into long strands so she could feed it into her spinning wheel to make the yarn. Then she'd be busy knitting jackets, caps, and mittens all winter. Most of the items she knitted she would sell at the zoo's store, but the rest would keep Harry and her warm, especially on the cooler mornings. Plus she had plans for some extra pieces of clothing. Maybe a blanket or two as well.

Placing her hand on her belly, she thrilled with the news she had to share with Harry before they headed for her cabin and the other llamas in Eldora. She watched Harry double-check the lock on the gate to the elephants' pen, and with Betta still following, he strode to the house and sat in the chair next to hers.

With his special smile just for her, he reached to take her hand but stopped when he saw where her hand rested. Concern filled his eyes. "What's wrong? Are you well, sweetheart?"

She felt her smile widen. Oh how she loved this man! She took his hand, resting it on her belly with hers on top. "I've never felt better."

"Then why—" His eyes widened. "Are you. . .are we. . . ?"

She nodded in answer to his unspoken question.

"Wh–when?"

"In the spring. About the same time as Mrs. Elephant, if I'm figuring right."

Harry let out a whoop of joy as he stood, drawing her with him. Then he gathered her into his arms and kissed her deeply.

When she pulled away, he still held her close. She felt his heart racing beneath her cheek as it rested on his chest. If she'd known marriage would be so sweet, she might have fallen earlier. But then, it wouldn't be so sweet with any other man.

Harry pushed her away with his hands on her shoulders. "Does this mean we need to get your parents home? Or. . ." His voice trailed off, and uncertainty etched lines around his eyes.

Maddy shook her head. "No." Her answer was firm. "Maybe your mom, but the only one I really want is Aunt Susie."

His grin of relief made her put her hands behind his neck and pull him down to her for another deep kiss.

This time he pulled back first. "We'd better get going then. The train isn't going to wait on us to get there." He took her hand and pulled her into the house where their suitcases waited for them just inside the door. "Now that we have the right 'ammunition,' we should be able to coax Aunt Susie down the mountain for the winter and spring."

Maddy grinned in response and, after shutting and locking the door behind her, followed Harry to the waiting wagon. She couldn't wait to see what the summer had in store for them at the ranch in Eldora.

Marjorie Vawter is a full-time freelance editor and writer. She is the author of many published devotionals, several devotional books, articles, and book reviews, plus four novellas and several nonfiction books. As the recently "retired" assistant to the conference director for the Colorado and Greater Philadelphia Christian Writers Conferences, Marjorie has had the opportunity to work with publishers, editors, agents, and publicity directors, as well as other writers. An avid reader, she also judges for several prestigious awards in the inspirational marketplace. Mom to two adult children and a daughter-in-love and Gramma to two grand-children, Marjorie currently lives in the Denver, Colorado, metro-area with her husband, Roger, and cat, Sinatra. You may visit her at www.marjorievawter.com.

Zola's Cross-Country Adventure

by Mary Davis

Dedication

To my wonderful parents, Zola and Allen.

Chapter 1

July 27, 1903
Seattle, Washington

Zola Calkin sat in the Fergusons' parlor with her cousin Vivian Newland and several of their friends, both ladies and gentlemen.

"Listen to this." Zola ruffled the newspaper to get everyone's attention and read aloud from the *Seattle Post-Intelligencer*. " 'Dr. Horatio Nelson Jackson, esteemed surgeon, along with his chauffeur and mechanic, Sewall K. Crocker, completed the first transcontinental automobile trip on Sunday, July twenty-sixth. The trek took sixty-three days, twelve hours, and thirty minutes.' Isn't that something? How exciting it would be to go on an adventure like that."

Garfield Prescott, who had been a school chum of Zola's, stood with an elbow resting on the fireplace mantel. He took the pipe from his mouth. "You? Ladies are entirely unsuited to drive automobiles."

She straightened. "Ladies drive automobiles." Granted, not many, but a few daring ones did.

"Down the street and around the corner in town maybe, but any farther than that would be. . ."

Zola stood. "Would be what?"

"Foolish." Garfield replaced his pipe between his teeth with a clack.

The other men in the room added their bit remarks. "And dangerous."

"To everyone else."

"On the road and off."

"The boardwalks would no longer be safe."

A roar of male laughter erupted around the room.

She ignored them all except Garfield, their ringleader. "You think women incapable of such a trip?"

Garfield snickered. "Yes, I do."

Zola turned to the dozen gentlemen and ladies in the' room. "Who here thinks women are capable of making such a trip?" She held her own hand high.

Most looked away or at the ground. All except Garfield, who smirked at her, and Vivian, whose hand raised halfway up, then slipped back down to rest in her lap.

She couldn't believe this. Everyone thought women inept and feeble. "I'll prove to you a woman can do just what Dr. Jackson has done."

Garfield puffed out a plume of smoke. "You aren't suggesting that *you* are going to drive across the country, are you?"

Well, she hadn't been. Hadn't really thought about exactly what she was suggesting. She figured there must be some way to prove a woman could do the same as a man. Some adventurous woman in the world who had already accomplished something similar. "No. I'm not silly enough to say that I. . ."The men all stared hard at her as though daring her. ". . .by myself. . .would undertake such a momentous feat. Vivian will go with me. After all, Dr. Jackson didn't go alone. So why should I?"

"Me?" Vivian choked out.

Garfield lowered his head and shook it. "Not only have you never driven an automobile, but you don't even own one."

"I'll buy one. And you'll see. Next summer, I—" She gripped Vivian's arm and pulled her cousin to her feet. "*We* will drive from ocean to ocean."

Garfield let out a boisterous laugh. "You and Vivian? Vivian, who thinks electricity is going to blow up the world?"

Vivian straightened. "I do not. I was repeating what someone else said and was wondering if there was any truth to it."

"You two and how many men? You'll need someone to make repairs when you break down."

Zola squared her shoulders. "None. We'll fix the automobile ourselves."

Garfield and the other young men roared with laughter again.

Though the other three ladies in the room didn't laugh, they offered no support, only looks of sympathy, defeat, and that's-the-way-the-world-is. When women couldn't stand by other women, the road to climb would be hard indeed.

"Women are as capable as men." Zola held out her hand to Garfield. "Shall we make the same fifty-dollar pledge that Dr. Jackson made with his friends?"

"I wouldn't be a gentleman if I took your money. I have a better idea."He pointed at her with his pipe. "If you quit before making it from one coast to the other, you take out a full-page ad in the newspaper extolling the superiority of men."

Shrewd. "And when I make the trip, you do the same, lauding the abilities of ladies." Her hand still hung in the air between them.

He gripped it. "May your journey be short."

"May your words be eloquent." She folded the newspaper. "You better get started on that full-page discourse. You'll want to get those words just right." She wiggled her fingers in the air. "I'm off to buy an automobile. Let's go, Vivian." As she left the room, her flowing chiffon day dress fluttered around her.

Vivian trailed after Zola out the front door. "When I raised my hand, I was saying I thought women were capable, not that I was volunteering."

The young footman on duty snapped to attention. "Miss Calkin."

"My carriage, please."

"I didn't expect anyone to leave before luncheon was served. It will take a few minutes. You can wait inside where you'll be comfortable. I'll send word when it's ready."

"We'll wait here."

"Yes, miss." He ran off.

Once in the back of her carriage with her driver at the reins, Zola smoothed her hands across her lap. "This should be fun."

"Fun?" Vivian shifted in the seat to face Zola. "What were you thinking? You've dunked us in another pickle barrel now. Not only do we not know how to drive an automobile, but we know even less about repairing one."

"Don't worry. We have nine months to learn both."

A frown line creased between her cousin's eyebrows. "I *don't* want to do this."

"Really?"

"All right. A part of me wants to go on this grand adventure, but I don't think we can succeed. They're all going to laugh at us."

"Would you rather try and fail and have half of a grand adventure or have no adventure at all? Think about the exciting stories you could describe afterward. Or would you rather tell the story of simply finding a husband and having children?" Zola wanted to recount thrilling stories.

"What gentleman would want to marry a lady who would partake in such an unladylike activity?"

"Gentlemen who aren't stuck in the Dark Ages. Men will be lining up to ask for your hand. You'll have so many proposals, you'll have a hard time deciding whom to marry."

"Highly doubtful." Vivian caught her bottom lip between her teeth. "But it would be kind of fun to see how far we can get."

"How far? From coast to coast."

"So, what's your plan for making this happen?"

"Plan? Good question. First, we'll need to buy an automobile."

◆— · —◆

May 1, 1904
New York City

Allen Basart sat at his desk at the *East Coast Herald*, tapping away on his typewriter. Another society piece. The Garden Club's annual Festival of the Flowers planning meeting. Did anyone really care?

He'd written an article on the working conditions in factories. His editor said someone else was covering it. He wanted to write about several people getting ill after visiting the hospital. Someone else was covering it. The treatment of children in orphanages. Someone else was covering it.

He could write any one of those stories as good if not better. If his editor would only give him a chance.

Carl Ghetty poked his head out from his chief editor's office. "Allen, get in here."

Allen jumped to his feet and darted into his boss's office. "Yes, sir."

Mr. Ghetty had a handlebar mustache, fiery red hair, and a temper to go with it. "You ever drive one of those newfangled automobiles?"

"Yes, sir. Several times. I know a lot of people think they're a passing fad, but I hope not. They're a lot of fun."

"Good. Sit down." His boss settled in his chair behind the desk. "I have an assignment for you."

Allen sat. "A real news story?" This could be his big break.

Mr. Ghetty scrunched up his face. "Suuure."

This was what Allen had been waiting for. The chance to write a serious piece. "What is it? I'll do the paper proud."

"Two ladies from out west are going to attempt to repeat Dr. Horatio Nelson Jackson's historic trip last year from coast to coast, driving from New York City to Seattle."

"So?"

"You are going to be there alongside them every mile of the way."

He'd heard about the two foolish socialites. "I thought you said this was a real story. Ladies driving an automobile? A waste of time. That's not news."

"Real enough, and this *is* important. You won't be gone for very long. A day or two. I doubt those women will last even that long. A week at most."

"Give me some real news. A foreign dignitary. Or corruption in government. Not garden parties and what one snobbish family is serving at their son's tenth birthday party. And not foolhardy aristocrats who have something to prove."

"Do a good job on this story and you'll have proven to me you have what it takes to be a serious reporter."

Allen huffed out a breath. "All right." It wasn't like he had much of a choice if he wanted to keep his job. "When do they leave?"

"In the morning. We already have an automobile packed with all the supplies you'll need. Gear, food, everything. I want each failure of theirs recorded. Women need to see that automobile driving is a man's sport."

"So you anticipate they'll fail?"

"Of course. They're women."

"What if they don't? What if they actually complete the entire trip?"

"That could make for a good story too. In that case, you'll be gone for more than a week." Mr. Ghetty jabbed a finger in the air. "You can't help them. If they want to prove they can do this, then they can't have men helping them at every turn."

"And who's going to help me if I get stuck or break down?"

"Barney Cuttels. He'll be your photographer."

"Cuttels? Didn't you just hire him? He has no journalism experience."

"Hired him for this story, and he has his own camera. That's good enough for me." Mr. Ghetty stood. "A special event is being thrown tonight in honor of these daft ladies. Be there. Take Cuttels. Interview the flighty females, write it up—pictures, the whole works—and drop it off on my desk before you leave in the morning."

Allen stood. This was not going to be good. "Then you'll give me real news to cover?"

Mr. Ghetty came around his desk and slapped Allen on the shoulder. "Of course. Hurry up. You need to change. The dinner is a formal affair."

At the event, Allen and Cuttels waited their turn to speak to the two female motorists. Miss Zola Calkin wore a flowing peach-colored gown bedecked with feathers that gave her the appearance of floating. Miss Vivian Newland wore a blue satin gown. "Miss Calkin, Miss Newland, I'm Allen Basart from the *East Coast Herald*, and this is my photographer, Barney Cuttels. May we ask you a few questions?"

"Why, of course. We'd be happy to answer any questions you may have." Miss Calkin gave him a smile he suspected she'd used to charm and disarm many men.

He would *not* be swayed by it nor her twinkling hazel eyes. "Why are you undertaking such a treacherous journey?"

"To prove women are as capable as men. But I don't think it's all that treacherous. I'm sure we'll run into a trouble or two. We aren't fooling ourselves that the trip will be easy, but we are confident we'll make it."

A trouble or two? This lady had no idea what she was in for. His boss had been right. Within a few days, he'd be right back at his desk, working on a serious news piece.

Ghetty had given him a dossier on the two socialites who had never had to work a day in their lives. No way they would complete this trip. They'd be lucky to make it out of town. He actually felt sorry for them. They seemed like nice ladies and were going to become a laughingstock and the target of many jokes for years to come. Should he try to talk them out of this? No. That wasn't his job nor his business. "Is it true you'll be driving the same model of automobile that Dr. Horatio Nelson Jackson drove last year on his historic trip?"

"We will. A two-cylinder, twenty-horsepower Winton. We considered many different models of automobiles and drove several."

"Dr. Jackson named his automobile the *Vermont*. Did you name yours?"

"The *Atlantic*, because we intend to have the Atlantic meet the Pacific."

Cute, but it wasn't going to help them succeed. "Is it true that neither of you had driven an automobile before last summer?"

"It is true, but once you learn the basics, it's not so difficult. I think every woman should learn to drive."

He didn't doubt that, but he, for one, hoped most women were smart enough not to attempt it. Leave the driving to men. "Besides learning to drive, what did you do to prepare for this undertaking?"

"We've spent the past nine months preparing. Most recently we visited with Dr. Jackson and his lovely wife, Bertha. We acquired a great deal of knowledge about his trip and have learned much from it. We will take the same route between here and Chicago, but then we'll head north to Minneapolis and follow the Northern Pacific Railroad line west."

"Dr. Jackson drove from the West Coast to the East Coast. Why are you driving from east to west? Wouldn't it have been smarter to follow his route exactly so you would already know all the pitfalls and troubles?"

"That trip has already been done, but going from east to west hasn't. We won't be following his exact route. We are going to end in Washington State rather than California. Dr. Jackson proved that driving toward one's home, rather than away from it, had been a good choice. He said it was as if his heart was pulling him onward and toward his wife."

"Do you have someone special your heart will be pulling you home toward?" Why had he asked that? Whether the pretty socialite with an infectious smile and charming personality had a special fellow or not had no relevance to the story. On the other hand, it might give a nice human-interest slant if he needed it.

"Yes and no. If you're asking if I have a husband or beau, the answer is no."

That answer pleased him.

"But my heart will draw me forward by all the women, young ladies, and girls who will see that they are only confined by the limitations they allow others to bind them with."

Ah, a suffragette. "Dr. Jackson picked up a dog, Bud, along the way. Will you take a dog on your trip?"

"Of course. I wouldn't dream of leaving Lady Beatrice Goodings behind. Ladybug for short. She loves riding in automobiles and will make an excellent companion on the trip. I even had special goggles made for her."

"What kind of dog is she?"

"A white Pomeranian."

Several snickers rippled through the room.

That was a lot of name for such a little dog. One more thing for people to make fun of these ladies for.

Miss Calkin waggled her index finger in the air. "Never underestimate a small dog."

Allen pointed toward Barney Cuttels. "May we get a photograph of the two of you?"

"Of course. We want our trip well documented."

So did Allen, or rather his editor, but for a different reason than these ladies did.

"We'll be taking photographs ourselves all along our adventure."

No need to tell them now that he too would be documenting their trip the whole way. However long that was. They would find out soon enough that they would have tagalongs. A part of him looked forward to this trip as it could be interesting. Another part wished these refined ladies would reconsider rather than face humiliation.

Chapter 2

Day 1

Zola stood in front of the standing mirror in her hotel room. This would be one of the last few decent places she would lay her head for a while. She'd found the closest New York City hotel to the Atlantic Ocean as she could. Garfield had agreed that this counted as starting at the ocean without having to dip the automobile tires in the salty water, risking getting the vehicle stuck in the sand.

She picked up her start-of-the-trip hat. Not to be confused with her driving hat she would wear most days, her meeting-people-along-the-way hat, and her victory hat to wear as she crossed the finish line, waving to the cheering crowd. A lady couldn't be photographed in the same hat at the end of the race that she started in.

She settled the stylish wide-brimmed hat with flowers and feathers on her head. She pulled the two sides of the netting around on each side of her head, crossed them in front, and let the ends trail down her back. The hat went well with her cream-and-pink silk garden-party dress. She draped her matching velvet shawl around her shoulders. The spring morning would start out chilly. "Are you almost ready, Vivian?"

"Coming." Her cousin appeared in her blue lace dress, equally suitable for afternoon tea. "Do I look all right?"

"Picture perfect."

Vivian donned her hat and shawl.

Zola walked over to the bed. "Come on, Ladybug. It's time to go meet our fans."

The white Pomeranian pranced across the coverlet and leaped into her arms. "Good girl."

Ladybug licked Zola's chin. She had been well groomed and had black polka-dotted red bows on her head.

Vivian held out her eyewear. "Are you going to put on your goggles here or wait until we're in the automobile?"

"After we're out of town and have left all the observers behind. We may be going on an adventure, but we're going to look good doing it."

With a nod, Vivian tucked her goggles into her reticule.

Zola held out her free hand. "First, let's pray. We don't want to go anywhere without the Lord." She asked God for blessings on this endeavor.

Their other luggage had already been taken down earlier. They'd packed prudently, not including anything they didn't absolutely need. They headed downstairs.

Dr. Horatio and Bertha Jackson met them in the hotel lobby. Dr. Jackson stood in front of them. "You've chosen a great automobile, that Winton. Remember, don't think about how hard things are getting—keep your focus on the finish line and arriving home."

Zola nodded. "We will. We can't thank you enough for telling us your story and the pitfalls we might run into along the way."

"It still won't be easy."

"We know."

Mrs. Jackson took one of Zola's hands and one of Vivian's. "Women everywhere are counting on you. I know you two can do this."

"Thank you." It bolstered Zola's confidence having these two believe in them. She'd already wavered many times and thought of giving up before even starting. No standing down now.

As she stepped outside, she drew in the salt air. Circling seagulls screeched overhead.

Garfield Prescott met them at the Winton automobile. "You're really going to do this."

Zola gave a delicate laugh. "Why, of course. Why do you still doubt me?" Not that she hadn't doubted herself and the feasibility of this whole adventure, but he didn't need to know that.

He opened his mouth several times to apparently say something but settled for a shrug.

She would show him. "See you at the finish line."

He shook his head. "I doubt you'll make it that far, but I give you credit for not giving up before you start."

Zola stood with Vivian beside the *Atlantic*. A vibrant green banner on each side of the Winton had bold black letters that read SEATTLE OR BUST, and underneath WHERE THE ATLANTIC AND PACIFIC WILL MEET. With Ladybug in her arms and her cousin at her side, she posed while several cameras flashed, including that of the handsome reporter with sky-blue eyes and his photographer from the previous night.

Mr. Basart stepped forward. "Is this Lady Beatrice Goodings?"

"You remembered her full name. Yes, it is." She lifted Ladybug's paw to make her wave.

He pressed his lips together as though trying to contain a smile.

She knew people didn't think much of her little white Pomeranian at first sight, but Ladybug was a trouper. "Mr. Basart, will we be seeing you at the finish line?"

"Most definitely. If you make it that far."

"We will. We will indeed. Until then." She climbed in the right side of the open Winton behind the steering wheel, and Vivian got in the passenger seat. This horseless carriage had no top or glass windscreen.

Zola put Ladybug's red with black polka-dotted goggles on her to match her bows. It had been a challenge to get Ladybug to tolerate the eye protection. At first she pawed them off. With enough treats of cooked chicken, she became more obliging. And once she experienced the exhilaration of riding in the automobile, she didn't mind the goggles at all and seemed to look forward to them. They meant going for a ride.

She moved the Pomeranian over to Vivian's lap where the dog put her front feet on the dashboard, and her tongue lolled out. She was ready for this adventure.

Mr. Basart put his forearm on the Winton's door and leaned forward. "I'll see you a lot sooner than Seattle. My photographer and I will be trailing you the whole way. However far that is."

Had she heard right? "You're what?"

"Following you in a vehicle of our own, taking photographs and writing about your trip. But we've been instructed not to help you. Just observe and report."

"I wouldn't expect any assistance from you or anyone else. Vivian and I are quite capable of making this trip without you tagging along. Toodle-oo."

Zola cranked the engine, and it sputtered to life. As she pulled forward, she waved her hand over her head. "See you all on the other side of the country."

Once away from the crowd and tooling down the main street of New York City, Vivian turned around backward then faced forward again. "That reporter and dashing photographer are following us."

"Let them. I know what they want. They want to document our failure, but the joke will be on them, because they will be documenting our success."

The reporter and photographer were going to put a crimp in her style. She'd planned to stop before every town, no matter how small, and clean up before entering. That would leave all the wide-open spaces in between to get dirty and throw a fit if she needed to. She couldn't very well wear her dresses the whole way. Vivian and she had planned to wear trousers on the days no one was around.

But now someone would always be around.

At the edge of the city, Vivian dug out their motoring hats. "Do you want me to put yours on you now?"

Zola had the great plan of Vivian removing her fashionable hat and replacing it with the motoring one without stopping, to save a bit of time. Her schedule had them driving one hundred fifty miles today. Averaging twenty-five miles an hour, they would arrive in six hours or so.

She knew they would be making enough stops that eliminating as many as possible would help. "I fear we would look silly. Could you imagine if they took a photograph and what they would write about it? I'm fine. I'll drive without it until you take over at the wheel."

Five miles out of the city, the last of the crowds had been left behind. The road had changed from paved to packed dirt.

"I know. Take the wheel."

"What? Why?"

"So I can switch hats myself." If those men were indeed going to follow them, they would eventually see the unadorned piece of millinery.

Vivian grabbed the wheel.

Zola removed her flower-and-feather-bedecked hat and tucked it on the floor between them. She put on her goggles. After securing the functional headwear in place with hatpins, she lowered the netting over her face and tied the ends behind her. That would keep things from flying in her face. She put her hands back on the wheel. "Your turn."

Vivian glanced behind them, then faced front again. "I'll wait. They're still back there."

"I was afraid of that. I'd hoped they would stop at the edge of town and catch a train to the next town. Then they could take a picture of us whizzing by while we waved and kept going. This is going to be tedious if they watch us every inch of the way."

Vivian glanced back again. "I don't know. That photographer is kind of cute."

"It won't do us any good for you to be mooning over one of our tagalongs."

"What could it hurt?"

It could cause her cousin to get distracted, lose focus, decide that looking presentable for a man was more important than finishing the trip. "You realize he will eventually see you in your motoring hat, don't you?"

"But he doesn't need to see it just yet."

POP!

The front right tire wobbled on its rim. Zola braked to a stop.

The tagalong vehicle pulled up beside them. Mr. Basart, behind the steering tiller, leaned forward to look around Mr. Cuttels. "Is everything all right?" They had a left-steering automobile with a tiller instead of a wheel.

Zola had tried one of those but preferred directing the vehicle with a wheel. "We have a ruptured tire. That's all."

He pulled his automobile forward to the side of the road and parked in front of them.

Zola and Vivian climbed out, as did the men. Zola lifted the netting from her face. "Do you gentlemen have a problem with your vehicle as well?"

Mr. Basart sauntered toward her. "No. Our Oldsmobile is tiptop. If you'll direct us to your spare tire in all this, we'll get started." He motioned toward the tarp covering the heaping back half of the *Atlantic*.

She stared into his blue eyes a moment. "Get started with what?"

"Changing your tire."

Did he think her foolish? "We appreciate your offer, but we are quite capable of taking care of this little mishap ourselves. What happened to not helping us?" Under normal circumstances, she gladly would have accepted help from this handsome man, but this was not a normal situation.

"We wouldn't want you to give up before you've even gotten started."

She didn't like that he thought so little of her abilities. "We have no plans to give up."

He put his hand on his chest. "What kind of gentlemen would we be if we didn't give you a hand?"

"The kind who believe we can do this ourselves. Our agreement with our gentlemen friends back home was that we make this trip on our own without aid from men at every turn. You would have us lose before we even get started?"

Mr. Cuttels stood beside his companion. "Have either of you ladies changed a tire before?"

Just like men to think ladies incapable of such a task. A year ago, she wouldn't have had a clue as to how to change a tire.

Before Zola could reply, Vivian did. "I'll have you know that we have each removed and replaced all the tires on this automobile more than once."

Mr. Basart held up his hands. "Then we'll leave you lovely ladies to your task. We wouldn't want to cause you to suffer a loss on our account."

"We appreciate that. You men can carry on." Zola waved her hand toward them. "We'll catch up to you."

The men walked back to their vehicle but didn't move to get aboard or prepare to leave at all.

Vivian untied a corner of the tarp protecting their supplies and dug out the jack and wrench. Zola did the same on the opposite side to retrieve one of their spare tires.

Vivian wedged the jack under the vehicle's frame. "I do wish they wouldn't watch us. It makes me nervous."

"Pretend they aren't there." Zola leaned the spare against the side of the Winton.

Vivian worked the jack and had the flat tire off the ground, then she tapped Zola on the shoulder. "Look. They're getting out a camera to take our picture."

Zola fitted the wrench over the wheel nut and glanced in the men's direction. "Let them. Photographic evidence that we took care of ourselves."

◆━━ · ━━◆

Allen had thought the flat tire would have shaken the socialites' resolve. But they had that tire changed in a trice.

They climbed into their automobile and drove off, waving as they passed by.

Allen had to admit these ladies had gumption. "When do you suppose Miss Calkin changed her hat?"

Barney shrugged. "Had to be while they were driving. Are we going to go after them?"

"Pack up your camera. We wouldn't want them to get lost."

Unlike the ladies, who had changed drivers, Allen sat behind the steering tiller again. He preferred to be in charge of the automobile since his photographer had never operated one before.

The rest of the day went by uneventfully. He pointed to the ladies' vehicle with a bulbous tarp covering a heap of stuff in the back end of their automobile. "What all do you think they have under that tarp?"

Barney shook his head. "I was surprised they had a tire and jack. I figured it would be a bunch of useless stuff."

"I thought so too, but now I think they might just surprise us a time or two in the next couple of days."

"You don't think they'll make it all the way across the country, do you?"

"Just look at them. Changing a tire in those fancy dresses? What will they do when something more serious happens? What about when there's no hotel to check into? This end of the trip is the easy part with packed roads, signs to keep them going the right direction, and towns with comfortable beds. Their finishing schools and debutant balls didn't prepare them for a trip like this."

"I guess you're right. They don't really stand a chance of succeeding. I wish they'd let us help them. Then maybe they could make it."

"You really want them to succeed, don't you?"

Barney shrugged again. "They seem like nice ladies."

"Well, if they don't give up right away, I'm sure they'll give in soon enough and accept our help."

"You'd help them? Would Mr. Ghetty allow that?"

"Truthfully, he expects them to fail. Hopes they'll fail. But honestly, he wants a good story more than anything. So helping the ladies succeed would make us all winners." Except Allen himself. If they made it all the way across the country, he would be gone longer than a few days or a week.

Chapter 3

Day 7

Next stop, Chicago! One week into the trip and things had gone smoothly. Everything according to plan. Zola sat in the passenger seat petting Ladybug on her lap. Thus far they had managed to wear dresses, but that couldn't continue for much longer. In the early afternoon, she pointed. "Let's stop there."

Vivian pulled over and parked the Winton at a French bistro in Chicago. So far providence had shone kindly on them. Breakfasts and suppers had been eaten in the cities and large towns at stops along the way with overnight stays. Half of the noon meals had been taken in smaller towns. Other times they ate while driving. One drove while the other ate, and then they would switch. And each night a comfortable hotel bed cradled them so they woke refreshed.

The men weren't as prepared and stopped in towns here and there to grab something to eat. After a couple of times of having to hurry to catch up, they bought food for lunch on their way out of town. Not having expected Zola and Vivian to have lasted this long, the men had wired for more money from their editor at the paper. That first time, Zola had loaned them some until they received their funds.

Zola made sure to keep to her stringent schedule of 150 miles a day, on the average. Maintaining speeds between twenty and thirty miles an hour meant five to seven and a half hours of actual driving time each day with necessary stops along the way. Dr. Jackson had cautioned not to overwork the Winton or wear themselves out too early in the trip, needing to save their strength, because the most taxing part of this endeavor would be at the end of their journey—the Rocky Mountains of Montana and Idaho and the Cascade Range in Washington State.

Zola wasn't worried about the Cascades. She and Vivian had driven over the passes of those mountains last autumn in preparation, so she didn't see any problems there. Once they crossed the Rockies, the worst of the trip would be over with. And there weren't any real mountains between Chicago and western Montana, only some minor ones, hills, really, in comparison.

Having the benefit of others having already made this trip almost felt like cheating. All three of the men's teams last summer didn't have the benefit of knowing for sure this kind of endeavor was indeed possible. The men had proven it so. She wasn't out to prove it over again. She wanted to prove that women were as capable as men. Maybe then men would realize that women had the capacity to vote and do all sorts of things that only men traditionally did. Women had become doctors and scientists, even sailors and pirates. Not that she wanted to try her hand at being a pirate. This trip would prove to herself that she could do anything she set her mind to.

Zola sat in the French bistro with Vivian, Mr. Basart, and Mr. Cuttels. While waiting for the food to arrive, she opened her map. "It's only about eighty-five miles to Rockford. I know we thought we might stay here the night, but I think we can get to Rockford. What do you think, Viv?" So far they had made good time without much trouble.

Her cousin smiled. "Let's do it."

Mr. Basart set down his glass of water. "It might be dark before you arrive."

"I think we can make it before nightfall, and even if we don't, we have head-lamps on the sides and an acetylene lamp attached to the front. Is your automobile equipped for driving at night?"

He offered her his charming smile that sent her insides dancing. "We'll do just fine."

"Then it's all set. We eat, then telegram Rockford to reserve a room, and we're off."

Allen shook his head, no doubt thinking them foolish. "I need to send a telegram as well. To my editor."

"What is it you tell him every day?"

"We report your progress."

"And what does he do with the information?"

"Puts it in the paper so everyone can see how well you're doing."

Or how poorly. Fortunately, troubles had stayed away so far. "I think I'll wire the paper and get copies sent to Minneapolis so I can read what's being said about us." People were probably amazed at what they had already accomplished.

Vivian piped up. "Oh, that will be exciting."

"And while we're at it, let's get the other major papers as well."

An hour later, Zola sat behind the wheel as the *Atlantic* puttered out of Chicago. If we keep up this pace, we'll be in Seattle in two weeks. So much faster than any of the men's teams."

"Wouldn't that be a boon for us."

"For women everywhere."

Two hours later, Vivian opened her locket watch. "Time to switch drivers."

"Let me get us up this hill, then we'll trade."

Just as the Winton crested the top, the engine came to a shuddering stop, with a clunk and sputters. Zola tried restarting it to no avail.

Vivian put her arms around Ladybug. "What do we do now?"

"I'm going to coast to the bottom. There appears to be a good spot to pull off and take a look at the *Atlantic*."

"Can you do that? Just coast without the engine running?"

"We're doing it, so I would say we can."

✦•——•✦

Allen squinted at the automobile in front of them. Something was different. Exhaust no longer puffed out the back of the vehicle. He couldn't tell if their engine had stalled above the noise their own made. The two women exchanged several furtive glances.

Barney tapped Allen's arm. "What are they doing?"

"I'm not sure. It appears their automobile has quit."

"That's what I thought, but they're still moving. Do they think they can coast the rest of the way to the Pacific Ocean?"

Allen chuckled. "I doubt it. They're too smart to think that. They're probably heading for that wide spot near the clearing. That's what I would do if I were them."

Sure enough, they coasted to a stop right where he would have.

He pulled the Oldsmobile up behind them and jumped out. "We thought your engine had quit." He didn't want to offer help, because that would be against the rules and be turned down. "Anything we can do? Not that we're offering help."

Zola gifted him with a smile. "We sincerely appreciate your offer *not* to help us. We'll figure out the problem and be back on the road in a jiffy."

"We'll just stay out of your way."

"Thank you. And thank you for not assuming we couldn't handle this."

Allen gave her a nod and strode off. He did assume they couldn't handle it. Repairing an engine wasn't the same as changing a tire. How long before they gave up? As a gentleman, he would, of course, help them in their time of need. But as a reporter, he'd been ordered not to.

He sat on the bank on the side of the road.

Barney sat next to him. "What are they doing?"

"Trying to repair their automobile."

"Do you think they can do it?"

"Nope. But they have to try. Fixing one of these engines isn't something a person can just do like sweeping the floor or cooking a chicken. If it's not done right or one little detail is missed, the whole thing won't work."

"So what'll we do then?"

"Offer them help and hope they accept it."

"And if they don't?"

"I don't know. Drive them back to Chicago and deposit them at a hotel."

"But then their trip will be a bust. They will have lost."

"I know." His spirit sagged. He hadn't realized he'd started cheering for these two headstrong ladies.

"I hope they can fix it."

"Me too. But honestly, I don't hold out much hope." Allen didn't look forward to returning to his editor's smugness at being right.

"We could peer over their shoulders and tell them how to fix it."

"That would be considered helping." He lay back in the grass. "We just have to wait and see what happens." He didn't want to jeopardize their endeavor by being impatient. Whether they repaired their automobile or not, he still got paid by the paper. If he thought they would accept his help without repercussions, he'd be there in a trice. But since they wouldn't, it was best if he didn't get too close, where he'd be courting temptation.

Miss Calkin was some kind of lady. Brought up in privilege but not afraid of adventure. He didn't know one single other woman who would even consider attempting—even on a smaller scale—what she and her cousin were actually doing. For all intents and purposes, they had already succeeded. Just planning and starting out was more than a lot of *men* would have undertaken.

He could never hope to have a genteel lady like her give a ruffian like him a second look.

Sometime later, the sputter of an engine coming to life rousted him out of his musings.

Had they actually fixed their automobile? Amazing. The sputtering came to an abrupt halt.

He worked himself onto his feet and walked to the ladies' vehicle.

The two women had changed into trousers and had their heads over the engine compartment.

Barney stood behind them a few feet, biting his thumbnail.

Allen strolled to his photographer. "How are they doing?"

"They almost had it. I think they actually know what they're doing."

"How can you tell? It starting could have been a fluke."

"It's the way they talk, like they know what all that stuff is in the engine. Stuff I know nothing about."

Hmm. Interesting. He sauntered toward their automobile and listened. They indeed sounded as though they knew what they were doing. "How's it going?"

Miss Calkin straightened. "Obviously not well, or else we'd have the *Atlantic* up and running. It's a clogged carburetor."

Atlantic. Their frivolous name for their vehicle. "It sounded like it almost turned over. That's something."

"Yes, but we'll have to remove the carburetor again and clean it. We'll clean the lines running to it while we're at it."

"A clogged carburetor? Do you know what a carburetor is?"

She glowered at him, then turned and placed her dainty index finger on a part of the engine. "*That* is the carburetor."

He peered over her shoulder. She was right. As far as he could tell. Actually, he didn't know the particulars of this engine. He'd tinkered a little with one, but never anything serious, and certainly not to the extent that these women apparently knew. "How do you know so much about automobiles and their engines? You must have been learning about them for years with how much you know."

"We really don't know all that much. When we undertook this challenge, we had each ridden only a few times in an automobile. That was the extent of our knowledge."

"I find that hard to believe."

Miss Newland wiped her dirty hands on a rag. "It's true."

Miss Calkin nodded. "We really don't know much except where this particular model of vehicle is concerned. Once we decided which automobile we would be driving, we bought one. After we learned to drive it, I hired a mechanic to teach us how to repair it."

"He seems to have done a thorough job."

"He made us take the whole thing apart, every nut and bolt, including the engine. When we put it back together—which took three weeks—it wouldn't run. So he told us what we'd done wrong and made us do it again."

Barney leaned in. "Did it run then?"

Both ladies shook their heads. "After the third time—"

"It ran?" Barney said.

Miss Calkin shook her head. "We had damaged so many parts, it wasn't likely to ever run, so we bought another one."

Miss Newland smiled broadly. "The second time we put that one back together, it ran. And we were faster at reassembling it. We got it down to two and a half days!"

Miss Calkin motioned to the back of the automobile. "The good parts from the first one are under the tarp, as well as parts we purchased. From talking to Dr.

Jackson and hearing stories from other motorists, we would be foolish to think we would never break down."

"You two are truly amazing." Allen's editor hadn't anticipated these two being so prepared. "I don't know that I would have had the tenacity you've had to keep at this for a year."

"Tenacity. I like that." Miss Calkin picked up a wrench. "Our tenacity needs to get back to work if we're going to get this running."

After several hours of working, the ladies stopped. Zola brushed the hair from her face with the backs of her hands. "We need to eat."

Allen bowed to her. "You're in luck, ladies. We have prepared supper for you."

Miss Newland's expression brightened. "I'm ever so hungry."

Miss Calkin put her hand on her cousin's arm. "I don't think we can. Wouldn't that be considered helping?"

Allen swept his arm in front of him. "Nay, milady. What we offer isn't help, assistance, nor aid. Like in towns you've stopped in and eaten at a restaurant, we welcome you to the Basart & Cuttels Café. We have a varied menu at a penny a plate. Each full-course meal consists of cooked beans, half-burned biscuits, cold creek water, and sliced apples for dessert."

Miss Calkin laughed at his antics. "Since you put it so eloquently, how could we refuse?" She had a nice laugh.

He'd like to hear it again. And often. He was surprised she hadn't turned up her socialite nose at their pitiful offering they claimed to be food.

She batted her eyelashes playfully. "Shall we dress for supper?"

He laughed this time. "What you're wearing is dressy enough."

"Let us wash up, and we'll be right there."

He waited until they were ready. "Right this way." He led them to where he and Barney had made a makeshift table and covered it with a blanket. A fallen log and a couple of large rocks served as seats.

"Miss Calkin?" He pulled his handkerchief from his back pocket and shook out the folds.

"Please call me Zola. If we are to be traveling companions for some time, it's only fitting."

"Then you must use my first name as well. Allen." And with their knowledge of automobiles, it actually could be *some time*.

"Well, Allen, are you surrendering with that white flag, or did you retrieve it for another purpose?"

He glanced down at the handkerchief in his hand and held it up. "You missed a smudge of dirt on your cheek."

She took his offering and wiped everywhere but where the smudge resided.

He held out his hand. "Let me."

She relinquished the cloth.

He wrapped it around his finger and dabbed at the spot until it yielded. "There." He gazed into her hazel eyes.

She gazed back.

"I've never known a lady of your station to not mind getting a little dirty."

She gifted him with her smile again. "It's only a little dirt, not an angry grizzly bear."

Miss Newland chuckled. "Or Mrs. Pendleton when she doesn't get her way on the charity auction committee."

And then it happened. Miss Calkin laughed again. "So true. She can be a bear."

"You'll have to point out this Mrs. Pendleton when we arrive in Seattle so I can be sure to avoid her."

"Then you believe we'll succeed?"

He couldn't bring himself to lie, so he said, "You've made good time so far. Shall we eat?"

In the waning light after supper, Allen approached the ladies. He stood in the middle of the dirt road and looked both directions. "As far as I can figure, we're closer to Chicago than Rockford."

Zola's expression turned quizzical. "And your point is?"

"I was just wondering if you wanted us to return you to Chicago on roads we're a little familiar with or push on to Rockford in the dark on completely unfamiliar roads."

"Neither. We'll camp here."

A laugh chuffed out. "Outside?"

She folded her arms in challenge. "Why not?"

"Well, because. . . You know, people like. . ." Any way he phrased this, it would come out sounding critical and demeaning. "Not everyone is suited for camping and sleeping on the ground."

"Are you suited for it?"

"Probably more so than you and your cousin."

"I—we appreciate your concern for us, but we'll do just fine."

Allen wasn't so sure of that. But this could turn the tide of whether or not they continued this escapade. Repairing a vehicle was one thing. A socialite being uncomfortable was another.

She flashed him a smile. "Do you believe us incapable?"

"Miss Calkin, you have proven to be nothing but capable. Do you two honestly intend to sleep outside overnight?" He couldn't imagine that.

Zola smiled. "Of course not. We'll sleep in our tent."

Another laugh coughed out before he could stop it.

"Something funny?" Zola didn't appear the least bit offended.

"I'm having a hard time picturing either of you sleeping in a tent."

"Well, you won't have to picture it. You'll see it for yourselves soon enough."

He guessed he would, *if* they could get it set up. "Since it has nothing to do with your automobile, I don't think it would count against you if we pitch it for you."

Zola planted her hands on her hips and thinned her lips, then looked at Miss Newland. "After all we've already accomplished, these men still think us incompetent."

"Dear cousin, don't be hard on them. They can't help ascribing to the social stereotypes." Miss Newland turned to Allen. "If I would have been asked a year ago if I could set up a tent, let alone make this journey, *I* would have been the one telling *you* that not only I couldn't, but I wouldn't."

"And now?"

"Setting up the tent will be one of the easier things we do on this adventure." Miss Newland put her arm around Zola's shoulders. "You see, my cousin is very determined. She's a hard taskmaster. She's made me put up our tent by myself a dozen times. She wasn't going to let me hold us back from succeeding. Without her planning and pushing me beyond anything I thought I was capable of, I wouldn't be here."

Allen shifted his gaze to Zola.

She shrugged. "If a person is going to do something, there's no point in doing it if one can't do it right. If we don't succeed, it won't be for lack of planning— something we could do in advance." A smile pulled at her sweet rosy lips. "How about a race?"

"A race? What kind?"

"To see who can set up their tent first."

He hadn't pitched a tent in some years, but he and Barney could surely best them, or at least match them. "You're on. We'll set up camp as well. You will allow us to dig ours out first, won't you?"

"Of course. It wouldn't be a fair race otherwise."

He walked with Barney to their Oldsmobile. "Do you know all that is packed in there? Do we have a tent or any other gear for staying out overnight?"

Barney shrugged. "We haven't had to dig any farther than our small traveling bags and my camera gear."

"Well, we best see how comfortable Mr. Ghetty planned we'd be."

It took all of five minutes to plunder the contents of their vehicle and determine they had no tent. Two wool blankets and the thin tarp covering their minimal gear was the best they found. They hadn't needed much before now. Obviously, Mr. Ghetty hadn't thought they'd need much.

He faced Zola. "It appears we have no tent."

She scrunched up her face. "You must have one. You didn't expect to travel all the way across the country and not have to sleep outdoors at least once, did you?"

He hadn't expected any of this. Certainly not for this journey to still be continuing. "This automobile and everything in it was provided by the newspaper and packed for us. I didn't even find out I was going on this excursion until the day before we left. And our editor didn't expect you to last more than a couple of days, so I'm surprised we even have blankets."

Zola gave him a sympathetic look. "I'm sorry. But at least it appears to be a clear night, so no rain."

She truly seemed sorry for their situation.

"We'll be just fine. Since we don't have a tent, we would be more than happy to set yours up for you."

"No need. Stand back and watch."

Allen stood next to Barney. He hoped they were able to set it up on their own without trouble. He'd been hoping more than he thought he ever would that they succeeded at even these small tasks. What he saw amazed him.

After unbuckling the rolled-up back end of the rubberized tarp that covered the mound of stuff they had packed in the rear of their vehicle, they unrolled that portion of the tarp. The rest of it remained attached behind the front seat of the automobile. Then they unfolded a bottom section of it, which freed six three-foot sections of wooden poles. Each pair had a metal tube attached to one end of one of them. They put the three pairs together and proceeded to slide the first into a pocket along the top edge. The other two pairs were fitted into shallow pockets perpendicular to the first pole. The opposite ends had a spike attached, which they jabbed into the ground.

Both ladies turned in unison. Zola waved a hand toward their strange contraption. "All done." The whole process had taken them two minutes—three tops.

"That's your tent?"

She gave a vigorous nod and held the flap open. "Come see for yourself."

Allen and Barney peeked inside. Though the "tent" stood six feet at one end, the other sloped down and attached to the middle of the vehicle. They could reach everything in the back end while inside. The bottom of the "tent" unfurled beneath the automobile so that when they slept, their feet would be underneath.

Allen had never seen anything like it. "Where did you find such a specialized contraption that would fit on your vehicle?"

Miss Newland clapped. "Zola designed it and had it made."

He stared hard at Zola. "You did? How? Where did you get the diagrams for it?"

"I created them. Setting up those awkward tents took too long and was something extra I didn't think we needed to carry. We already had a tarp, and I figured it could be used as a tent as well. It has a threefold functionality. One, it keeps all our stuff from getting rattled off and lost along the way, as Dr. Jackson's had. Two, it keeps everything dry—not that we've had any rain so far. And three, it's our tent."

Miss Newland held her hands out to the sides. "And incredibly easy to set up."

Zola nodded. "That was a must. I didn't want to waste time day after day setting up and taking down a tent. That would be impractical. Remove the poles and separate them, roll them up with the tent section, and buckle the whole thing in place. And we're done."

Allen realized something. "If we *had* a tent, there was no way we were going to win a race, were we?"

Zola shrugged. "Not likely."

"This is really ingenious." Smarter than he'd ever given her credit for.

"Thank you." She gifted him with another one of her darling smiles.

She needed to stop doing that, or he'd get the idea she could start thinking of him as something other than an underling. Or dare he consider, liking him? The chances of that happening didn't exist.

Chapter 4

Day 10

After driving for two days in the rain, the next dawned sunny.

Allen stopped the Oldsmobile behind the ladies. Ahead of them sat a long, wide puddle that spanned the breadth of the road, hemmed in by rocky landscape on both sides. But this body of water was no bigger than ones they'd forged before. Unfortunately, there wasn't a way to go around it. The rocky terrain would eat up their vehicle. The only choice was to plow on through.

He put the Oldsmobile into reverse to make room for the ladies to back up as well so they could get a running start. They did and floored it, getting up a good speed before hitting the water and coming to an abrupt stop, which nearly threw Miss Newland over the hood.

The poor dog yelped, having gotten tossed to the floor.

Allen pulled up to the edge of the puddle and got out. He stepped as close as he dared to the mud-bound automobile. "Are you two"—he pointed to Ladybug—"you three all right?"

The ladies nodded to each other before Zola spoke. "We're fine. I thought this was simply water like all the ones before."

"That's how it looked to me. A sheen of water must have formed on the top of the mudhole. Let us pull you out. There's no harm in that."

"There is a great deal of harm. Everyone will say we needed men to help us. That we weren't able to do this on our own."

She was too proud for her own good but awfully cute.

The mud would dry around their tires, and they'd never get their automobile out.

"We won't tell anyone, will we Barney?"

The photographer shook his head. "Not a word."

"And what will you say when someone—some *reporter*—asks you if you helped us?" He opened his mouth, but she held up her hand to stop him. "You'll tell them we couldn't manage on our own, and every man will consider us a failure."

Allen put his hand on his chest. "I won't think you're a failure."

"But if you tell them you didn't help us—as you suggested—that would be a lie. I won't have that on my conscience. If we can't make it on our own merits, we won't make it at all. That is the whole point of this endeavor."

Stubborn woman. "Then how do you plan to get out of there?" She should just let him and Barney help them.

◆•——————•◆

Zola studied the terrain surrounding the mudhole. "We will be fine. We have a block and tackle. We can pull it out ourselves."

"What are you going to put your rope around? The nearest tree is back there."

There wasn't much in their immediate vicinity. Except rocks.

She looked around and pointed. "That boulder up there." The largest one—that would be close enough.

He waved his arm for her to proceed.

"You don't believe we can do this, do you?"

"I think it would be challenging for Barney and me to do it under these circumstances."

"We're just as capable." But she wasn't as confident as she made herself sound. She opened her door and stared at the mud. She should have let him offer to carry her across the mire, but she'd have to get in it eventually if she was going to free the *Atlantic*. Good thing she wore laced-on boots that couldn't get sucked off her feet in the mud.

After getting one block pulley attached to the front of the Winton and the rope threaded through both of the block pulleys and attached to a large, upright rock, she and Vivian heaved on the rope. The automobile didn't budge. They pulled harder and harder until they had movement. With a final heave-ho, the tautness on the rope gave. Zola and her cousin fell back with the release of the tension. They had done it.

She stood, brushing off her trousers, and turned to their freed automobile. Only it wasn't free. It still sat firmly in the mudhole. However, the boulder was upended from its foothold, toppled onto its side.

Vivian stood next to her. "That wasn't what we intended."

"No, it wasn't."

The men came up to them. Allen patted the toppled rock. "That took some strength to move this. I'm impressed."

"Don't patronize us."

"I'm not. I'm seriously impressed. That's a significant boulder. Moving it even a little is a remarkable feat."

"Thank you." She appreciated his encouragement. "But it doesn't get our Winton out of the mud."

"No, but it will make for a nice piece to send to my editor. Barney, take a photograph of their accomplishment."

"Oooh. That's a good idea." Vivian tromped through the mud to the Winton and returned with the box camera.

Zola shook her head. "But we didn't do what we had intended. Why would you want to document our failure?"

"How many ladies do you know who have overturned a boulder?"

"Well, none."

"Exactly. Now, go stand beside it." Vivian looked down at the top of the camera through the view window.

"Since you're so excited about this, you stand by the rock, and I'll take the photograph."

"All right." As Vivian held out the camera to her, Allen took it.

"Both of you stand there, and we'll take the photographs."

"Well, at least let us change into something more suitable." Zola didn't want photographic evidence of her wearing trousers. And muddy to her knees.

"You can't put on one of your fancy dresses. No one would believe you moved that thing then."

She supposed he had a point and stood properly with Vivian in front of the boulder.

Mr. Basart held up the camera. "Show us your muscles."

Vivian raised both of her arms with her hands fisted.

Zola was not going to do that. It was enough that she was allowing this photograph to be taken.

Vivian tipped her head toward Zola. "Come on. This will be fun."

Zola couldn't resist them all egging her on, but one of them posing like a muscleman was enough. She picked up the end of the rope, letting it dangle from her upturned hand, and put on a coquettish smile.

"Got it." Allen lowered the camera. "Will you let us help you now?"

Vivian nodded. "I think we should. I don't have any more strength left."

Zola was reluctant to admit defeat, but she didn't know what else to do. It would be easy to have the men pull out the *Atlantic*. "What if you weren't assigned to follow us?"

"What do you mean?"

"If you weren't here, what would we do then?"

"But we are here. You can't let your automobile sit there until the mud dries around it. You'll never get it out then."

"We could walk to the nearest farmhouse." And then what? Ask a man there to help them? There had to be another way. "I'm hungry. Let's eat while we think on it."

No sooner had they begun to eat, when an old farmer in bibbed overalls strolled up. He led a large dapple-gray horse with a girl of about twelve perched atop it. The man inclined his head toward the Winton. "You folks need some help?"

"We're stuck in the mud."

"We call that Buffalo's Wallow. We can pull you out."

An apt name. Zola ached—in more ways than one—to accept aid from this kindly gentleman but didn't know how without losing the whole point of this trip. "We appreciate your offer, but we have promised to make this trip without aid from any men. We're trying to figure out another way."

His mouth pulled up into a pleasant smile. "You're them two ladies set out to drive across the country, aren't you?"

"Yes, we are. And to prove that women are as capable as men, we need to get ourselves out."

"So you can't get *any* help at all?"

"No. Just not from men."

The old man thumbed toward the girl. "But you could receive some from my granddaughter?"

"Yes, but I don't see what she'll be able to do." One more female pulling on the rope wouldn't likely make a difference.

"This here draft horse is hers. Not mine. Minnie lost most of the use of her legs when she got powerfully ill. She gets around with her horse. If you were to give her one end of your rope, and tie the other to your vehicle, she can haul you out."

Zola walked up to the girl on the horse. "Good afternoon, Minnie. Would you be willing to help us?"

The girl nodded vigorously. "Radish is a girl too."

Zola petted the horse's neck. "Do you think Radish is strong enough to pull us out?"

"Oh yes. She does all sorts of work around our farm."

"When we're out, we'll give you a ride in our automobile. Would you like that?"

The girl beamed and nodded again.

Once the rope was secured at both ends, Zola and Vivian slogged through the mud to the back of the Winton. "Ready! Pull!" She and her cousin leaned into the back end of the *Atlantic*.

Vivian's feet slipped, and she fell to her knees.

Zola gripped her arm and helped her up.

Minnie goaded her horse. "Come on, Radish. Come on, girl. You can do it."

The Winton inched forward.

"It's working! Keep it up!"

Radish whinnied.

Then the vehicle broke free and rolled forward with a lurch.

Zola tried to keep up, but the mud held her feet sucked in place, and she fell forward into the muck, all the way up to her chin. She managed to keep her face above it.

Vivian only went down onto her knees again.

The Winton continued to roll forward all the way out of the mire.

Zola pushed up to her knees. "That's it! You can stop!" She turned to her cousin. "We did it! The *Atlantic* is free!"

The old man whooped.

Allen held up Vivian's camera. "We got photographic evidence that you didn't have help from men."

Great. Also, photographic evidence of being stuck in the first place and covered in mud. Zola pushed to her feet. "Don't you dare show that to anyone."

He furrowed his eyebrows. "Why not? It's proof the two of you are capable."

"We're a mess and all muddy. I'll pay you for yours."

Allen smiled and shook his head. "You'll thank me for it."

She doubted that. "Your turn to traverse the dangerous Buffalo's Wallow. Let's tie the rope to your Oldsmobile and have Radish and Minnie pull as you drive so you don't get bogged down in the middle and stop. I'll push from the back as well."

"I can't let you do that."

She held out her mud-covered hands. "I can't get any dirtier at this point. Don't argue with me. I'm going to do it whether you approve or not."

With the help of the draft horse, the men's vehicle rolled right on through.

The old man pointed. "There's a crick over yonder. You can worsh off there."

"Thank you." Zola and Vivian found the creek and washed, fully clothed, in the frigid water.

"Brrr. That's cold." Vivian climbed the bank in her soaking wet clothes.

"You still have mud on your back."

"I don't care. That's too cold for me."

Zola climbed out as well, her teeth chattering. "How can it be that cold in May? It must be running off from some mountain or something." She sloshed back to the Winton.

Allen stood, talking to the old farmer, but turned toward her as she approached. "I assume you ladies will want to change into something dry."

Zola shook her head. "We've lost too much time." But when she went to start the *Atlantic*, it wouldn't.

Minnie and Radish towed them all the way to their farm five miles away.

Chapter 5

Day 12

Two days later in the early morning, Allen trailed along behind the ladies away from the farm. Good wishes went with them, and they all waved.

He had spent the previous day on the farm with Minnie, Radish, Gramps, and the rest of the family, giving automobile rides to them and their neighbors while Zola and Vivian struggled with yet another repair to their automobile. They removed the drive chain, cleaned the mud off it, regreased it, and put everything back together. They were simply amazing, but both ladies were quite peeved at the length of time they had lost.

He wished they'd let him help them, but he could see their point in doing it on their own. If they were men and were aided, no one would think poorly of them, but since they were ladies, it was a different story. If they received assistance, they would be looked upon as inadequate and inferior. Neither of which they were.

Halfway between the farm and the next town, the Oldsmobile clunked to a stop. He tried restarting it.

Barney pointed ahead of them. "They're getting away."

"I know, I know." He honked the horn. Not that he thought they could hear it over their own engine and road noise. And even if they did, would they stop? This could be the perfect opportunity for them to escape from the prying eyes of a reporter and a photographer for good.

The ladies tooled on down the road and out of sight around a corner without glancing back to see that their unwanted entourage had fallen behind.

Allen climbed out. "We best see if we can get this beast running again." If the ladies could do it, then certainly he could.

As with the absence of a tent or sleeping bags, no tool kit could be found. How had Ghetty expected them to make this trip with such inadequate supplies? But Allen knew the answer to that. His editor hadn't initially expected him to be gone this long. *A day or two. A week at most.* Ha.

Allen looked back the way they'd come and blew out a breath. "I suppose we should start walking."

"Why?"

"To see if we can find someone to help us."

Barney stared the direction the ladies had gone. "But they'll come back for us. Won't they?"

"They never wanted us on this trip in the first place. Coming back would only slow them down. Would you come back if you were them?"

Barney slouched. "I suppose not. But could we wait just a little bit to see?"

Allen didn't like the idea of putting off the inevitable. If they waited, they would lose precious daylight. He puffed out a breath. "We can wait a few minutes."

◆ ◆ ─────── ◆ ◆

Zola couldn't believe they'd lost so much time between being stuck in the mud and cleaning up the engine from that event. And all that after the delay of the repair outside of Chicago. She would push them today to make up a little time. Drive farther and longer. She doubted they could reach Minneapolis today, but definitely Dubuque and possibly La Crosse.

Vivian tapped her arm. "The men are missing."

"What do you mean?"

"I don't see their automobile."

Zola glanced over her shoulder. The road behind them was clear. "They're probably just hanging back to avoid the dust we kick up."

"I don't think so."

Zola eased off the accelerator. "I'll drive slower until they catch up."

After five minutes, Vivian faced forward. "They still aren't back there."

Zola stopped in the middle of the one-lane dirt track. If a horse and wagon came along, she would move the Winton to the side. Another five minutes passed.

Vivian bit her bottom lip. "What should we do?"

Zola didn't like the looks of this. "They might have broken down. They're due. I don't want to take the time, but we should go back and see."

Vivian nodded. "Do you think they'll accept help from us? We have turned down their offers many times."

"That will be up to them. And for them, accepting help is different." She wheeled the *Atlantic* around over the bumpy grass along the side of the road and drove back on the brown ribbon they'd just traveled. She backtracked over five miles before catching sight of the men, stopped with their hood folded back.

She parked nose to nose with their automobile, stood on the floorboard, and leaned over the steering wheel. "Need any help?"

Allen chuckled. "You don't happen to have a spark igniter in your back end, do you?"

Zola turned to Vivian, and they both laughed. "We certainly do. We have most of another Winton back there. Don't know if it will fit your Oldsmobile, but we can try."

"Would you really give up one of your parts to help us? What if you need it later?"

"We actually have more than one. You can replace it in Minneapolis. They're likely big enough to have some automobile parts." Zola unfolded the diagram of parts, equipment, and gear in the back end. It saved them time when hunting for something.

Vivian untied the tarp closest to where the part was stored and held it up.

Zola grabbed the portable handheld electric light, turned it on, and poked her head under the tarp into the blackness. If not for this light, she and Vivian would need to untie half the tarp and fold it back to see anything. She retrieved the part and backed out.

Allen accepted the spark igniter. "We didn't expect you to return. Thought you'd be glad to be rid of us."

"True. At the beginning, we would have rather not had you along, but to have witnesses to our triumph will make success all that much sweeter and less likely that our accomplishment could be invalidated by naysayers. Provided you don't give false witness, but I don't believe you would do that."

"Even though I suggested I would withhold confessing if you accepted our offer of help."

She waved her delicate little hand in front of him. "That was a momentary lapse in judgment. I can hardly blame you for trying to be gallant in helping damsels in distress."

He chuckled. "I have learned since then that though you two may be damsels and you have been in many distressing situations, you are anything but helpless. Quite capable, in fact."

"Why thank you, kind sir." She winked. "Now, would you like some *help* installing that part? I would like to get moving again."

"Thanks, but I can handle this."

"Then we shall point the *Atlantic* back toward the Pacific and be ready when you are."

"Um. One more thing." He kicked at the ground. "This is embarrassing, but could we borrow your tools?"

She retrieved the tools and handed them to him. "It's a crime that your employer sent you off on this mission so ill equipped."

He nodded and got to work as rain sprinkled down one drop after another.

Chapter 6

Day 17

With continuous rain the next two days, the block and tackle had to be used more than twenty times to get both vehicles unstuck from mud, get past treacherous places where the road had been washed out, and move boulders and branches from the pathway. Then three days off and on with more minor repairs on both vehicles. In all, it took them more than ten days to travel between Chicago and Minneapolis. It should have taken them only two or two and a half.

Zola pointed. "There's the post office. I want to pick up the newspapers I requested so we can read all the wonderful things being written about us. We'll pick up supplies for the next portion of the trip, then head out of town."

Vivian turned to her. "What? I thought we were going to stay the night here. That's what we always planned."

"But we didn't plan to take over a week to drive four hundred miles. It's still morning. There's a lot of the day left. I know we're both tired, but don't you want to make up for some of that lost time?" When her cousin still looked hesitant, she continued. "We have the most difficult parts of the trip ahead of us. There isn't going to be much in the way of towns between here and Seattle, even with railroad stations and towns along the Northern Pacific line." The railroad tracks gave them a clear course to keep them from wandering off in a wrong direction.

"I suppose you're right." Vivian sighed. "Let's get supplies and eat. I want to eat at a nice restaurant if this is going to be the last I'll have for a while."

"I'm all for that." Though in reality, she would prefer to eat half-palatable food while driving to save time, but this was a good compromise.

Vivian parked. "I'll wait here for you."

Zola jumped out. "I'll be quick. Decide where you want to eat." Anything to save time.

The men pulled in behind them, and Allen got out. "Where are you two staying tonight?"

Zola waved her arm west. "Somewhere along the road."

He chuckled. "I told Barney that's what you'd say."

"He didn't believe you?"

Allen opened the post office door. "He was sure you two would go for the comfortable beds."

She slipped through the doorway. "But you didn't think so?"

He followed her inside. "I told him that you were too determined to make headway to choose comfort over progress."

She liked that he knew her so well already, but it also concerned her. Did her determination make him think less of her?

He pointed to the telegraph operator at the left end of the counter. "I'm going to send my latest story about you to my editor."

"I can't wait to read your stories. I hope at least some papers have arrived." She walked up to the mail side of the counter. "I'm Zola Calkin."

The heavyset woman in her thirties brightened. "You're that lady who's driving clean across the country, aren't you?"

Zola smiled. "Yes, I am, with my cousin."

The woman leaned forward, resting her elbows on the counter. "That is really something. Do you think a woman like me could do a thing like that?"

"Well, I don't know you to know if you could or not, but if you put your mind to it and plan things out, I'm sure you could. The key is not to give up." Zola liked that women were gaining confidence in themselves to contemplate things they never would have before. She wasn't going to help this woman or any others feel emancipated if she didn't make it all the way to the West Coast. "I should have a few newspapers waiting for me."

The woman chuckled. "I'd say a few." She walked away and came back with an armload of newspapers nearly a foot high.

"So many?"

"This is just what's come in the last two days." The woman pointed to a two-foot-high pile in the corner on Zola's side of the counter. "Those are yours too. I didn't have room for them back here."

"Amazing. This is more than I expected."

The woman blew out a breath. "Wait. There's more." She left again and returned with a bulging canvas bag and plopped it onto the counter. "These here letters are for you too."

Zola opened the satchel and fingered through a few envelopes. Hundreds of letters. People were writing to her and Vivian?

Allen came up beside her. "What are those?"

"People are writing to us. Isn't that something?"

"You two inspire people."

The woman nodded. "I'll say they do."

"I never would have imagined."

Allen smiled. "Why not? You're doing something incredible." He pointed to the stack of newspapers. "Would you like me to carry those? I don't think that would be considered helping you make your trip across the country."

"Thank you. That would be nice." Zola pointed to the corner. "I have all those to carry out as well."

His eyes widened. "Where are you going to put them all?"

"For now, on the floorboard on the passenger side."

He retrieved half the pile in the corner and stacked them on the others on the counter. "If you would open the door, I'll put these in your automobile and come back for the others."

Zola hurried to the door and held it for him. She scooped up the remainder of the newspapers and hoisted them to the counter. After slinging the bag of mail over her shoulder, she reclaimed the newspapers and headed for the exit. *Oh dear.* She hadn't thought how she was going to get out.

With perfect timing, Allen opened the door. "You didn't have to get all those." He took the newspapers.

"Thank you. I could have managed if not for the door." But she was glad to be relieved of them.

He deposited them with the others in the Winton. "Are there any more?"

Vivian's eyes widened. "What is all this?"

"The newspapers from across the country running stories about our trip." Zola hefted the bag of mail on top of the papers. "And these letters are for us."

Mr. Cuttels let out a long whistle. "That's a lot of mail."

Zola smiled. "I know. Apparently we inspire people."

◆— · —◆

Allen sat across from Zola in the cafe. She had brought the bag of mail in with her. They each took an envelope.

Zola read a letter from a twelve-year-old girl who wanted to be just like them. She pressed the letter to her chest. "Isn't she sweet."

Barney read from a woman who encouraged them not to give up.

Vivian read from an eighty-eight-year-old woman who wished she was young enough to go with them.

He read from a woman who left a job where her boss mistreated his workers.

The other letters were similar. Encouragement after encouragement. Women being daring and brave to better themselves.

Zola and Vivian were changing lives. That's what he wanted to do with his news stories. He had been so wrong. What these ladies were doing *was* real news.

Like the twelve-year-old girl, he wanted to be like them.

Zola folded the latest letter she read and addressed him. "Did you get your telegram sent?"

"I did." And had received three terse ones in return. Ghetty wasn't pleased that this "fiasco" was still continuing. Allen had let his editor know these women were very capable and just might make it all the way. He hoped so. They deserved it.

A few miles outside Minneapolis, the men's Oldsmobile fell behind again and stopped.

Zola directed Vivian to pull off to the side. She jumped out and walked back to the other automobile.

After a short assessment, they discovered the two front springs had broken.

Though she loathed to lose any more time, Zola said, "We can tow you back to Minneapolis."

Allen raked a hand through his hair. "Are you sure? I know you wanted to get farther down the road."

"We can't leave you stranded out here."

"Thank you. I wish we could make it up to you, but I'm not sure how without it appearing as though we're helping you. Maybe I'll think of something."

Zola drove the Winton while towing because Vivian wasn't comfortable doing it. She stopped at an automobile garage.

Allen thanked her. "We really do appreciate this, but we don't expect you to wait for us."

"Vivian and I talked about it. We are both exhausted and welcome the respite. We'll sleep in a comfortable bed tonight and leave at first light."

"And if our vehicle isn't repaired by then?"

"I'm sorry, but we need to keep moving if we are going to meet our deadline."

"I understand deadlines. I didn't realize you had one."

Vivian shrugged. "I got caught up in the moment and said we could make the trip in sixty days or less."

"And we can do it," Zola said, "but we still have the hardest part of the trip ahead of us. We calculated averaging fifty miles a day going over the Rockies and Cascades."

Though Zola didn't like this waiting, it would give her a chance to read the stack of newspapers. She would keep only the pages that had stories about them.

Leaving the men in the garage, she and Vivian went back out to the *Atlantic*. Zola plucked out all the *East Coast Herald*s and put them in order. She wanted to read Allen's stories first and revel in them.

Opening the first, she read aloud to Vivian. " 'Miss Calkin and Miss New-land seem to be intelligent. So why they want to undertake such a journey is beyond this reporter.' "

Vivian frowned. "Not quite glowing."

"That was from the party the night before we left. He didn't know us yet." She turned the article toward her cousin. "The picture of us is fantastic."

The next few articles were better, with stories full of hope, but all with under-tones that he didn't believe they could make the trip without help. After that, they got progressively more antagonistic. As they went on, his reports became disheartening, full of cynicism and negativity toward her and Vivian for even attempting such a trip. And even that horrid photograph of them in the mud pushing the Winton had a negative slant. Minnie and Radish had been cropped out, and the caption read, "Socialites caught in a dirty situation."

She couldn't believe the things Allen had written. He really had it in for them. One article stated, "These flighty females have no business being behind the steering wheel of an automobile. They should go back home and stick to needlepoint and garden parties."

Tears pooled in her eyes. "I thought they were rooting for us. But this whole time they've been against us."

Vivian's eyes glistened as well. "The other papers are much the same."

One called them "silly socialites," another referred to them as "daft damsels." Newspapermen did seem to like alliteration.

Allen—Mr. Basart—and Mr. Cuttels approached. "The mechanic should have it repaired in a couple of hours."

Zola brushed the backs of her fingers under her eyes to remove the escaped moisture. The men had it easy with someone else repairing their vehicle.

"Is something wrong?"

She shook her head.

Vivian thrust a newspaper at him. His newspaper. "It seems you've shown your true colors."

" 'Flighty females?' " Zola choked out.

He took the paper, and as he read, his face paled. "I didn't write this."

Zola couldn't believe he was denying it. "Isn't that your byline?"

"Well, yes, but. . ."

She stood. "We've changed our minds. We'll be leaving right away. Good day." She strode off.

Allen caught up to her and stepped into her path. "Zola, please listen to me. I didn't write those words."

She wanted to believe him. Truly she did.

"I believe the words are those of my editor." He sounded earnest. "He never thought you could nor should make this trip. He doesn't like to be wrong. He's taken my progress reports and twisted them. Please believe me."

"I want to. Those words are hurtful." She recalled the articles from the other papers. "Your editor isn't alone."

"What do you mean?"

"The other papers had similar stories. Why do men want so badly for us to fail?"

"They're insecure. If women can do everything men can, then what need would you have for us?"

"That's silly. God designed people—male and female—to need each other. 'It is not good that the man should be alone.'"

"Not good at all." He gave her a tentative smile. "Do you believe me?"

She nodded. "I do, and if I wasn't so tired, I probably would have realized those words weren't yours to begin with." None of those words had sounded like him. Not one. Except that first one from the prestart event. "Would you help me dispose of every last one of those newspapers?"

He flashed his genuine smile this time. "Gladly."

A warmth spread through her, and she smiled back.

Chapter 7

Day 23

After crossing from Minnesota into North Dakota, the ladies—in front as usual—stopped at a shallow, fast-moving river.

Zola and Vivian got out and stood in front of their automobile.

Allen and Barney joined them. Getting from one side to the other would prove challenging.

Allen pointed. "You could attach the block and tackle to one of those trees on the other side."

"No way to get them over there." Unlike in towns, the only bridge out here in the country was a train trestle a few yards up the river. Zola pointed. "We can go across on the tracks."

Allen shook his head. "I don't think that would work."

"Dr. Jackson drove on the tracks several times during his trip. He didn't advise it but said if we had to, to be extra careful. The terrain is flat here, so we can see a train coming for miles except for those trees. I'm willing to risk it." She turned to her partner. "What do you say, Viv?"

Vivian stared for a long time. "All right, but I'm not driving."

Allen sputtered. He couldn't believe these women. "You're serious, aren't you?"

"I'll only stay on the tracks as long as necessary. When we get to the other side, we can tie a rope to a tree and see if we can get the other end to float downstream and across to you. Then you can try to drive your automobile through the water, but it could be a little deep in the middle."

Allen shook his head. "If you're going across on the tracks, then so are we. Let us go first to make sure it's safe. And no, this isn't helping. We're just cutting in front of you." He waved a hand toward Barney. "Trot across and go beyond the trees to make sure the track is clear up there."

Barney scurried off and disappeared behind the trees, then reappeared and waved him forward.

With a deep breath, Allen maneuvered the Oldsmobile up onto the tracks several yards away from the bridge so he could get a feel of how the vehicle handled over the railroad ties. Bumpy, but manageable. He took it slow, holding his breath most of the time. As soon as he was across, he steered off the tracks. That hadn't been so bad. Zola would easily be able to manage.

He parked and jogged back across the bridge. He leaned on the top of her automobile door. "Keep it slow and steady, and you'll do fine."

She beamed a smile at him. "Thank you for not telling me I can't do this."

He shook his head. "I doubt it would do any good." He straightened and cupped his hands around his mouth. "All clear?"

Barney hollered back. "Clear!"

Allen patted the side of the Winton. "Slow and steady. I'll trail behind."

Zola started back where Allen had and seemed to get comfortable bumping over the ties quickly.

He held his breath again several times as they crossed.

Once on the other side, she drove off the tracks, stopped, and jumped out. She threw her arms around him. "I did it! That was fun but nerve-racking." She stepped back.

He'd liked holding her if only for a brief moment in her excitement. That had made not breathing while she crossed worth it. "I must admit I'm surprised you did it."

"I had to. There was no other way to get across, so I didn't think about it too much. But I hope we don't have to do that again."

"I agree." But if there were some other daring event that would cause her to end up in his arms, he wouldn't be opposed to that.

Chapter 8

Day 43

The trip across North Dakota proved to be the most difficult to date, fraught with one repair after another, storms, mudholes, punctured tires, and all sorts of trouble. They were visited upon by numerous wildlife. Prairie dogs and squirrels constantly begged for handouts, but the raccoon, a pair of weasels, and a coyote just took what food they wanted. One morning a skunk waddled through camp. Ladybug had to bark at it and nearly got sprayed.

The repeated breakdowns had slowed them considerably. Some of them were not due to wear on the Winton or rough roads, but sabotage. Twice their fuel line had been cut and once their oil line. The men's vehicle was never touched. Why were some people determined that they fail?

The *Atlantic* chugged to a stop.

"No! Not *again*." Zola got out and threw up her hands. "Why can't we get out of North Dakota? We've been in this dreaded state for *twenty* days. *Twenty!* I'm never getting out of here. I'm going to die here." It had all been too much for her.

Vivian came up beside her. "We don't even know what's wrong yet. Surely we can fix it."

"We don't have any more spare parts. We brought everything we thought we might need and then some, and it wasn't enough. We haven't even gotten to the hardest part, the Rocky Mountains and the Cascades." Zola walked off, needing to be alone. Ladybug pranced at her side.

After a few minutes, Allen tentatively approached.

Zola didn't want him to see her crying. She attempted to blink her tears away but only succeeded in pushing them out of her eyes to roll down her cheeks. "I can't do this. I'm exhausted. I can hardly move. I'm tired of being dirty and muddy. I'm tired of sleeping outside. We were hoping to be in Seattle long before now. All you men were right. I can't do this. I want to give up."

"There is nothing wrong with wanting to quit." Allen pulled out his handkerchief and dabbed the tears off her cheeks.

That was sweet of him.

"You want us to fail?"

"I didn't say that. What I was going to say is, there is nothing wrong with *wanting* to quit. But *wanting* to and actually doing it are two very different things. Most days, *I've* wanted to quit, but I have a job to do. And *you* and Vivian have a job to do. You have driven more than halfway across the country. You've made it this far. Are you really going to give up now?"

"But that was the easy half."

"You *want* to give up. But are you going to?"

"Why are you trying to encourage me? Don't you want me to fail like all the other men in the world do?"

"I never wanted you to fail. My boss did. Did I think this endeavor was foolish? Yes. But you have made it farther than I ever imagined you could. You have proven that anyone—man or woman—can do anything they put their mind to. Dr. Jackson wants you to succeed. Are you going to let him down? Let yourself down?"

She wanted to finish this journey, but she didn't want it to be so hard. It was a lot more difficult than she'd imagined. She'd started out with high hopes and grand ideals.

Ladybug put her front paws on Zola's leg.

She picked her up. "Do you want to quit too?"

Her Pomeranian licked her face.

Allen chuckled. "I think that means she wants you to finish what you started."

It was nice of him to say that. "I'm ready to go back to the Winton."

He fell into step beside her. "Does this mean you're going to continue?"

"I don't know. It might depend on what's wrong with the *Atlantic*. I'm tired of repairing it."

Back at the automobiles, Vivian stood near the photographer, smiling up at him. Her cousin was smitten.

Zola cleared her throat to get Vivian's attention.

Her cousin turned but didn't step away from Barney. She looked as tired as Zola felt.

"What do you want to do?" Zola asked her. "Go on or quit? I'm all right with either."

Vivian heaved a sigh. "I want to quit and go home and sleep in my own bed. I wanted to quit after the second day. Then after the first week. And every time we had to sleep outside."

If Zola didn't have Vivian's support, could she make it on her own?

"But I want to go on. In this stupid automobile. I never thought we would actually start this adventure. Even with all our planning and preparing. Then once we started, I never thought we'd get this far. I never imagined myself capable of doing everything we have already done. I never thought myself strong enough, but you have shown me that I am. I'm not the same woman I was when you told Garfield that women could drive clear across the country. I don't even recognize that timid girl anymore. I don't want to be the woman who quit. I want to continue this trip and become the woman I'll be when we cross the finish line."

"That was a really good speech." Zola took a deep breath and squared her shoulders. "Let's see what's wrong with this beast and figure out how to repair it. *Again*."

The line feeding oil to the cylinders had clogged—again—but was an easy fix.

Later, after dark, Zola drove over the state line into Montana and stopped a mile in. She raised her hands high. "Finally! A new state."

Chapter 9

Day 47

Montana was not without its troubles. But even with a hub and bearings giving out, which they needed to replace, and cleaning out a dust-clogged carburetor—again—most of the state lay behind them in just over four days. Tomorrow they would head up into the Montana side of the Rocky Mountains and cross into Idaho the next day.

Allen pulled in behind the ladies' automobile. Zola had stopped in a nice clearing with some trees for shade and some rocks for sitting on.

She climbed out from behind the steering wheel a bit stiffly. "Washington isn't far off now. I can't wait."

He was glad she'd perked up after having been so down in North Dakota.

Ladybug jumped to the ground and trotted off. She liked to explore each new camp.

Allen got out of the Oldsmobile and strolled toward an outcropping of rocks. From on top of them, he could get a better view of the surroundings. "You've chosen a good spot to camp." She always did.

Ladybug raced toward Allen, barking and yapping.

When he took a step back, she advanced. "Zola, could you call off your dog?"

"Ladybug, come here."

The Pomeranian kept barking. She turned and barked the other direction.

"Lady Beatrice Goodings! Get over here and leave Allen alone." Zola strode toward him. "I don't know what has gotten into her."

What indeed. Then he saw it. "Freeze! Don't move!"

Beyond the little white dog sat a coiled rattlesnake shaking its tail angrily.

"I'll get her. She doesn't norm—"

"No! A snake! Stop!"

Zola froze and gasped.

"Step away slowly."

"But she'll get hurt. I can't let that happen."

Ladybug continued to bark at the snake.

The little dog had likely saved his life.

Zola patted her hands together. "Come here, Ladybug."

"Stay back." He couldn't let Zola get hurt.

Zola picked up a long stick. "I will not let that thing bite my dog."

Then everything happened quickly, almost at once.

"Ladybug!" Zola commanded with the stick held high.

The Pomeranian turned to her mistress.

The rattler lunged and struck at the side of the white fur ball.

"No!" Zola swung her stick and made contact.

The snake flew through the air and landed a few feet away, limp.

Allen snatched up the dog, hurtled her toward Zola, and took her stick.

"Is it dead?" Barney asked.

Allen shook his head. "I think it's only stunned." He inched over to the lifeless form. When it woke, it would be madder than before. He tromped on the head and crushed it under his boot.

With Ladybug in one arm, Zola hugged Allen with the other. "Thank you for saving my dog."

"You have it wrong. It was she who saved me. If not for her barking, I would have walked right into that snake. Did she get bit?"

Zola gasped. "I don't know."

"Sit, and we'll take a look."

Zola sat on one of the rocks.

Vivian sat next to her. "That was scary." She stroked Ladybug's head. "You were so brave."

"She certainly was." Allen dug in the dog's fur, trying to feel where the snake bit her.

Ladybug lapped her tongue at her fur, but Allen blocked her. "Keep her from licking herself. There could be snake venom on her."

Zola held the Pomeranian's face. The dog nipped at her. "Behave yourself."

Was the dog upset because her mistress was confining her? Or because she had been injured? He prayed she was fine.

Allen parted the fur. And parted the fur. And parted the fur. "How thick is this stuff?"

Ladybug snarled at him.

"She has a double coat, so pretty thick."

He dug down to her skin. Four-fifths of this dog was fur. He probed around. "I can't see any puncture wounds or blood. The snake must have gotten only her fur." How fortunate.

Zola hugged her canine friend. "Oh good. She's safe."

"Not quite. There could still be venom on her coat. We should wash her thoroughly. Don't let her lick herself until we do. Where are your cooking pots?"

Vivian jumped up. "Over here." She went to the *Atlantic*, untied the tarp, and pulled out two large pots.

Barney stepped back. "I'll get ours as well."

Allen took the pots. "We'll fetch some water and be right back."

Zola thoroughly washed the dog once, then a second time. Soaking wet, Ladybug was a third of her fluffy size. The dog shook herself several times, causing water to spray everywhere.

With the stick Zola had wielded, Allen picked up the snake body, walked it far from camp, and buried it. When he returned, Zola sat on a rock with Ladybug wrapped in a blanket on her lap. "Is she all right?"

"I don't want her to get cold."

"Let me build a fire."

Once crackling flames blazed, Allen held out his hands. "May I hold her?"

Zola gifted him with a sweet smile as though he'd just paid her the most glowing compliment. She handed the white fluff ball to him.

He sat on the ground close to the heat and unwrapped Ladybug so her fur could dry in the warmth. "I will never in my life poke fun at a little dog again."

Ladybug raised up and licked his face.

Zola gave a gentle laugh.

He loved that sound.

"She likes you."

He hoped the dog wasn't the only one.

Zola gazed at him tenderly.

He wanted to savor this moment forever.

Chapter 10

Day 52

Allen stood with Barney at the telegraph office in Missoula, Montana. He had sent another request for money from the state's capital yesterday. The clerk handed him a telegram from Mr. Ghetty.

NO MORE MONEY *Stop* THIS HAS GONE ON LONG ENOUGH *Stop* STOP THEM NO MATTER WHAT IT TAKES *Stop* OR ELSE *Stop*

Stop them? Did he mean sabotage them? People had tampered with the ladies' automobile on several occasions already.

He handed the telegram to Barney.

The photographer read it. "What does he mean by 'or else'?"

"I suspect he means our jobs."

"I thought he wanted the story whether they succeeded or not."

"Apparently he would rather have it be *not*. Maybe he feels he can sell more papers that way. Or maybe he's getting pressure from the newspaper owner. Either way, our funds are cut off."

Mr. Ghetty had been more than happy to send the needed money all through North Dakota when the ladies were having so many troubles. Knowing how the editor had twisted his words, Allen had been careful not to provide many of the negative details, just that the ladies had succeeded at yet another difficult repair to their automobile.

Barney handed back the message. "Are you going to do what he said? Stop them?"

Allen was *not* that kind of journalist nor that kind of person. "These ladies have earned the right to make it if they can."

"Then what are you going to do? Go back to New York?"

Allen shook his head. "I'm going to see this through. I want to be there when they cross the finish line, but I also want to complete this drive for myself."

"What if you get fired?"

"That will more than likely happen. I'll drop you off at the next train station.

You can tell Ghetty that I skipped out on you during the night."

Barney stood still and silent for a moment, then shook his head. "I want to continue with you, with them. I agree that they have earned the right to make it. I want to see that."

Allen gave Barney's hand a hearty shake. "Few people have done what we're doing."

"How are we going to make it without the newspaper's backing?"

"Fortunately, we don't have that much farther to go, just the panhandle of Idaho and across Washington. We still have the rest of the money from the last wire. I'll have the money I have in savings wired to Spokane. We should be there in a day or two. You have any money?"

Barney nodded. "Not much, but I'll donate it all, and I'll see if my parents will send some."

"No more hotels, not that there will likely be many opportunities for the remainder of the trip. We'll sleep with the automobiles. No restaurant meals. We eat jerky, crackers, cheese, and cold cuts."

Barney nodded. "If we do that, we could actually make it."

Allen crumpled Ghetty's telegram and crammed it into his pants pocket, then stepped back up to the telegraph counter. On the pad of paper, he wrote, "*Everything is being taken care of.*"

Barney peered over his shoulder. "That makes it sound like you're going to do what he says."

Allen smiled. "Yes, but it's also true. We are going to take care of all our expenses from here on out. We can't help it if he misinterprets our message."

Barney's mouth stretched into a wide grin. "Can't help it at all."

Chapter 11

Day 54

Zola returned from scouting for firewood. She dropped her pile with what had already been collected. The others must have gone out for another load, which was what she should do.

A piece of crumpled paper by the wood caught her attention. She picked it up and unfurled it. A telegram. Must be one of the many Allen had received from his editor.

She started to fold it up so she could return it but halted at the words on the page.

STOP THEM NO MATTER WHAT IT TAKES *Stop*

She had a terrible thought and shook her head. *No.* He couldn't have been the one who sabotaged their automobile. But who else could have done it? He had been given the order to do whatever it took to stop her and Vivian. Tears welled in her eyes. Had all his kind words and pep talks been a ruse? How could she have allowed herself to care for such a scoundrel?

The cracking of a twig caused her to whirl around. Barney approached with an armload of wood. He had to be in on the deception as well. She crumpled the paper up in her hand and held her fist behind her back.

She went to the Winton and crammed the paper up under the seat in the springs. She would show it to Vivian later. For now she needed to pretend nothing was amiss, to be as good an actor as Mr. Basart.

Once the campfire was going, Zola got out the food for supper. She wished they didn't all have to share the meal tonight. She put the grate over the fire and the cast-iron skillet on it to heat while she peeled and cut potatoes.

Allen came over and held out his hands. "Hand it over."

She froze. Hand what over? Did he know she'd found his telegram? "What are you talking about?"

He cast her his disarming smile. "The knife. It's our turn to cook. Yours to clean up."

"Oh." She handed him the knife and the potato and walked away. She needed time to think about what she was going to do.

"You don't have to run off," he called after her.

"I. . .need to take Ladybug for a walk." She picked up her pace before he could delay her or ask what was wrong. Ladybug trotted along beside her.

Would Allen have stooped to tampering with their vehicle? How else could the incidents be explained? He had been quick to suspect the men who had taunted them in one of the towns of being the culprits. Wasn't it more plausible that a man who was with them all the time and had plenty of opportunities to sabotage their automobile would be the prime suspect? Not to mention that his boss had given him orders to stop them *"no matter what it takes."* She didn't want to believe he would do something so cruel, but what other conclusion could she come to?

After supper, Zola finished drying the dishes and packed all the cooking gear in the Winton. She proceeded to pack up everything else they had taken out.

Allen came up next to her. "You aren't thinking of continuing on tonight, are you?"

"What?" She'd considered it. "Why would you ask that?"

"You're stowing away all your gear."

"Oh that." She let out a nervous laugh. "I just wanted to get a jump on things. I take far too much time in the morning packing. I want to leave as early as possible."

"But won't you have to unpack your cook kit again to make breakfast?"

"We could skip breakfast and eat in the first town we come to. It'll save time."

Once everything was tied down except the tent, Zola needed to get Vivian away from the men without raising their suspicions. "I have a headache." It had started immediately after she'd found the telegram. "I'm going to turn in. Good night." She lit a kerosene lamp. "Are you coming, Vivian?"

"I'm going to stay out here a bit longer." Her cousin smiled at Mr. Cuttels.

Zola hoped he wasn't in on the deception, for Vivian's sake. She sauntered to the Winton and fiddled around the front interior of the vehicle. Reaching up under the seat, she snagged the telegram, then circled to the back end and ducked inside the tent. Ladybug trotted in after her.

She didn't change into her sleeping attire but sat on her sleeping bag, waiting for Vivian. With her arms wrapped around her bent knees, she listened to the murmurs coming from around the campfire.

Ladybug pawed at her arm and whined.

She petted the Pomeranian and kept her voice low. "You know something's wrong, don't you?"

Ladybug tilted her head to the side.

Zola patted the blankets next to her. "Lie down."

Ladybug circled five times before settling, then huffed a huge doggy sigh.

Zola didn't know what to feel, or rather which feeling to focus on. The hurt? The anger? The humiliation? The betrayal?

She still sat there with bent knees and the light low when Vivian pulled back the flap.

"Oh. I thought you would be asleep by now."

Zola motioned her inside. "Keep your voice down."

Vivian crawled in and closed the flap. "What's wrong? Do you still have a headache?"

"It's a whole lot worse than that." Zola pulled the wrinkled telegram from under her blanket. She'd done her best to smooth it out. "Read this."

Vivian tilted the paper toward the light and gasped. " '*Stop them no matter what it takes.*' What does that mean?"

"It means that at least one member of our tagalong team has plans to see to it we don't finish this trip. It also means that the saboteur is closer than we anticipated. A whole lot closer."

Her cousin's eyes widened. "You can't think Barney or Allen would have done anything to our automobile, do you?"

Zola nodded. "I hadn't until I read this telegram. Their Oldsmobile was never tampered with."

Vivian shook her head. "They wouldn't. I won't believe that."

"Then how would you explain the telegram?"

"I. . .I can't." Her cousin's shoulders slumped. "What are we going to do?"

"We have two options. We either leave in the middle of the night without them. . ."

"That's why you packed everything up."

Zola nodded.

"What's the other option?"

"Drive along as though nothing has changed and keep a very close eye on those two. They'll be desperate to obstruct our progress. Maybe they'll slip up and we can catch them in the act. But if they are indeed out to sabotage our trip, do we really want them so close?"

"We could show them this telegram and make them explain it."

Zola had contemplated doing that. "And what do you think they'll say?"

"That it doesn't mean what we think it means."

"And if they say it means something completely innocent, you'll believe them?"

292

"Why shouldn't I?"

Zola wanted to believe they were innocent but at the same time didn't want to find out they weren't. "Let's say they're guilty. What do you think they would tell us if we confronted them with the telegram? Do you think they would admit to any wrongdoing?"

Vivian's mouth worked back and forth. "I guess not."

"There's no way to know for sure. Whether they're guilty or innocent, they'll say the same thing. I want them to be innocent as much as you do, but any way I think about this, it always comes out the same."

Vivian heaved a sigh. "I know what you're going to say."

"What?"

"That we should leave without them."

It was the best solution. "I won't unless you want to too."

Chapter 12

Day 55

In the morning, Allen crawled out from the lean-to, twisted one direction and then the other. He hoped Zola's headache had gone away with a good night's sleep. He glanced toward their automobile and tent.

And froze.

The place sat empty.

He scanned the area. Not a sign of them. Where had they gone?

He ducked his head inside the tarp. "Barney, get up!"

Barney rolled over and yawned. "What is it?"

"The ladies are gone."

"They might just be out getting more firewood or something. They'll be back."

"No. They are *gone*. Everything. Them. Their automobile. The dog."

Barney scrambled out of the lean-to and looked around. "Where did they go?"

Allen shook his head.

"Do you think they've been kidnapped?"

"Out here? Not likely. Zola was acting strange last night. Let's head out and see if we can catch up to them." He and Barney broke camp faster than they ever had and were on the road in record time.

Allen stopped in the first town and inquired about the ladies driving an automobile.

Several people had seen them about three hours earlier.

They were farther ahead than he'd imagined. But why had they left without him and Barney?

After buying gasoline and nothing else—because they couldn't afford to—Allen drove on.

Barney stared intently out the front. "At least we know they haven't changed their route."

"Unless they did after that town, knowing we would ask about them and assume they were continuing on their same course and then went a different direction."

"You're just full of good news today, aren't you?"

"Those women are smart. I'm just trying to think like they would."

"That sounds dangerous."

Allen chuckled. "You're probably right."

Another hour of driving. Barney pointed. "Look. Their automobile."

They were stopped alongside the road, hood folded back. Both ladies pulled their heads out from the engine compartment. His insides relaxed. Zola was safe. He hadn't realized he'd been feeling like her protector.

Allen pulled up and stopped. "Need some help?"

Zola put on a fake smile. "We are quite capable, thank you."

Something was definitely wrong. He didn't know why he'd asked to help. Not only would they not accept it, they *were* more than capable of handling any issue that came up with their vehicle. Allen parked in front of them and got out.

Ladybug met him, wagging her swirly tail, then raised up on her hind legs and waved her paws in the air. Though she still resembled a fluffy ball, her white fur was dingy with dirt.

"Well, at least someone's glad to see me." He picked her up and walked back to Zola and Vivian. "What's the problem?"

Barney followed.

Zola dipped her head back into the engine compartment. "Clogged oil line again as well as a flat tire."

"That's not what I meant. Why did you leave without us?"

Vivian gave Barney a woebegone look.

Allen stepped closer. "Zola, look at me."

She straightened and swiveled toward him.

"Why did you leave in the middle of the night?"

"We didn't leave in the middle of the night. It was early morning. We didn't want to disturb you gentlemen."

"I don't believe that. You know we're in this as much as you."

She pulled her eyebrows together and tilted her head. "Do we? Are you?"

For a conversation, he certainly wasn't understanding much of it. "You've been acting strange since last night. I can't think of anything I said or did to upset you."

"You can't think of anything?"

Vivian gave a little whimper. "Oh, you might as well tell them."

Zola turned to the vehicle, retrieved a folded paper from her little handbag, and thrust it toward him.

He took it and unfolded it. The worst of the telegrams from Mr. Ghetty.

"I didn't want to believe what it said but can't come up with any other explanation. Tell me you didn't do what that suggests, that you didn't sabotage our automobile those times. Or was that the plan all along?"

"No. I didn't. I promise."

Zola turned her gaze on Barney.

He choked out, "I didn't do anything either."

Allen wiggled the paper. "This wasn't our idea. Our editor sent this. We had nothing to do with his plan."

"I want to believe you. Truly I do, but I don't know how."

Allen slumped his shoulders. "I don't know what else to say."

Barney stepped forward. "We're getting fired for not following our editor's orders."

"What?" Zola's gaze shifted between the two.

"We don't know for sure." Allen shrugged. "But it's highly likely we'll lose our jobs over this. It was a choice we both made. We couldn't do what he was asking."

Barney pulled a dollar bill from his pocket. "And we're using our own money to continue on this trip."

Allen nodded. "He cut off our expense account. That's why we quit eating in the restaurants—not that there were many after that—and why we slept outside rather than in the hotel that last time."

Vivian twisted her hands together. "I believe them."

He could tell that Zola wanted to but wasn't quite convinced.

"When I was given this assignment, I didn't want it. Do you know why?"

Zola shook her head.

"Because I wanted to report on a *real* news story. One that was important. One that mattered. I didn't want to follow after some flighty socialites—"

Zola opened her mouth and held up her hand as though she was about to speak, but Allen wasn't done.

"—who didn't know what they were doing. I quickly realized you both *did* know what you were doing. You had everything planned out. You didn't wake up one morning and decide to head across the country. You were very smart about every aspect of this trip. I'm ashamed to say that you have surprised me at every turn."

"You didn't think we could do it, did you?"

"No, I didn't. I'm not ashamed because you can repair your automobile better than I can—better than most men would be able to, but because *I* was repeatedly surprised. You proved yourself over and over, and still I didn't expect you to be capable. Flighty? You two are anything but. Your story matters more than many of the stories my paper covers. Your story is more important than I ever imagined. And more real. I thought this was a story about two ladies driving across the country. I was wrong. It's a story about ingenuity, strength of character, honor, encouragement, and courage. You have shown women and young girls all over the country—all over the world—courage. Courage to do what they dream. Courage to not let anyone tell them they can't do something. Courage to try. Courage to rise up to their potential. You have shown me that I can do more than I ever thought possible."

Allen stepped forward. "I had a job to do. Report your progress. But now I want to write stories that make a difference. I don't want someone else telling me what I can and can't write. You have empowered me to write what I feel God telling me to write. You have inspired me."

Zola stared at him. "I've inspired you?"

He nodded. "Very much."

She huffed out a breath. "I hope I don't regret this, but I believe you too."

Allen put his hand over his heart. "You will have nothing to regret." He would make sure of that.

Chapter 13

Day 60

Despite having driven late into the night, Zola felt surprisingly refreshed this morning on the last day of their journey. Only twenty miles to go.

After breakfast and with most everything packed inside the *Atlantic*, she and Vivian donned their crossing-the-finish-line outfits. She wore a flowing, feathery confection in lavender. Vivian's dress had layers of chiffon in pink. They both sported fancy hats to match their outfits, and their overall looks gave the appearance they were floating. Perfect for the end of this adventure.

Allen and Barney gaped at them.

Zola twirled once around. "What do you think?"

Allen opened his mouth several times before any words would form. "I think you two will be the prettiest ladies in Seattle."

Her mouth stretched wide. "Thank you."

"Shall we be off, ladies?"

"We need to strap down our tent first."

"I would help, but I'm forbidden." He put his hand on his chest. "Just know that this gentleman would be more than honored to offer assistance in any way you would accept."

"There is something you could do."

"Name it."

"Would you pray for us?"

He smiled. "Gladly." He bowed his head. He asked God to bless this final leg of the journey and give them a triumphant entry into Seattle. "Amen. See you at the end."

Zola put her gloved hand on his. "That was beautiful. Thank you. For everything. See you at the end."

He nodded.

On each side of the vehicle hung their *Seattle or Bust* banners. Though they had started the trip in vibrant green, they were dirty, tattered, and faded now. But like her and Vivian, they had made the whole trip.

With everything secured in place, Ladybug leapt into the passenger seat and barked. Time to go.

Vivian reached for the driver's side door. "Since you drove late last night, I thought I'd take us the rest of the way."

Zola's spirits sank. "But this trip was my idea. I'd hoped to drive over the finish line."

Vivian studied the ground.

Oh dear. She'd made her cousin feel bad. "If you want to drive to the finish, that's fine."

"It's not that I *want* to. I *had* expected you to."

"But?"

"Do you realize that every single time we've broken down, gotten stuck, or been given the wrong directions and sent miles out of our way, you've been driving? What if something happens again today?"

Zola thought hard. She *had* been the one driving all those times. "You don't think I'm to blame, do you?"

"No. Of course not. Things just happened. I was always relieved when they happened to you and not me. I don't know if I could have handled being the one driving during a breakdown. You were always so calm and took it in stride."

She was glad to hear her cousin didn't blame her. "If it makes a difference in us completing this journey or not, I'm keen." She walked around, ducked under the oversized umbrella affixed behind the seats, and got in on the passenger side. First one raindrop, then another ushered in a light sprinkle.

Barney closed the driver's door and smiled at Vivian. "We'll be cheering you on all the way."

Allen tapped the edge of the umbrella on Zola's side. "It looks like you'll both stay nice and dry."

"I wish we had another one for the two of you."

"Don't worry about us."

"Maybe it'll stop and the clouds will part."

"Maybe." He stepped away.

It was Seattle. Who were they kidding?

Vivian headed the Winton down the road.

Five miles outside of Seattle and seven from the finish line, an assortment of conveyances sat along the sides of the road, some horseless carriages and the others horse-drawn ones. People stood by and cheered as Zola and Vivian drew closer.

Had all these people come out to see them? And in this weather? Rather than the clouds parting, the sprinkling had turned into a steady, gentle rain that tapped continually on their umbrella.

Both kinds of vehicles fell in behind the Winton and the men's Oldsmobile. Women and children lined the street, waving little flags and holding banners. Men jogged alongside the *Atlantic*.

Ladybug greeted the people with barks.

Zola waved to the crowds. "We made it. We succeeded. And with five hours to spare."

Vivian took one hand off the steering wheel to wave. "I never thought we'd actually do it. You should drive the rest of the way."

Zola shook her head. "No, you deserve to take us the last bit to the finish. I'll wave to all these people."

"I can't believe so many are out this far."

One of the men running alongside the Winton hopped up onto the running board. Garfield Prescott. "I didn't think you two could do it. I'm impressed."

Zola hadn't either. "I expect that full page declaration in tomorrow's paper."

He chuckled. "You two deserve it. I'll see you at the finish." He hopped off.

Just outside the city, the *Atlantic* came to a noisy and sudden stop.

Vivian looked at Zola. "I'm so sorry. I should have insisted you drive."

Zola put her hand on her cousin's arm. "Nonsense. It's not your fault. It would have happened if I were driving. Let's fix it as fast as we can. We can still make it."

When Zola inspected the problem, she found that the stud bolts holding the connecting rod to the crankshaft had sheared off and pierced through the crankshaft cover. No fixing this fast or in time. Her spirits sank.

The race was over.

They had lost.

She gazed at the buildings of Seattle. So close. They had almost made it.

Allen leaned closer. "What's the trouble?"

She blinked moisture from her eyes. "We lost." And her fluffy, feathery dress hung in wet tendrils. A soggy mess.

"What do you mean?"

"Even if we had the parts, we can't repair this fast enough. It will take days."

"That bad?"

She nodded.

Allen squinted. "Who says you have to repair it?"

Zola tilted her head. "How can we go on if we don't?"

"What was your agreement?"

Zola looked to Garfield, who had been trailing them in his roadster.

Garfield shrugged. "That you ladies couldn't make the trip across the country in an automobile."

Allen's eyes widened. "Nothing about the automobile running when they crossed the line?"

Garfield shook his head.

Hope bubbled up in Zola and just as quickly plummeted to her feet. "Minnie and Radish aren't here to tow us this time, and we can't exactly have someone around here—a man—tow us to the finish."

"But you *could* push it."

Zola cast a glance toward Seattle, then back at Allen. "We have another three or four miles to go. I'm not dressed for such strenuous work." She held out a delicate shoe from under the hem of her feathery skirt. "These are *not* the best footwear for such an endeavor."

"You could easily change into your boots."

"Out of the question. They would look atrocious with this dress. Besides, we would never be able to push the *Atlantic* that far."

"How do you know unless you try? You didn't think you could make this whole trip, but here you are. So close to the finish you can almost see it. Even if you made only one mile an hour, you'd get there with time to spare."

Garfield chuckled. "I'll even help push."

Allen held up his hand. "No men." He gave her a nod. "I know you can do this."

Allen's belief in her made her hope soar again, and she faced Vivian.

Her cousin smiled. "We have been through too much not to try."

Zola stood at the driver's side and manipulated the steering wheel to keep the Winton on the road. Vivian pushed on the other side. With her teeth, Ladybug grabbed a dangling end of the rope that held their tarp in place and pulled. Though her doggy efforts didn't make a difference, she was a trouper.

The crowd fell silent.

Zola, Vivian, *and* Ladybug were barely able to make the more than five-hundred-pound vehicle inch forward for a moment. They weren't strong enough. She wasn't dressed for this. Her heeled slippers skidded on the dirt road that was quickly turning to mud, and Vivian didn't appear to be faring any better. Zola wished now that she hadn't insisted upon looking her best to cross the finish line. If she were in her trousers and boots, this would be a whole lot easier, but trousers and boots were out of the question. Such attire on a lady in public was wholly unacceptable. An utter disgrace. Even her bedraggled appearance was better than that kind of scandal.

A man ran up and held out his hands as though he would push, but Allen waved him away. "They have to do this without men helping them."

Zola appreciated Allen looking out for their interests. She also appreciated that a man had been willing to help them succeed.

A lady in a fancy white walking dress, large hat, white gloves, and a suffrage sash fell in behind Zola and pushed with her. "You have proven that women can do anything."

A woman in a plain black skirt and white blouse with leg-o'-mutton sleeves came along behind Vivian. The automobile rolled forward.

By ones and twos, women crowded around the vehicle and pushed. The Winton moved faster. At this rate, the journey would conclude within the hour.

Tears filled Zola's eyes. They were going to make it after all.

A convoy of cars trailed in the *Atlantic*'s wake.

When the end came into view a half mile ahead, the lady with the suffrage sash tapped Zola on the shoulder. "Climb in, both of you. We'll get you there."

Zola and Vivian got in. Someone picked up Ladybug and deposited her inside as well. A hint of sadness cast a brief shadow on Zola's elation. With the thrill of this adventure behind her, she would miss the excitement and challenges of the past year. How would she ever return to her ordinary life?

Vivian held the white Pomeranian on her lap. "It's fitting that you are behind the wheel for this."

"You know we look like drowned rats, don't you?"

Vivian beamed. "I don't care."

Surprisingly, neither did Zola. So much for perfection.

As the Winton crossed the finish line, Dr. Horatio Nelson Jackson smiled and saluted them, and Bertha Jackson waved vigorously.

The hushed crowd erupted into deafening cheers. Ladybug barked.

Zola parked in front of the Palace Hotel and hugged her cousin. "We did it."

Vivian squeezed back. "Thank you for asking me to do this with you."

"I don't recall asking."

Vivian giggled. "I could have refused if I really wanted to."

"I'm glad you didn't. We made a good team."

A throng of reporters crowded around the *Atlantic*, throwing questions at them.

Zola looked for Allen. His was the face she wanted to see in this moment of victory.

He came and opened her door.

She took his offered hand and stood.

Garfield joined them and spoke to the reporters. "Everyone inside out of the rain. You can ask your questions after they give a speech." He held the door open.

Allen escorted her inside and to the hotel's ballroom.

Zola picked up Ladybug. "I'm not prepared to give a speech."

Garfield laughed. "I've never known you to lack for something to say. You'll do fine." He went up onto the platform at one end of the room.

Allen and Barney left her and Vivian at the two steps where their parents waited. Zola's parents as well as Vivian's hugged them and told them they were proud.

Once on the platform, Vivian whispered, "What are you going to say?"

"I have no idea. You want to give the speech?"

"No. That's one crazy thing you're not going to talk me into." Vivian patted her arm. "But I'm right beside you. For moral support."

Garfield introduced them. "When Miss Calkin declared she and her cousin were going to drive across the country, I didn't believe they would even attempt it. I expected them to back out the next day or the next or the next. She and Miss Newland have surprised me every step of the way. Zola, Vivian, tell us why you did it. Though I'd love to take credit, I don't believe my goading you into this spurred you on all this time." He stepped back as the bystanders clapped.

Zola dipped her head to Garfield and then to the audience. They quieted. She took Ladybug's paw and waved. The crowd chuckled. "Mr. Prescott, thank you. We certainly never expected all of this. Sorry for my bedraggled appearance. We ran into a few troubles along the way." That was an understatement.

"I would first like to thank the Lord for making this trip possible and getting us through all the hardships and for the friends we made." She smiled at Allen.

"When we started this adventure, I had a clear picture in my mind of what it would be like every mile of the way. The reality was nothing like I imagined. It was so much harder and so much better. I am a different person than I was two months ago when I started, and that lady was different from the one a year ago when Mr. Prescott provoked me into taking up his challenge." She nodded to Garfield.

"If I had known how difficult this endeavor would turn out to be, I *never* would have undertaken such an arduous journey. But then I would have missed out on becoming the woman who stands before you. I thought I was capable of doing only a few things. This trip has taught me that I can do anything I set my mind to.

"A part of me is glad for this adventure to be over and to sleep in my own bed again. But another part of me is sad to have it all end. I imagined crossing this finish line to cheers"—she took Vivian's hand and raised it—"for *us*. What I heard were cheers for women everywhere.

"Men, don't get me wrong. We women don't strive to be better than you—we just want to be seen as your equals. Men are strong. Women are strong. Together we are stronger.

"I have done things I never imagined. This past year, I have had dirt and engine grease under my fingernails for the first time in my life. Sorry, Mother. I'll get them clean. I promise."

Laughter rippled through the room.

Her mother acknowledged with a nod and proud tears glistening in her eyes.

She didn't know what else to say, so she turned to Vivian. "Do you want to speak?"

Her cousin shook her head. "I think you covered it beautifully."

Zola faced front again. "Thank you."

The reporters pressed in from one side and threw their questions at her and Vivian. When the inquiries died down, she realized that Allen hadn't asked anything. Not surprising, since he had traveled with them for the last two months. He already knew the answer to anything he might ask. "Mr. Basart, have you no questions?"

He shook his head then held up his hand. "Wait. I do have one."

Oh, the curiosity of what it could be after spending so much time together. "What would you like to know?"

As though anticipating his question would be important, the people in the room hushed.

He straightened and took a deep breath. "If a lowly reporter were to ask an adventurous socialite to spend the rest of her life with him, what would her answer be?"

Yes! She cleared her throat and schooled her emotions. "The socialite would tell the reporter that if he were truly a gentleman, he would ask the lady properly."

Allen bent down on one knee, and the hushed crowd stepped back. "I haven't had time to buy you a ring, but I will. Zola Calkin, will you do me the honor of becoming my wife?"

"The honor would be mine."

He stood, leapt up onto the platform, and dipped her into a kiss.

How improper in public! But she didn't care.

The crowd erupted in applause.

Her adventure across the country had meant more than a boost for women. It had driven her straight into the arms of the man she loved.

She kissed *him* this time.

Most improper.

Historical Note

Dr. Horatio Nelson Jackson's transcontinental trek in 1903 is an actual historical event. Only 150 miles of paved roads existed in the entire United States, most of those in large cities. He, along with his chauffeur/mechanic, Sewall Crocker, traveled from San Francisco to New York City in a twenty-horsepower automobile. Along the way, Horatio bought a dog named Bud who enjoyed the trip immensely. Dr. Jackson and Mr. Crocker left San Francisco on Saturday, May 23, and arrived in New York on Sunday, July 26, at four thirty in the morning, completing the first American cross-country road trip. The journey took sixty-three days, twelve hours, and thirty minutes. Two other two-man teams left California in the following weeks of the same year, but Dr. Jackson's team was the first to make it. Other endeavors to drive across the country in an automobile had been attempted in years prior to Jackson's trip without success. I thought it only natural for ladies to follow suit and join in the fun.

Mary Davis is a bestselling, award-winning author of over a dozen and a half novels in both historical and contemporary themes, eight novellas, two compilations, three short stories, and has been included in ten collections. She has two brand-new novels releasing in 2019. She is a member of American Christian Fiction Writers and is active in two critique groups.

Mary lives in the Pacific Northwest with her husband of over thirty-four years and two cats. She has three adult children and two grandchildren. She enjoys board and card games, rain, and cats. She would enjoy gardening if she didn't have a black thumb. Her hobbies include quilting, porcelain doll making, sewing, crafting, crocheting, and knitting. Visit her online at www.marydavisbooks.com, or www.facebook.com/mary.davis.73932 and join her FB readers group, Mary Davis READERS Group at www.facebook.com/groups/132969074007619/?source=create_flow.

Detours of the Heart

by Donna Schlachter

Dedication

Dedicated first and foremost to God the Father, God the Son,
and God the Holy Spirit. Without Him, no story is worth telling.

To Patrick, the love of my life.

To my agent Terrie Wolf, who believes in me
when I don't believe in myself,
and who reminds me—it's all in the timing.

To Pastor Adam Bishop for the great teaching on healing.
You see, I *am* paying attention.

In all thy ways acknowledge him, and he shall direct thy paths.
PROVERBS 3:6

Chapter 1

Y ou will marry him, or you'll not spend another night under my roof, you ungrateful child."

Millie Watkins focused on the vein in her father's temple, the one that emerged, pulsating in tempo with the staccato timing of his words.

He was angry for sure.

She stepped back, putting another foot or so between them. Just out of reach of his ham-sized fists. One of the cats—Mouser or Calico, she wasn't certain— screeched when her foot made contact with its tail. She staggered to regain her balance, grabbing at a kitchen chair to stay upright.

His hobnailed boots were weapons as formidable as his hands, and she'd not fall victim to either today.

She raised her chin. "I won't marry that pimple-faced child cleverly disguised as the postmaster's assistant. Angus Portman is rude, lewd, and crude, as well you know."

"That boy is as fine a catch as you'll ever hope to hook. It's not like you're any great shakes, girlie."

Despite hearing these words—and others like them—all her life, they still stung, and she blinked back tears. No, she wasn't as beautiful as her mother— God rest her soul—but few women were.

"You can't force me."

Her words rang hollow in her own ears, and rather than convincing her father to do as she wished, they fueled the sneer that started with his eyes, then made its way down to his mouth, revealing teeth yellowed by tobacco, worn down through use, and missing because of bar fights. "Git your things and be gone then. Cain't afford to feed you no longer."

She exhaled. He spoke the truth, for he was a hardscrabble widower farmer with four children younger than her. The next in line, Anna, was of an age to leave school and take care of the house.

He was right. He didn't need her. Couldn't afford to keep her.

Didn't want her.

She nodded. "I'll be gone in an hour."

"You ain't got that much stuff. Git now."

She turned and left the kitchen, climbing the ladder to the loft she shared with her sister and brothers. Thankfully, they were in school and wouldn't see her humiliation. She was more of a mother to them than a sister, and her heart ached that she couldn't say a proper goodbye. Let them know she wasn't leaving them forever, the way their ma had. There in the morning, dead by the time they came home from school.

No, she'd leave them a note. Assure them she'd keep in touch. Send money when she became famous. Bring them to live with her in California.

Because that's where she was headed—the silver screen in Hollywood. As she shoved her few belongings into a pillowcase—she didn't even own a proper carpet bag or trunk—she revisited the glamor of the movies as depicted in the few dog-eared magazines the pharmacist traded for sweeping the shop and stocking the shelves.

The secret she kept from everybody.

The only thing she owned that she didn't have to share with anybody else.

That, and her dreams.

Images of Greta Garbo greeting her on the movie set of their next feature film. Of John Barrymore holding her hand in the dark. Of a comedy routine with Charlie Chaplin.

She shivered with delight. She'd show her father, that ugly Angus Portman, and the whole neighborhood that she was better than they thought.

The last items to go into her makeshift travel bag were three editions of *Hollywood Glamour*. Not much to show for the hours of work she put in to earn them, but a treasure house of information on hairstyles, dresses, heel heights, and makeup tips.

Not that she had any makeup, of course. Her father would never stand for that. *Painted women* he called them when he saw them in town hanging around the saloon. As though applying a little kohl on her eyes or rouge on her cheeks would suddenly transform her into a loose woman.

She took a final glance around the room she had called hers for the past eighteen years, then headed for the ladder, dropping her pillowcase to the floor below before climbing down.

Or rather, out.

Out of the poverty of her childhood.

Out of the promise of endless hours of backbreaking work and a passel of kids that put her mother into an early grave despite the belief that God would heal her.

Out of boredom and drudgery and the bleak landscape of Terrace Addition, a mile from the city, surrounded by desert hills and coyote packs.

She stepped through the screen door—hanging by a single hinge for as long as she could remember—and pointed her toes toward town. In about three hours from now, she'd reach her goal: the Alvarado Harvey House Hotel.

The first stop on her journey west.

＋●━━・━━●＋

Sick and tired.

Peter Duncan jerked on the wheel of the Indian Detours bus, avoiding another bone-shuddering pothole in the dusty road ahead.

Sick and tired.

Of always moving around. Never having a place to call his own. Sharing a room—and often a bed—with a stranger.

Raucous laughter from the fat guy with dark stains under the arms of his white linen suit filled the hot, cramped vehicle, and Peter wondered for about the tenth time today if he should give up this job and move on.

But where? Not back home to his family in Arizona. Or Texas. Or wherever they were this month.

Not that there really was a home to return to. As itinerant farmers, his folks and six sisters followed the crops, season in and season out, in a wide swath of country from California to Florida. Two weeks here, three weeks there. Sometimes subsisting off the fruit or vegetables they picked. Oranges every day, every meal, grated on a man's nerves and failed to fill his belly for long.

Although he'd kill right now for one, sweet and juicy, fresh off the tree.

Seemed the greatest component of his diet lately was dust.

And rude comments from rich passengers who thought they were better than him because they paid him to drive. Who grumbled when they didn't think they got every penny's worth. Like today. No tour guide again.

He shook a lock of hair from his eyes. That wasn't a very Christian attitude on his part. After all, God was good to provide this job, a roof over his head every night, and three meals a day. Even if they were the leftovers from the Harvey House Restaurant, picked over, sometimes dry and a little crusty. Still, they were something to be thankful for.

As was the tin containing his tips for today, an amount that often doubled his earnings as a driver. Which he didn't have to share with the tour guide, since he did both positions today. His regular guide was out sick. Again. Another thing to be grateful for. Not that he wanted to benefit at another's expense.

He made the final turn from the Acoma Tribal Lands onto the road leading back into Albuquerque and the hotel on First Street. These folks had put in a full day, and his stomach told him that five o'clock rapidly approached.

Once on the more level and even track, the rocking and rolling of the bus acted like a pacifier for the passengers, sending them to sleep. Which suited him fine. An hour of peace and quiet, giving him time to think and plan and sometimes even to pray.

He sighed. Yes, he should do more praying and less complaining. Unable to take his eyes off the road, he turned inward for a moment. "God, thanks for takin' care of us today. And for gettin' us all back safely. And Lord, if You could see fit to send me a wife, I'd appreciate that. I need a helpmeet, and I surely do want to settle down before I'm too old to enjoy my children. Anytime You're ready, God. Amen."

Over a little rise in the road, he spotted somebody walking toward town.

Must have come from Terrace Addition.

A woman. Or a young girl. Totin' a sack of somethin'.

He checked the rearview mirror. Sure enough, heads lolled, confirming his passengers slept. No harm in offering her a lift.

He slowed then pulled over to the shoulder, working the lever to open the door. "Want a ride into town?"

She stared up at him with brown eyes so dark he thought they were black, until the sun caught the golden bits that danced like fairy dust. A straw hat protected her face, and a smattering of freckles dotted her cheeks framed by hair the color of honey fresh from the hive.

She craned her neck around to the rest of the vehicle. "Got no money for a ticket."

Peter shook his head. "Not a commercial bus. Work for the Alvarado."

"Where you comin' from?"

"Indian Detours bus of visitors to the Acoma Tribal Lands."

Her eyes widened. "People pay to go out there?"

"Sure do. Folks like to learn about nature and the land. And buy Indian jewelry."

She stepped in, clutching the railing. "Folks sure have strange notions."

He nodded. "Where you headed?"

"The Alvarado. Gotta get me a job."

"That's where I'm goin'. I can show you around."

She settled into the single seat directly behind him, which suited him fine. That way he could keep an eye on her in the mirror.

Because she sure was a sight to behold. Pretty. Strong too by the looks of her. Brave. She had to be, setting off on her own to find work.

Just the kind of woman he was looking for.

Now, the final requirement: Did she believe in God?

He caught her watching him in the mirror, and heat crept up his neck. What was he thinking? He just met her, for crying out loud, and already he was evaluating her qualifications as a wife?

He smiled at her. "What kind of work you lookin' for?"

She shrugged. "Dunno. I can read and write. I'm used to hard work. Cooking. Cleaning. Laundry. Sewing. The like."

He knew exactly what she meant. The same kind of life for most women around here. Everywhere, he reckoned. His mother's life described in a single sentence. "That what you want to do forever?"

"Nope." She turned to stare out the window at the gray and brown landscape flashing past at more than ten miles an hour. "Just until I get enough money to buy me a ticket."

"To where?"

She perked up at this question. "To Hollywood. I'm an actress."

His heart thudded all the way to the toes of his boots. Just when he thought he'd found himself a keeper—or at least one he wanted to get to know better—she turned out to be another highfalutin fancy woman.

Funny how looks could be deceiving.

He turned his attention back to the road ahead.

No point in even asking about her faith in God. What did she need Him for? She was an actress.

◆━━━━━◆

Millie's heart raced like a runaway horse, thundering in her head at the audacity of her words. There. She'd said it.

"I'm an actress."

Well, it's what she wanted, wasn't it? What she dreamed of. Why she worked so hard for those magazines. Why she practiced memorizing entire chapters of romance stories, exercising her memory for when she needed to learn her lines.

But to say it out loud.

She let out a deep breath.

That took courage. More than she thought she had in her.

But if that's what was needed to get her what she wanted, she'd shout it from the rooftops until she was hoarse.

She leaned forward, dangling her arms over the rail separating her from the driver. "What's it like, the Alvarado?"

His eyes jerked back to the mirror, connecting with hers. Blue eyes. Blond hair. A space between his front teeth. He could be actor material too, if he was as smart as he was good looking. "I dunno. Nice, I guess."

Her brow pulled down. Is that all he could say? "I hear it's like a mansion. The Jewel of the West. Fancy rooms. Gilded chairs. Carpet so thick you can drown in it."

"S'pose so. Don't spend much time in that part of the hotel. Drivers eat in the servants' area."

She closed her eyes and leaned back. "Doesn't matter. Got to be better than where I grew up."

"Terrace Addition?"

She stared at his reflection in the mirror. Was her past painted on her like a billboard? One as big as the Hollywood sign, maybe? "How'd you know?"

"Not much else out here within walkin' distance."

She relaxed again. "Silly me."

He slowed the bus as they crossed a bridge just outside town, then turned toward the downtown section. Millie had been here but once, for a Veterans Day parade about five years ago. A day trip with her parents and siblings. A fun day filled with cotton candy and bands in the park and swimming in the lake.

The next year, her mother was gone, and overnight her father turned into a bitter, angry man. One more able to express his feelings with his fists than with his words. One who figured a slap more profitable than a tender touch.

No more. A man would never treat her that way again.

Now the town—without the oversight and protection of her family—seemed overwhelming. More tall buildings reaching for the sky. More cars than she'd seen in her entire life combined, parked on every street, filling every lane of travel. Mixed in with horses and wagons and carriages. Horns tooting. Brakes squealing. Horses neighing at the intrusion into their domain.

All of a sudden, a wave of something she'd never felt before washed over her. Had she made a huge mistake? Maybe marrying Angus Portman wasn't such a bad idea. Perhaps she could convince him to move to California with her. Help her achieve her dream of stardom.

Then the bus pulled to a stop in front of the biggest building she'd ever seen. The train station. Bigger, surely, than Buckingham Palace. Or the White House. And over there, a train chugged into the station, its wheels screaming against the tracks. Men in black uniforms scurried around. Women in silk dresses and matching parasols strolled along the wooden boardwalk.

And over there, nestled in the midst of the activity like a queen bee surrounded by her workers, the Alvarado. Red tile roof gleaming in the sun. Fountains shooting water. Flowers and plants as plentiful as a garden. The tantalizing aromas of beef, chicken, *and* pork wafting on the evening breeze, all at the same time. Surely the restaurant didn't offer three kinds of meat at the same meal?

Had she died and gone to heaven at this very instant, she'd enter the pearly gates happily. Not that she had any worries of such a thing happening. A God who'd let her mother die wouldn't have any interest in spending time with her. Not on earth, not in heaven, not anywhere.

Chapter 2

"Miss Watkins. A moment, please."

Millie sighed and tucked a lock of hair behind her ear. Not once in the past three days had Mr. Ramirez, the restaurant manager, found anything to compliment her on. The simple act of touching her hair was just another item on his list of complaints, for sure. She forced a smile. "Yes, Mr. Ramirez."

She set her tray of dirty dishes on the table nearest the kitchen—one used for paying customers only when the restaurant was filled to capacity—and crossed the dining area. The three other Harvey Girls avoided her glance as she passed. Once again, she felt like Typhoid Mary.

The manager looked down at her through a monocle, an obvious affectation, since he didn't use spectacles to read the newspaper, the menu, or her tally book. Still, the gesture served its purpose—to remind her of her lowly position in relation to his. "Miss Watkins, what were you doing?"

"Clearing the table, sir."

"Before that."

"Serving the food, sir."

His eyes narrowed. "You were talking with the customers at table twelve."

So he'd caught that little banter, had he? "Sir, it was harmless. They were telling me about California. And Hollywood." She closed her eyes and clasped her hands in front of her, swaying in time to music only she could hear. "Mr. Carter, the younger man, climbed up to the Hollywood sign and left his autograph there."

"Miss Watkins. You are not here to fraternize with the customers. You are here to serve them. Mr. Harvey Jr. is specific about his rules. You signed a contract to obey those rules."

"But, Mr. Ramirez—"

"No buts, young lady. I warned you repeatedly yesterday about this kind of behavior. You may consider yourself relieved of duties. Permanently. Go to the pay office to collect your wages, then clear out your room."

Millie studied the floor as she swallowed back a lump the size of a baseball. Without a job, she couldn't get to Hollywood. Without a job, she'd be forced to return home.

She looked up to entreat the manager once more, but he'd already dismissed her from his mind and turned to straighten a place setting on a nearby table.

She pivoted and headed out of the restaurant, around the corner, and down the corridor toward the pay office. Not that she expected much. Two or maybe three dollars at most, including tips. That might get her a ticket to Flagstaff.

Loud voices reached her ears, and she paused. A woman exited the office and pushed past her, brushing against her.

The woman, her neck wrapped in a scarf and her mouth covered by a handkerchief, stopped. "Forgive me."

"No, excuse me."

The woman scurried off, her heels clicking on the wooden floor before exiting through the employee entrance at the rear of the hotel.

Strange. It had to be more than seventy degrees outside. Why would she wear a scarf?

Millie entered the pay office and waited at the wooden counter while two men in an office to her right huddled together, deep in conversation. After a few minutes of head shaking and murmuring, the two men separated, with one sitting in a chair, staring out the window.

The other man crossed to the pay wicket. "Can I help you?"

"Yes. I've been working here as a Harvey Girl in the restaurant—"

"Payday isn't until Friday. We don't give advances unless you've been here at least six months, and then Mr. Harvey Jr. will need to approve your request."

The man's staccato tone served like nails in her heart. "I don't need an advance."

He peered at her. "Then what do you need?"

"What was wrong with that woman?"

He blinked several times. "She has the mumps."

Ah, that explained the scarf. "I'm sorry to hear that."

"Not half so sorry as the Indian Detours bus tour that goes out again this afternoon without a tour guide because she can't work today. The driver did a good enough job on the morning tour, but a few passengers complained and wanted their money back."

The mention of the tour reminded Millie of Peter Duncan, the strange man she met on her way to town. "Has she been out sick for a while?"

"This is her third day. Said she'd be well enough to work today, which is why we booked two tours. Mr. Harvey Jr. doesn't like getting complaints. And he likes even less having to refund tickets and apologize to his customers, some of whom are leaving in the morning." He leaned across the counter. "Lots of folks come here especially for the tour, you know. They will be most disappointed."

"What did she do for the tour?"

"Why, the guide runs the story about the tribe, the hotel, the jewelry. All that stuff."

Perhaps this was her chance to show she was capable. Despite what her father said. "Does the guide chat with the customers on the tour?"

"Of course. The friendlier the guide is, the better the sales. And the tips. And the happier the customers."

"Could I try out for the job?"

"But you're a Harvey Girl. I don't think—"

"I don't think we have much choice, Walter, do you?"

The voice at her elbow made her jump, and she faced the speaker. Tall, thin, with a dark, receding hairline, he reminded her of the painting in the front lobby of his father.

"Mr. Harvey, sir."

He peered down at her, but not in the unkindly manner of Mr. Ramirez. "What are your qualifications? Besides being bold to spot an opportunity."

She hoped that was a compliment. "I can memorize anything I read and recite it back to you."

Walter scratched the back of his head. "Mr. Harvey, the Indian Detours bus leaves in less than thirty minutes. Nobody could remember the two-hour script that quickly."

"Let's give her a chance, shall we? And if she passes muster, we'll allow her to carry a cheat sheet this one time."

Millie licked dry lips and accepted the bundle of pages Walter handed her. She scanned the first page. What was she getting herself into? She didn't know anything about the Acoma people, their jewelry, or their traditions.

She drew a calming breath. She could do this. She must.

She studied the first sheet, committing the facts to memory. Then she closed her eyes and began reciting.

About four paragraphs in, Mr. Harvey Jr. cleared his throat.

She opened her eyes. "Did I miss something?"

He smiled. "Not at all. You're hired. For today only." He turned to the man behind the counter. "Walter, is the tour sold out?"

"No, sir, there is one seat left."

"Good. I'll go along this time to see how Miss—" He turned to her. "What is your name?"

"Millie Watkins."

"To see how Miss Watkins handles herself."

Great. A brand-new job, and the boss himself there to test her.

Oh well, it was nice while it lasted.

◆―――――◆

Peter checked his watch. He had about ten minutes before reporting for the next tour of the day. And he wouldn't waste a single precious moment.

Miss Carlita Espinoza, oldest daughter of the train conductor, snuggled against his side on the park bench overlooking the pond where swans floated past. She was a nice girl, from a good family, born in Albuquerque, and eager to please.

Perhaps too eager.

She leaned in, eyes closed, lips puckered to receive his kiss. Shallow breaths and flared nostrils might be attractive in the movies, but here, now—well, he was just a little scared of her. He had little experience with women at all, and even less with an aggressive one.

Perhaps it was her Hispanic blood.

Perhaps he was a coward.

While the petite senorita seemed shy and demure, the mere act of sitting on this bench awakened behaviors he hadn't anticipated. And as pretty as she was, Carlita was a cheap copy of that Millie Watkins. He wrinkled his nose and shifted away from her, putting another inch of space between them. Must be circumspect, particularly in public. And this was certainly not the place to awaken any amorous emotions in either one of them.

What would people say? He wanted to serve God, perhaps pastor his own church someday. He couldn't do that in good conscience knowing he'd stirred lustful thoughts—or heaven forbid, fleshly passions—all while sitting on a park bench.

A shadow passed on the ground before him, and he looked up. The object of his thoughts strode past him, her attention caught up in the handful of papers she carried in her hands. Her lips moved silently, and once she shook her head, frowned at the words, then closed her eyes as she walked on.

He extracted himself from Miss Espinoza's grip and hurried after Millie. "Hello again."

She stopped and faced him. "Hello, yourself."

Now what? He hadn't thought about what to say next. "Fancy meeting you here." He sighed. Did that sound as dumb to her as it did to him?

She glanced over his shoulder at Carlita. "Are you with her? She looks upset. I think she's. . .pouting."

That was another thing Carlita did well when not pleased. And while at first endearing, the affectation soon grated on his nerves. Particularly once he learned Carlita was seldom happy. "She wants me to stay."

Millie dropped the hand holding the papers to her side. "Oh. Sorry. Well, see you later."

But Peter knew by the smile dancing at the corners of her eyes and her mouth that she was anything but sorry. "I was just leaving. Got to get to the tour bus."

"Me too."

"Huh? Is it your afternoon off?" After all, how else could she have the time—or the money—to take a tour? "Didn't know you're interested in the Acoma."

"I didn't know it either. But isn't their history fascinating?"

He shrugged. "I don't know. I don't listen to the tour guide. Sally's been out sick for a few days, but she's due back today."

"Actually, Sally's still sick. Mumps. I'm taking her place. For today only."

Peter's heart did a double take. To think that not only could he conjure Millie up simply by thinking about her, but now they'd spend the afternoon together—well, it was simply beyond wonderful. He quirked his chin toward the papers. "Is that your script?"

"Yes. Mr. Harvey Jr. said I could use it since I didn't get much time to memorize it. But I've got most of it now."

"How long have you been studying?"

"What time is it now?"

"About five till one."

"Oh, then about fifteen minutes."

His admiration for her grew another degree. "You're kidding me. It took Sally three weeks to get that into her head."

"I told you. I'm an actress."

Thunk!

His feelings for this woman took a nose dive. Right. She was an actress. Headed for Hollywood.

He nodded toward the garage and the bus parked outside. Best to rid himself of Clinging Carlita, and keep Millie Watkins at arm's length.

So far he was batting a thousand when it came to choosing the wrong woman.

◆•————•◆

Millie's first tour went almost without a hitch. Even though Mr. Harvey Jr.'s presence made her a little nervous, she managed to make it through her talk without a glitch, looking at her script only twice. The passengers seemed to enjoy themselves, smiling and taking pictures of her in her buckskin shift and headband, complete with a feather. Mr. Harvey Jr. said she did well, and if she wanted it, the job was hers.

To say she was thrilled was an understatement. Less time on her feet, no more of Mr. Ramirez's disapproving stares, and better wages and tips promised a ticket to Hollywood sooner than expected.

And working with Peter today was fun, even if he was a bit standoffish. Then again, maybe the Indian Detours had the same kind of rules as the Harvey House—no fraternization with staff. No courting. No marriage. Absolutely no shenanigans or getting into trouble, as Mr. Ramirez phrased it.

When the bus pulled into the courtyard in front of the hotel, she smiled and acknowledged each passenger as he or she disembarked. While she and Peter cleaned the bus—picking up a stray handkerchief, sweeping the floor, cleaning the glass—in preparation for the next morning's tour, they chatted. Peter shared his desire to serve God, while she remained silent on the topic of a deity who'd never been anything but silent with her.

When she stepped down from the vehicle, a familiar figure strode toward her. Carlita.

Apparently the girl couldn't take Peter's very obvious hint.

He wasn't interested in a relationship.

Well, that was fine with her.

She wasn't either.

As nice as he was, she was headed for Hollywood.

And nothing would stop her.

Peter exited the bus practically into Carlita's arms as she waited at the bottom of the steps for him. She whispered something into his ear. He shook his head, but she persisted, then looped her arm through his, waving to Millie as though they were bosom buddies.

An ache passed through her chest, there one minute, then gone. What a handsome couple they made, although it appeared as though Carlita was leading and Peter followed reluctantly. Perhaps she'd been hasty to dismiss him. A temporary beau, perhaps, at least until she left for California and the brand-new film industry.

But no. She'd be better off not getting even tangentially attached. She had a job to do, and that's all that mattered. Earn the money to buy the ticket to stardom.

And she wouldn't let any man—or any God who let her mother die—get in the way.

Chapter 3

Peter glanced in his rearview mirror for about the hundredth time in the past minute. Millie perched on her seat, looking as fresh as when she set out on the Detour more than three hours before. Not a hair out of place—well, except for the lock that fell over her left temple and curled a bit on the end. Seemed she spent half her time tucking it behind her ear.

Which she did right now, almost as though his thinking conjured up the action.

He smiled, but she didn't return his gesture. She was too intent on her job.

That was Millie, all right. As focused as one of those telescopes that searched the heavens for—for what? Stars and planets. Comets and meteors. But were they looking for the most important thing—for God?

He doubted it.

And neither was she, apparently.

He turned his attention back to the person who constantly competed with his thoughts of his Creator. Millie Watkins.

Spending every day with her for the past week made it difficult for him to keep his focus on his job or on his calling. Because he certainly had no intentions of driving for the Indian Detours bus for the rest of his life. No, he longed to preach in the pulpit, to share his love for God with others.

If only Millie shared that passion with him.

By far the most beautiful girl he ever met, that wasn't her only attraction for him. She was also caring, compassionate, and fun to be around. She made him laugh. She made him think. She made him examine his beliefs, and her questions deepened his faith.

And right now, her mere presence tantalized him with a longing to gather her into his arms and quiet her tour speech with a passionate kiss.

But was it all an act? Something she put on like a fancy dress as if she were playing a part? After all, she was an actress, wasn't she?

He turned his attention back to the road ahead. They were on their way to the second of the Acoma tribal towns, Sun City. The first went well, with the twenty-four passengers strolling through the pueblos and buying up a few knickknacks that would likely languish in an attic or gather dust in a parlor. But Sun City was known for its quintessential Acoma-pattern pottery that celebrated the sun god, and its turquoise jewelry, both highly sought after by collectors and tourists.

The winding road led up to the top of a mesa where the town perched as though preparing to jump onto the desert floor below. Almost invisible, the small clay huts dug into the steep cliff sides. With no modern amenities, such as running water or electricity, life out here was harsh and short.

He navigated a particularly sharp turn and thought about the previous evening. Carlita Espinoza didn't give up easily. When Millie turned down his offer of coffee—again—and the eager Carlita met him at the parking area, he decided to go with her.

Much to his chagrin, she cajoled him to join her in the town square at some kind of folk festival, and after three cups of a fruity punch—certainly laced with tequila or another equally strong drink—he tossed aside his hat and his inhibitions and danced with her.

The rest of the evening was hazy, although he was fairly certain he hadn't completely humiliated himself.

The early hours of the morning found him on the steps of the church, where he vaguely recalled her dumping him when he insisted he would be a minister someday.

Peter pulled the bus to a stop and opened the door, disembarked, and lowered the step, then assisted the passengers—beginning with Millie first—from the vehicle. The touch of her fingers in his palm sent a tingle up his arm as though he'd hit his funny bone, and when she pulled away from him to answer a passenger's question, a feeling akin to jealousy arose in him that she would pay more attention to a stranger than to him.

Did she know how he felt about her? That what he knew about her fit perfectly into his ideals for both a wife and a helpmeet?

Or was she playing the part of one of those alluring sirens he heard about in the movies?

He stepped into the shade of a tree while Millie led her tour participants into the first adobe where they could sample and purchase baked goods. What exactly did he feel?

Surely not love. For all the hours they'd spent together in the past week, he knew little about her plans for her future except that she was headed for California.

Which was in direct competition with his dreams and goals.

No, it would never work out between them. He should simply forget her and move on to someone else.

As if.

◆— —◆

Millie led the way from the bakery to the next shop, her favorite. Hannah Blue-Sky was a master artisan when it came to working with silver and local precious stones like turquoise and apache tears. Inside the small building, Hannah bent over a piece, her only illumination coming from a nearby open window.

The tourists gathered around the workbench, asking questions and exclaiming over various articles, while several studied finished pieces on display on tables set in a horseshoe shape. Millie stood to one side to give them room while keeping an eye on them. She and Hannah had an unspoken agreement: Millie protected her wares from light-fingered tourists, and Hannah spun the tales that sold the pieces.

From the corner of her eye, Peter moved into view, then leaned against a tree. She definitely could have done worse when it came to a driver. Several of the other Detours that visited the Lakota and Laguna lands had drivers who drank or swore or harassed the guides.

And while Peter was good looking, personable, and even presentable, she held him at arm's length. And why not? He wasn't part of her plan. He wanted to settle down, get married, preach.

Her complete opposite in every way. Travel, acting, handsome leading men, and real life were on her agenda.

Sure, he told corny jokes that made her laugh, but that wasn't enough on which to base a relationship—if she ever thought of a future with him.

Which she didn't.

Wouldn't.

So why did the sight of him dancing with Carlita last night cause her to grit her teeth and clench her fists? Not that she was following him or anything like that. No, she turned him down. He had every right to ask another.

But Carlita? It was obvious what she wanted. Marriage to a good boy. Settle down. Have babies.

Right in line with Peter's goals.

Didn't bother her at all.

The tour party moved on to a pottery store, and Hannah stepped outside. A lingering tourist, smelling of dust, sweat, and cheap cologne, sidled up to her in the empty shop. The man's cigarette, clenched between his lips, dropped ash onto the dirt floor of the shop. "Hey honey. This here jewelry would look great against your skin." He lifted a finger to touch her where her peasant blouse exposed her neck. "How's about I buy you a little somethin'?"

She stepped back, forcing the snarl in the back of her throat down. If she offended the customers, they wouldn't buy. And they'd complain about her. She pasted on a smile. "Thank you, but no. These pieces are out of my price range."

His brow raised. "Oh I see. You're *that* kind of girl." He dug into a pocket and pulled out a roll of bills. "No problem, girlie. I can pay cash." He shoved a five down the neck of her blouse and stepped forward, pinning her against the wall. "Now, give over."

She pressed her hands against his chest, her scream caught in the lump of fear in her throat. She twisted her head from side to side to avoid his lecherous mouth. *Where was Hannah?* The man grabbed her behind, pinching. She closed her eyes and shuddered when his lips made contact with her cheek.

And then he released her.

Her eyes snapped open.

No, not truly released her.

He shrank against the wall beside her, a fist aimed at his nose, a hand around his throat.

Peter.

The tourist's pale face contrasted with the reddish brown of the adobe, making him seem whiter. The dark look from Peter pinned him in place.

She exhaled and stepped out of reach.

Peter shook the man. "Apologize to the lady."

"She–she's no lady. I paid good money for her."

Millie removed the offending bill and tossed it at him, relishing the sight of the money falling to the ground. Like dust. She glared at her tormentor, whose cigarette burnt near his lips. "Take your no-good money back. And never touch me again. Do you hear?"

The passenger nodded, sweat dripping from his nose. Peter released him, and the man scurried outside.

Millie turned to her knight in shining armor. "Thank you."

He bowed. "Always pleased to help a damsel in distress."

His sentiment rankled. Is that how he saw her? A woman in need of a man? She pushed her shoulders back. "Time to move to the next shop."

His smile fell—again, to the ground like dust—and she wished she could snatch back her words. But it was too late. He pivoted and exited the adobe, returning to his place under the tree. She huffed. Seemed that the future man of the cloth had a thin skin.

As she exited Hannah's shop, a glance at the bus confirmed that the odious passenger sat in the very last seat, arms crossed, a scowl indicating his displeasure.

Serves him right.

And the man's twin in expression and mood slouched against the tree he occupied when they first arrived. She nodded as she passed Peter, but he didn't so much as nod or bat an eye to acknowledge her.

Men! They could be so infuriating. Fawning and helpful one minute. Cold and aloof the next.

She jutted out her chin. Fine. She could play that game.

Besides, she didn't want a man who would be more married to the church than to her. Who'd spend every waking minute in prayer or Bible reading. That wouldn't be much fun.

And fun is what she wanted more than anything. Along with fun would come happiness. Happiness at being free of Terrace Addition. Happiness at being her own woman, with the world at her feet. Happiness at not having to answer to a man—or to anybody, for that matter.

Maybe it all came down to freedom.

Freedom to choose for herself.

✦•————•✦

Later that evening, Millie curled up in a chair in the room she shared with Kay, a laundress in the hotel. Her book, one discovered on the shelves of the hotel library, offered her several hours of reading enjoyment: *The Acoma of New Mexico.*

Written as a travelogue to memorialize the travels of the author, and filled with dozens of photographs, the book was both compelling and informative. In particular, the chapters about the native jewelry, including insights into the importance of animal and nature symbols, fascinated her. Before today she thought a bird was a bird and a cactus simply a plant. But now she read of legends and tales that went along with each symbol, and the symbol's meaning to the Acoma people.

Starting tomorrow she planned to pay more attention to Hannah's stories—and the ones told by the other artisans in the village. Knowing more about the subjects of the Indian Detours provided fodder for her talks. Understanding the minute differences in style and design of the crafts meant she could help each tourist purchase the piece that suited his or her own personality.

Not only that, but her spiel wasn't merely a pitch for the passengers.

She saw her talk as training for when she got to Hollywood. Memorizing details now would improve her memory, like working a muscle. After all, producers were certainly looking for someone just like her: a great memory and a pretty face.

Isn't that what Miss Garbo said in one of her many magazine interviews?

Millie stuck her index finger in the book to save her page and picked up her *Hollywood Glamour* magazine. Flipping through several pages, she found the article she remembered. Yes, there it was. *"Miss Garbo credits her success with being able to catch a producer's eye with her comely figure as well as her photographic memory."*

Millie's cheeks heated at the mention of a comely figure. She wasn't quite sure what that meant, but if it had anything to do with how she looked, she had the job nailed. Simply walking down the street garnered her wolf whistles from the locals, and Mr. Sweaty Nose today thought she was worth five dollars for a few minutes of her time.

She fanned herself with the magazine. Not that she was that kind of girl. And never would be. But five whole dollars. For a grope and a squeeze in an Indian jewelry shop. Why, she'd have to work an entire week and include her tips for that kind of money.

Surely Miss Garbo must earn far more than that.

She sighed. What she could do with a lot of money right now.

First off, she'd head straightaway to Hollywood. No more spending hot days on the Indian Detours bus. Then she'd have a trunkful—no, a roomful of beautiful clothes. Flapper clothes, like in the magazine. Long, sequined shifts and matching hats and shoes. Black taffeta for cocktail parties. Silk and satin for lounging beside her pool.

And swimming costumes. Lots of them. One for every day of the week, because surely she'd swim every day in her own private pool. No more sharing the creek with her siblings after a hard rain.

And her own personal bathtub.

And bedroom.

And bed.

Maybe she'd even have her own house. One she didn't have to share with anybody.

Oh, life in Hollywood was going to be so glamorous.

◆━━━◆

Peter strolled along the alley behind the hotel, whistling a tune he'd heard on a phonograph through an open window down the street. He didn't know the name of the song, but it made him happy to imitate the orchestra with his only musical instrument, his mouth.

Was that what the Bible meant when it said that God's people were to be a holy instrument? He paused. Maybe whistling music outside of church music wasn't right. As a man called to be a pastor, perhaps he should focus on something more—well, more churchy.

He thought a moment, then launched into the chorus of "Amazing Grace."

Next came "The Old Rugged Cross," and then "A Mighty Fortress." When he got to the end of what he remembered of that song, he stopped. Would God be offended that one of His preachers only knew the chorus of three pieces of holy music? Maybe he needed to pay more attention on Sunday.

Lately his thoughts often strayed to Millie Watkins. Even in the middle of church.

He kicked aside a rock, enjoying the clatter as it skipped across the dirt, struck the side of the hotel, and rolled a few feet before bouncing off a rusted old tin can.

A window high above slid up, and a head popped out. "Hey, what's that racket down there?"

Peter looked up at the disembodied face of the object of his thoughts. "Hi, Millie. Just me. Whistlin' and kickin' a rock. Whatcha doin'?"

She harrumphed, sounding a lot like his former schoolteacher when he gave an incorrect—or incomplete—answer. "Planning my future. Not wasting my time or frittering away my energy."

Her words bit into him, and he shoved his hands in his pockets and dropped his gaze. "Not fritterin'. Thinkin' and prayin'." While not entirely true—at least not the praying part—maybe God would overlook his little white lie. He looked up again. "Whatcha readin' about?"

She held a magazine in one hand. "Hollywood. Makeup. Etiquette."

"Hollywood? And you're makin' me feel bad about whistlin'?" Didn't sound like she knew what she was talking about. "What's makeup and manners got to do with education?"

"Knowing more about the movie picture business will get me roles faster." She sniffed. Just like his teacher. "So I can become a famous actress when I go to Hollywood."

That dreaded H-word. Every time she mentioned her plans, he shuddered. When she saved up enough money, she'd be gone from his life. Six months, maybe less. As though she never was there.

He swallowed down the lump threatening to choke him. If he didn't tell her how he felt, she wouldn't know, and he'd lose his chance. He drew a deep breath. "Millie, you're a swell girl."

She tipped her head like the little puppy on the phonograph label. He was hopeless.

He tried again. "What I mean is, I like you a lot."

"And I like you, Peter."

"You know I want to be a preacher."

"I do know that. You've told me pretty much every time we've talked."

He stared at her, trying to discern her thoughts. "Will you go for a walk with me?"

"No."

His hopes for his future slipped through his fingers like motor oil through a rusty pan. "Why not?"

"Must I have a reason?" She disappeared inside, and he feared she'd simply close the window and never speak to him again. Then she reappeared, this time without her magazine. She held out one hand, fingers clenched, and counted each digit off, starting with her index finger. "One. I'm busy." Next came her middle finger. "Two. I'm not interested." Her ring finger. The one he'd love to slide a wedding band on. "Three. I have bigger plans than New Mexico." Her pinkie. "Four. That don't include you." Then her thumb. "Five. I'm not interested." She studied her hand. "Oh wait. I mentioned that already, didn't I?" She shrugged. "Doesn't matter. You get the idea."

His hope melted and dissolved into vinegar on his tongue. How to convince her? "I'll go anywhere you like. Just say you'll go for a walk with me."

"No."

"Why not?"

"I don't need the extra baggage."

Chapter 4

Millie slammed the window shut and collapsed onto her bed. Tears burned hot behind her eyes. Tears she swore she wouldn't let him see. Tears that had no basis in reason or in any emotion she could identify. So why did they now threaten to overflow both her lids and her will?

She blinked rapidly to quell the onslaught, but to no avail.

They rolled down her cheeks, dampening her pillow.

No modern woman should cry over a man. Particularly one that threw himself at her so often. Unrequited love—now that was a reason to bawl. Lost love—but she had neither.

What she had was the first decent man she ever knew who was head over heels in like with her—at least according to his words. Like. Not passion. Not love. Not even strong emotional attachment. He'd used none of those words to describe his feelings.

Like.

Well, wasn't that what she wanted? After all, she had plans. And those plans didn't include the son of itinerant farmers hanging on her coattails.

Well, she told him where to get off.

If he never spoke to her again, she deserved nothing more.

And for sure and certain, nothing better.

She rolled over on the bed and stared at the ceiling. She could spend the rest of the evening feeling sorry for herself, or she could make good use of her time.

Her magazine called to her, as did her book. But the thick tome lost the battle. She'd read that another night. When her heart wasn't aching. She propped up her pillow and pulled the blanket over her feet and plunged into another article about meeting the perfect agent.

To acquire the perfect agent, you must be willing to work diligently, to take roles that at first may seem below you, and to never act like a diva. Difficult actors and actresses soon earn a reputation in the industry and, as a result, are offered fewer movie opportunities.

Oh, she would never want that to happen. No, she'd listen to her agent, and the producer. She'd do exactly what they told her to do. Why, she wouldn't even argue if they said she needed to wear that dark red shade of lip color that most folks said were for streetwalkers and soiled doves.

Kind of like the shade she saw a female tourist wearing last week.

Although, it was becoming on her, even if her mouth looked a little pinched, like she was sucking on a lemon.

Now, if she were Miss Greta Garbo, or someone famous like her, then she could do what she liked. Wear the clothes she wanted. Turn down a role that didn't suit her.

But until she was rich and famous, she'd bide her time.

That was one thing she had lots of.

Because she'd keep working hard. Save her money.

She set the magazine on the bed beside her.

Wake up, Hollywood.

Millie Watkins would be the newest silver screen star in town in no time.

The next morning, Millie arrived at the lobby of the hotel a few minutes early. She sauntered through the gift shop. Not all guests of the Alvarado took the Indian Detours trip, so Mr. Harvey Jr. offered them the opportunity to purchase genuine Acoma jewelry, pottery, and woven and leather items without leaving the comfort of the city.

Even those who took the tours often checked on prices before they left, although Millie tried to tell them the natives undersold the gift shop on every item. She'd overheard several snide comments about "thieving Indians," words that pierced her heart because they were both untrue and unfair. Still, she checked her temper and her tongue, preferring to let those tourists learn their lesson the hard way—buy at the hotel, then see the lower prices on the reservation.

She studied several pieces, including a squaw blossom-patterned necklace and a silver-and-agate belt buckle. Hannah really did good work. She ran her hand along a tooled leather belt from one of the other artisans, admiring the intricate pattern celebrating a successful wild pony roundup. Early on she learned that every article contained a story, sometimes more than one, and she practiced training her eye to see beyond the mere decoration.

The bus horn tooted, alerting passengers—and the tour guide—of the bus's departure. She sighed. As much as she loved the reservation, some days she'd love to stay here in the shop and reorganize the displays. Sort the items. Peruse the catalogs.

But that was not for her.

Hollywood beckoned.

As did Peter and a busload of curious tourists.

◆•——•◆

This must be what hell is like.

Peter opened his lunch box and pulled out a slightly mushed ham and wilted lettuce sandwich.

He sighed. He'd ordered neither.

Roast beef, hold the lettuce, mustard.

Seemed the hotel kitchen was off-kilter again, which happened at least once a week, usually because the chef quit. Or the kitchen manager got drunk. Or the hotel manager scolded one or the other one time too many times.

If he were the hotel manager—which he never would be, not in a hundred years—he'd treat the employees better. Listen to them when they had a problem. Look for a solution instead of a reason to harangue.

No, he was going to be a preacher. Although, he supposed, he could be both, so long as his church was small and his duties not too time consuming. Like the little church he attended on Sundays. The pastor there ranched during the week. Said he liked being self-sufficient, not dependent on the congregation for his living.

Peter bit into his food. Yes, living this close to the woman he loved—for despite her harsh words of last evening, he was in love with Millie Watkins— and not being able to voice his feelings, speak to her, or show his devotion truly felt like hell on earth.

Several times during the ride out here this morning he caught sight of her in the rearview mirror. His surreptitious glances usually netted him only the back of her head. His fingers itched to reach out and brush that errant lock of hair that always stuck out no matter how much pomade she used. Or to hold her hand when she alighted from the bus at each stop.

Instead, she ignored him. Brushed past him. And the one time he summoned the courage to speak, she stared at him as though he spoke a foreign language.

He sighed and chewed. There she sat, over by herself on the low wall outside the leatherworker's shop. A couple strolled past, back toward Hannah's workshop. He nodded in their direction, but they didn't respond.

Maybe he was invisible today and didn't know it.

That was for sure how he felt.

He didn't really care about a set of strangers he'd never see again.

If only Millie would take notice of him.

◆•——•◆

The ride back that evening was almost intolerable as Peter struggled to keep his attention on the road and off Millie. She kept up a steady stream of information, details, and banter with the mostly drowsy passengers, taking care to stay in her seat as they bounced along the highway.

After the last tourist stepped down, he gathered his few belongings and headed for the door, but Millie called to him.

"Peter. Can I have a word?"

He sighed. He was tired, hungry, and in no mood for her to list off on her fingers again why she wanted nothing to do with him. He'd just have to get over it.

Or die of a broken heart.

He paused at the top of the steps. "What is it?"

"I'll help you clean the bus tonight."

Well, this was a change. It wasn't her job. She didn't get paid to help. Sure, once or twice she picked up a discarded candy wrapper or took an item to Lost and Found, but clean? "Why?"

"You have lots of questions, don't you? Ever heard of not looking a gift horse in the mouth?" Her lips tipped up in a half smile, which brightened her entire face. And it was all for him.

That decided it. "Sure. I'll take whatever help I can get."

He groaned inwardly. Did that sound as desperate and pathetic to her as it did to him?

Apparently not, because not a single wisecrack came from that delicious mouth. At least he envisioned it as delicious. Not that he had any firsthand knowledge.

Yet.

Hope bloomed again.

She led the way to the rear of the bus, and they spent a companionable fifteen minutes or so wiping down seats, cleaning the windows and closing them for the night, and sweeping the floor. By the time they worked their way almost to the front, they enjoyed an efficient and comfortable routine.

At least he did.

When she sat in her usual seat behind his, he slid into the seat opposite her. "You look like there's something you want to say."

"There is, and I don't know where to start."

He held up his hand. "If it's anything to do with our conversation last night, I don't think I can bear it, unless you want to tell me you've changed your mind and will go for a walk with me tonight."

Her mouth formed a straight line at his words. He'd said the wrong thing. Again.

He shook his head. "Go ahead."

"Did you notice that couple in the third row? The ones with the matching sombreros?"

He chuckled. "Does anything scream 'tourist' louder than a sombrero and sunglasses?"

"You're right." She laughed. "One or the other, but both?"

"Sure, I saw them. What about them?"

"They went back to Hannah's shop today during lunch."

"Right. I noticed them walking that way."

"I followed them. Just to keep an eye on things. Hannah was home cooking lunch for her family, and I didn't want any of her pieces going missing."

The hair on Peter's neck bristled. "Did they try to steal anything?"

Millie shook her head. "No. But I overhead them talking about jewelry designs. Before they got to Hannah's, they ducked into the chief's adobe."

This was sounding curiouser and curiouser, as Alice would say. "What did they want?"

"They asked the chief about designs and stones and settings. The stories behind the designs. Popular pieces. What Hannah sold most of. Things like that."

"Sounds like they want to open their own jewelry store."

"You might be more correct than you think. I saw the man taking photographs of Hannah's pieces."

"What do you think they're up to?"

Her brow pulled down. "Not sure. But the man said they should plan on staying a couple more days. And the wife said yes, that he could take care of that, and she'd make sure to get tickets for the Acoma Indian Detour for tomorrow. That's strange, because that means they'll take the same tour two days in a row."

"Does sound suspicious. Do you think they're trying to bargain Hannah down? Maybe they think if they go back tomorrow, she'll recognize them and lower her prices to get them to buy."

"I don't know for sure. All I know is the chief said he'd send a jewelry maker from another village into town this evening to meet with them."

"Did they say what time?"

She glanced up at the town clock. "In about five minutes."

"We should check this out. Where?"

"At the fountains."

Peter rose, brushed off his pants, and held out his hand. "Then I say we have a date."

As soon as the words were out of his mouth, he wished he could sink into a hole in the ground. What would she think of him? She asked for help, and he turned it to his own advantage.

But she slipped her hand into his and followed him down the steps, around the corner, and into the courtyard to where the fountains whooshed and gurgled.

And all the while, his heart threatened to burst at the sheer joy of having her so near.

This must be what heaven is like.

◆•———————•◆

Millie groaned. Only the wife showed up at the fountains, sitting on the edge, trailing her hand in the water, looking every bit the tourist. Then a light-skinned man, dressed in white man's clothes, entered the courtyard, head high, shoulders back, as though he belonged there. Which, if he was a New Mexican or Mexican native, he very well could.

But Indians weren't permitted in the nonemployee areas of the property.

Millie's studies of the Acoma people alerted her to a discrepancy between who this man purported to be and who he was. The sunburst tattoo the size of a quarter behind his left ear.

He was Acoma.

And if anybody else spotted him, they'd throw him out on his ear.

She edged closer from her hiding place in an alley doorway, and Peter gripped her arm. She nodded and waited, straining to hear.

The woman looked up from the fountain. "Funny tradition. Tossing pennies in the water and making a wish."

"Yes." The native glanced around. "We must talk fast. If I am discovered—"

"The mere fact you're talking to a married white woman gives you credibility you might lack otherwise. What information do you have for me?"

"I can make the pieces you need."

"How many, and how much?"

He shrugged. "As many as you want. One dollar each."

"I want a thousand. Five hundred dollars. Half up front. Half when we receive the final order."

He blinked several times. "Very well."

The woman handed him an envelope. "Here's the first payment, along with photographs of the pieces we want made."

A lazy smile covered the native's face. "You were very sure of yourself."

"I know who I'm going into business with."

The man stepped closer. "And I know who I am in business with." He spat out a phrase, then stepped back and folded his arms over his chest. "White people all the same."

She sneered. "I suspect that wasn't very complimentary." She stood. "Doesn't matter. You do your part—make the pieces. And I'll do mine—pay for them. In two weeks. Not a day later. Understand?"

He nodded, a single brisk motion, then pivoted and strode away. The woman remained where she was for a few more minutes until the man's footsteps died away. Then she sauntered across the courtyard and out of view.

Millie exhaled. She wasn't certain what they just witnessed, but whatever it was, it couldn't be good. Otherwise, the woman and man would have made their deal on the reservation. She needed time to figure out what to do. She turned to Peter. "I'll see you tomorrow."

His face fell. "I thought—I thought maybe we could—"

"Not tonight. We'll talk more tomorrow."

He brightened, and she regretted her words. No point in giving him any reason to hope for anything more between them than friendship. Still, she needed his help.

For the next few days at least.

She scurried down the alleyway toward the staff rooms. As she passed a doorway, an arm reached out and grabbed her by the wrist, and another hand clamped over her mouth to stifle the scream already in her throat.

A gruff voice whispered hoarsely in her ear. "You're looking for trouble, aren't you?"

She shook her head.

"I think you are. I saw you watching my wife. And I know you followed us today."

Another shake of her head.

He squeezed her wrist tighter. "Don't lie to me. If you say anything, I'll tell the manager you stole my watch. It's my word against yours. Understand?"

She nodded.

She understood very well.

Her love for and desire to protect the Acoma people could cost her everything she held dear.

Her reputation.

Her job.

Her ticket to Hollywood.

Chapter 5

Peter arrived at work early the next morning. He liked this time of day best. Before the heat. Before the tourists. Before the boss. He checked over the bus, including fluids, listening to the purring rumble of the engine for a few minutes before shutting it off.

He lounged against the side of the vehicle, taking advantage of the shade offered, while eyeing the sky. Looked like another warm day. Not that he minded. The dry heat didn't seem nearly as oppressive as when he lived with his family in Mississippi, picking cotton for twelve and fourteen hours, forehead almost touching the ground. Fingers pricked by the thorns, his blood staining the cotton, reminding him of the price Jesus paid for his sins.

Of course, when he was five or six years old, he always struggled to pinpoint exactly what those sins might be. Not nearly so difficult now.

He sighed. If only he could go back to that age of innocence.

But wishing in one hand and spitting in the other demonstrated the futility of his efforts.

Spitting always won out, as his father would say.

There were two other reasons why he liked this time of day. The quiet allowed him time to meditate on the scriptures he read on rising each morning. Today's verse was from Proverbs, about acknowledging God and letting Him direct his paths.

Another sigh. That was a tough instruction. So many times God seemed to move at a snail's pace. Or at least slower than he wanted.

The other reason approached. Millie Watkins. She strolled along, notes in her hand, her lips moving silently as she rehearsed another tidbit of information. She spent a lot of time reading about the Acoma and New Mexico, always increasing what she told the tourists. If she wasn't careful, she'd work herself into a full-time job.

Her step slowed when she looked up, then a smile lit her face and she hurried toward him. "Peter. I have something interesting to share."

He wouldn't have cared if she wanted to stare at the sky, so long as she had a mind to do it with him. He pulled out the step stool. "Take a seat."

She did. "Last night when I left you, that nasty tourist followed me."

"The woman?"

"No. Her husband."

"What happened?"

She quickly filled him in, and with every description of the despicable way that lout treated her, Peter's ire increased. By the time she finished her tale, his fists itched to set the man straight.

But Millie laid a hand on his arm. "Beating him up won't do any good. He'll simply tell his ugly lie. You'll go to jail for assault, and I'll still lose my job."

He drew a deep breath and counted to ten. "You're right. We should pray for wisdom and ask God what to do."

Millie snorted. "I don't know why we'd waste our time."

Peter blinked a couple of times. "Prayer is never a waste of time or energy. It connects us with the God who loves us."

"Oh really?" She planted a fist into one hip. "Is it love to ignore a person's question? Or to say no to everything they ask?"

"Well, I don't know. I guess it depends on what you're asking for."

She glared at him, color rising in her neck and cheeks. "You're just like all the rest of those Goodie-Two-shoes. Saying I must be asking for something God doesn't want to give me."

Her words stung. "I guess that might be one reason. Another could be He knows it's better if He answers at a different time."

"Well, my mother ran out of time. And all His answers now won't change that."

Movement from the corner of his eye caught his attention. The passengers for the Indian Detours approached. Their discussion would have to wait until later. "I'd love to talk with you more about this. Maybe give you some examples from my life when I felt God was far away. Would you meet me for coffee after dinner tonight?"

She stared at him so long he was certain she'd turn him down—again. Then an almost imperceptible dip of her head affirmed her decision to give him—and God—another chance. "Fine. Doesn't mean I'm going to change my mind. I'm still angry."

She stomped up the steps of the bus and plunked into her seat, her notes gripped in her hands.

He plastered on a smile and greeted each passenger, offering a steadying hand to each one who boarded. Once or twice he glanced in her direction, but she kept her head bowed over the pages, almost as though in an attitude of prayer.

Or defeat.

He wasn't certain which.

He prayed the former.

Millie entered Hannah's shop after the rush of tourists left, tossing a quick smile to the older woman hunched over her work. "Did you do good business today?"

Hannah smiled, her teeth white against her bronze skin. "Yes. Very good." She gestured to the tables. "Many empty places. Much work to do."

Millie grinned. "If it's too much, we could encourage them to buy in another village."

The woman's eyes widened, and then she relaxed. "You tease me. I understand your white humor."

"You really do good work. And the tourists are getting a great deal. Maybe you need to increase your prices a little."

"I want everybody to take home some Acoma with them. Don't want cost to be a problem. They pay good money to come here, come on tour. They like stories. I like telling them. We all win."

"That's a lovely way to think about it. Maybe you should write a book about your stories too."

Hannah laughed and shook her head. "White humor. That one I do not understand." She looked up from the piece in her hand. "If I write book, I not have time to make you this." She held out a piece of silver and turquoise that dangled from her hand like a satin ribbon. "Please. Take this. I make it for you."

Millie stepped back. "Oh I couldn't. I'm saving my money to—"

"Not to buy. As gift. I talk to the others. They say you speak kindly of us to the tourists, and you encourage them to buy. Is our way of saying thank you. Then I tell you the story."

Tears threatened to spill over at the woman's generosity. Not in a month of Sundays could she hope to save enough to purchase such a piece. She nodded, and Hannah slid the bracelet around her wrist and fastened the clasp. The two embraced, Millie enjoying the solid feel of the woman in her arms, a reminder of her own mother.

And another reason to end the hug before she really wanted to. She didn't need to get attached to Hannah. She'd be leaving soon. And saying goodbye was never easy. For any reason.

Millie exited Hannah's shop, toying with the delicate silver and turquoise bracelet. She held it up to the sunlight, marveling at the tiny reflections and the intricate patterns worked with the stones in their settings, and the story echoing in her mind. It was about a young girl who got lost in the desert. A wolf came to her, but she was afraid, so she hid. A coyote came to her, and still she hid. When a rabbit found her shivering in a mesquite bush, it asked her what she was afraid of. The girl said she thought the animals would hurt her. The rabbit led her over a small hill, and down below was a village. The animals were trying to show her the way home.

Hannah nodded in her sage-like way. "The moral of the story is that sometimes what scares us the most is meant to help us."

One of the female passengers paused on her return to the bus. "Oh, what a lovely piece."

"Thank you. It was a gift."

"Someone must think you're very special."

"Yes. They do."

Yes, they do.

Well of course anybody who met Millie Watkins would think her special.

Peter strolled down the boardwalk, away from the hotel, pondering the overheard conversation. He hadn't meant to eavesdrop. He had been simply waiting for the passengers, sitting on the bus, eating his lunch. Millie was more than special—exceptional, delightful, a treasure. Just a few of the words he'd use to describe her.

So who thought so highly of her? Jewelry was a personal gift. Intimate almost.

Had a man purchased it? Who else would buy such a gift for a woman?

Well, if that's what she was like—accepting pricey presents from men—he couldn't keep up with that. He had no intention of buying her affections. Perhaps he'd do well to simply forget her. And forget their date after dinner. Not that it was actually a real date. More of him begging for another chance to explain why God wouldn't forsake her the way she thought He had.

God didn't need him to defend Him. He was God, for crying out loud.

If she didn't see God at work in her life, how could he possibly convince her otherwise?

A faint cry reached him as he crossed an alleyway. He paused and listened again. This time a scream—feeble and muffled—reached him, and he turned into the narrow passageway. Two figures struggled at the far end, one larger and looming over the smaller, huddled in a corner.

Peter dashed in their direction. "Hey. Does anybody need help?"

The larger person turned, fist still in the air. Dark hair, dark eyes, a bottle in his hand. "Get away. We don't need no help!"

Peter looked down at the other figure, who stared up at him, eyes wide and mouth open. Blood trickled from the painted lips, and dark streaks of kohl ran down her cheeks.

A woman.

A saloon girl, likely, judging by the feather in her hair and the skimpy outfit, cut low in front and high on her thigh.

Still, a woman.

Peter grabbed a broken board propped against a wall. "Leave her alone. I'll call the police."

The man turned and strode toward him. Peter stopped, hefted the board in his hand, and waited. When the attacker got within reach, Peter jabbed the sharp end into the man's midsection. He doubled over, and Peter whacked him aside the head. The man fell to his knees, shaking his head like a stunned grizzly, before scrambling to his feet and rushing past him, turning right at the street, and disappearing from view.

The woman whimpered, and Peter tossed his makeshift weapon aside, then hurried to her. "Are you all right?" He shrugged out of his jacket and wrapped it around her shoulders. "Let's get you to the doctor."

She shook her head as she sagged against him. "No doctor. Just get me home."

He peered at her in the gloom of the alley. "I think you're going to need stitches on your lip."

"No doctor."

He pulled his handkerchief from a pocket and handed it to her. She pressed it against her mouth, and they made their way out of the alley. He slowed at the street and glanced around. Fraternizing with a saloon girl could cost him his job.

Or his parish.

She quirked her chin to the saloon. "I live upstairs. Sure you're not embarrassed to be seen on the streets with me? I'd understand if you were."

Rankled that she read his mind, he lifted his chin and aided her across the street. Nobody—regardless of their station in life or the color of their skin—deserved to be mistreated that way. If anybody thought less of him because he helped her—well, that was between them and their God.

He would do his Christian duty.

He shook his head. "If you want to get out of this life, I know people in town who'd help you."

She peered up at him, sniffling. "Really? You think someone would help the likes of me?"

"Sure. The pastor and his wife, for two."

"I dunno."

"Let's go there and at least get you cleaned up. Then you can decide what you want to do next." He glanced around. Several women eyed him, and a couple of men outside the mercantile looked in their direction and snickered. "Maybe you want to go home to family. Start over again. Do they know what you do?"

She shook her head. "They think I work in a bank. That's what I tell them when I write. Which ain't often. Not much to write about apart from lies."

"Then home is where you should go. Nobody need know about your life here. Where's your family?"

"Arkansas."

"Never been there. But I bet it's beautiful."

She smiled. "It is. I'll surely think on it."

He helped her toward the pastor's home at the end of the street, recalling a recent sermon preached about aiding the downtrodden and weary. This woman in his arms—no, more of a girl, really—definitely qualified as both. The pastor and his wife would help her until she healed, and then likely send her home.

If only his own problems could be solved so easily.

❖ ━ ❖

Millie sank onto the bench in the small park next to the hotel, her book beside her. Dinner would be called in about ten minutes, and after that—well, after that, what? She was supposed to meet Peter for coffee, but he'd been particularly quiet on the ride home from the reservation.

Which was fine with her. She made notes on a slip of paper from her pocket about the story Hannah told her, as well as several others, and tonight she'd write them into her script.

She smiled. Pretty soon she'd need a longer tour so she could get in everything she wanted to say.

Still, it was good exercise for her memory, in preparation for her acting career.

The tourists seemed to like her chattering on and on, and they demonstrated their appreciation in the tips they left.

At this rate, she'd be able to leave a month earlier than planned. But for now, her book called to her.

A hair ribbon substituting as a bookmark peeked out of the top of the book, and she flipped back to her favorite subject, the Acoma jewelry.

Recently, with the growing popularity of all things Indian, criminals have copied these sacred patterns and produced nickel-based replicas, even mimicking the original artist's signature. These inferior products cause customers to doubt all forms of the jewelry, since they are not educated in discerning the real from the counterfeit. As well, they steal from the natives, who live a subsistence lifestyle and are not privy to government assistance in these difficult times.

Millie's hand rested at the base of her throat. How could somebody want to steal from these sweet and gentle Acoma by making substandard items? Why would they choose to drive down the prices of the real product? Why, if she suspected one of her passengers of doing such a despicable thing, she'd—she'd— what would she do?

She stared at the words on the page. What was described here fit in with the conversations she'd overheard in the village and in the courtyard. Perfectly. Like pieces in a puzzle.

The two tourists, the chief, and the Acoma man were planning to steal from the Acoma people.

But what could she do?

She could report them. Confront them. Perhaps tell Hannah, who might get some of the tribal warriors to threaten them.

But who would believe her?

If she made a mistake and accused the wrong person, she'd lose her job.

And that would never do.

Her dreams of Hollywood would be over.

That was too high a price to pay.

No, she'd keep quiet. Work hard. Save diligently.

She'd leave changing the world until *after* she was rich and famous.

Satisfied she made the right decision, she glanced around at the early evening traffic and pedestrians around the station and the hotel. Albuquerque—and the Alvarado in particular—were nice enough. If she didn't have big plans, she might even be happy to consider this her forever home. Settle down but still travel the world. Have a family but keep her identity. Maybe she could do all that with someone like Peter.

She straightened. Why did his face always pop into her mind's eye when she thought of men? Or marriage? Sure, he might be interested in her, but really, they had nothing in common. He wanted to escape the life of an itinerant farmer, while she wanted to see Australia and the Continent. Maybe even China. And he likely had stick-in-the-mud ideas about a woman's role in the family. None of which included holding down a job outside the house. Or choosing her own way.

No, Peter was not the man for her.

He and his little senorita would absolutely be better for each other.

Speaking of Peter and a woman, he stepped into view.

Holding a woman in his arms.

With his coat draped over her shoulders, as any gentleman would do to ward off a chilly evening.

Except this woman was no ordinary one. And certainly not Carlita.

This was a soiled dove. Likely from the saloon.

She was right about him.

He wasn't the man for her.

And if that's how a man who believed in God behaved, she wanted nothing to do with either of them.

Chapter 6

Millie tucked a penny notebook into her skirt pocket, making sure she had a pencil at the ready. After a night of tossing and turning, worrying through the problem of counterfeit jewelry, she came to a decision. She couldn't simply ignore what she knew.

Or what she thought she knew.

But if she was going to risk her entire future, she needed more evidence.

Settling into her seat behind Peter, she flattened her notes on her thighs and scanned the notations she'd made the previous evening. Feeling like a modern Sherlock Holmes—minus the meerschaum pipe and deerstalker hat and cape of course—she considered what she already knew.

Counterfeiting Indian artifacts and new pieces was profitable. Enough to risk prison and disgrace. That's what the magazine articles said.

She also observed the strange couple studying Hannah's pieces and taking photographs. They were on the tour for the third day in a row. No matter how enamored they were of the Acoma people or their artisanship, surely they'd learned all they could about the reservation by now.

The objects of her thoughts boarded the bus and headed for the last seats, as was their custom. Millie shifted a few inches to her left to get a better view of them in the rearview mirror. They sat close, whispering from the corners of their mouths, smiling and nodding at the other passengers.

Millie pulled out the notebook and jotted a note. She'd keep an eye on them today and write down their actions.

Peter slid into his seat, his mouth set in a grim line. She stood him up last night. And why shouldn't she? After the way he brazenly waltzed that girl down the street in front of the entire town—well, she wanted nothing to do with the likes of him.

She never needed anybody before.

And she didn't need anybody now.

❖—❖

There she was, writing something else in that little book of hers.

What was she up to?

All day long, he'd kept Miss Millie Watkins in his sight. While not an unpleasant task under normal circumstances, this was far from ordinary. So far she trailed the passengers—no, not all the passengers, just the woman who met the Acoma man at the hotel and the man who threatened Millie if she interfered in—in what? They didn't know. She followed them, hovering in the shadows while the woman looked at some pieces in Hannah's shop.

For the third time on this trip.

Had this stranger been so engrossed on the previous tours? He hadn't paid them much attention except to ensure that the man didn't bother Millie.

Millie glanced his way, and he melted into the recess in the wall where he stood. If she knew he was there, she'd want to know why. And he had no good reason, except he wanted to be sure she stayed safe.

But a modern woman like Millie couldn't possibly understand his desire to protect her from—from what? Even he didn't know. She'd more likely interpret his actions to mean he didn't think she could look after herself. That he somehow saw her as weak. Or inept.

Which he absolutely didn't.

In fact, he didn't know a stronger or more capable woman than Millie Watkins.

The couple in question sauntered a little too casually from the shop, with Millie in their wake. Peter melted out of sight around the corner. But instead of moving on to the next shop or returning to the bus, the two rounded the building, Millie close behind.

When the suspicious pair returned a few minutes later, a sneer on the man's face and the woman's cheeks colored pink, Peter waited. They made their way to their customary places on the bus. And still he waited.

No Millie.

He headed in the direction the three went, around the side of the building and following a barren path to the rear of the adobe.

Nothing back here but an empty clothesline and an old shed. Almost ready to topple over, its roof looked askance and its foundation washed out.

But a shiny new lock ensured the door—hanging from its hinges at an angle—stayed secure.

He turned to go back when a muffled scream caught his attention.

He whirled around and aimed for the shack.

More screams. Something about a snake. And somebody paying for what they'd done.

Millie!

And she was madder than a wet hen.

He jiggled the lock a couple of times in hopes it wasn't really secure, but it was. So he pried his fingers under the hinge-end of the door, and pulled.

At first the nails and wood protested his attempts, but after a couple of hard yanks, he overcame both.

The door opened, and Millie fell into his arms.

While the feel of her in his arms should have thrilled him, it didn't.

Her red, tearstained face stared back at him, her mouth clamped shut, her nose wrinkled as though in distaste.

He set her back on her feet and offered his handkerchief, which she refused with a swipe of her hand. The square of cotton fell into the dust at their feet.

She huffed. "I can't believe you'd do such a despicable thing."

"What? Save you?"

"Save me?" She jabbed a forefinger into his chest. "You are the reason I was in there in the first place." She dusted off her blouse and skirt, then flounced away, pausing at the corner to glance over her shoulder. "And if I never see you again, it will be too soon."

◆————◆

The next day, Millie debated whether to go to work. Maybe she should just take her earnings, buy a ticket, and go as far from Albuquerque—and Peter Duncan—as she could get. Start over again. There were lots of jobs out there for a personable young woman like herself.

The nerve of Peter. Following her around all day. Getting into her business while she tried to figure out what that couple was up to. Waiting until she peeked in through the boards, then sneaking up behind her. Pushing her into the shed filled with snakes. Okay. Just one snake. But still, that was—that was just—

She exhaled so hard her bangs lifted then settled back onto her damp forehead.

And then she had to go and make a fool of herself by crying. And screaming. Just like a girl.

Well, she *was* a girl, but that didn't mean she had to act all weak and scared like one. She worked hard not to act like the other girls. Because she wasn't like them. Didn't want to be. Never would be.

Girls like that needed a man to keep an eye on them. Get them out of trouble. Make their decisions for them. That wasn't her.

Well, she'd put Peter in his place yesterday. He proved himself to be just another man who would go to any lengths to get a woman. Putting her in danger, then rescuing her. How pathetic.

The only problem was, none of what she believed lined up with the Peter she knew. The Peter who made her laugh. Who saved her from the lecherous tourist. Who acted as her trusty sidekick when they watched the meeting in the courtyard.

She smiled. Watson to her Sherlock.

Perhaps she needed to rethink this whole situation. Because if Peter didn't shove her into that shed—as he so vehemently insisted—that meant somebody else wanted to see her hurt.

And right now, she could think of only two people who fit that description.

Peter sighed, the ache in his chest making breathing difficult. How would he survive? He hoped once Millie calmed down, she'd listen to reason. To his explanation. But twenty-four hours later, she still wouldn't talk to him. She finished up the tour yesterday, a smile pasted on her face for the passengers. If he didn't know better, he'd think she was happy. She bantered with the tourists, included interesting bits in her talk, and visited some with Hannah. But for him, nothing.

She didn't make eye contact and, as far as he knew, didn't ever look at him. Not a word, kind or unkind. As though he didn't exist. And if this shunning continued, he might not.

Food had no pleasure. Sleep offered no respite, and he awoke this morning more tired than when he laid his head on his pillow. Even the attentions of Carlita, once a pleasant distraction, proved tiresome last evening, and now he avoided her as much as possible.

All he could do with any sincerity was pray.

And pray he did. Continuously, as scripture admonished. Pouring out his heart to God. Seeking direction. Clarity. Even being so bold as to ask for a sign whether Millie was the one for him. Because right now, the only thing he was certain of was that God would never leave him or forsake him.

Still, without Millie, he felt so alone.

Finally, the suspicious couple left the Alvarado. Millie stood at the large plate glass window in the gift shop as they boarded the train, suitcases and trunks and boxes galore stowed in the luggage car. They waved to the porter as though they were royalty.

Then the man caught sight of her and pointed his finger at her and then at his eyes. *I see you.*

She stepped back from her observation point, a shiver running up and down her spine. Heart racing, she left the shop and headed for the bus loading area. Would the man really carry out his threat to get her fired? She was fairly certain she knew what they were up to. But still she hesitated. Maybe they *were* simply tourists, interested in the Acoma.

No, that would be too simple. And that wouldn't explain the clandestine meeting with the Acoma man and the exchange of monies or the deadline for delivery. And it surely wouldn't explain the husband's behavior or his threat.

She needed help if she was to learn the complete truth. Unfortunately, the only person she knew well enough to ask wasn't in her good graces right now. Peter had played a nasty trick on her, one intended to win her heart—but she saw right through it.

At least, she was fairly certain that was his plan.

Unless—no, surely the tourists wouldn't have tried something so dastardly. Did they think Peter would simply leave her there?

The past few days of little to no contact with him—wasn't that her plan all along?—hadn't produced the expected result. She believed that if he moved on to another and left her to her plans, she'd feel better. But she didn't.

What did that say about her?

It's what she wanted all along, wasn't it?

Should she give him the chance to explain? Maybe suggest he apologize? Isn't that what his Christian faith required? Forgiveness. She supposed she could extend that to him, if only to unravel this mystery.

Fine. If he was at the bus ahead of her, she'd talk to him. Let him speak for himself. She was pretty certain she wouldn't like his answer, but she could at least be the adult in this situation.

When she exited from the alleyway between two buildings, he stood beside the bus, almost as though waiting for her.

Which he wasn't, of course.

However, she could let him think she thought he was. She was an actress, after all. But he'd have to make the first move.

She strode along the walkway like she'd done on a dozen or more mornings before, slowing when he fell into step beside her. "Peter."

His eyes widened and his nostrils flared.

She'd surprised him.

Good. Catch him off guard.

She stopped. "I think there's something you want to say?"

He nodded. "There is. And I don't know where to start."

"You could begin with apologizing for the shed and the snake."

"I'm sorry you got locked in the shed."

But not the snake? "And?"

"I'm sorry things have been so tense between us."

Would he never get to the part about trying to make her think she was in danger so he could rescue her? "And?"

"And please forgive me."

Well, not exactly what she expected. But he appeared contrite enough. Almost docile. She gifted him with a nod and a smile. "Done."

He exhaled then assisted her onto the bus, and she accepted his hand, even thanking him.

He'd done as she wanted. Yet she felt no pleasure in his acquiescence. Which, she was fairly sure, said more about her than about him.

Chapter 7

Two tense weeks later and matters still hadn't improved much between her and Peter. She saw no way to bring him around to apologizing for his behavior in locking her in the shed. Millie perused the hotel gift shop at the end of her shift. Her bracelet from Hannah still decorated her wrist, and every time she saw it, she joyed in its simple beauty and its story.

Recently she'd taken to reciting the tale to herself as she fell asleep at night, and just this morning she awoke with the moral on her lips: sometimes what scares us the most is meant to help us.

Apart from the usual things—guns, knives, and rattlers—not much frightened her.

No, that wasn't exactly true.

Dying alone. Never knowing true love. Not being a famous actress. All of those scared her spitless.

She stopped in front of the jewelry case and compared the bracelets on display with her own, finding those wanting. The store manager nodded in greeting, and Millie returned the gesture, noting the stack of boxes on the floor. She quirked her chin in their direction. "Looks like you have a big delivery."

Nancy swiped at a lock of hair and cut the string on another box. "Yes. Huge. Got to get it all marked and on display. Boss said it's important to move it quickly."

"Maybe I could help. I have a few minutes. I'll open the boxes and set them out for you."

"Thanks so much. That would be swell."

Millie cut the string and opened the next box while Nancy wrote out the price ticket. The first packet contained earrings, and the second one bracelets.

Similar to her own.

She paused and picked one up, then turned it over. She was right. Hannah's signature mark decorated the back of the piece. Delicate, much like her own bracelet, but different. An inferior design. The clasp not so well done. The pieces of turquoise smaller and chipped in places.

She fastened the clasp and compared it to her own. She liked hers better. Not only was it gifted to her personally by the craftswoman, but Hannah designed it especially for her.

She opened the next packet. Another almost exactly like the one she just put on. Which was also strange. Hannah never made any two pieces alike. Each one its own story. Each one its own symbolism.

She picked through the other packets. Of the thirty or so pieces, only three designs. All with Hannah's mark. All shoddy when compared to her own original piece.

Perhaps Hannah took more care with Millie's bracelet because she knew it was a gift. Perhaps she felt more rushed with this order. Perhaps she couldn't afford the best raw materials and substituted lesser quality.

Perhaps Hannah didn't make these at all.

She glanced around. Nancy was busy on the other side of the counter with a customer. Millie headed for the kitchen. According to the book she read, one way to tell real silver jewelry from the fake stuff was to weigh it. Silver weighs more than nickel.

In the kitchen, she caught the chef's eye. "Could I borrow your scales for a few minutes?"

He eyed her up and down. "You want to check your weight?"

She held out her arm. "Not mine. These."

He nodded and pointed. "Herb scale is on the counter. Make sure you put it back where it belongs. And the weights too."

She hurried over, pulled the miniature scale toward her, and removed both bracelets. She needn't bother with the weights. The actual measurement wasn't important.

What she wanted to confirm was that her bracelet was the genuine article.

Her piece on the left, the new one on the right.

The new bracelet—the suspect version—hung in the air like a kitten dangling from a tree branch.

No doubt about it—hers was the heavier one.

She returned to the gift shop and showed the piece to Nancy. "This is a large order for Hannah to fill. She must have been working night and day."

Nancy shrugged. "I don't know. The hotel manager orders. I put it out and sell it."

"Is it silver?"

Nancy turned the piece over. "Says it is. Just like the ones we always carry."

"I just compared my bracelet to this one. Mine is an original from the artisan. I believe this one is a fake. Probably nickel."

Nancy's brow drew down. She scooped all the pieces back into their shipping box, then set her pen on the counter. "Well, that's not good. I'll go talk to Mr. Larkin right now."

She stepped out from behind the counter and hurried from the store.

Millie's earlier suspicions were correct. Somebody was stealing from the Acoma. And using the Alvarado to do it.

◆◆————◆◆

Peter set his coffee cup down when Millie burst into the staff kitchen, her cheeks red and her fists clenched. He rose to meet her. "Millie, what is it?"

"I think somebody is making counterfeit jewelry and trying to pass it off as the genuine article."

"How do you know this?" He led her to the table and poured coffee for her, pushing the cream and sugar toward her. "Drink this and start from the beginning."

She took a couple of deep sips before placing her hand, palm down, on the table. The bracelet—a gift from a suitor, perhaps—decorated her wrist. "I've done some research into the Acoma jewelry styles."

"Right. For the Indian Detours."

"A large order came in today at the gift shop, so I offered to help Nancy—"

"Nancy?"

"The store manager."

"Continue."

"I offered to help her. I opened the packages, and she put the price tags on the items. One was a bracelet similar to mine, so I laid it on my arm to compare them. It didn't look right. Or feel right. So I weighed it. And mine was heavier. Much heavier. Proving mine is silver and the others aren't. But they're marked as silver, and even have Hannah's mark."

He needed to get some things out into the open. It was now or never.

God, help me say this in a loving way that she can receive.

He drew a breath and exhaled. "Where did your bracelet come from?"

She waved off his question. "Hannah gave it to me as a thank-you for encouraging tourists to buy at her shop."

A wave of relief flooded him, washing away his suspicions and his worries in a tidal wave of peace.

She continued. "What's important is that the maker's mark on the back of my bracelet, which I saw Hannah make, and the mark on the reverse of this other bracelet are almost identical. And the sterling silver label is there too."

"Maybe it's a mistake. Some costume jewelry pieces got marked as silver by mistake."

She shook her head. "I could see that happening to one piece in the order. But not all of them. And when I asked Nancy about it, she acted strange. She took all the pieces, then left. Just like that. Didn't come back. Didn't close the shop." Millie snapped her fingers. "Poof."

Peter thought about her words. One strange event could possibly be explained. The couple could have been eccentric collectors of all things Acoma.

But two incriminating events, both involving Acoma jewelry, was one too many.

He nodded. "We need to talk to the hotel manager about this. After all, it's Mr. Harvey Jr.'s and the hotel's reputation at stake here."

"If we're wrong, we'll both lose our jobs. Maybe I should go to him on my own. No point in both of us being unemployed."

He shook his head. "We're in this together. If tourists purchase counterfeit jewelry, believing it to be real, and learn later they were duped, this won't be good for the hotels all along the line. And in the meantime, it will call into question the authenticity of the real thing."

She stood. "You're right. Should we go now?"

"Let's. There's no time to waste."

Chapter 8

No time to waste.

Right. Millie's shoulders slumped at the unfairness of the situation. To Hannah and the other Acoma craftsmen. To the Alvarado. To Mr. Harvey Jr., who had been so kind to her. For about the hundredth time in the past few days, she wished she knew what to do.

While she waited with Peter for their passengers to arrive, they discussed the events of three days ago. The hotel manager, Mr. Larkin, had listened politely, read through Millie's journal, tsk-tsked at the mention of the couple taking photographs of Hannah's jewelry, expressed amazement at her ingenuity to compare the weights, and promised to check into the matter.

Since then, when they asked for him at the front desk, he was never available.

Millie wrung her fingers into knots. "I think he's just trying to put us off."

"But why? It's his job on the line if Mr. Harvey Jr. discovers we reported this and he neglected to look into it."

"Unless he's part of the scheme."

Peter nodded. "Hadn't thought about that. I guess I was trying to avoid putting faces and names into the counterfeit pot. I'd rather not know the people involved."

"My thinking too. But denying it hasn't worked. Every time I look at an employee, I wonder if it's him—or her."

He chuckled. "You don't look at me like that, do you?"

"No. There are at least two innocent people here. You and me."

She brushed at her skirt. She really liked this job. And since she and Peter reconciled—sort of—she enjoyed working with him. Maybe she needn't rush off to Hollywood. Perhaps she could stay on, practice her memorization, and save more money so she could live comfortably once she got to California.

Not that they could ever be more than friends. She'd seen another side of him with that saloon girl.

But should she give him another chance?

She glanced up at Peter. "We never went for coffee. You were going to explain why God wouldn't answer my prayers."

His mouth curved up. "I may not be the best person to answer that question. Sometimes I feel like He doesn't hear mine either."

"Really? I never heard anybody—at least not a Christian—admit that before. I guess I kind of thought that when you got your act all cleaned up by Jesus, everything was fine after that."

He slid into the seat opposite her. "If anybody tells you that, they're lyin'. No siree. If anything, once I asked Jesus into my heart, things got worse."

That didn't make a lick of sense. "Why?"

"My pastor told me it was because the devil didn't mind when I went around doin' what I wanted to do. But now that I was tryin' to follow Jesus, well, it made that old devil plumb mad. So he's goin' to pick on me more."

She chuckled. "If that's your grand attempt to convince me to give my life to God, you need to change your sales pitch. Honestly, that's not very inviting."

He nodded. "I guess you're right. But it's the truth."

She looked up. "Here comes Mr. Larkin now. Maybe he has news for us."

The man crossed the courtyard and stood in the doorway of the bus. "Good. I'm glad you're here. I need your help."

At last they would finally take action. Millie's heart pounded and her thoughts raced. Would they go undercover? Contact the Acoma man who made the deal with the woman? Because surely the two were connected. "What can we do?"

"I need you to take a bus to the far corner of the Acoma lands, to where the Laguna reservation meets it at the wash. A tour bus from Winslow broke down on the Laguna reservation. But the Laguna won't let us on their land, so the group is hiking toward Acoma land. They should be there by the time you arrive. If not, wait for them and bring the passengers back here."

Peter's brow drew down. "But we're about to leave on our own Indian Detour."

"I'll get somebody else to take that one. You take the old bus. Not so pretty, but beggars can't be choosers. Get out there right away. One of the passengers has heart trouble, and we don't want him dying in the heat or from stress."

Millie stood. Something didn't seem right. Why make a man with heart trouble hike in the heat? They should simply defy the Laguna and go. This was an emergency. "What was the bus doing out there this early? Normally the Detours don't even start out for another thirty minutes."

"This special charter went out yesterday and camped overnight in the desert. Don't ask me. These crazy tourists will do anything for a gag. Now go."

She glanced at Peter, indecision mingled with suspicion cementing her feet to the floor. He lifted one shoulder in concert with his eyebrows. He didn't like the order either, but he was right.

What could they do?

If they didn't go, they'd lose their jobs.

◆━━━━━◆

Talk about being caught between a rock and a hard place.

Peter gritted his teeth three hours later, when, for about the umpteenth time, the steering wheel wrenched from his hands when the front of the bus ground to a halt. High-centered in yet another rut in the road, no doubt. Good thing he wasn't going much beyond five miles an hour.

He'd best keep his eyes on the road—and not on Millie.

He groaned. At this rate, they'd both be collecting their pensions by the time they arrived at their destination. He checked the sky. Nothing but blue as far as he could see. Not quite noon and already over ninety degrees.

At least.

He swiped at the sweat running down his forehead into his eyes and took another swig of water. Millie sat behind him in her usual spot, peering out the window to her left, then the windshield, then the window across the aisle. Upon completing the circuit, she made eye contact with him in the rearview mirror.

A cycle she'd repeated every few seconds for the past seventeen miles.

And still they hadn't seen a sign of a bus, stranded or otherwise.

Or another human being, for that matter.

He depressed the clutch and wrangled the gearshift into reverse. If he could get out of this impediment, they could continue on their way.

The transmission groaned as metal encountered metal, but the bus didn't budge. His arms and shoulders ached with the tension of the difficult ride, not to mention the rickety old vehicle's propensity to veer to the right. Nothing at all like his regular bus. Already they stopped twice to add water to a leaking radiator.

He sighed, engaged the clutch again, yanked the lever into first, and tested the gear. The bus inched forward but caught against the far side of the hole in the road.

This was no ordinary rut.

He fiddled with the lever and eventually found the sweet spot for reverse. The rear tires spit gravel, and he eased up. When he added gentle pressure on the gas pedal, the engine groaned, then the bus backed away like a turtle from hot pavement—slowly. Painfully slow. The undercarriage scraped on the sunbaked clay, hardened by heat and the last of the spring rains into a cement-like texture.

Thank goodness he didn't blow a tire. That would surely put them in a bad situation. If it were just him, he wouldn't be so worried. But Millie. . .and the ill passenger they had yet to meet. . .

He closed his eyes for a split second and offered up a quick prayer for protection for everybody concerned. And for the bus.

"Do you think we've much farther to go?"

He snapped open his eyes and met her gaze in the mirror. "Not really sure. Never been out this way. You?"

She shook her head. "Don't even know where we are."

"The Acoma and Laguna reservations meet at a tiny point of land about ten miles past Sun City. I'm pretty certain we're almost there."

She stretched her arms over her head. "I feel like I've been on this bus for a week."

He chuckled. "Me too. And I don't expect the ride back to be any picnic either. Particularly if the radiator keeps losing water."

Millie repeated her vigil out the windows. "I haven't seen any sign of civilization for a while now."

"Let's focus on something else to make the time pass faster."

She settled into her seat. "Like what? There's no sheep to count."

"How about singing?"

She fanned her face with her handkerchief. "I don't know many songs. None of the popular ones anyway."

"And I only know church songs."

She raised her eyebrows. "And just because I don't go to church, you think I don't know any of your songs?"

He wished he'd never brought up the topic. What was he thinking? "Do you know 'Jesus Loves Me'?"

"Everybody knows that one." She scooted forward, holding the rail between their seats. "You start, and I'll chime in. What I don't know, I'll hum."

For the next few miles, they sang other songs too, including "Amazing Grace," where Millie hummed more than she sang, and "Where He Leads Me." She sat perfectly still for his slightly off-key rendition of that one, clapping when he ended.

Whether she was glad he stopped singing or was touched by the words, he wasn't certain.

He prayed the latter.

By that time, he spotted a fence in the near distance and pulled the bus to a halt. The vehicle shuddered to a stop, steam hissing from under the hood. Now that they stood still, the desert heat invaded the shell, and dust motes danced in the sunbeams dotting the floor.

He opened the door and stepped onto the desert, stretching his back and arms after the rigorous drive, glad the bone-rattling motion was ended. At least temporarily.

Millie followed close behind, and he offered her his hand, which she accepted.

Using one hand to shade her eyes, she scanned the area. "Don't see anything."

"Me either." Glancing at the sun, he confirmed their approximate position and pointed to his left. "That's south. Forward is west. They should be coming from there, but even if they got off track, we should be able to see them by now."

"Unless the ill passenger got worse through the night and couldn't travel."

"I guess we'll give them some time. Can't see what choice we have."

"You're right. If we return empty-handed, Mr. Larkin will have our hides. And our jobs."

He chuckled to lighten the situation. Which didn't help much. "True. Although right now, I'd pay him to fire me."

She punched his arm. "You're tired and probably hungry. Good thing I packed some snacks."

He rubbed his hands together. "That's what I want to hear." Bowing, he gestured toward the bus. "Join me in my fancy horseless carriage, milady?"

She curtsied. "Yes, sir, I shall. Lead on."

Their lighthearted banter lifted his dour mood, and he helped her board. She was right. He felt much better once he ate.

Or maybe it wasn't the ham sandwiches and warm tea.

Perhaps it was the company.

Chapter 9

Peter kicked a rock, sending it skittering across the desert floor.

Could things get any worse?

He swallowed down the lump of irritation. Complaining wouldn't solve their current dilemma.

Or dilemmas, rather.

The picnic-like atmosphere of a few hours before evaporated like a puddle when the sun came out in full force, beating down on them for hours. He and Millie ate their lunch, and before he knew it, he fell asleep, his hunger and thirst satisfied. When next he opened his eyes, the sun kissed the horizon. He woke Millie with a tap on her shoulder.

She sat up, glancing around. "What? Are they here?"

"No. The sun is going down. We should head back."

That was an hour and about five miles ago.

Which brought them to this place. Stuck on the road in the middle of nowhere with a flat tire.

At least the bus had a spare.

He hoped.

He checked the luggage compartments built into the sides of the vehicle, finally locating a worn tire on a rim, the treads smooth as a baby's—well, never mind that. Smooth.

But they didn't have any choice.

He rolled it to the ground and pulled out the jack and lug wrench. The tire danced in a half circle around him, then flopped to its side.

Something didn't look right.

He stepped on the rubber, then groaned.

Flatter than the one already on the bus.

Millie peered out a window. "Everything all right?"

"Spare's flat."

"Do we have a pump?"

"No."

"Can we drive on the flat?"

"Already did that for the last mile or so. Down to the rim. And that keeps digging into the road, pulling us off center. Not to mention the damage to the rim and maybe the axle." He kicked the tire on the ground. "I don't have enough strength to manhandle this bus all the way back to the first repair shop. And we'd be a menace on the highway since we can't keep up to speed."

"Can we at least get closer to the highway?"

He considered her idea. "Good idea. All aboard!"

But less than a half mile later—and still some ten miles or more from the highway, the bus ground to a halt once more, the engine temperature needle beyond the red zone.

Peter turned off the key and leaned his head on the steering wheel.

Things definitely *could* get worse.

Millie stood beside him, dark circles of worry decorating her eyes. "Now what?"

"Overheated. Again."

Her brow drew down. "We don't have any more water, Peter."

"None?"

She shook her head. "I gave you the last of it the last time this happened."

"Okay, that does it. We'll have to spend the night here."

"The sun isn't quite down. We should walk."

"It will be dark in about fifteen minutes. We don't have a lamp or a lantern. No food. No water. No weapon. The desert is a dangerous place. Especially at night."

As though to reinforce his words, the yipping of coyotes wafted across the desert floor.

Millie wrapped her arms around herself. "I still think we should try."

"It would be foolish."

She drew herself up to her full height and jutted out her chin. "And who made you the boss?"

"Nobody." He sighed. "We'll be safer in the bus than out in the open."

"Nobody will find us here."

"Sure they will. Mr. Larkin will know we should have been back by now. He'll send another bus to find us."

She sank into her seat. "I wouldn't count on it."

"Why would you say that? He sent us out here on this fool's errand. He knows where we went."

"There was something wrong with this entire trip right from the beginning. You thought so too."

"I didn't like the idea of being pulled off our regular route."

"Right. And one of the other employees could easily have done this. If there ever really was a passenger in trouble." She sat up straighter. "I think he sent us out here because we went to him about the jewelry."

He peered at her in the gloom. "Do you think he and Nancy are working together in this?"

"When she left the gift shop, she said she was going to tell the manager about the forgeries. And she said he was the one who placed the orders. She simply put out what was received. And once we talked to him, he kept himself pretty scarce. Doesn't that strike you as odd?" She sighed. "He's probably spreading a bunch of lies right now about how we stole the bus and took off with hotel property. So when they find our desiccated bodies, everybody will believe him."

"Wow, I hadn't thought of that." Where did she get her ideas? "Sounds like a murder mystery."

"I've read a lot of books. That's the kind of movie I want to star in when I get to Hollywood." She stared out a window. "*If* I get to Hollywood."

"Well, let's look on the bright side. The sun will be up in less than eight hours or so. Just enough time to catch up on our sleep."

She stepped away. "I don't care if we are stuck here. I am *not* that kind of girl."

He grinned. "I wasn't suggesting anything like that at all." He rummaged around in the same compartment where he found the tire and tools. "Here's a couple of blankets. We can stretch out on the seats for the night."

For a moment, he was certain she'd come up with another argument, but instead, she nodded and accepted the worn covering.

"Fine. But as soon as the sun comes up, we head east."

"Agreed."

It was going to be a long night. Sleeping mere inches from the girl he wanted to hold in his arms would be tough. Perhaps the hardest thing he'd ever done. Because she'd made herself perfectly clear. She was not *that* kind of girl.

So why did she think he might be *that* kind of guy?

◆━━━━━◆

Millie stared at the cracked paint on the ceiling of the bus, along with the pattern of shoe prints—really, how had those gotten there?

"Peter, are you awake?"

"Yes."

"I'm cold."

Rustling in the dark. Footsteps. Then he stood at her feet. "Slide over. We can sit close to keep warm."

"I am not—"

"I know. That kind of girl. No worries. You stay inside your blanket, and I'll stay inside mine."

That should be safe enough. Visions of him carousing with the soiled dove filled her mind, but she scooted over and allowed him room to perch on the seat. She sat rigid beside him, ignoring the smell of him, a curious combination of sweat, grease, and—and something else. Something masculine.

More likely mildew from the old blanket wrapped around his shoulders.

She pressed her nose against the window. "I'm exhausted, but I can't sleep."

"Nerves will do that. How about I tell you a story?"

"No ghost stories. I'm already scared enough."

"Okay. How about a story about being rescued?"

"Sure." She leaned her head back against the seat and closed her eyes. "Begin."

"Well, there was this one guy named Moses. . ."

For the next hour, Peter told her story after story about people in need of saving. From evil rulers. From hateful brothers. From lions. From giants.

Using all manner of circumstances. Including plagues. And prison. And prayer.

Most of all, prayer.

When he paused for breath, she turned in her seat and faced him. "So why didn't God answer my prayers?" She choked back a sob. "Why didn't He save my mother when she was sick and dying?"

"Did your mother know Jesus as her Lord and Savior?"

The question turned bitter in her heart. "What difference does that make? Dead is still dead."

"One more story." When she opened her mouth to deny him the opportunity, he placed a forefinger across her lips. "Shush."

And she did. She wasn't certain why. Nobody since her mother had managed to quiet her when she wanted to speak.

Perhaps it was the intensity in his look. Or the hoarse pleading in his voice. Or the tender touch of his finger that sent a shock of electricity through her.

She sat back, arms crossed, bottom lip jutted out. "Fine. But this better be good."

"Jesus had a really good friend named Lazarus." He paused. "Do you know this story?"

"No." She kept her cold stance just to remind him she was simply humoring him. "Carry on."

"Jesus loved Lazarus. A lot. Like a brother. Then Lazarus fell sick. His sisters sent word to Jesus to come if He wanted to see him before he passed.

But Jesus didn't go right away."

That didn't make any sense. "Doesn't seem like something a friend would do."

Peter held up his finger again. "There's more." He drew a breath and exhaled. "Then Lazarus died. And when Jesus got word, He said to his disciples, 'Let's go.'" He squinted at her in the dark. All she could see were the whites of his eyes and his teeth where he offered a tiny smile. "Following?"

"Yes. Still doesn't make any sense."

"The disciples said basically the same thing. And Jesus said He'd show them the glory of God."

"All the glory of God isn't going to fill the dead guy's sisters' hearts. Or the loss in their lives."

"Exactly. Jesus went. And Lazarus's sister Martha came out to meet him. She said her brother wouldn't have died if Jesus had been there. He could have healed him. Jesus said she'd see her brother again, and Martha believed that. In heaven. Then Jesus asked if she believed in Him, and Martha said yes."

"Believed in what?"

"That Jesus was the resurrection and the life, and so could raise Lazarus from the dead."

"And she agreed?"

"She likely had already seen, or at least heard, about Jesus doing exactly that a couple of times before."

"So what happened next? Did Lazarus come alive again?"

He smiled again. "Patience. Now, where was I?" He planted a finger on his chin as though deep in thought. "Oh right. Martha took Jesus to her sister, Mary. Mary said essentially the same thing—that if Jesus had been there, Lazarus would be alive. And all her cryin' and the wailin' and mournin' of the other friends and family touched Jesus' heart. He asked, 'Where is Lazarus?'"

"Well, he was dead, wasn't he? Buried in a coffin and all."

"Not quite. In a tomb carved into a hill. So Jesus went to the mouth of the cave and told them to open up the grave. And everybody was disgusted, because by this time he'd been dead four days. Can you imagine the stink?"

Millie nodded. Apart from her mother, who started to smell even before she died, she only had experience with a dead cow they came across in the back pasture. Maggots and flies and nasty stink was right. Dead four days, well—she waited for the rest of the story.

Because there had to be more.

"They rolled the stone away that blocked the cave to keep the animals and the like from the body, you see." He waited until she nodded. "Then Jesus prayed and called to Lazarus. And out he came."

Out he came. There had to be more to it than that. "Then he wasn't really dead."

"Oh yes, he was. The Jews were most particular about that kind of thing. They made sure there was no breath. No heartbeat. They had some traditions they followed to make certain the person was really dead. And if he wasn't really dead, don't you think he could have woken up, made his way to the stone, and just been sittin' there when the cave was opened?"

"Well, I guess so."

"Sure. But he didn't come alive until Jesus called his name."

"So where is all this going? That doesn't answer my question about my mother."

"Well, do you imagine Lazarus died again, maybe years later?"

"Of course he did."

"Right. So although Jesus raised him, it was only a temporary healin', right? Because we're all subject to time and age."

She began to see where he was going with this. "So what you're saying is that even if God answered my prayer to heal her, she'd still die at some point?"

"Yes. In your mother's case, she experienced a permanent healin'. She closed her eyes in pain, and she opened them in heaven, with God, completely healed. Forever. Which do you think she preferred?"

"The permanent kind."

"And what would you have chosen for her?"

"The same." The words stuck in her throat because she really would rather her mother was still here for her. At the same time, knowing her mother was healed and free of sickness was good news. "Yes, the permanent kind."

He held her hand as gently as though she were made of delicately spun glass. "This is one way God demonstrates His love for us. For your mother. For you."

"I never understood it that way before." She stared out the window at the stars. "You told me the story of Joseph, how God told his grandfather that He knew every star by name. Think a great big God like that would know my name?"

Peter gripped her hand tighter. "Not only does He know your name, but He sent His Son to redeem you from this world and receive the next, when you're ready."

Tears burned her eyes. "I want to know a God like that. I want to know that if I ever get sick, God might choose to give me a permanent healing."

"I can help you with that. Close your eyes and repeat after me."

After leading her through a prayer and encouraging her to take a few minutes to talk to God—which she did—a huge weight lifted from Millie's shoulders. Nothing on the outside changed—they were still stuck in a broken-down bus in the middle of the desert with no assurances that anybody would come looking for them—but now she knew the God who loved her as He loved no other.

A sense of peace settled over her like a warm blanket, and she fell asleep watching a shooting star pierce the darkness of the night.

And of her soul.

Chapter 10

Peter woke the next morning with the strains of "Amazing Grace" in his head. He glanced at Millie, whose head rested on his shoulder. A soft whistle akin to a snore came from her mouth.

He smiled, joy building in him until he thought he'd burst. Through their circumstances, their conversation of the night before, and her decision to receive Christ, he sensed a new closeness in their relationship that had little to do with the fact they'd slept in the same bus seat the previous night.

This intimacy came about because she was now part of his spiritual family.

The sound of a rock skittering across the ground drew his attention to the world beyond the bus window. A circle of Indians, decorated in war paint and feathers, guns and arrows at the ready, faced him. Their ponies danced in place, kicking up dust, bobbing their heads also adorned with feathers, leather tassels, and silver amulets.

He poked Millie's arm. "Wake up. We've got visitors."

She opened her eyes and smiled up at him, and for a moment, he wished they could stay right where they were.

But they had more urgent matters to attend to. Like saving their scalps.

Millie followed their gaze. A soft moan escaped her lips. "Oh no."

"My thoughts exactly."

"I feel like I'm in a wagon train of old. A wagon train of one."

"Me too. Any ideas?"

"Well, we're still on Acoma land. Maybe we know them from the Indian Detours."

"Better question is do they know us? They look mighty menacin'."

"Remember what the guidebook says. Assume positive intent when making contact with natives."

Peter blinked at her. "You mean you actually read that?"

"Of course I did. They told us to, so I followed orders."

"Good."

"Good?"

"Two reasons. One, it shows you can be a submissive wife if you set your mind to it."

"Oh it does, does it? Pity the man who believes that. And the other reason?"

"Because maybe it also gave you some ideas on how to react in this situation."

She pursed her lips.

Her very attractive lips. That under other circumstances he'd take as an invitation to kiss. But later. Once they were safely on their way.

She shook her head. "Nope. They didn't say what to do." She nudged him. "Move over."

"Why?"

"I'm going out to talk to them."

"They have guns. And arrows. And bows."

"Assume positive intent, remember."

"Right. Positive. I'm positive they're goin' to kill us."

"Don't be silly. Let me get out."

Despite his misgivings of her plan, he did as she asked. She ran her fingers through her hair, smoothed the wrinkles from her blouse and pants, and headed for the door. Unable to watch, certain she'd be the first to go, he closed his eyes and prayed.

After he ran out of things to pray for, he opened his eyes. Millie stood near the largest pony with the most decorations and laughed up at the warrior on its back.

Laughed!

She'd get them killed.

Oh well, if that happened, at least they'd both meet Jesus together.

The warrior returned her laugh, slapping his thigh and gesturing to the others. Who joined him. Then two slid from their mounts and handed her the reins, which she accepted.

Peter held his breath. She needed to be careful. She could be agreeing to marry one of these natives.

The two warriors on foot waited while two others rode next to them, then mounted behind the riders. The entire group rode away, leaving nothing behind but the two horses and a cloud of dust.

Millie turned back to the bus and waved to him. He lowered the window. She pointed to the ponies following docilely behind. "They lent us these horses to get back to town once I explained our situation."

"You speak their lingo?"

"Of course. Hannah's been teaching me. And they know some English. We managed to make ourselves understood. Come on. Daylight's wasting."

He lifted his eyes heavenward and sent up a quick prayer of thanksgiving, then did as she bid. Perhaps this experience was also teaching *him* to be a submissive child of God.

＋━━━・━━＋

Racing across the desert at breakneck speed on surefooted Acoma ponies was the thrill of Millie's life. She clamped her thighs tight to her mare's sides, bent low over its neck, and basically let the pinto carry her along. A couple of times she glanced over at Peter, who concentrated on staying aboard by gripping his stallion's mane and the reins in both hands.

Almost an hour later, they slowed to a lope as they reached the town limits. The city was just rousing. Windows opened, dogs ran in the alleys, delivery vans and wagons began their routes, and a factory on the outskirts blew the start of a shift horn.

Seven o'clock.

Millie sat upright and reined her mount to a brisk walk, then halted at the Alvarado. She dismounted and helped Peter down, then they hitched their horses to the rail. A car coming from the other direction also stopped, and a uniformed chauffeur stepped out and opened the rear door. Mr. Fred Harvey Jr. stepped out.

Oh what a day for the owner to make one of his surprise appearances. Here she was, a mess to look at. Mr. Larkin's sharp tongue would surely tear a strip off her for this. Staff poured out of the hotel, gathering around Mr. Harvey Jr., offering their greetings, led by Mr. Larkin and Mr. Ramirez. The gift shop manager, Nancy, hung back in the shadows, wringing her fingers into knots.

Millie pressed in closer, unable to break through the crowd, but catching snatches of conversation. "Surprise inspection." "Leaving in an hour." "Making sure everything is running smoothly."

Well, things certainly weren't running smoothly. No matter what anybody else said.

Millie gripped Peter's hand and pushed in, excusing herself, infiltrating herself in layer by layer, until she stood face-to-face with the great man himself. Mr. Harvey Jr., his suit looking as fresh as though he'd donned it just minutes before, not a bead of sweat on his face, his mustache neat and his collar tight but not choking him, smiled at her, one eyebrow raised in question.

She extended her hand, which he shook. "Mr. Harvey, I simply must speak with you. I believe there is a problem at the Alvarado with counterfeit Indian jewelry."

His brow pulled down. "That is a serious accusation. Millie, isn't it? I remember you from the pay office. What proof do you have?"

She held out her arm to show him her bracelet. "This is a piece given to me by a local artisan."

"And?"

And she had no physical proof. Only her word. But would that be enough? "I compared the weight of my bracelet to the ones in the most recent shipment."

"And?"

"Mine weighed significantly more."

He peered at her. "What does that mean to you?"

She drew a deep breath.

Oh God, give me the words.

"According to a book I read about Acoma jewelry, which is all silver, and the various counterfeit pieces identified recently, which are usually nickel, the silver pieces will always weigh more than the nickel ones."

He gestured to her bracelet. "May I?"

She nodded.

He undid the clasp and examined the maker's mark and metal signature. "What marks were on the bracelet you say weighed less than this one?"

"The same. Although the pattern and materials were different. Chips in the stones. Not so intricate a design. Almost as though it were stamped out instead of being worked."

"And you could tell this how?"

Mr. Larkin appeared at Mr. Harvey Jr.'s elbow. "Mr. Harvey, I'm sorry these young people are bothering you."

Peter stepped in close, his nose mere inches from the hotel manager's. "Don't you mean you're sorry we're here at all? You sent us out into the desert in a decrepit vehicle, hoping we'd fall victim to a mishap and never return."

Mr. Larkin sputtered, his face growing redder by the second.

Mr. Harvey Jr. laid a hand on the manager's arm. "I want to see the inventory in the gift shop."

"But, but—"

"Now! My father invested a lot of time and money to ensure the products we offer are of the highest standard. Show me."

Inside the gift shop, following a stern command from Mr. Harvey Jr., Nancy produced the items in question. He pulled a jeweler's loupe from a pocket and examined each piece, taking them out of their packets. He set some to the left, some to the right. When finished, he tucked the loupe into his pocket and pointed to the grouping on the left. "Just as in the Bible, when God talks about separating the sheep from the goats, these 'goats' on the left are counterfeit. The 'sheep' on the right are genuine. Yet I see the goats bear tags and maker's marks claiming they are silver." He scoured Mr. Larkin and Nancy with his gaze. "Who is going to tell me what's going on?"

Nancy pointed at the manager. "I told you this was a stupid idea."

"Shut up, woman. They can't prove anything."

The gift shop manager shook her head. "I'm not taking the fall for this. I'm tired of falling for crooks." She faced Mr. Harvey Jr. "It was all his idea. He found an Indian who wanted to make enough money to get off the reservation."

Mr. Larkin lunged toward her and grabbed her around the throat. Peter stepped in and pried his fingers off, landing a solid upper cut that sent the manager sprawling.

Nancy clutched at her neck. "I'll tell you whatever you want to know." Her voice rasped in her throat. "I thought he loved me."

Mr. Larkin stirred, then his head flopped back. He was out cold. Nancy slumped against the counter, her face white.

Mr. Harvey Jr. nodded. "Somebody call for the police to take care of these two. Get them out of my sight."

Nancy wrung her hands. "Please, have mercy. I didn't mean any harm."

Mr. Harvey Jr. frowned. "Well, you and your accomplice here very nearly accomplished much harm. You stole from the Acoma people through your activities."

"I did not. We paid good money for these. To one of those Indians."

"But you knew it wasn't genuine. So you stole from the true craftspeople. And you stole from Mr. Harvey Sr."

"No, never!"

"Yes. You were willing to risk his reputation and standing in the community and with the local natives in exchange for money. Crude, rude, temporal money. Disgusting."

The police arrived and handcuffed the pair, then escorted them out to their wagon.

Mr. Harvey Jr. smiled. "I'm suggesting that the first one to testify against the other receive a deferred sentence. I carry a lot of clout here in town."

Peter gripped Millie's hand, sending her a quick squeeze now and then as encouragement. While her heart raced at the intensity of the moment, she thoroughly enjoyed watching the police haul the two away. She smiled over at him. "Now are you glad those warriors found us?"

One side of his mouth lifted in a smile. "Am I ever."

Mr. Harvey Jr. faced them. "Peter and Millie, I can't thank you enough. My father would surely want me to reward you in some way."

Millie shook her head. "We were just doing our jobs, sir."

"No, you went above and beyond your jobs. You put your lives into some danger, and you overcame your fear to be here today. I suspect there's a great story in there somewhere."

Peter smiled. "It was all Millie, sir. She discovered the crooked tourists, insisted we follow them, got threatened by the husband, then figured out that Mr. Larkin was tryin' to get rid of us. And if it wasn't for her speakin' Acoma to those warriors, our scalps might be decoratin' a teepee now instead of bein' firmly attached to our heads."

Mr. Harvey Jr. laughed. "Son, you make it sound like a movie."

A movie. Yes, Millie supposed it did sound a little fantastic at that.

She smiled. "I guess that's pretty much how it was though."

"Peter, I'd be right pleased and feel a lot more secure if you'd take over as hotel manager. And Millie, you have an eye for detail. Would you consider working for me as gift shop manager?"

Peter's mouth worked as though he wanted to answer but was biting back the words.

Millie stared at him. Whatever was wrong? It's what he always wanted. To settle down. In a good job. Now he could afford to get married and have a family. She nudged his arm, and he finally came out of his trance.

"Sir, thank you for the kind offer."

"I hear a 'but' in there somewhere, young man."

Peter nodded. "Yes, sir. You see, sir, Millie plans to go to Hollywood and be an actress. And me, I plan to follow her wherever she goes. If she'll have me."

Millie smiled at his words. He really was a dear. One she wanted to be around all the time. She faced Mr. Harvey Jr. "Sir, I'd be honored to accept the offer, and I believe Peter would be too. Because I plan to stay right here. If Peter will have me."

Peter grabbed her hands. "But Millie, what about California? And your dreams of the silver screen?"

"I finally figured out that God's path is the best one. But I have one question for you."

"Anything. Ask away."

"What about your soiled dove?"

His brow pulled down and his head tipped in question. "What soiled dove?"

"The one I saw you with, coming out of the alley. You waltzed her down Main Street wearing your coat, bold as brass."

His cheeks colored. She held her breath. Would his answer be enough to convince her to stay?

"I found her in that alley. Some man beat her up. I helped her to the pastor's house. He and his wife raised the money to get her back to Arkansas."

She studied his face. His honest face. He couldn't lie to her if he tried.

He leaned close. "I have one question for you. Are you goin' to Hollywood or stayin' here?"

She pulled him close, and he tipped her chin up and lowered his mouth to meet hers. After a breathless kiss, when they finally came up for air, she whispered in his ear. "No more detours for me. Just the straight and narrow from now on. At your side."

Donna Schlachter lives in Colorado, where the Wild West still lives. She travels extensively for research, choosing her locations based on local stories told by local people. She is a member of American Christian Fiction Writers and Sisters in Crime, and facilitates a local critique group. One of her favorite activities is planning her next road trip with hubby Patrick along as chauffeur and photographer. Donna has been published twenty-four times under her own name and that of her alter ego, Leeann Betts, and she has ghostwritten five books. You can follow her at www.HiStoryThruTheAges.wordpress.com and on Facebook at www.fb.me/DonnaSchlachterAuthor or Twitter at www.Twitter.com/DonnaSchlachter.

Riders of the Painted Star

by Kathleen E. Kovach

Dedication

To my cowboy, Jim, who makes me feel like a star every day.
And to Daddy, your love of Zane Grey novels did not go unnoticed.

Chapter 1

1936
New York City

"You good fer nothin' snake in the grass! I'm gonna teach you a lesson." Deadeye Pete drew his six-shooter and pointed it at the bearded cowboy he had just culled from the posse. "Dance, you varmint!"

Bullets peppered the dust near the cowboy's feet, and he high stepped to avoid getting hit.

"Boo!" Zadie Fitzpatrick joined her voice with those in the darkened movie theater. Nobody likes a villain, and Deadeye Pete was the worst of them all, at least in this latest Bret Masters movie, *Long Arm of the Law*, featured at Nobel Theater in Midtown Manhattan.

"Zadie, control yourself," Marvin Hinkle hissed into her ear. This was the first and last date with the bank clerk from Yonkers. Zadie looked at him in time to see him roll his eyes behind thick lenses encased in black frames. He'd just failed the first round in her litmus test for men worth pursuing a relationship with. They first had to enjoy the cinema, particularly Westerns.

If they passed that test, they had to appreciate art. When Zadie wasn't in a movie theater, she could be found in front of a canvas painting the New York skyline, life in Central Park, midtown shoppers. Her art expressed where she lived.

"Marvin, everyone boos the villain."

"Well, I don't think it's proper for a young lady such as yourself to engage in such behavior."

Strike two.

Annie leaned in on Zadie's opposite side. "The Last Roundup?" Code for *Could this fellow be the one?* Annie apparently thought she and Marvin had been whispering sweet nothings to each other.

"Tumbling Tumbleweed." Zadie whispered back the code to her best friend. *Moving on.* They had used song titles to talk secretively ever since high school.

She glanced over at Annie's fiancé, Raymond, and then down to their hands, where he gently cradled her palm and absentmindedly wiggled the brand-spanking-new engagement ring hugging her finger.

"You're so lucky to have found your keeper."

"Shhh!" Marvin, the self-proclaimed etiquette police, glared at the two of them. "If I must endure this tripe, may I at least do it in silence?"

Strike three.

Her blood reached 212 degrees Fahrenheit, threatening to burn Marvin if he dared look her way. But she dialed back the heat out of self-preservation to avoid embarrassing herself in the packed theater.

Marvin had seemed a nice enough guy when she first met him on a ferry crossing the Hudson River. His home was in New Jersey, and her destination was an art exhibit in Hoboken. She had been sketching faces of passengers when he expressed curiosity about her art, and as they spoke of her other interests, he seemed to share her passion for Western movies. Although she should have been tipped off when he didn't know Tom Mix from Gene Autry. If anything could produce a strike four for the relationship test, it would be phoniness. Or maybe that should be number one. Zadie hated when a man put on a different personality just to get her to like him. Marvin wasn't the first to try that. Why couldn't people just be themselves?

When the movie was over, the two couples left the theater and wandered into a warm spring evening. Marvin seemed agitated as the audience spilled out onto the sidewalk and began hailing cabs. Zadie pulled him aside.

"Listen, Marvin. You're a nice guy and all—"

"But we're not suited for each other."

Zadie took a step back. That was her line. "No, we're not, so I think it's best—"

"—if we don't see each other again."

Strike five. He could at least be a gentleman and let her break up with him first.

Raymond flagged down a cab and helped Annie inside. "Coming, you two?" He had one foot inside the vehicle.

Marvin gently squeezed her shoulder. "You go on. I'd like to walk a little bit. There's a stamp symposium a few blocks from here. I had thought to ask you to go, but then you suggested the movie." He offered a lopsided grin.

"I remember you mentioning your love of stamps. You should go. My friends will see me home."

His face lit with excitement. He had a pleasant face, but not a spend-my-life-with, have-babies, and grow-old-together face.

She kissed him on the cheek. "I'm sure there's a woman somewhere who would love to collect stamps with you."

He gave her a hopeful look. "Do you really think so?"

"The Lord will lead you to just the right person. I'm sure of it. Now go and find that rare one."

"Stamp?"

"Sure." She meant woman, but either would apply.

He shoved his hands into his pockets and disappeared into the moving river of people.

Once inside the cab and heading home to the Upper East Side, with Annie and Raymond on the seat next to her, Zadie gazed out her window. If she were to paint this scene in her current mood, she'd opt for dark watercolors, muting the faces. Couples walked arm in arm, groups laughed merrily. She'd paint the lone woman in the forefront, maybe in red, to show she hadn't lost all hope. Zadie glanced down at her red dress. Alone yet still with hope.

She shouldn't complain however. Other than her love life, she had it pretty good. After all, this was 1936. The country was valiantly fighting the Great Depression. Her parents, children of Irish immigrants, faired quite well as Dad climbed up the political ladder. They had all lived through the War to End All Wars and survived.

And she had just survived Marvin.

She sighed more heavily than she had intended. Annie must have heard her and emerged from her cocoon of bliss. "I'm sorry, Zadie. I didn't think Marvin was the One, but it would have been nice if he could have been the One for a While."

"I don't know. I think I'm the problem. I'm bored. Bored with big-city men. Bored with big-city life. Bored with the big city. I think I need a change of scenery." She leaned her elbow on the window jamb and pressed her fist to her cheek. With a sigh, she thought about the movie she'd just seen. What she needed was big, open spaces and a cowboy to share them with. A cowboy like Bret Masters. Now *that* was a man.

"Oh! Why didn't I think of it?" Annie slapped her own forehead. "What a dummy I am sometimes." She slapped Raymond's shoulder. "She needs a change of scenery."

"Oh!" A lightbulb went off somewhere in his brain as he caught on to what Annie was talking about. "Of course!" They both looked at Zadie with huge grins on their faces.

Annoyance niggled at Zadie's nerves. "Do you two want to share?"

Annie gripped Zadie's knee. "You know my cousin who lives in Arizona, the one married to Holden Chase?"

"The famous Western novelist and my favorite author? Uh, yes. He's the one who sparked my interest in cowboy movies."

"Well, he's approached the publishing company where we work." She pointed at Raymond to include him. "He needs a new illustrator for his latest book."

Zadie already liked where this was headed. Anticipation pulled at her painting fingers, and they tingled with new possibilities.

"My boss promised to search our files and will give him an answer on Monday."

"Canvas work? Ink line drawings? That sort of thing?"

"Yes, all of it. With an in-house assignment at their dude ranch."

"I could do that." Zadie's heart fluttered with excitement as she caught the vision. "I'm not an artist on file with your publishing company though. I would probably have to submit my portfolio."

"If I remember right, Holden was impressed with your work when they visited a few years ago. Remember when your impressionist work was featured at the gallery? He may have even bought one."

Zadie rested against the seat cushion and gazed at the cab's ceiling as if she could see her future played out on the cinema screen. No more concrete sidewalks. No more tall buildings shutting out the natural light. And best of all, no more spoiled or neurotic city boys. "*Cowboys.*" She sighed. "Tell your boss to put away his files. I'm going."

❧ ⸺ ❧

Zadie had finally ended her long trip across the country. Annie's cousin, Theresa Chase, an amiable middle-aged woman, met her at the train station. "My husband regretted not being able to pick you up. He's in a meeting today with a Hollywood executive."

"That's exciting."

"Yes, we're on pins and needles. A producer has approached him to make a movie of his book that hasn't even been published. The one you're here to paint the cover for."

"Mr. Chase's stories made me fall in love with the Old West. And when Western movies started showing at the cinema, well, I couldn't think of a better way to spend an afternoon. A Chase novel made into a movie? The best of both worlds."

A porter helped to load her luggage into the car, a roomy four-door Cadillac.

Theresa swept a red-checkered scarf over her silver-brown hair. "You ready to see the Novel T Ranch?"

Zadie pressed a fist to her chest, trying to still the millions of butterflies trying to burst out. "More than ready."

She took an immediate liking to her host. Her yellow wraparound day dress flapped in the breeze of the open window. Large white sunglasses completed the ensemble. She drove with one hand and hung her elbow out the window. "I hope you like our little dude ranch."

"How many acres is it?" Zadie sat in the front passenger seat, having tied on her hat with the blue scarf attached to it. All the windows were down, blowing in hot, dry air, and she had to raise her voice to be heard.

"We're a working ranch on ten thousand acres."

"Really? I can't even imagine that much land. Central Park has only eight hundred and forty-three acres. And it's huge. I've painted there many times since they cleaned it up a couple of years ago."

Had she not been in an automobile, she could have imagined herself in a stagecoach, traveling through the desert, tall cacti on either side. "So, it's a working ranch and a getaway spot. What does that look like?"

Even though there was no traffic whatsoever, Theresa tapped her blinker and turned left onto a dirt road. "We cater to city slickers who want fresh air and relaxation as well as people who love hard work. Depending on their skill level, they can go on a cattle drive and be immersed into the larger part of the ranch. Or they can participate in hay rides and classes we offer. Horseback riding is popular, and of course we have our Saturday barbecue with smoked beef straight from our own herd."

"It all sounds lovely." Zadie's stomach growled at the mention of food. The sun was just beginning its descent to the west, and she hadn't eaten for several hours.

Soon the car began to pass outbuildings and the ranch house came into view. Made of adobe, it blended well with its environment—a beautiful terra-cotta color offset by green cacti of various shapes and sizes. Cedar posts held up the porch, and a carved double door stood as the focal point.

"I hope you're okay to stay in the house. We offer rooms for guests, and also cabins. The rooms are more luxurious than the cabins."

"I'm fine sleeping on the couch if it means staying on this beautiful ranch."

Theresa parked in front of the house, and Zadie opened her door. A young cowboy of about fifteen years of age burst from the house and loped to the back of the car where he promptly began removing the bags. He'd have to make a couple of trips but seemed determined to do his job without any help.

Zadie untied the scarf and removed her hat. She slowly turned in a circle to take it all in. Her dream gift. A delicious, made-to-order diamond cut just for her.

A fountain sprang from deep inside her soul, refreshing and spouting new life. She couldn't stop the grin stretching from cheek to cheek as she followed her hostess into the sprawling ranch house. Immediately her skin, warmed by the dry heat outside, cooled inside the large structure.

"I heard adobe homes made the desert heat bearable. I'm happy to learn this is true."

"Oh, my husband loves his creature comforts. He may write dusty stories of cattle drives and desperados, but when he built this ranch, he made sure his den was on the north side, where the sun never hits." Her hearty laugh bounced off the walls of the spacious room furnished with warm timber and soft leather. She led Zadie up the wide staircase where a red, patterned carpet runner protected the dark wooden steps.

Theresa stopped at the first room, one of six off a veranda overlooking the area below. Zadie held back a whistle as she entered the place she'd be staying. She was no stranger to opulence, having grown up in an affluent family, but the rustic beauty of this sanctuary took her breath away. A tribute to days long gone, handwoven blankets adorned the walls as if they were fine works of art. The large bed was made of pine logs, and a small step stool awaited dutifully to help the guest climb up into the decadent folds of the comforter. Oil lamps turned into electric lights gave the space a soft glow, and a chamber pot used as a planter decorated a corner.

Zadie placed her hat on the dresser and walked to where two easy chairs and an artist's easel beckoned her near.

"We thought this room would suit you best, what with the natural light from the window."

"It's perfect. Thank you."

Theresa patted the dresser. "Feel free to make yourself at home. Dinner is in an hour. If you'd like a tour of the grounds afterward, Holden should be here in time. Tomorrow he plans to take you on a ride into the desert to show you what he has in mind for the cover. Springtime in the desert is not to be missed." She started to leave the room but stopped. "Oh! Do you ride?"

"If I'm with someone who knows what they're doing. It's been awhile, but my family used to vacation upstate, and we did a little horseback riding."

"Wonderful! He will be pleased."

Theresa shut the door behind her, and Zadie squealed as she launched herself onto the bed. "I'm in my own Western! Thank you, Lord!"

Zadie freshened up and changed out of her traveling clothes. She considered the cocktail dress she had packed but, after seeing the ranch and the relaxed atmosphere, opted instead for a skirt and blouse. She tied a blue scarf around her neck to complement her short auburn curls. After an approving peek in the mirror, she left the room to find dinner.

The savory scent of roasted meat wrapped her in a hug. The eating area was al fresco under a pavilion. On the shaded crushed rock were three sets of three tables that sat fifty-four people. Benches served as chairs in the informal setting.

People milled about chatting and getting to know one another. Families, couples, and single men, maybe fifty in all, took their seats when Theresa rang the dinner bell. They were served family style, with large bowls of mashed potatoes and green beans, and glorious meat served on platters—beef rib roast, Zadie learned, that had been cooked over a fire on a spit.

Holden Chase arrived home just as everyone began passing the plates. He wasn't quite what Zadie had expected. She had envisioned a tall man with a ten-gallon hat, fancy cowboy boots, and a huge silver buckle on his belt. But Holden was about Zadie's height of five feet seven inches, and robust. He sported a business suit with the coat slung over his arm and his tie askew. The only thing remotely Western about him was brown cowboy boots and a graying bristle-brush mustache that completely obliterated his upper lip.

"My apologies, folks." He raised his hands. "Just had an excellent meeting that I'll tell you all about in the days to come. In the meantime, enjoy the meal."

Holden and Theresa disappeared and didn't reappear until close to dessert. Zadie imagined he was telling her the exciting news in private.

After the peach cobbler, some people stood and stretched, while others remained seated and patted their stomachs. Zadie had maneuvered her legs around the bench when someone held out a hand to help her. She looked up to see Holden Chase acting the gentleman.

"You're Zadie Fitzpatrick, I assume." His eyes crinkled at the corners, much like the dancing Irish eyes she loved back home.

She stood and placed her hand in his. "Yes, sir. Thank you—"

With a tug, Zadie suddenly became enveloped in an embrace by this stranger.

When he pulled away, he patted her upper arms. "I've been shaking enough hands today. Here on the ranch, we treat each other like family."

When she finally found her voice, she responded with a breathless, "Okay."

"Would you like to see the ranch?"

"Yes, sir."

He frowned, and his mustache twitched. "Young lady. If you call me sir one more time, I'm going to take you to the desert and leave you there."

She fought her tongue not to say the offending words in reply.

Holden chuckled and led her away from the house and toward the building where the horses were corralled. "So, you know Theresa's cousin."

"Annie. She's very special to me."

"And to us. We were quite happy when she called us about you. I was losing hope of finding someone."

"I'm happy to do it. It gives me a new perspective for my art. I can't tell you how many cityscapes and Statue of Liberty paintings I've created. I need new scenery."

"I bought one of your paintings the last time I was in New York. It hangs in my den."

"May I ask which one?"

"It was of a street musician, his tattered clothes belying the pure bliss on his face."

"I love that one. I'm happy it found a good home."

"That painting was the reason I hired you. I was thrilled to hear you were available. I may be able to tell a good story, but the cover art is what sells books."

Zadie wanted to argue. She bought Holden Chase books because of Holden Chase. He always delivered an entertaining escape from her sometimes dull life. "What was it about the art that spoke to you?"

"The musician's face. I found I wanted to laugh right along with him. I want that detail on my covers. I want the reader to see a story before he even cracks open the book."

Zadie had to admit, capturing the lives of New Yorkers made her happy. But now the wide-open spaces called to her. She longed to paint cacti and red earth. Horses and cattle. And yes, cowboys.

"I assume, then, you will want more than just scenery on your covers. I work best with a model when drawing real people."

They had meandered over by one of the corrals. Two men stood near a horse. The tall one held the reins while the second patted the horse's neck. A third, pudgier cowboy, sat on the fence while playing a jaunty tune on a harmonica.

Upon seeing Zadie and Holden, the one patting the horse's neck grabbed the reins from the tall one and swung himself into the saddle. In a fury, the horse took off at the man's urging and galloped to the far side of the corral where two barrels had been set up. The horse rounded one and then the other, then rushed the fence where the two spectators stood. Dust flew, making Zadie cough.

"Dirk! What have I told you about showing off for the guests?" Holden brushed his clothes as he sputtered through his mustache.

"Sorry, Mr. Chase. I was just putting Chester through his paces."

Zadie would have been impressed by this cowboy's skills had it not been for the tall one now leaning against the fence with his boot heel hooked on the lower rung. His dark hair feathered from beneath his Stetson. His plaid shirt barely concealed arms the size of sturdy oak logs. But his face, handsome with a cleft in his chin, held the quality she looked for in her painting subjects.

Vulnerability.

She could work with a face hard as stone, but if that something extra didn't show through the tough exterior, then she wasn't interested. Much like the street musician. One could tell he'd led a rough life, but when he played his concertina, his face opened up and showed his soul.

"Holden." She pointed toward the tall cowboy. "Who is that? The one leaning on the fence."

Holden waved him over, and the other followed, tucking his harmonica into a shirt pocket. The closer they got, the more Zadie made up her mind. The taller man was the one she wanted to model for the cover. This was her real cowboy.

Chapter 2

Royce Rutger, I'd like you to meet Miss Zadie Fitzpatrick. She's here to illustrate my books."

Royce touched the brim of his hat. "Howdy, ma'am." New Jersey bred, he played the part, pleased to try out his new cowboy role on a civilian.

Dirk had dismounted and now hung close, as if he were about to snatch the next available taxicab.

"And these gentlemen are Dirk Cunningham and Jack Burnett."

"Flapjack to my friends, ma'am." The round face held a genuine grin. "They call me that because I love flapjacks."

Holden cleared his throat. "Yes, we have a hard time keeping pancakes on the table at breakfast."

Miss Fitzpatrick seemed to scrutinize Royce's face. She tilted her head and squinted one eye. "Pleased to meet everyone." What was wrong with the woman? Did she recognize him? Surely not. He had decided to stay clean-shaven, forgoing the itchy beard and mustache. He hated those anyway.

The only reason the movie studio insisted he wear a beard was because, in their words, "You have the face of a leading man. We can't have the young ladies in the audience swooning over you instead of our star, now can we?"

In truth, the star was the one who had complained, Royce was sure.

Bret Masters was walking on thin ice with the studio, and the studio heads had taken Royce aside. If he could learn more about horses and riding, he'd be perfect for the next craze. The singing cowboy. He could already play the guitar and sing. Gene Autry had made a big splash, as did others, and it seemed the smart way to go. He had not traveled from New Jersey to Hollywood to become a bit player, lost in the pack playing everything from a member of a posse to one of a plethora of train robbers riding with Jesse James.

"Holden." Miss Fitzpatrick turned to his boss. "On our venture tomorrow, may we bring Mr. Rutger with us?"

"If you don't mind, the name's Royce, ma'am." He tilted his hat just as he'd done in his last movie, *Long Arm of the Law.*

"And I'm Zadie." Her delicate fingers touched her chest. "If I may be so bold, I love your blue eyes. Not pale, but deep and full of life."

An ember glowed deep in his heart at the compliment.

"Thank you kindly, ma'am. No one's ever noticed my eyes before."

"Surely not. That's a travesty. Men with dark hair and blues eyes are rare."

He liked her green eyes too. Not only because of the color but because they sparkled with enthusiasm.

Dirk thrust himself between them. "My eyes are light brown. Some have described them as yellow."

"Interesting."

Flapjack grabbed Dirk's shirt and yanked him backward. He blustered behind Royce while Zadie continued her scrutiny.

She placed the tip of her finger next to her chin. "You'll make the perfect model for Holden's covers."

Royce groaned inside. No. Not modeling. Not again. He'd worked for Gibson Patterns, a sewing company in Newark. Morning coats, sport coats, and suits. Even smoking jackets for the businessman to relax in when he came home. Standing still while someone sketched his likeness—nope, never again.

Not even to be near the pretty Zadie Fitzgerald.

Holden stroked his mustache. "Good idea."

Before Royce could object, Dirk shoved Royce's shoulder. "What do you want with this yahoo?" He draped his arm over the fence in front of Zadie and wiggled his eyebrows. "I'd be happy to join you in the desert."

Something boiled in Royce's belly. Jealousy? Protectiveness? Both? He'd seen others like Dirk in the big city. Though they didn't wear cowboy hats, their attitudes were the same. Conquest. See a pretty girl and all of a sudden she became part of a game.

Royce looked at Holden with determination. "I'll do it. It'll give me a break from *this* yahoo." He thumbed toward Dirk.

"Perfect." Zadie smiled, and that ember she'd already started in his heart glowed brighter. "I look forward to working with you."

Dirk continued to hang on the fence and ogle the woman. "If you should change your mind, you know where I live." He finished his greasy statement with a wink.

To her credit, she merely nodded, then addressed Holden. "I'll bring my sketchbook. With Mr. Rutger there, I can see how the whole picture will come together."

"Excellent. Royce, we'll leave right after breakfast."

"Yes, sir."

"It was nice meeting you, Flapjack, and *Dirk*." She'd said Dirk's name with attitude. Royce needn't worry about her around the smarmy cowboy.

As they walked away, Royce realized what he'd just agreed to. They'd be riding horseback. Sure, he could ride, but should anything out of the ordinary happen, he'd reveal himself as a greenhorn. Good thing Holden knew his secret. Maybe he'd cover for him if he blundered.

The next day in the stable, as Royce tossed a saddle onto Sonora, Holden approached him. "Theresa has decided to go so we can pick up some rocks while we're out."

"Rocks?" He'd seen polished rocks, such as turquoise and agate, for sale in town. A local tribe sold them as jewelry. "How many?"

"Only two or three. She's had her eye on a red heart-shaped sandstone boulder by the north mesa. She wants to put it in her rock garden, but it's too heavy for me to lift by myself."

Oh. Big rocks.

"So, you'll have more to do today than just look pretty." Holden winked. "Think you can hitch up the buckboard?"

"Yes, sir. That was one of the first things I learned when I got here. That, and saddling a horse." He indicated Sonora and the not-quite-cinched leather strap hanging from the saddle.

"Excellent. You and Miss Fitzgerald will follow on your horses. How's it going?" Holden glanced around to assure they were alone. "I know you haven't been on the ranch long, but is your instruction going well?"

"I'm getting the hang of things. You'd think I'd have picked up some tricks on movie sets, but you do your scene and then either stand off to the side or hit the food. I appreciate you allowing me to train here. And for going along with my request to remain incognito."

"The wife doesn't even know. I love her, and she has many great qualities, but keeping secrets isn't one of them."

"I appreciate that, but I'm sorry to have to do it to you."

"After meeting with the Hollywood types yesterday, I can understand the need to build your image. They seemed overly concerned with marketing and numbers when talking about my project. You and I are both nothing but products."

"Very true." Royce chuckled. "Speaking of that, I called the studio, and they gave the go-ahead to model. They said it'll do my career good and might sell you a few more books if they turn me into the next singing cowboy star."

"Yep, gotta keep the product from getting tainted." Holden shook his head, but his smile suggested he understood the process. Before he left, he added, "Can you saddle Sierra for Zadie? She fell in love with the paint yesterday."

Royce glanced around the stable at the stalls, some occupied. "Right. The paint." He removed his hat and scratched his head.

"The one in the corner over there." Holden strolled to where a beautiful horse waited, its white and brown head reaching beyond the half door for a pat. "So named because of the multicoloring."

"Ah. Got it." So much to learn. "What type of horse is Sonora?" All he knew was that they had given him a white horse when he'd first gotten there a couple of days prior.

"He's a quarter horse. Strong, durable, bred for ranch work."

Holden left and Royce saddled the paint, then hitched two horses to the wagon.

He waited outside the big house and muttered, "Lord, please don't let me make a fool of myself today. Help me retain all I've learned, and please keep me in the saddle."

"Talking to the animals?" Zadie wore a riding habit with the extra material at the hips, and tall black boots. Except for the cowboy hat, she looked more suited for cricket than a ride in the desert.

"Um, no. Just going over last-minute reminders." *Like reacquainting myself with the Lord.* He took in her outfit. "Nice trousers."

She pulled on the sides. "There is no place in New York to buy authentic Western wear. But I wanted to be prepared. I'll go to town soon and get something more appropriate." She tapped her cowboy hat. "I borrowed this from Theresa."

"You look nice."

"Thank you." She walked over to Sierra and patted her nose. "Isn't she a beauty? I chose her because I'm an artist, and she's a paint. Get it?" Her dazzling smile issued an electric jolt, the likes of which he hadn't felt since that bumper car shocked him on the boardwalk when he was young.

Royce cleared his throat and strode near her with his hands behind his back. "Yes, she's a paint, so named because of the multicoloring."

Holden appeared at the end of the buckboard, laughing. No doubt because Royce had just repeated him word for word.

Zadie eyed Holden suspiciously. "You're happy this morning."

"Just eager to show off my desert."

Theresa followed with a large basket. "I made us lunch."

Holden hefted it into the wagon bed. "You do realize, my dear, it's just the four of us and not the entire ranch."

Royce could eat a whole basket of camp food just by himself. He'd never been so hungry or eaten so well in his life.

"Just thinking of you and your appetite, my sweet." Theresa patted Holden's stomach.

Zadie removed a flat leather bag from her shoulder and laid it in the bed next to the basket. "I didn't realize you'd be joining us, Theresa. Now I won't feel so outnumbered." She flicked a playful glance toward Royce.

Theresa scampered into the wagon. "I wanted to be sure Holden picked up the right rocks for my garden."

"The only thing I've ever planted was a philodendron in a pot. I grew up in a flat surrounded by impossibly tall buildings."

So did Royce, but he wagered her flat in Manhattan had been big enough for an indoor orchard. The tiny apartment he shared with his mother, and where she still lived, only had room for a windowsill herb garden.

"About all we can grow here are succulents." Theresa climbed into her seat. "And wildflowers, but they're only pretty in the spring."

"I'd probably have more of a chance at a beautiful garden if I simply painted it."

Royce pointed to the satchel. "Is that your canvas and paints?"

"No, it's a notebook and sketching materials. Just pursuing ideas today. But be prepared."

To model. Great. Just great.

He mounted his horse with ease. Thankfully, he'd learned that much on set and during his few days at the ranch. He laughed inwardly at a memory from his first movie. The director was as much of a greenhorn as he was, and when he called "Action!" and the dozen or so actors all stepped into the left strap, he hollered, "Cut!" He wanted the cowboys to vary their mounting, some on the left and some on the right, for aesthetic purposes. Royce saw nothing wrong with that at the time, but the uproar from the saddle-bred actors, letting the director know in no uncertain terms that a real cowboy never mounted from the right, helped him to remember that the left was the proper side.

Zadie also mounted after refusing help from Holden.

"You seem at ease around horses." Royce was impressed. "How long have you been riding?"

"I'm from New York City, but my family occasionally vacationed in the Adirondacks."

His mother never had the time or the means for a vacation.

"We had family friends who owned a small ranch up there," she continued. "I gained basic riding skills, but it's been forever since I've been atop a horse."

She moved the reins, apparently to test her skills. The paint responded well. "I'm thrilled to be getting some tips from a real cowboy."

Guilty flames rushed up his neck. "Yes. . .well, we'll keep it gentle until you're more comfortable."

He nudged the horse to follow Holden through a weathered wooden gate and out into the open desert.

Anxiety niggled at Royce. He hadn't been in raw, rugged terrain without a team of people surrounding him, some behind cameras, some on horses next to him who knew what they were doing. It helped that Holden could handle a horse, but should he have to step in, Royce's cover would be blown.

Chapter 3

Zadie trailed a smidge behind the wagon and the chiseled cowboy riding alongside on the pearl-white stallion. She took in this tall drink of water in the saddle. He held himself differently than those she'd seen on the silver screen. His straight back showed off his muscles as the horse rocked underneath him. He held the reins high in both hands instead of relaxing into the saddle, draping one hand over the horn. He made her think of a cavalryman or someone too disciplined to slouch.

"Where is home for Royce Rutger?" Theresa asked once they were well under way.

Royce's shoulder blades stiffened even more, if that were possible. Zadie's observation skills, honed by hours of painting live subjects, kicked in. Did that question seem distressing to the cowboy?

"Right now, home is Los Angeles."

"Like a tumbleweed, eh Royce?" Holden chimed in. "You go where the wind blows?"

"Uh, yeah. Exactly." Royce chuckled and rubbed his neck. "Where the wind blows."

Holden gave Theresa a side hug. "My wife's family hails from Oklahoma, and whenever she visits, she comes home sounding like an Okie."

Teresa swatted him in the chest with the back of her hand. "I do not." She feigned an indignant air, but Zadie spotted a grin tugging her lips.

"What about you, Zadie?" Holden asked. "Have you always lived in New York?"

"Yes, Manhattan. As much as I love it there, I'm finding your desert absolutely beautiful."

"Springtime in the desert. Nothing like it in the world."

"I can't wait to paint these plants. So much color. I thought the desert would be dry and thorny."

"Cacti bloom this time of year." Theresa indicated the typical flora. "Early morning is the best time to see it, or after a good rain. That's a saguaro. I call him the 'old man of the desert' with his arms held high. I don't know why, but these cacti seem like sage sentinels, keeping watch over the rest of the desert."

Zadie had seen them in many movies. These had white blossoms. "You should be a writer."

"Oh, thank you, but I'll leave that to my famous husband." Theresa waved the idea away.

Holden chuckled. "I've told her she should write children's stories. She keeps the grandchildren entranced with her tall tales."

Theresa shook her head and pointed to another plant with multiple spindly tendrils raised to the sky. "That's an ocotillo."

"What a perfect name." Zadie particularly enjoyed the brilliant red blooms on the ends of each branch. "I was thinking it resembled an octopus."

"Or a sea urchin. When the wind blows, they bring to mind sea life on the ocean floor, waving to the whims of the water. Oh, be careful of those." She indicated a cute little cactus that looked soft to the touch with chartreuse flowers. "That's a type of jumping cholla. The teddy bear. But don't be fooled by its cuddly name. If you get close enough to touch it, pads of cactus will seemingly jump off and stick to you. It has barbs that sink into the skin and are very painful to pull out."

Royce steered his horse clear of the plant. "It looks so innocent."

"It is beautiful." Theresa nodded. "They grow up to eight feet tall. At sunrise and sunset, they will catch the sun's rays just right and take on an ethereal golden glow. The needles look soft, like the fur of a stuffed toy."

Holden shuddered. "One of my cowboys fell into one. Those nasty pieces stuck to him. Spiny snowballs all over one side of his body. They even penetrated his clothes. When the spines touch anything with moisture, like skin, the barbs curl, making them very difficult to remove."

"Ouch! Is he okay?" Zadie rubbed her arm, imagining tiny needles piercing her skin.

"We eventually removed them, but he was in excruciating pain. A comb is the best way to pluck them out. The Apaches used the cholla as weapons. If the enemy got one near his heart, it could kill him."

Zadie eyed the cactus as she rode by, making note of other patches of the dreaded plant as the group moved along.

"There, Holden! There are my rocks." Theresa pulled on her husband's sleeve and pointed to the right at a cluster of sandstone. She jumped out before Holden could stop the horses fully.

"Woman, don't do that. You'll give me a heart attack someday," Holden muttered under his breath as he directed the team of horses to a small grove of trees.

Zadie dismounted, as did Royce, and they both joined Theresa.

There didn't seem to be anything special about the rocks, but upon closer inspection, one of them did look like a large heart, perhaps three feet tall.

"Be careful, dear," Holden, now on foot, called as he caught up. "No telling what critters lurk under that pile." He searched the ground and retrieved a long stick. "Everyone, stand aside."

They all complied, Zadie the first to distance herself from whatever could be living under the pile.

Holden poked the stick into one of the spaces. "I don't hear a rattle."

Suddenly a small green head peeked out from the other side of the heart rock.

Zadie yelped and sprinted to the wagon, jumping in. Royce joined her. She cocked her eyebrow at him.

"Just keeping you safe, ma'am." He tipped his hat.

"Mm-hm. You nearly beat me to this spot."

Holden laughed at both of them. "Relax, it's just a little lizard."

Sure enough, the tiny, four-legged creature scampered from its hideaway, no doubt indignant over the disturbance.

"Should be safe now. Royce, you want to help me with this thing?"

Royce appeared to take tentative steps toward the pile, but once there, lifted the heart-shaped rock with Holden on the other side. They managed to get it into the buckboard and returned for another one.

"These three, and that one over there." Theresa directed her laborers, and soon all the rocks were loaded. Leaning on the wooden side of the wagon, she gazed adoringly at her treasures. "Oh, those will adorn my garden nicely."

Zadie also admired them. "You chose perfect specimens. I can't wait to see what you do with them."

Holden shook his head. "I just see a pile of rocks. How 'bout you, Royce?"

"Yep. Along with more spine-breaking work to get them where she wants them." He rubbed his back before mounting his horse.

"You got that right." Holden chuckled and, once Theresa was settled in her seat, whipped the reins gently to move the horses forward.

After another half hour, Holden tugged on the reins and brought the horses to a stop. "This is the spot. See that mesa over there?" He indicated a perfect tabletop rise of land with steep sides, thousands of feet high. "This is the backdrop I imagined for the book."

Theresa reached for the picnic basket. "Let's have lunch before you three talk shop."

They had stopped at a little oasis of land near a creek swollen with spring rains.

While Holden and Theresa unpacked lunch, Royce unhitched the horses. Zadie joined him as he led them to the water.

She perused the area, taking in the colors of the land. Vivid purple, red, and yellow wildflowers that Theresa had said were lupines, poppies, and owl clover, carpeted the desert floor. Blossoms adorned formidable cacti, from barrel to prickly pear, and they all contrasted with the red dirt leading up to the burnt sienna mesa and cerulean-blue sky.

"This is a dream come true for me."

"Watering horses?" Royce had taken off his kerchief and dipped it into the water. With a swipe, he rubbed his face and neck.

"No." She bent near him and cupped water into her hand, then touched her warm cheeks. The moisture cooled her skin but was gone all too soon from the dry breeze. "Although I guess watering horses is part of it. I mean being here. In the West. With a cowboy." She stood and breathed deep. "We don't have anything that smells this wonderful in New York."

"Lots of automobile odors and the construction smell of progress"—he cleared his throat—"I would imagine."

"Yes, exactly."

He glanced around. Finding what he was looking for, he reached out to a bright green bush and pulled off a leaf, then crushed it between his fingers and handed it to her. "Here. This is what nature intended for us to breathe."

She took it and sniffed. Her eyes widened, and she sniffed again. "It smells like rain."

"It's a creosote shrub. Thirsty fellow. It'll suck up all the water around it, cutting off the moisture from other plants. When we give tours, Flapjack, in particular, loves this plant and points it out to the guests."

"Thank you. I always think in colors, forgetting there are other senses." Like Royce's ultramarine-blue eyes and hair the color of burnt umber. "Impressionism is my favorite form of expression."

"Ah, Monet."

She scrutinized this conundrum of a cowboy. "Yes, and Renoir. How did you know?"

He shrugged. "Cowboys can have culture. Depends on how you're raised."

"Well, I commend your parents."

A shadow drifted across his face, but he cloaked it quickly.

"Woohoo! Hey, you two." Theresa waved her arms for them to come over. "Lunch is ready."

Even though Zadie was starving, she joined the other couple reluctantly. Time alone with Royce contributed to her cowboy dream. Of course they'd spend more time as artist and model, but it wouldn't be the same as standing close enough to—

"Got some wooden chairs here." Holden interrupted her musing. Probably a good thing, considering where that trail was leading her.

"My bride prefers to dine in comfort." He gave Theresa a peck on the cheek. "I'm afraid we only have two. The ladies can use them." He hopped onto the tailgate and let his feet dangle. Royce remained standing.

Theresa handed Royce a sandwich. "I hope you like leftover pot roast. Cookie outdid himself on this one."

"Cookie?" Zadie accepted her meal from Theresa and sat in one of the chairs. "As in the trail cook? I thought that name was only used in the movies. I love Westerns."

Royce choked on his sandwich, and Holden quickly poured water from a canteen into a small tin cup.

Theresa jumped to his side and patted his back. "Heavens! Are you all right?"

"Yes." Royce squeezed the word from his closed throat. "Just breathed in when I should have swallowed." He swigged the water and seemed to return to normal, then raised his food in a toast. "Good sandwich, if it's not in my lungs."

Royce glanced toward Holden, who seemed to telegraph something in return.

What was it with those two? All morning something crackled between them. Theresa didn't seem to notice, but she had been chattering most of the time about her beloved desert. Of course, it wasn't any of Zadie's business, but she determined to keep an eye on them.

◆━━━━━・━━━━◆

Royce joined Holden in the wagon and accepted another splash of water in his tin cup. Cool, healing, refreshing, it slipped down his throat and soothed.

"So, you go to the movies often then." Theresa had quit fussing over Royce and now asked the normally innocent question.

But for Royce it could signal the death knell for his disguise. He hoped he wouldn't suck in another surprised breath with food in his mouth.

"Oh yes." Zadie's beautiful green eyes lit up. "Every chance I get. I particularly love Bret Masters."

Royce cleared his throat louder than he intended, and everyone glanced his way, no doubt concerned. "Sorry. Still a little tender." He pulled on his collar. How could he change this subject? He'd been in the last four Bret Masters movies. Thankfully, the beard and mustache he'd had helped him stay incognito now with his clean-shaven face.

"The last one was particularly exciting." Zadie continued the excruciating prattle. "Someone stole a strongbox from a cattle baron, and Bret's best friend was a suspect."

And Royce was one of the extras in the villain's gang.

"Bret Masters is so handsome. And he plays his guitar while riding on his horse."

Bret Masters was also egotistical and spoiled. Which was why the studio wanted to groom Royce. The popular actor's days were numbered at Western Empire Film. He had cost the studio thousands with his antics, showing up late on set and demanding expensive treatment.

"Royce, here, plays the guitar." Holden jerked his thumb.

"Can you play while riding?" Zadie bounced in her seat.

"If you got a guitar and you got a pony, there's nothing finer than a song or two on the trail."

That sounded authentic, didn't it?

Holden grinned, then tried to hide it.

"That's so romantic." Zadie pointed to her bag. "Royce, can you please hand me my satchel behind you?"

"Oh sure." He retrieved it for her.

"While you finish eating, I'd like to sketch you. Get down your facial characteristics. Is that okay?" She pulled out a sketch pad and rummaged around until she found a charcoal pencil.

"Sure, I guess. Just don't show the food in my teeth."

She smiled. "I won't. Only your best features. I promise."

Was she flirting? He could have his pick of Hollywood starlets. They threw themselves at him as if they were seagulls and he was popcorn on the Jersey Shore. But he liked it when Zadie did it.

Her pencil *shush, shush*ed furiously on the sketch pad while he finished his apple pie. She had declined a piece, probably to get right to work. By the time he finished eating, she had several pages of parts of his face. His eyes all on one page, all different expressions. He didn't even know he had that many thoughts in his head. Another page was his nose from different angles. And so it went, page after page. His ears. His chin. His hair. On the last page, she drew his entire head.

She flipped the pad so he could see it better. "What do you think?"

"It's good. Why just my face?"

"It's a nice face." Her cheeks turned the color of the pink cherry blossoms in Branch Brook Park.

The likeness was remarkable. He hadn't known what to expect, but she was definitely talented. In fact, he'd seen similar work in galleries with his mother. What was Zadie doing in the dusty desert sketching book covers?

"Holden, if you're through eating, perhaps you could show me your vision of the backdrop."

Holden hopped to the ground. "Will do." They wandered off, Zadie raising her arms and forming a square with her fingers, apparently to show him where the mesa would best fit on the cover.

Royce and Theresa packed up the lunch items for the return trip. She wrapped the last of the dirty tin dishes and placed them in the basket. "Let's go arrowhead hunting while those two talk shop."

Theresa led the way, scanning the ground. Royce followed suit but doubted he'd find anything. Theresa explained that this spot was a hunting ground for the Apache because of the water source. To Royce's surprise, he found one arrowhead and Theresa found five.

Zadie called Royce over to where she and Holden had been talking. "And bring your horse."

He excused himself from Theresa and walked to where he had tied Sonora along the creek. Now he hoped to keep the beast still so Zadie could get good sketches of him.

Zadie glanced toward the mesa. Then, gauging the right spot for her model, drew a line in the sand with the heel of her boot. "Royce, please bring Sonora here." Royce mounted and complied. "See how I have the line? Try to be sure his front hooves are close to it. This will put you in the correct position."

While Zadie grabbed her materials and positioned her chair, Sonora seemed to want to follow her. Royce struggled to get the horse to understand. The animal got close to the line in the sand and then pawed at it, as if no one could fence him in, even if it was just a mark.

Zadie went to Sonora, stroked his neck, and whispered something in his ear. He instantly settled down and became the perfect model.

"What did you say to him?"

"That he was a handsome horse, and if he let me paint him, Sierra would probably want to get to know him better."

Was the encouragement meant as much for him as for Sonora?

◆━━━━━◆

Zadie pulled the chair around to face them, positioning herself to see part of Royce's face.

With horse and rider finally in position, Royce turned slightly to see Zadie. "Any particular way I should sit?"

"Yes. The title of the book is *Mesa Marauder*. I envision you, as the hero of the book, scrutinizing the mesa as if watching for signs of the outlaw. How are your acting skills?"

A tentative grin tugged at the corner of his mouth. "Fair."

"Well, do the best you can. I have the sketches of your face to fall back on if needed."

"Is that why you went into such detail?"

"It's a technique I use when I do portraits. That way I can work on the piece when the subject isn't able to sit for me."

Though true, she had to admit this time she'd taken extra care to get every detail because this subject pleased her. Very much.

Within minutes, she had a rough sketch of the marshal atop his trusty steed, watching for signs of the dastardly villain. "You're quite good at this."

"I've done my share of modeling." He scowled, then turned his face away.

"Face forward, please." When he complied and resumed his expression, she continued. "When would a cowboy have the opportunity to model?"

He hesitated, and she wondered if he'd heard her. Finally, he spoke. "It was a sewing pattern company."

"Really?"

Royce offered a mirthless chuckle. "A cowboy's got to eat."

Zadie sketched quickly, getting the basic lines down. She'd add detail later. "Sounds like fascinating work."

"It wasn't. Standing around for hours is boring."

"So, not fulfilling?"

He shook his head.

"Where do you find your fulfillment?" Zadie found hers in the Lord. He'd been her constant companion as long as she could remember. Everything else, the art, her love of movies, even her excitement of visiting the Wild West and meeting a real cowboy, were simply gifts from her heavenly Father.

"I have certain pursuits."

While curious about his cryptic remark, another subject interested her more. Should she approach him about the Lord? She didn't want him bolting away, either physically or mentally. Still, she needed to know because this man was seeping into her heart.

With her pencil, she put shading along his firm jawline. "For me, I could be doing anything, as long I know the Lord is pleased with it."

The jaw relaxed instead of becoming rock hard. A good sign.

"You sound like my mother."

Zadie's spirit did a little leap of joy. He had a praying mama.

"Sounds like a smart woman." She winked when he cocked his head toward her.

"She's a strong woman, for sure. Raised me by herself."

What about his father? Zadie wanted to ask but knew he'd tell her if he wanted her to know.

"Mom did everything in her power to assure I had a normal childhood. And when I was old enough to work, I contributed, despite her protests."

Guilt stabbed at Zadie. She had been born to privilege. All of her pursuits lined her own pocket, save for the tithe she gave each week at church. Perhaps she should pursue causes beyond herself.

"What about you?" He turned the tables on her. "How did you manage to find yourself here all the way from New York? I know you took the job, but why?"

"I was restless. I was born and raised in the big city, and the buildings were beginning to close in on me." She sketched his left hand on his hip, envisioning a marshal's six-gun there. Were the fingers strong from years of roping cattle? Was his palm rough? "Don't get me wrong. New York is full of wonderful people, genuine people, but lately I'd found myself among phonies. Particularly the men I dated. Particularly Jersey boys. Don't get me started on Jersey boys." She huffed a breath.

His hand slipped from his side. "Sorry. Cramp." He reset his pose. "So. . . uh. . .then you left?"

"I knew there was a big world out there, and I wanted to explore it. The Lord takes good care of me, and this opportunity landed in my lap. So I took it. Do you feel that way? God must have brought you here, to such a beautiful setting."

Sonora's ears swiveled back, as if he'd heard something behind him. He shifted a few feet to the right, and his hind leg brushed against a shrub.

"Whoa, boy." Royce pulled on the reins and spoke gently to calm Sonora. But the horse only grew more agitated. With wide eyes and nostrils flaring, he kicked the shrub and then reared up.

Royce tumbled off, saddle and all, and landed hard on his shoulder.

Zadie ran toward the horse to keep him from trampling the handsome cowboy.

"Get back!" Royce called.

She slapped Sonora's rear flank, and the horse sprinted away.

Then she heard it.

A menacing rattle.

Chapter 4

Royce lay on the ground, helpless, still clinging to the saddle. Well, he'd prayed for the Lord to keep him in it.

Zadie raised her hands. "Don't move."

Why was Zadie still there? She should have run far away with the horse.

The rattler sounded only inches behind him. He froze.

Beyond Zadie, Holden and Theresa ran toward them.

Theresa bore down with intent in her eyes and a six-gun in her grip. When she neared, she lifted her arm and aimed just above Royce's hip.

At the single *bang*, he instinctively curled, hoping her shot rang true.

Theresa lowered her gun, a triumphant gleam in her eyes.

Blessed silence. No sinister rattle.

A peep over his shoulder assured him the snake no longer posed a threat. Not only dead, but no longer had a head.

He relaxed, only to have his relief cut short by a severe stabbing pain radiating from his left shoulder. Embarrassed, he realized he hadn't finished cinching the saddle that morning when Holden interrupted him.

The two women surrounded him, clucking like mother hens. Soon a strong arm gripped his right hand and hauled him to his feet.

"Mighty lucky there, son." Holden's pale face spoke of the seriousness of the situation. "You okay?"

"I did something to my shoulder, but considering the alternative. . ." He let the thought trail away, not wanting to consider what could have happened. One of the scenarios being Zadie trampled under a frightened horse.

"We need to be mindful of nature. Everything here has either thorns or fangs." Holden's sage advice came too late, but Royce chuckled at the irony.

Zadie had slipped under his good arm. "I'm so sorry. I should have seen it there."

He looked down, her face so close she surprised him. Emerald-green eyes shimmered with tears. He wanted to say, *Don't worry your pretty head, little lady*, but cowboy speak seemed inappropriate at the moment.

"Not your fault." He tried to assure her. "That thing blended in remarkably well with its environment."

After retrieving Zadie's sketchbook and supplies, Theresa stuffed them into the satchel. Royce inclined his head toward her. "Nice aim."

Theresa grinned. "We're both packin'. We may not have outlaws in our stretch of the desert, but other dangers lurk. That's just one of them." She thumbed behind her toward the dead snake.

"Glad it wasn't my head that got blown off."

Holden chuckled, pride lighting his eyes. "Naw, my Theresa's the best there is. She teaches sharpshooting at the ranch."

"Well, I'm grateful." Wait a minute. He'd had a ride. "Where is my horse?"

Holden placed his hand up to shade his eyes. "Probably halfway to the ranch."

"I'm so sorry. I hope he'll be all right."

"Not to worry. Most all the horses know the way home."

Holden slung the saddle into the wagon, then boosted Royce next to it where he used it as a pillow and a buffer against the rocks.

Before leaving, Theresa checked Royce's arm. "I don't think it's broken."

"Me neither. I've had a broken arm before. I'll probably be sore for a while though. Hopefully this won't affect my train—er, work much."

He'd almost said training. How far would this set him back?

As they neared the ranch, Royce heard Dirk's voice. "Woo-ee! We're starting our tour with a good one, folks."

Royce tried to blend in with the rocks, but to no avail.

Dirk and his horse came into view, and he trotted past, going the opposite direction. A group of guests followed for a tour of the desert. Dirk leered at Royce. "I thought that was your horse I saw making a beeline for the barn—without a saddle. How'd you lose him? Get tired of riding? Need a little nap?" He cackled. "Or maybe the time ran out on your merry-go-round?" He gave an exaggerated wink.

He pointed to the saddle in the buckboard and roared with laughter.

Royce felt heat rise up his collar and flame at his ears.

Dirk settled down to an annoying chortle and tipped his hat at Zadie as they passed each other. "Hey, Miss Fitzgerald. I told you I'd be the better choice."

Royce groaned. He wouldn't live this down anytime soon.

Zadie tugged the reins to turn around and block Dirk's horse. "I'll have you know that this man was quite brave facing down a rattler that wasn't more than a foot from him. Didn't even flinch. Which is more than I can say for his horse."

He remembered it differently. He didn't face it because he couldn't bear to look at it. Had he known how close the snake had been, he'd not only have flinched but would've beaten Sonora back to the ranch.

But he loved Zadie's spitfire spirit in facing down another snake. One who smirked while sidestepping Royce's defender. One whose haughty behavior had to have broken some kind of cowboy code. One who began whistling a tune.

A familiar tune, but in Royce's state of mind, he couldn't find it in his memory.

Flapjack rode behind the tour group. "Sorry, buddy. Dirk is out of line."

"I can handle him."

A few minutes later, Holden hauled back on the reins in front of the main house. "Come on in. I'll track down the camp doctor."

Royce refused help and scrambled out on his own. His tender shoulder already felt better. Hopefully he just got a good jar from his fall.

"I'll set up pillows on the couch and put together an ice bag." Theresa bustled into the house.

"I can walk to the bunkhouse. No need to fuss over—" Royce couldn't even get the whole sentence out before Theresa disappeared.

Holden chuckled. "Enjoy the attention, son. You can't buck a woman with a cause."

Zadie held Royce's arm up at the elbow as he took each porch step gingerly. He could feel her nearness, and while he didn't need two females fussing over him, he didn't mind this one. She placed her hand on his back, and the comforting warmth felt better than anything the doctor could give him.

True to her word, Theresa led him to the cowhide sofa and padded it with pillows to rest his arm on.

"Would you like anything?" Zadie hovered near. "Lemonade? Maybe some leftovers from the lunch served while we were gone?"

Theresa walked toward the kitchen. "Come with me, Zadie. We'll find something for him. I also want to get an ice pack on the shoulder, pronto."

The two women left, and Royce drew in a deep breath. As he contemplated hollering that he was fine and leaving, the house manager, Constanza Vega, entered the room.

"Meester Rutger? Phone call for you. Follow, please."

He rose gingerly and trailed the colorful skirts toward the rear of the house.

She stopped and indicated for him to enter Holden's office. The receiver lay on the desk. With a polite grin, she shut the door.

"Hello?"

"Royce, this is Ernie." E. B. Merrill, studio executive and holder of Royce's career. Some days he was Ernie, others Ernest Bernard. On serious days, he was Mr. Merrill. He must be in a good mood today. "How are you doing way out west?"

Royce chuckled. "Los Angeles is farther west than Arizona."

"Semantics, my boy. We have civilization, and you have cows."

"I'm learning a lot." Like following through when saddling one's mount.

"Glad to hear it. Wanted to give you a heads-up. We're in talks to make Holden Chase's book into a screenplay. Masters wants to do it, but we're at a stalemate. If things go south, will you be ready to step up to the part?"

The chance Royce had been training for. He rubbed his sore shoulder. "Uh. . .sure. I'll be ready."

"Glad to hear it. I'll be in touch."

Royce set the handset on the base and blew out a breath. First he's asked to model, then he hurts his shoulder. When would he find time to continue training? Had he already learned enough? Probably not.

That night Royce's dream returned him to the desert where teddy bears whizzed past him on arrow shafts. Some stuck, and brushing them off proved difficult. More attached themselves to the point of near suffocation. He fell to the ground where a rattlesnake met him face-to-face. The face on the reptile belonged to Dirk, leering and scoffing. Royce managed to scamper away sans teddy bears and tried to mount his horse. But how? This foot? That foot? Where was the horn? While puzzling over it, the snake methodically slithered closer, its tongue darting like a whip.

It coiled and struck.

Royce jerked awake. Had he screamed in his sleep? Had his bunkmates been disturbed? In the bunk on the far wall, Flapjack slept soundly with his mouth wide open, unearthly sounds coming from within. Above him, Tin Star, so named because his last name was Testar, lay quietly taking deep, even breaths. Joe and John, the twins in the bunk to his right, both slept with their backs to him. Royce pulled himself up and gingerly stepped from the bed. No one seemed disturbed. But what about Dirk?

Royce peered over the mattress of the top bunk, not wanting to come head-on with the ugly mug but, still in the haze of the nightmare, needing to see for himself that Dirk was human.

The bunk was empty.

Royce jumped back into bed, jerking his feet under the covers in case Dirk was slithering around.

Sleep eluded him, and five thirty came early. His shoulder had stiffened up overnight. The camp doctor had told him it was a strain, and if he iced it and kept to his normal duties as much as possible, it would work itself out.

Even on Sunday, basic chores needed to be done, like feeding Sonora and mucking his stall. The shoulder protested, but he got it done. He should have gone on to check the horse's hooves, but the *clang-clang* of Cookie's chow triangle sounded the call to breakfast. Royce must have taken longer than he thought. By the time he cleaned up and made it to the meal pavilion, most of the bacon and potatoes were gone. Tin Star and the twins sat at one end of the long table chatting and drinking coffee. Flapjack entertained Zadie at the other end while shoving pancakes into his mouth. She laughed at something he said, a refreshing sound, like water bubbling over rocks in a stream. Neither noticed Royce as he scraped the last of the gravy from the pan and poured it over his biscuits. He savored the sight of her a moment longer before making his presence known.

Dirk appeared from around the corner. Royce's nightmare in the flesh. All he needed was a rattle trailing behind him.

Zadie spoke to him in cordial tones, but her spine had stiffened, as if she remained on alert. Oh how he hoped she would tear into him again. Royce had found that quite enjoyable despite the pain and embarrassment.

He joined the group, and Zadie's genuine smile rewarded him, but before he could savor it, Dirk opened his big mouth.

"How's it goin', Buck?"

Royce glanced behind him but didn't see anyone else Dirk could be talking to. "Excuse me?"

"That's your new nickname." Dirk swung one leg over the bench and plopped himself down next to Zadie. "You got bucked off your horse, and you came home in the buckboard. Yep. Buck it is."

Royce wanted to nickname him Snake-in-the-Grass.

Zadie tapped her fork on the table, and her flushed cheeks reminded him of a volcano about ready to blow.

But Flapjack came to his rescue this time. "Now, Dirk. You know any one of us could have been in that position."

"Which one? The *prone* position?" Dirk cackled. Had he inched closer to Zadie?

"You weren't there. It was awful." Zadie folded her hands on the table and squeezed them until the knuckles turned white, and then she slid to the other end of the bench. Why was she working so hard not to explode? Maybe trying to remain ladylike?

"I'm sure it was for a little city gal like you, but us *real* cowboys should know how to handle ourselves." Dirk started to scoot near her, but Royce placed his booted foot on the bench between them.

A growl formed in Royce's throat. "Back away."

Dirk hopped up and stood nose to nose with Royce but took a step back when Theresa approached from the main house. "I need some volunteers if you're not doing anything else later this afternoon. Maybe two men to unload the rocks and place them in my garden?"

The twins volunteered. Tin Star swigged the rest of his coffee. "I'll come help. My daddy was a landscaper. Maybe I can give a few tips."

"Wonderful!" Theresa clapped her hands.

"What would you like me to do?" Royce had to finish his chores, but he could get to those later if Theresa needed him for something.

"I want you to rest that shoulder. There's an ice pack ready for you in the camp icebox."

Dirk snickered. "Yeah, take care of yourself. . .Buck."

He turned his attention to Zadie again, but she stood and reached for her wide-brimmed hat with a blue scarf tied around the outside. It blew in the slight breeze, and Royce envisioned her as an angel.

"Royce, since you can't work on the rock garden, I'd love to explore the town. Would you like to accompany me and perhaps take in a matinee this afternoon?"

Dirk's demeanor wilted. Zadie had never been more attractive.

"It'd be my honor to escort you to the cinema."

As long as it wasn't showing a Western.

Chapter 5

Zadie climbed into the long wagon provided by the ranch, excited to further her Western experience by worshipping in a historic mission chapel. She sat on one of two long benches that ran the length of the bed. Where was Royce? Would he join them? She was sure he said he'd be there after completing his chores.

Theresa climbed into the front and pivoted to address the passengers. "The chapel we're going to was a mission outpost up until the early nineteenth century. It was established by a Franciscan order primarily to bring the Gospel to the Apache tribes. When we bought this land, we were thrilled to see most of it still standing, although the courtyard walls and some outbuildings had succumbed to the weather. Holden and I restored the chapel and have been holding Sunday services there ever since we started the Novel T Ranch. Our motto is, 'We provide an authentic Western experience,' and what's more Western than worshipping in a real mission?"

Zadie tingled with anticipation. How many movies had she seen where a mission was part of the setting?

Holden hopped into the driver's seat and called over his shoulder. "Everybody ready?"

"Ready!" Zadie joined in the unanimous response.

"Hold on!" He whipped the reins, and the four-horse team lurched forward.

Zadie rolled to one side into a pleasant woman she had met the day before. Lena and her husband, Alf, had decided on a second honeymoon and thought the dude ranch sounded romantic. "We love the Old West," she had said, enthusiasm oozing from her words. "We've been married for twenty-five years and have talked of nothing but this type of vacation."

She and Zadie giggled as they rocked to the rhythm of the road and shared shoulder space.

"How 'bout a rousing hymn?" Holden called out. "Any suggestions?"

" 'Bringing in the Sheaves.' "

" 'When the Roll Is Called Up Yonder.' "

" 'Victory in Jesus.' "

"Great songs. Let's sing 'em all." Holden led the songs with a boisterous, off-key voice. By the time the last strains were sung and everyone was "plunged to victory beneath the cleansing flood," they pulled in front of a small adobe chapel. Trees sheltered the oasis, and Zadie could imagine children playing under their limbs.

Zadie and the others headed inside. She filed in to find a spot on one of ten wooden pews. Five down each side with an aisle in the middle.

Outside the heavy wooden door, the sound of approaching horses drifted in. She had seen a hitching post outside near a well and assumed that's where they'd tie the horses. The well even had a bucket on a rope.

Royce, Flapjack, Tin Star, and the twins, John and Joe, entered, removing their hats. With the sunshine behind them, dust glittered gold as it billowed from their clothes. Four of the cowboys slipped into a back pew, but Royce sought her out. He held the neck of a guitar and leaned it against the outside of the pew. She slid over to accommodate him, and he lowered himself next to her. Even though she had cooled off from being outside, a flush of warmth radiated from her rapidly beating heart.

When everyone was seated, Holden stood up front. "We had a good hymn sing on the way here. You all can join my choir anytime."

Everyone laughed.

"Now, to start our little service, I'd like to ask Royce Rutger to come forward and lead us in 'Amazing Grace.' "

Royce whispered, "I'll be right back." He stood and grabbed the neck of the guitar, then made his way to the front.

Thankfully, Zadie had remembered her sketchbook. She slipped it from her bag, hoping she could be discreet since she was in the house of the Lord. Royce pulled the guitar strap over his shoulder, wincing from his injury, and positioned the instrument in front of him. From the first strum to the last, Zadie sat captivated. Royce's rich baritone filled the small space and rolled off the walls. Some in the congregation had started to sing along, but their voices trailed away as they must have decided to listen.

The message of the beautiful old hymn spoke to Zadie as if for the first time. She had heard it on many occasions in her own church, played from a powerful organ and led by a large choir in robes with gilded yokes. But the simplicity of the message, grace, had never come through before now.

Royce ended the hymn and returned to his seat, once again leaning the guitar against the pew. He raised an eyebrow at the blank paper in Zadie's sketchbook. She closed it and replaced it in her bag.

"I was mesmerized." She whispered her excuse.

"As am I when I watch you sketch."

Oh, he says all the right things. Nothing phony about him. And Lord, he's a real cowboy!

Royce joined Zadie in the pew. Her hands shook as she put away her materials, and her cheeks had blossomed to that pleasant pink.

Holden once again stood, this time with an open Bible cradled in his palm. "I'm not a preacher, never been ordained, so today the Lord is in charge. I'm just going to flap my gums until He tells me to quit." Among a smattering of chuckles, he lifted the worn, black leather Bible to a readable height. " 'And be ye kind one to another, tenderhearted, forgiving one another, even as God for Christ's sake hath forgiven you.' This comes from Ephesians 4:32. Royce sang about amazing grace, the grace our Father extends to us. He also expects us to extend grace to each other. Whatever He has done for us, He wants us to emulate here on earth. Do you feel anyone has wronged you? Forgive. It's not worth holding a grudge."

Forgive?

Who?

Bret Masters who treated him like dirt because he was an extra at the movie studio?

Dirk who had slithered into his life to make him miserable?

His father who had left his mother to care for an infant?

He'd have to pray long and hard about all of those.

When the service ended, he led one last hymn, then helped everyone into the wagon, lingering in assisting Zadie. He liked the feel of her slender hand in his and the warmth of her back as he steadied her.

On the return to the ranch, he rode alongside the wagon. He'd have liked an intimate conversation with Zadie, but others wanted to talk to him.

"Where did you learn to play like that?" This came from a woman sitting next to Zadie.

"At church as a kid. A pastor played the guitar, and I asked if I could strum it. That led to lessons. He taught me hymns but also popular music."

"Oh Royce," Theresa called from her seat next to Holden. "Would you be kind enough to play for our next barbecue?"

"My pleasure." Playing the guitar and singing had been an escape growing up in New Jersey. With no father and a mother who worked two jobs, he found music was a lifeline. The other boys enticed him with stickball, and he'd play, but nothing made him happier than being behind his guitar.

Music had helped him pave the way to Hollywood. He earned money singing in dance halls, but Mom always had him in church the next Sunday to help erase whatever he had seen. Movies helped fill the time too, and he worked in a theater during the summer. That's where he got the idea to move to Hollywood. He'd hoped his talents would be beneficial there, but he'd been stuck as an extra for Western Empire Films under contract for two years. Meanwhile, he saved money for the day he could buy a house and bring his mother to California. He wanted to put her in a mansion and assure her she'd never have to work another day. That dream had seemed far off until this latest offer. All he had to do was learn about being a cowboy, and he could potentially be the next big Western star.

The ranch rose from the desert as he neared. His musings had made him lag behind. The other ranch hands rode far ahead, no doubt ready to take advantage of their day off.

With a nudge to Sonora, he caught up to the wagon and dismounted as they pulled up to the house. Again he helped people out. Zadie lingered nearby until the last passenger had touched ground.

"So, how about that movie?" She stood near the porch with her hands behind her back and swaying her shoulders.

He tipped his hat. "Yes, ma'am. I'll bring my car around."

"You have a car?"

"We all have our own transportation. Do you think we ride horses to town?"

She giggled and pressed her hand to her cheek. "I guess I never thought about it."

Soon he had the pretty Zadie Fitzgerald in his 1928 Chevrolet Landau Coupe, heading for lunch and then the two o'clock matinee.

At the café, they were discussing which movie to see when Dirk slithered in, followed by Flapjack.

The Snake-in-the-Grass smirked and approached their table. "Fancy seeing you two here."

Flapjack shrugged an apology. "We saw your car out front."

Royce's nemesis swung his hips into the red vinyl booth, next to Zadie, making her slide to the left. Royce reluctantly indicated for Flapjack to take a seat.

"Relax." Dirk waved his hand. "We're not staying. If you haven't decided on a movie, I thought I'd suggest the Liberty Theater. It's just around the corner. Some of the boys and I went there last week."

"That's nice of you, Dirk." Zadie spoke as if she meant it, but Royce interpreted the glint in her eye as, *What are you up to?* "What's playing?"

Even though Zadie had asked the question, Dirk pointed his answer toward Royce. "The new Bret Masters movie, *Long Arm of the Law*." There was no mistaking the challenge in his voice. Dirk knew Royce's secret. He had to.

"He's my favorite." Zadie changed from suspicious of Dirk's motives to a bouncy admirer. "Yes, let's see that one, please."

Royce couldn't disappoint her. But how could he keep her from recognizing him on screen?

Dirk relaxed against the booth and swung his arm behind Zadie's shoulders. "I like Bret Masters too. You could say I *relate* to him." He cackled at his own private joke.

Despite Royce's misgivings, he could never allow Dirk to sense fear.

Royce spoke directly to the snake. "The singing cowboy it is."

Challenge accepted.

Dirk grabbed a toothpick from the small glass bottle on the table and flicked it in and out of his mouth. With a toothy grin, he rose. "Excellent! My good deed is done. Come, Flapjack, my man. We have other roads to explore."

Flapjack had been swiveling his head between his two buddies, slack-jawed, as if he were puzzled about what had just happened.

Royce had his suspicions. Dirk was toying with him. But why?

After lunch Royce offered his arm on their way to the theater, torn between enjoying Zadie's presence and wanting to run screaming the opposite direction from the theater. Would she recognize him on the screen? His role in *Long Arm of the Law* was the usual. As one of ten bad men who rode with the villain robbing banks, he was usually in a cloud of dust. Except for that one scene where Deadeye Pete shot at his feet to make him dance. Would that blasted beard be enough to keep her from recognizing him?

He thought of confessing right there on the sidewalk but remembered the studio's threat. No one must know he was being groomed to take over for Bret. If it got out, he could lose it all. Then he could never send for his mother, and she would never see her son on the silver screen like he'd promised. She didn't care about such things, but he had bragged about it and felt the need to prove himself.

The two quarters weighted his hand like lead as he handed them to the ticket girl. His feet dragged at every step. His stomach turned at each pop of popcorn. He wanted to punch every seat in the theater. Unaware of his dread, Zadie bounced and twirled in her excitement. He pretended that his presence— not Bret Masters—had created such a lovely sight.

The movie rolled, and he found himself enjoying it despite his nerves.

Zadie made that possible. She whistled with two fingers in the exciting parts and booed the bad guys. Royce loved her excitement but tensed whenever he was on screen. As the scene neared where Deadeye Pete made him dance, his mind whirred.

Think, man!

Just before the confrontation, Royce leaned over to whisper. "May I have some popcorn?"

She passed him the bag but he *accidentally* knocked it from her hand.

"I'm so sorry."

"Shhh." Oh great, now he was disturbing the rest of the audience.

They both went for the bag. Just as her fingers neared it, he pushed it farther away. "Almost got it." He strained to reach it.

He heard the gunshots on screen and knew his part was almost over.

"Um, Royce?"

"Yes?"

They were still bent over. She had the bag, but at some point he had placed his hand between her shoulder blades and was holding her down. "Oh. Sorry."

"Shhh." From behind him again.

They sat up, and he raised his hand to apologize again but thought better of it. "I'll get you more popcorn."

When the movie was over, Royce apologized once more.

"That's okay," she said as she stood and kicked popcorn away from her feet. "I've seen it before."

Dread hit his gut. She'd already seen the part he'd tried to cover.

She didn't seem to make the connection however. Relieved, he followed Zadie from the theater and into the lobby. She paused to gaze at the movie poster. And at Bret Masters. "What a great cowboy."

"He probably isn't as heroic in person." No probably about it. Royce had personally seen how he treated people on set.

"Oh, don't spoil my image of him. He's one of the reasons I took this assignment with Holden Chase."

"Then I'll have to thank him."

She blushed. "It's because of him that I wanted to meet a real cowboy." She peeked up at him from under her hat. "And here you are."

Guilt smacked him in the gut. To recover, he changed the subject. "How about a piece of pie and cup of coffee before going back to the ranch?"

"That would be lovely. Thank you."

Across the street, Dirk leaned against his battered pickup truck, his arms coiled across his chest. Zadie didn't see him, but Royce glared over his shoulder as he steered her away. Dirk offered a sloppy salute and a sneer. Then he began to whistle as he had in the desert. Royce couldn't recall the song then, but he'd just heard it in the movie they'd seen.

He knows, but why would he care?

Royce resolved to confront the snake sometime when Zadie wasn't around.

Chapter 6

Zadie glanced out the window of Holden's office while talking on the phone to Annie. "And he's a real cowboy."

"No fooling? Just what you wanted."

A dream come true. Her cowboy stood in the corral with Flapjack and their horses. "We went to a Western movie yesterday. Talk about a surreal moment."

"The best of both worlds, eh?"

Flapjack ran up to the rear of his horse, acted like he was going to jump on, but bounced off the hindquarters. *Curious*. Royce laughed as he helped Flapjack from the ground. The two men seemed to discuss what had just happened. Flapjack made a running motion with two of his fingers and "leaped" with his hand to the saddle of the horse. Then they both stood there rubbing their necks.

"Which movie did you see?"

"*Long Arm of the Law*. The one we saw the night you clued me in on this assignment."

Now Joe, one of the twins, led his horse into the corral. The three of them talked, with Flapjack scissoring his fingers again in a running motion. Joe nodded, then walked away from his horse. A second later, Joe ran up to his horse and leaped over the rear and into the saddle.

Oh, that's what they were doing. Royce was probably trying to teach Flapjack how to do it, but his arm was still tender. So Joe had to show him.

She turned from the window and sat in the desk chair. "The movie was really good, but I'm finding that with Royce by my side, Bret Masters is fading."

"You've gotten what you wanted. No need for fantasies now."

"I don't have him yet, but I'm hoping. We'll have to do another modeling session so I can finish Holden's cover. The first one was cut short due to a snake." She told the story.

"Be careful out there in the Wild West, Zadie. I want my maid of honor alive. And then if a certain cowboy steps up, I may be in *your* wedding in Arizona."

First thing she needed to know though, was something important to her.

He knew the words to those hymns they'd sung yesterday, but did he know the Lord?

Zadie finished the call and returned to the window. Now all of the cowboys were in the corral except Dirk. All were running at their horses' behinds and jumping into the saddles, all but Royce. He must be a pretty good teacher.

Later that evening, after Zadie had worked on smaller drawings for the inside pages of Holden's book, she sought out Royce with her sketchbook in hand. She found him at the stable about to ride into the desert on a sunset tour with Flapjack and six guests.

"May I join you?" she called to Royce, who glanced up from cinching a stirrup to accommodate a child. He gifted her with a smile. A sudden burst of sunshine warmed her within, and much to her embarrassment, without. Her cheeks must have been the color of Flapjack's red-checkered shirt.

"Absolutely. I'll saddle your horse."

Soon Sierra and Sonora ambled along side by side, following the others on horseback. Flapjack led the family of four and a middle-aged couple.

"I'm happy you joined us." Royce seemed less tense than he was last week on the first modeling excursion.

The guitar slung over his back swept Zadie into her own personal singing-cowboy movie. "I'm glad I caught you," she said. "I've been so engrossed in my work, I forgot I was on a dude ranch where fun is right outside my door. How's the arm?"

He rubbed his shoulder. "A little stiff but much better. I'll be a hundred percent by the end of the week."

"I'll bet it's hard to do your work while laid up like that."

His laugh was gentle. "Yep."

"Royce, I started to ask a question our first time out, but we were rudely interrupted."

He shuddered. "Don't remind me. I've sworn off reptiles forever."

"I was wondering where you stand with God."

He jerked his head toward her and quirked an eyebrow.

"If you don't want to answer, that's okay. I've probably overstepped my bounds. I just thought I'd try again since you seemed so comfortable in church."

His gaze drifted forward. "My mother made sure I went to church clear up until I was an adult. It made her happy, so how could I refuse?"

"But you wanted to refuse."

He shook his head. "I didn't mean that." He sighed, and his shoulders drooped. "She raised me alone. I barely knew my dad."

"Oh Royce, you don't have to—"

"No, that's all right. I don't mind talking about it. He left. She did the best she could but knew the only way I'd grow up okay is if I could have the positive influence of the church. I accepted Christ as my Savior when I was a kid." He side-eyed her. "Was that what you wanted to hear?"

"Well, yes, but. . .how are you now? I mean. . .well. . ."

"Are God and I still talking?"

His smile let her know he was fine with the conversation, so she pressed on. "Yes, I guess that's what I'm wondering."

What words was he forming in his head to create such a long pause? Finally, he spoke. "I changed my address, but I'm not sure He followed me."

Ah. A prodigal. She could work with that.

"How about you?"

"Also raised in the church. Mother headed the women's auxiliary, and Father always prayed before meals. I don't remember a conscious decision to follow the Lord, but I've never felt far from Him."

After riding in silence for a moment, he finally spoke. "I guess when things are going well, I know He's there. But a lot has happened in my life, and I've questioned His part in it. It felt as if He abandoned me, like my dad."

"I'm so sorry." Zadie considered her next words carefully. "My life has always been relatively stress free. Father had a career that kept me comfortable, art always came easy to me and paid well enough for me to have my independence. And of course, that led to this." She swept her hand to include their desert ride. "I hope if faced with something hard, I'd know He had my best interest at heart and was working to alleviate the pain."

"Well, to tell the truth, I suppose in those kinds of moments, I was probably the one to turn away from Him. I never really expected Him to fix my problems."

"Maybe if there is another challenge, for either of us, we'll take it to Him and see where it goes."

His shoulders lifted as if he had received new hope. "Maybe. I guess it comes down to where we want to focus our attention. On the test or on the One with the answers."

"Well said. I'll remember that."

Flapjack had been showcasing the flora occasionally as Theresa had done. They followed a worn trail through tall saguaro, ocotillo, and mesquite trees. Birds of various colors landed on cactus needles, and a bobcat caused some excitement when the group disturbed his search for dinner. The trail circled, so the riders saw new terrain during the entire trip.

About halfway, Flapjack hollered over his shoulder. "Sun's settin' low, folks. Looks like we'll have a beautiful evening to enjoy a spectacular show."

"Hey Flapjack." Zadie caught his attention. "We've seen colorful sunsets at the ranch. I'm enjoying the ride, but why come all the way out here?"

He offered a knowing grin. "You'll see."

True enough, the heavens took on a lavender hue that burst into vibrant magenta and golden yellow. It covered the entire sky, a sight to behold without any buildings, or even the natural adobe structures on the ranch, to get in the way. Zadie imagined herself inside an impressionist painting, the artist God Himself. She imagined Him painting His sky with the diffusion method, blending colors right on the canvas, leaving no clear lines. Only vivacious shades straight from heaven.

"I want to paint this, but I don't think I could do it justice."

"Sometimes it's better to be a spectator." Royce lifted his head with the others, pure joy radiating from his face.

After enjoying the sky a moment longer, Zadie pointed to the guitar. "You going to play that thing, or is it some sort of fancy necktie?"

Royce smiled, swung the guitar around, and serenaded the desert—and dare Zadie think—her.

By the time they reached the ranch after their ninety minute ride, the sky had taken on a cerulean blue, deepening to indigo until nighttime officially swallowed the evening.

The group stabled their horses, and Royce instructed the group on how to give them a quick rubdown. Afterward, despite the full moon, Royce found a lantern and offered to walk Zadie to the house.

They reached the porch and climbed the steps. Zadie did not want this day to end. Instead of heading inside, she led Royce to the railing of the wraparound porch, toward the corner, and gazed into the growing darkness beyond the ranch. Where a short while ago the world had seemed caught up in a glorious ball of fire, now in the moonlight, the desert took on velvet shades of gray.

She gazed up at him. "Thank you for the beautiful evening."

"Thank you for making it more beautiful."

A gasp floated in her throat as he faced her and placed his left hand on the small of her back. He drew her near and traced her jawline with his fingers. Surprisingly smooth, callous-free fingers. With a slight hesitation as he searched her eyes, silently asking permission, he dipped his head and covered her lips with his own.

Sweet, delicious, and all too short.

He pulled away, but where she expected to see joy on his face, she saw something else. Something darker. A struggle perhaps.

"Zadie Fitzpatrick, you've reached into my soul."

Then he turned and stomped off the porch, leaving a vacancy she knew no other man could fill.

＊·———·＊

What had he been thinking?

Royce berated himself all the way to the bunkhouse. He wasn't the man she thought he was. He'd lied to her. Even if it were possible, how could he tell her the truth without destroying her perception of him?

He kicked at a small grass clod, creating a cloud of dust. All for a stupid movie career. Why did he want to be a part of it? Fake sets, fake stories, fake people. Zadie was real, and at the moment, her world beckoned him with far more appeal than the one for which he'd worked so hard.

He wished he had told her the truth in the beginning. She'd have kept his secret. Even so, once all was revealed and she knew the truth, what would her reaction be? She'd already confided her desires. She thought he was a real cowboy. He'd watched how she reacted around a phony. Dirk. She could see right through him.

And what about fellows from New Jersey? That first day Royce modeled, she'd alluded to a bad experience with one. Royce was two for two. Not a cowboy. And from New Jersey.

No. He'd blown it. He'd painted himself into a corner where not even the pretty artist would want to tread. Best to keep her at bay, no more sunset rides, no more movie dates, no more gazing into her green eyes. He'd model if she needed, but definitely no more intimacy.

But after that kiss, how could he stay away?

A groan tore through his throat.

He needed to punch something.

Where was Dirk?

Chapter 7

Royce awoke the next morning, his shoulder feeling much better, and ready to resume his training. He hadn't found Dirk the night before. Probably a good thing. He couldn't become the next big Western star if he was in jail for assault.

With new resolve to finish this chapter of his life, he completed his morning chores, then looked for Tin Star, who was slated to teach him some roping.

The day before, he'd hoped Flapjack could help him with something he'd seen the stunt men do on set. Mount his horse from a run and jump over the hindquarters. Bret Masters could do it with ease. If Royce were to replace him, he needed to be as good or better. Flapjack, however, proved to be useless, if not entertaining. He kept bouncing off his horse and sliding to the ground. Good thing Biscuit was a docile animal, or Flapjack might have been the next one to see the camp doctor. When the other cowboys had shown up, they all enjoyed mounting their horses like stunt men, and he received some good tips. When his arm healed a hundred percent, he'd test what he'd learned.

He found Tin Star behind the barn, already corralling a sawhorse. A head had been fashioned from a plank of wood and nailed to the end. Two steel pipes had been affixed for the horns. "Whoa there, cowboy," he called to Tin Star. "Best watch that steer. He seems mighty frisky."

There were, in fact, a herd of imitation calves. Five of them, scattered around the yard.

Tin Star held a coiled rope and threw a perfect circle over the horns, whipped his arm back, and tightened the line. "Nah, just needs broke, that's all." He retrieved the lasso from the docile sawhorse. "Your turn."

"What? So soon? Show me what you did."

The lanky cowboy, not much older than Royce but with a whole lot of living in his leathery face, handed the rope over. "It ain't that hard."

Royce took the stiff lariat and attempted to make it into a circle in the air. The center closed and acted like a girl's jump rope. Still, he thrust it at the "horns," and it landed a foot from the target.

"That was pitiful."

"How was *your* first try?"

"Cain't remember. I was four." Tin Star cracked a grin, revealing his impish side. He gave Royce a quick lesson, and he tried it again. But the rope flew past the rigid livestock.

"You really are a greenhorn, aren't you?"

"Not dark green. I know some things."

"Uh-huh. I seen you on a horse."

Before Royce could defend himself, Flapjack showed up with a handful of children. "This here's where y'all are gonna learn ropin'."

Royce pulled Tin Star aside. "You didn't tell me this was a class. A *kids'* class."

"Don't you check the schedule on the blackboard every morning?"

"No. It's my day off."

To rub salt in his wound, Zadie appeared around the corner with her sketchbook.

Royce wanted to head her off, but she was too quick and entered the corral. He pulled her away from the group.

Meanwhile, the class started. "Gather 'round, buckaroos." Flapjack pointed to his chest. "You know me. This here's Tin Star, and that feller over there sweet-talkin' the artist lady is Royce."

Royce didn't feel like sweet-talking. He wanted to get rid of her but made the mistake of looking into her eyes.

Eyes the color of spring grass.

Zadie broke the awkward silence. "Flapjack told me you were over here. I'd like to sketch you roping. It would go well with one of the chapters."

Royce scratched his neck. "Okay. But just to warn you, I'm better at roping real steers and not these scrawny things."

Lies. All lies.

"Really? Well, I'm sure you're an expert at other things."

He chuckled. "Well, I can play the guitar while riding a horse."

"I sketched that too, even though there are no singing cowboys in Holden's story."

There would be when they made the movie, and Royce hoped he'd be the one doing the strumming.

He turned his attention to Tin Star, realizing he should be learning along with the kids.

Tin Star proceeded to demonstrate the parts of the lariat. The knot being the holt, the short part of the rope the shank, and the bottom of the large loop the tip. He taught them how to coil and how to layer the rope in their hand so they wouldn't capture themselves while twirling the loop over their heads. Lastly, he showed them how to snap their wrists while twirling overhead, just before letting go.

The children took turns, none making it on the first try, but some eventually getting the hang of it.

While they were engrossed, Royce coiled his rope, hoping he'd paid enough attention. He didn't make it the first time, and shrugged in Zadie's direction. She smiled her encouragement but continued to sketch.

He made the second one and yelled, "Yes!" Everyone turned his direction. "Uh, yes. Everyone is doing great."

Flapjack approached Zadie. "You wanna try?"

"Sure. It looks fun."

"Fun?" Royce hitched his pants and wished he knew how to spit tobacco for effect. "When you're out on the range and it's time to brand that big boy"—he pointed to the wooden bovine—"and it's just you and your horse, one wrong move and you could be smiling up from a daisy-covered mound, telling your loved ones goodbye."

Zadie pulled her mouth to one side and narrowed her eyes, as if she were trying to figure out where that came from.

He was too, frankly. Here he'd been berating himself for lying to her, and he spouts a line from his first movie. Great. Just great.

Flapjack also scrutinized him, then handed the rope to Zadie. "Want me to show you how?"

"No, I was listening." She asked Royce to hold her sketchbook and pencil.

She made her coils, pulled the shank, found the tip, twirled the loop, snapped her wrist, and let go. The rope landed perfectly, and she jerked the line to tighten the holt.

All three men dropped their jaws to the dusty ground.

"You don't watch every Bret Masters movie ever made without learning a thing or two." She handed the rope back to Flapjack and retrieved her materials.

Royce had never been more attracted to her.

Roping lessons lasted another half hour. During lunch, Royce asked the other cowboys about Dirk.

"Don't know." Joe scratched his head. "I haven't seen him either."

Flapjack arrived at the table with a mound of fried chicken and baked beans. "You talkin' about Dirk?"

Royce nodded. "Do you know where he's gotten off to?"

"Yeah. Ran an errand to California for the boss man. Was supposed to return today, but he called this morning, asking if he could stay until the end of the week."

"California? Something to do with Holden's book being made into a movie?"

"I think Holden needed to sign something or other and get it to the studio quickly. No time to rely on the mail. Dirk is from Los Angeles, so Holden asked him since he's familiar with everything there."

Dirk was from Los Angeles? Royce assumed his home was in Arizona like the others.

"Isn't Dirk a regular on staff here?"

"No," John answered after ripping into a drumstick. "He showed up about a week before you did. Good thing he knew his way around a ranch, or we'd have two greenhorns to contend with." He nudged his brother, and they guffawed in harmony.

Royce didn't find that funny. "Any of you know where Dirk might go in the middle of the night? I've noticed his bed empty several times."

Standing with his plate in hand, Tin Star placed his boot on the picnic bench and leaned in. "I hear tell he's got a lady back home. One day I overheard Holden call him in on the carpet for using the office phone and racking up long-distance charges. Maybe he sneaks into the big house and talks to her after midnight."

Royce's brain whirred. Dirk and he were both from Los Angeles. Dirk knew his way around. . .where? The city, or the movie studio? Could that be the clue to why Dirk held such animosity toward him?

Chapter 8

As much as Zadie studied Royce's face, for business and for pleasure, the sketch of him she would later add to the canvas still didn't seem right. In the picture his back was to her, but the left side of his face could be seen as he gazed off into the distance—presumably to watch for the mesa marauder.

She tried not to interfere with Royce's work, although she wasn't quite sure what he did. The other cowboys not only ran the ranch but gave desert tours and held classes on everything from cattle cutting, where they taught students on horseback how to choose a bovine for branding, to hatchet throwing—a skill she wasn't convinced was useful on a ranch. But Royce always seemed to be the extra hand, sometimes getting involved but other times acting like one of the guests.

Zadie shook off her silly musings. No doubt his arm still needed pampering.

She found him at a barrel class in the south corral. He stood outside the fence with his boot resting on the bottom rung. Inside the corral, fourteen adults and teenagers sat on horses off to the side while John, atop his horse, rode around four large barrels set apart to form a square. He went slowly, even though Zadie suspected he and the students would go faster as the day wore on. He motioned to the first rider, a young man, who copied his every move up until the third barrel, where the horse seemed to forget its right from its left. It sidestepped away from the barrel, and the man admitted defeat, reining in the horse and joining the others.

Royce's position as he observed the activity was perfect. Zadie stood behind him, to the left, and sketched the side of his face. By the time she finished his neck, collar, and cowboy hat, Tin Star and Joe flanked her, watching over her shoulder.

"What do you think?" She held the drawing at arm's length.

Joe squinted, then eyed Royce, who was still oblivious to being the object of so much attention. "I didn't think it possible, but you made him even purdier than he already is."

Tin Star elbowed him. "Yep, I agree. Maybe you should put a beard on that face to give the rest of us a chance."

They had a point. The man in the sketch was Royce times ten. Perhaps she should give the hard-edged marshal on Holden's cover a week-old beard and mustache.

While Zadie pondered, Royce appeared by her side. "What are you doing?"

She startled and nearly dropped her materials. "I didn't see you there."

"You were concentrating mighty hard." He moved to see the sketch. "I thought you'd already drawn that pose."

"I did but can't quite get the proportion correct. Would you consider a sitting where I can draw you full face again?"

"Do I have a choice?"

"Not really." She nibbled the corner of her lower lip. When his gaze drifted there, she stopped, realizing how close he'd gotten. While she was all for a quick kiss in public, his eyes deepened from ultramarine to Prussian blue, and she feared the kiss might go longer than was appropriate.

"Hey, you two." Flapjack to the rescue. "Wanna turn at the barrels?"

Zadie stepped away, widening their distance, acutely aware of the magnetic pull.

Thankfully, she had dressed for riding, in the appropriate attire after a shopping spree with Theresa. "I'm game."

Zadie preceded the two men into the corral and stopped short at the sight of her horse saddled and ready.

Flapjack toed the dirt. "I got her ready whilst you was drawin'. Thought you might like to participate since you did so well with the ropin'."

"I would. That was very thoughtful. Thank you." She pecked him on the cheek.

He pulled his hat off and, with a goofy grin, placed it over his heart.

Royce passed him while escorting Zadie to her horse. "Get ahold of yourself. Act like a cowboy."

Flapjack replaced his hat and followed. "Oh, like you do every time you're near this filly?"

Zadie stopped and quirked an eyebrow, hoping her blush didn't betray her surprise.

Flapjack stuttered an apology. "N—no disrespect, ma'am."

She smiled to assure him. "No offense taken."

The barrel exercise proved cathartic as she led Sierra through the paces. The goal was to get adept at it enough to go faster and eventually race, but she liked the easy stride. The paint circled around every barrel without any difficulty, and Zadie returned to the other riders triumphant.

When it was Royce's turn, he nudged Sonora, and the two made the first barrel just fine. By the second, there seemed to be some miscommunication. Royce reined to the right, but Sonora wanted to go left.

"Show him who's boss," Tin Star called out.

Sonora clearly thought that directive was aimed at him, and he whipped his head the opposite direction from where Royce pulled. The horse's rear flank brushed against the barrel, and he kicked it over with one thrust of his hoof.

"Don't choke up on the strap—give him his head." Joe this time.

What was Royce doing? His face strained as he concentrated, and the more Sonora demanded his own way, the more agitated Royce became. The horse finally had enough and reared, like he had in the desert with the snake.

Zadie feared Royce would roll off and hurt himself again, but he held on.

When he finally gained control, he hopped off and kicked the dirt. As he stormed away, Zadie thought she heard him mumble, "I'll never get the hang of it."

Hang of what? Wasn't he a real cowboy?

◆——————◆

Royce marched into the bunkhouse and straight to his storage trunk. He yanked out his travel bag, threw it on his bed, and started to chuck in clothes.

"Whoa there, buckaroo. Where d'ya think you're goin'?"

"Leave me alone, Flapjack."

"I know that was a rough ride, but it happens to all of us."

"Come on. You all know what you're doing, and I—" He wanted to say he was a fake. A shallow phony, wasting everyone's time, including his own.

"You what? Got yourself into a little trouble out there? You think I ain't encountered a horse with a mind of its own once in a while?"

"Okay, but did you do it in front of—?" He again cut himself off, although he knew he'd said too much.

"In front of your filly—I mean, girl?"

Royce growled and hurled a pair of socks into his bag.

"You think she cares about that? Zadie's down to earth. I don't care where she hails from—she's us. She's family." He thumped his chest.

"You don't understand." Royce sat on the bed and lowered his head into his palms. Zadie had more of the cowboy spirit than this boy from Newark playing a part.

"Listen." Flapjack leaned against the bunk bed. "We all knew when you got here you didn't know near as much as you pretended. We were only told you were a greenhorn who wanted to learn ranching from the ground up instead of as a dude on vacation. Holden made it sound like you had the basics down, and you did, but maybe you were a little over your head."

Royce wanted more than anything to confide in his friend, but the studio's threats stilled his tongue. That and knowing his mother sat alone in her tiny flat, waiting for her son to make something of himself.

"I'll work with you. You and me. One on one." Flapjack laid his hand on Royce's shoulder.

"You're busy. You all are." However, a flicker of hope rose in Royce's chest.

"I ain't too busy to help out a friend. We'll steal away whenever we can. Of course"—he scratched his nose—"that means you may not have as much time with the filly."

Royce smiled. "I've already promised I'd sit for her one more time for Holden's book cover."

"Then you best put your clothes back in that there trunk."

The thought of facing Zadie after his outburst created pangs of anxiety that made Royce's palms sweat, but he owed it to her. He found her on the patio with her easel and paints.

"Hard at work?" He'd taken off his hat and approached as if she were a delicate butterfly on a leaf.

Her smile invited him to come closer.

"This is never work." She regarded the easel. Already, saguaro cacti sprang up in the desert setting, and the mesa stood solid in the background.

"Where am I?" He pulled up a ladder-back wooden chair, flipped it around, and straddled it.

"I'll get you in there as soon as I'm satisfied with your face."

He rubbed his jaw. "Nothing I can do about that. It's the only face I have."

She giggled. "And, it's a nice face. The fault lies with me."

He thought about that a moment. She was an accomplished artist, and yet she still struggled occasionally. It was as Flapjack had said. Anyone can encounter a horse with a mind of its own. For Zadie it was the sketch. He shouldn't have been so hard on himself. He knew more than he did when he arrived.

Zadie wiped green paint from her brush with a cloth. "Are you doing anything right now?"

"Actually, before we make any plans, I want to apologize."

"For what?"

"For losing my temper back there."

She capped one of her tubes of paint and placed it in her case where other tubes were lined up. Then she drew in a breath. "The reason I'm having trouble sketching your face is because it keeps coming out too perfect."

"I don't understand. Isn't that what you want?"

"No. The marshal in Holden's book is hardened by life. He has deep emotional scars, and probably a few surface ones as well. He's a living, breathing, flawed character. And I keep drawing him as I see you."

Royce choked on the lump in his throat. "You think I'm perfect? What you saw today certainly discredits that."

"You don't understand. I'm not seeing you with my eyes or my intellect." She walked to his chair and knelt so they met eye to eye. "I'm seeing you with my heart. The Bible says, 'charity'—that is love—'beareth all things, believeth all things, hopeth all things, endureth all things.' There is nothing you can do, Royce Rutger, to shake my belief in you or change my feelings for you. I will always behold you with the love in my heart."

She leaned in and kissed him.

He'd never had anyone declare her love to him in that manner. And yes, she used that word. *Love.* He stood, pulled the chair to one side, and they wrapped their arms around each other.

He found himself praying, *Please, Lord, smooth this path we're on, and help us through the thorny brambles I've created. Amen.*

Chapter 9

Saturday came, and Zadie regarded her cover art one more time. She'd finished it a couple of days prior but chose not to tell anyone until she revealed it on Saturday during the weekly barbecue. It helped to have Royce model one more time. After his concern from the failed barrel exercise, his eyes held pain. Not that it made her happy—she never wanted to see him miserable—but it had helped her paint a flawed character and yet a hero.

She enjoyed the week with Royce. After she had kissed him, he seemed more relaxed with her, although somewhat guarded. They took a sunrise ride with a group but managed to linger behind so their conversation could be private. When everyone stopped for a break, she stole some time with him behind a tall mesquite tree and enjoyed sweet kisses. Flapjack didn't seem to mind. In fact, she caught a not-so-secretive wink aimed in Royce's direction.

Now she stood in front of her closet, trying to decide what to wear for the Saturday night barbecue. She'd attended them every weekend since she'd come, but this one was special. Royce promised to play his guitar and sing, and Zadie planned to show the book cover painting.

She donned a dress in cobalt blue with short tulip sleeves and a large bow at the neck. A jaunty cap of the same color attached to her auburn hair finished the ensemble.

The aroma of smoked brisket enticed her down the stairs, reminding her she hadn't eaten lunch, and she joined the guests gathered outside under the dining canopy.

Royce stood near the campfire conversing with a group of three women, all of whom were married. Their husbands had gravitated toward the food. The way Royce wore blue dungarees, a perfectly pressed gold chambray shirt, and blue neckerchief, one would think him a celebrity. The moment he saw her, his face lit up, and he excused himself.

"Nice dress," he said as he approached her. "Trying to give this barbecue a little class?"

"You should talk. I haven't seen this shirt before." She fingered the sleeve and lingered, hoping to brush across a muscle.

"This old thing?" He pinched the front panels.

"If I had put the marshal in this shirt, you'd have thought he was going to see his best girl instead of trying to catch the marauder." She leaned in conspiratorially. "I finished the cover. Thought I'd show it to everyone tonight."

"May I see it?"

She shook her head. "Not until the reveal."

"But I'm the model."

"No exceptions, buster." She poked her finger into his solid chest.

"Hey Royce," Holden shouted from the group. "How about a song?"

Royce shrugged an apology. "My public awaits."

"Go get 'em, cowboy."

He grabbed his guitar from where he'd laid it and launched in. Surprisingly, he didn't start with a cowboy song. Instead, he sang a rousing rendition of "Happy Days Are Here Again" and invited everyone to sing along.

By the end of the next song, two guests had joined him, a man playing a fiddle and a woman with a banjo. The young man who had helped her with her bags when she first got there also brought a guitar and gazed with adoration at Royce as he strummed along. Soon Royce had a band surrounding him, including Flapjack playing harmonica and Tin Star on musical spoons. They played "I Got Rhythm" and "Will the Circle Be Unbroken?," and then Royce took Zadie's breath away with his heartfelt "All of Me" as he sang it directly to her.

They continued with "Tumbling Tumbleweed" and Zadie remembered the code she'd shared with Annie. *Tumbling Tumbleweed* did not apply to Royce. She not only wanted to date him, she was ready for *The Last Roundup* with him.

One of the female guests stood and whispered something to Royce. He nodded and played an upbeat introduction. The woman launched into "I Want to Be a Cowboy's Sweetheart," complete with perfect yodeling.

Zadie sang along, holding Royce's gaze to let him know she meant every word of the song.

As the concert continued, she slipped out to retrieve the canvas. Her stomach flip-flopped in anticipation. She'd never been this anxious to show off a piece of work. But this one meant more to her than anything she'd ever done. It could change the course of her career, just as the subject—Royce—could change the course of her life.

◆━━━━━◆

Thrilled the other musicians had joined him, Royce had begun the bouncy introduction to "Honeysuckle Rose" when a commotion sounded at the edge of the party. Dirk slithered in. Worse yet, under his arm, he wore Dottie Merrill,

Royce's former girlfriend. She was also the niece of studio head E. B. Merrill. The music silenced when yet another nemesis entered the party.

Bret Masters, in the flesh.

Suddenly it all made sense. Dottie must have learned what her uncle had planned for Royce—to prime him to take Bret's place—and she'd confided this to Dirk. Royce knew that Dottie wouldn't have said anything had Royce not broken off their relationship.

When the trio walked in, Holden and Theresa jumped up together from their spot near the fire. Holden shot Royce a silent question, and Theresa greeted the new arrivals.

Royce thought of retreating before Bret spied him, but something snapped inside. He was through hiding and lying.

A reporter and a photographer followed. Of course. Bret would probably color the whole thing in his favor. If Dirk was a snake, Bret was a dragon.

But why the subterfuge? If Bret knew what the studio was planning, why not throw his tantrum and be done with it?

Bret glanced Royce's way, then did a double take. He hadn't known. Was that possible? Had Dirk and Dottie planned the whole thing without Bret's consent?

Royce's head throbbed.

Bret made his way to Royce, ignoring his adoring fans, flicking them away like pesky flies.

Where was Zadie? Wouldn't she have been the first to greet Bret? She was nowhere around.

Royce and Bret stood like gladiators about to joust.

"Rutger."

"Masters."

Bret pointed at Dirk, still hanging on Dottie and clearly enjoying their little show. "He dragged me to the desert after convincing me that coming all this way would be good for my career."

Dirk preened at the attention. "Yeah, but Cousin Bret is really here because I told him about you."

Cousins. Could this get any better?

Bret jammed his hands to his hips. "Yes, he told me as we got out of the car about a traitor out to get my job. But I didn't believe it. Then I walk in here and see you. Not you, Royce. I thought you were faithful to me."

"What is it you think I've done, Bret?" If he'd said Royce had become employed at a dude ranch so he could become comfortable in a Western setting and eventually be *discovered* as the real deal when Bret lost his contract. . .then he'd be right.

"Do you seriously think you'll ever be the next singing cowboy star?" Bret motioned toward his publicity team. "These two will make sure that won't happen when I tell them what to write. I brought them to document me making nice with the owner of the dude ranch whose book is about to be made into my movie."

"That's news to me, Mr. Masters." Holden stepped forward. "No one contacted me about a publicity junket at my ranch."

"I don't run things by the studio anymore. They have a tendency to disregard my requests."

Demands, more likely.

The reporter wrote furiously in his notebook while the photographer clicked away. No doubt both would relay only what Bret approved.

Dottie extracted herself from Dirk. She'd seemed uncomfortable from the moment she walked in with the two slimes. "I'm sorry, Royce. Uncle Ernie told me he'd sent you here to train for Bret's job. I mentioned it to Dirk because I was mad at you, but I had no idea he would do something like this. Thing is, I don't think my uncle had any intention of allowing you to replace Bret. He only used you as a pawn in case he needed a bargaining chip to hold Bret to his contract."

"How do you know this?" Royce spoke, but both he and Bret stared down the trembling woman before them. Apparently Bret had also been duped by the studio.

"I was outside Uncle Ernie's office one day, waiting for him to take me to lunch. The door was cracked open, and I heard him talking on the phone."

Bret glared at the girl. "Why didn't you tell me?"

"And have you confront my uncle? I'm no snitch."

Royce tossed up his hands in frustration. "And yet you went straight to Dirk about me."

She grabbed the sleeve of his shirt. "Believe me, I had no idea the plan was to ambush you. I thought we were just joining Bret on a publicity stunt."

"I couldn't resist. . .Buck." Dirk threw down the gauntlet. "Knowing what you and the studio had tried to do to my cousin, I had to check it out. But the thought of you, a city boy from New Jersey, taking Bret's place, was laughable. Go back to your tall buildings and taxicabs. You're a horrible cowboy and could never fill Bret's saddle." He smirked and draped his arm over Dottie's shoulders again.

She shrugged him off. "Don't touch me. You used me as much as you used Royce for your childish vendetta." She uttered a sob, and Theresa took her under her wing and led her away from the group.

They walked past Zadie, her eyes wide, and gripping her artwork in two hands.

How much had she heard? Too much, by her pained expression. Royce's heart shattered for her.

◆━━━━━◆

The earth gave way under Zadie's feet. She'd gone to the house to retrieve the canvas while Royce sang. When she returned, a bizarre sight met her. Dirk and a strange woman were in a heated conversation with Royce, and. . . What was Bret Masters doing here?

From what she could gather, Bret Masters knew Royce.

Then it hit her.

She placed the canvas on the easel and slowly removed the cloth. Her world flipped on its head. The man in her painting was the same one she'd seen in at least four Bret Masters movies. She hadn't recognized him clean-shaven. But when she added the beard, and now, witnessing him with the actor, it all came rushing in like a New York blizzard.

Royce wasn't a real cowboy. No wonder he seemed uncomfortable that first day in the desert, and why he was thrown off his horse so easily. And why he didn't do as much as an employee of the ranch. And why he couldn't throw a rope or gain control of his horse around a barrel.

He was an actor.

From New Jersey.

A phony, like the other men she'd dated. Unlike them, she'd already lost her heart to this imposter.

Holden stepped between Royce and Dirk before fists flew. "Pack up your things, Dirk. You're fired."

"On what grounds?"

"For being an unpleasant fellow, for starters. And for presenting yourself under false pretenses."

"What about him?" He pointed to Royce. "He's more fake than I am."

"I knew why Royce was here. The studio approached me."

Zadie heard a gasp near her. Theresa brought her hand up to cover her mouth. Apparently she hadn't known Holden had been helping Royce. Oh how these men were going to get a good talking to by their women tonight.

Holden shoved his finger in Bret's direction, stopping short of poking him in the chest. "If the studio was just using Royce, then you can forget about playing the marshal in my book. I'm pulling the project."

"I don't think so." Bret gave a smug grin. "You signed the contract that Dirk shuttled to the studio."

"Actually," the woman said through her tears, "it's at my place. We never got around to taking it to the studio. Dirk wanted to party every day instead. I was going to give it to my uncle on Monday."

Bret turned on Dirk. "You fool."

"And now, gentlemen." Holden swept his arms forward. "It's time for you to leave."

Both men bristled but acquiesced.

The photographer snapped away, and Bret ripped the camera from him. "Don't take pictures of me getting thrown out, you dolt."

"Come on, Dottie." Dirk snapped his fingers and motioned to the woman who had been crying in Theresa's arms.

She reluctantly moved away from her shelter to follow the men.

"You don't have to go with them, Dottie." Theresa rested her hand on the woman's elbow. "You can stay here the night, and we'll take you to the train in the morning."

Dottie sniffed and wiped her eyes. "I'll be fine."

After the three left, one of the guests said, "That had to be the best drama ol' Bret Masters ever pulled off."

Everyone laughed, allowing the joke to ease the tension.

Holden wandered over to his wife, who retreated into the house without saying a word.

He glanced toward Zadie. "I think I'm in trouble."

Zadie nodded, not happy with him either. At least he'd only told a white lie with the intent to help. He wasn't pretending to be someone he wasn't, like the man in the painting.

"Is that my cover?" Holden gazed at it in awe. "It's beautiful, Zadie. Just what I wanted."

"Thank you."

"I'd like to talk to you more about a permanent artist-in-residence position."

Zadie softened toward him. She couldn't stay mad at such a sweet man, and she was sure Theresa would forgive him too. "I'd like that."

The party had ended, but everyone lingered, clustering in small groups and talking in hushed whispers. Zadie's big cover reveal had been spoiled, but several people commented favorably on it. All but Royce, who knew enough to keep his distance. Soon her adrenaline abated, and she contemplated going to bed.

Unearthly shrieks split the desert night. Coyotes? No, Zadie heard words.

"Help! Please, help him!"

Some of the guests headed in the direction the shrieks came from.

Dottie stumbled into the firelight. "We were driving away, and all of a sudden

I knew I couldn't bear the long ride with those two idiots. I jumped out of the car when we got to the main road, and Dirk followed me. I thought he was going to hurt me, so I ran into the desert. Then I heard him screaming."

Yelps echoed through the distance.

"Please, come help him. He got into a patch of cactus."

Holden, concerned for his guests, stopped the few heading to the desert to help. "We can handle this, but is there a doctor among you? Ours is gone for the weekend."

"I'm a doctor." A man broke from the group and hustled to his cabin. He came back with a black bag.

Holden, the doctor, and Royce, who had found a couple of flashlights, took off across the desert. Zadie trailed them.

Royce fell behind the other two men and stood in her path. "Please stay here. I don't want you getting hurt." He squeezed her shoulders. "Whatever you may think of me right now, know that I love you."

Rooted in place, she watched him leave until she could barely discern the bobbing light.

Chapter 10

Cries of pain like none Royce had ever heard sounded closer with every step.

"This way. Hurry." Dottie led the men straight to Dirk.

When Royce's flashlight landed on the source of the sound, he gasped. Dirk was barely recognizable with all the balls of teddy bear cactus clinging to every inch of him, including his face.

"Help me." His sobs tore at Royce's heart.

The doctor reached to pull them off, but Holden stopped him. "Don't touch them. They will stick to you too."

The doctor tried tweezers from his bag, but they proved ineffective. His eyes widened with confusion. "What can we do? He can't walk. They're stuck to his legs."

"Worse yet," Holden said, "they're stuck to his chest. We need to remove those before the spines reach his heart. They burrow for liquid."

Dirk whimpered.

Royce remembered the lesson Holden had taught that first day in the desert with Zadie. Natives had used the teddy bear cholla as weapons. "We need a tool to pull those off." He frantically searched his pockets, as did the other men. Finally, he remembered the girl. "Dottie, your hair."

Dottie's hands flew to her head. "What about it?"

"A comb is decorating it, right?"

She pulled the adornment from her short bob and ripped off the peacock feather embellishment. "Here."

Royce worked on the cholla closest to Dirk's heart, careful not to touch the cactus needles. The comb proved the perfect tool to pluck the spikes from his skin, although that apparently proved to be more painful than leaving them in. With that done, and Dirk out of immediate danger, Royce used the comb to pull at the ones on his face, and then on his legs so he could walk. While he toiled, the doctor applied salve to the wounds. Occasionally, a puff of cactus stuck to his hand, but he quickly combed it off. It hurt worse than a dozen bee stings. He felt for Dirk, who had become a pin cushion.

"Okay, Dirk, I got the crucial ones off. You want to finish this at the ranch, or should I keep going?"

"Keep going, please. I want to get it all over with."

Holden made a campfire to ward off "night critters," kicking the discarded cactus in for fuel. Dottie sat on a nearby rock, holding out her hands toward the fire for warmth. Royce continued until the last bunch of cactus fell off.

Dirk took a step and collapsed. Royce and Holden each pulled one of his arms over their shoulders. "Okay, buddy," Royce said. "Let's go home."

They reached the bunkhouse, and Royce pointed to their shared bunk bed. "Put him on my bed. He'll never make it to the top one."

Before they left him to the doctor's care, Dirk reached for Royce's arm. "I'm s—so sorry. Forgive m—me?"

Dirk had put Royce through the wringer with his callous, selfish nature. However, Royce no longer saw him as a snake, but as a pitiful animal who had been bested at his own game.

Royce offered up a silent prayer. *Lord, I have to admit, when I first heard Dirk was hurt, I felt vindicated. But seeing him in danger and hearing his pain helped me see the man inside the reptile. A man crying out to be loved. Help me forgive him, because I don't think I can do it on my own. Amen.*

The grip tightened on his forearm. Dirk must have been desperate to call up that much passion in his weakness. "Please."

"I forgive you, Dirk."

Dirk closed his eyes and relaxed. "Thank you."

Dottie moved forward to the bed and swept Dirk's hair from his forehead. "I forgive you too." But Dirk had already fallen into a laudanum-induced sleep. She glanced up at the men. "He tried to stop me from running into the desert because of this. I could have been the one in pain."

The top bunk looked mighty inviting, but Royce had his own person to seek for forgiveness before he could rest. That is, if she was still up. It was long past midnight.

When he turned around, she stood in the doorway.

◆━━━━・━━◆

"Hi." Zadie stepped aside as Royce led her to the small porch. He'd never looked more exhausted or more attractive. Or more uncomfortable. The ensuing conversation was necessary, but one she was sure both wanted to avoid.

"Hi. Did you wait up for us?"

"Yes. The cowboys held a prayer vigil at the campfire."

"I noticed they weren't in bed. That was nice of them."

"How's Dirk?"

"He'll be fine, but until he heals, he should be careful when he drinks water."

"Huh?"

"Let's just say, with all those holes in his body, he'd make a mighty fine sprinkler for Theresa's rock garden."

Zadie chuckled, then covered her mouth. "We shouldn't tease."

"Eh, he deserves it. But I think the experience changed him."

"I pray so. Miserable people tend to want others miserable."

"Too true." He glanced around. "Where's Bret? He might want to see his cousin."

"Believe it or not, he and his publicity team continued on, leaving Dirk and Dottie to fend for themselves."

"The wretch."

"Theresa sent someone to telegraph the studio. Hopefully they can get ahold of him to tell him what happened."

Royce shrugged, apparently not convinced it would matter to Bret Masters. He motioned away from the bunkhouse porch. "Let's take a walk."

She nodded.

"Royce—"

"Zadie—"

They laughed, having spoken at the same time.

"Ladies first."

She paused to gather her thoughts. Where to start? Best to launch in. "New Jersey?"

He looked away but not before she caught the eye roll. "Newark."

"Are you a cowboy?"

"Not technically."

"What does that mean?"

"I only play one in the movies, but I'm getting the hang of it."

"Then I was right. I had added a beard to your painting. When I saw you and Bret, I made the connection."

"I'm sorry for the deceit. I should have told you, but the studio forbade me to divulge my purpose in being here."

"You still should have told me. I wouldn't have given you away. But after hearing what went on between you and the uninvited guests last night, I can see why you had to keep it close to the vest."

Zadie's emotions swirled. She'd gone over it all in her mind while praying at the campfire. Royce should have told her, but then again, they'd only known each other for a few weeks. She could hold on to a grudge and dismiss him as she had the other tumbling tumbleweeds in her life, or she could stick it out and discover more about this man who had just spent the night plucking cactus off his archenemy.

"Apparently it doesn't matter. The studio was just using me to tame Bret."

"Theresa told me she wouldn't be surprised if Holden made good on his threat to take his book to a different studio. You may be the next marshal hunting down the *Mesa Marauder* somewhere else."

He shook his head. "I just signed another two-year contract. He'd have to wait."

"I'm sure he'd be good with that. He's already done so much for you."

"That he has." He chuckled. "I owe him a lot."

"However, neither you nor Holden may have to wait."

She wandered to the corral where Sierra and Sonora munched on hay. Sierra trotted over for a nose rub. Sonora followed, bobbing his head and nickering for attention.

"What do you mean?" Royce joined her at the fence.

"The man playing the fiddle last night? Turns out he's a lawyer. We were talking, and he knows some loopholes. What they did to you qualifies as a breach of contract if it says somewhere in the wording that they will protect your best interests."

He grabbed her shoulders and held her at arm's length. "Zadie Fitzgerald. I'm going to kiss you."

A giggle bubbled in her chest. "Don't kiss me—kiss the lawyer."

He seemed to consider it but pulled her close. "No, I'm pretty sure it's you I'm going to kiss."

She pulled his head down, and inches from his lips, she whispered, "Then do it."

"Wait." He lifted his head, and Zadie couldn't hold in the groan of dissatisfaction. "I'm not a real cowboy. You sure you want to continue this serial?"

She huffed an impatient breath. "The Lord reminded me of something while I was praying last night. I fell in love with cowboys by watching them on the silver screen. *Actors* playing cowboys." She raised her eyebrows, hoping he understood.

Dawn hit not only the eastern horizon, but also Royce's face. "Now, I'm going to kiss you."

And he did.

Epilogue

Summer of 1941
Painted Star Ranch, California

Zadie Rutger rode her paint, Renoir, to meet her husband as he turned up the drive to their ranch house in his alizarin-crimson Mercedes Roadster. Royce just called it red. In the back seat sat Holden and Theresa Chase, whom he had picked up at the train station.

Zadie squealed as she dismounted and ran to Theresa's waiting arms.

"I have something for you." Theresa led her to the trunk Royce had just unlocked. A box lay inside next to the Chases' luggage.

"Is this it?"

"Yes, all thanks to you."

"No, your talent speaks for itself."

Zadie reached in and lifted the flaps of the box. "It's real! It's really real!"

She removed the first edition of Theresa's new children's book, *The Old Man of the Desert*. Zadie had painted the cover, using a large saguaro cactus as the focal point. She flipped through the book, and there were her illustrations in glorious color.

"Did you bring enough?" She quickly counted the rest of the copies in the box.

"Twenty-five. That should cover the children coming with a few to spare."

"They'll love it. All these city children know about nature are the palm trees down Mulholland Drive."

Holden wrapped his arm around Royce's shoulder. "I'm mighty proud of our wives. Starting a program for underprivileged kids to come here in the summer and our place in the winter was pure genius."

"Yep. We married well."

The men grabbed the luggage, and Zadie and Theresa followed.

"And what about you, Academy Nominee Royce Rutger?" Holden climbed the steps to the porch.

"That's in large part due to excellent writing. An actor can only do so much with the material he's given."

"Well, I think you were robbed. Why would they pick that skinny James

Stewart for best actor when they had broad-shouldered Royce Rutger?"

Theresa pretended to swoon as they entered the house. "Jimmy Stewart in *Philadelphia Story*, my favorite movie."

Holden glared at her.

"I mean, it's my third favorite movie. *Mesa Marauder* and *The Marshal Rides Alone* are tied for first." She pecked Holden on the cheek. When she turned away from him, she fluttered her eyelashes and mouthed to Zadie, "Jimmy Stewart, oh my."

Zadie stifled a giggle. She agreed, but her favorite actor would always be Royce.

A tray with sugar cookies and tall glasses filled with cold lemonade appeared on the living room coffee table courtesy of Royce's mother. Holden picked up a glass and a stack of cookies, then headed to Royce's favorite leather chair.

Theresa hugged Zadie's mother-in-law. "How are you, Mrs. Rutger? I've not seen you in four years, since the wedding. You're looking well. California air must agree with you."

"I do enjoy it out here." Emily Rutger selected her own beverage from the tray and sat on the arm of the sofa, smoothing her house dress. "When Royce insisted I join him out here, I'm afraid I dug in my heels. Newark was the only place I'd ever known. But when he announced his engagement, I had to come. I've never regretted staying. Besides"—she shot a mischievous glance toward Royce and Zadie, who snuggled together in a wide easy chair—"I want to be present if I ever get a grandchild."

"Mom," Royce groaned. "When we're ready."

Zadie knew what Emily and Royce didn't. That she'd been harboring a secret she'd reveal when the time came.

"Best decision I ever made"—Holden continued his train of thought—"was to drop Western Empire Films and take my book to Maximum Pictures. They not only embraced you, my boy, but encouraged your singing career." He lifted his glass. "How many awards have you gotten for your records?"

Royce shrugged, but a grin tugged at his lips. "It's not about the awards."

"Of course it is."

"What about Bret Masters?" Theresa asked. "Anyone know what happened to him?"

Royce set his drink on a coaster atop the side table. He wrapped his arms around Zadie in a protective hold. A throwback reflex from when she was infatuated with the actor. "The studio dropped him," Royce said. "His luxurious lifestyle proved too much. I've heard he's gone into producing though. He might be better suited for that."

"What about Dirk?" Zadie still prayed on and off for him. Such a troubled soul.

Holden swallowed the remains of his third sugar cookie. "Not as wild as he was five years ago, but last I heard he was getting a divorce."

"Who did he marry? Not Dottie."

"No, she didn't last long. There were several after her."

Zadie shook her head. Poor Dirk. A victim of his own making. "And what about the others? Tin Star, the twins. Flapjack, of course, works here as our ranch foreman."

Holden waved another cookie. "Still at the ranch, plus we had to add a couple because you took two of them."

Once everyone had gotten caught up, Zadie and Royce took the couple on a horseback tour of their property. Holden seemed impressed when told they owned seven hundred acres. Afterward Royce grilled some steaks, and then they retired for the evening.

Early the next morning, while the household slept, Zadie and Royce slipped out for their daily sunrise ride. Zadie on Renoir and Royce on Autry. Their horses took them to the north pasture where their four hundred fifty head of cattle grazed on sweet summer grass.

They dismounted and walked a little while. Zadie wrapped her arm around Royce's lean waist, and he cradled her shoulders.

"We've done well for ourselves, Mrs. Rutger." Had Royce been thinking about the walk down memory lane with their guests yesterday evening?

"With God, all things are possible."

Royce stopped and faced her. "It's all due to Him. We wouldn't have the Painted Star Ranch if He hadn't intervened in both of our lives."

"And while we're counting our blessings, let's include your mother. I enjoy her so much."

"That makes me happy, especially since she's living with us." He winked.

"Besides, I love how she's included in the making of our ranch. What insight she had in naming it."

"*Painted*, for the artist in residence. . ."

Zadie curtsied. "And *Star*, for the actor who was my shining star before he ever won America's hearts."

"So. . ." Zadie tilted her head and squeezed his waist. "When *do* you think we'll be ready?"

"For what?"

"To make our mothers into grands."

He considered the sky for a moment. "We wanted to give our child the very best of us. With me off making movies and you busy painting Holden's covers, sometimes in residence, the timing never seemed right. But. . ."

"But what?"

"We're in a comfortable rhythm now." Did he mean that he didn't want children to upset his rhythm, or that he was ready now that things had settled down somewhat?

"You're still painting covers and I'm still making movies. But who knows when that will stop?"

"So, you're saying. . ."

"I could be persuaded in nine months to be a dad." He kissed her nose.

"Could you make that six months?"

His wide grin told her all she needed to know.

He pulled her close. "I'm going to kiss you now."

She lifted her face to her singing cowboy. Deep kisses kept her in rapture for a little while longer.

Then the riders of the Painted Star rode home in the sunrise.